A Scandal
in
Mayfair

ALSO AVAILABLE BY KATHARINE SCHELLMAN

THE LILY ADLER MYSTERIES

The Body in the Garden

Silence in the Library

Death at the Manor

Murder at Midnight

THE NIGHTINGALE MYSTERIES

Last Call at the Nightingale

The Last Drop of Hemlock

The Last Note of Warning

A SCANDAL IN MAYFAIR

A LILY ADLER MYSTERY

Katharine Schellman

NEW YORK

Published in the United States by Crooked Lane Books, an imprint of The Quick Brown Fox & Company LLC.

Crooked Lane Books and its logo are trademarks of The Quick Brown Fox & Company LLC.

Library of Congress Catalog-in-Publication data available upon request.

ISBN (hardcover): 978-1-63910-841-1
ISBN (ebook): 978-1-63910-842-8

Cover design by Nichole Lecht

Printed in the United States.

www.crookedlanebooks.com

Crooked Lane Books
34 West 27th St., 10th Floor
New York, NY 10001

First Edition: August 2024

10 9 8 7 6 5 4 3 2 1

To Mary Ann
Beloved mother-in-law, beloved friend
1954–2023

CHAPTER 1

London, 1817

The letter looked innocent enough when it arrived, nestled in the stack of the day's correspondence. Both the hot-pressed paper and the hand in which the direction was written declared that the sender had at least some money and likely a certain place in society. But Lily Adler still paused when she saw it, her fingers hovering without touching: it was addressed not to *Mrs. Frederick Adler*, but to *A Lady of Quality.*

Lily had kept a box at the general post office with that name on it for some years. *Discreet inquiries, confidential investigations, and mysteries solved* said the cards that she had, on rare occasions and with great care, shared with those who might need such assistance. And she had, from time to time, been engaged on such matters. But she did not need all her fingers to count the number of occasions on which her maid had brought home any such letters from the post office, and those she had so far received had concerned matters such as misplaced jewels or suitors of suspicious intentions.

Something about this one looked different from the others that had arrived. The paper was folded and sealed unevenly. The writing, though done by a well-trained hand, had a certain shakiness to it. Perhaps the sender had simply been rushed or careless or untidy.

Or perhaps—Lily felt a little shiver at the back of her neck—perhaps this time, whoever was writing to her was in true need of help.

"Mrs. Adler, are you attending at all?"

The question made Lily jump a little, and she glanced up to find both her guests watching her with curiosity and a little exasperation.

They were scattered about the sitting room of her cozy house on Half Moon Street, while, in typical fashion for a London spring, rain drummed at the windows. Amelia Hartley, Lily's temporary companion, sat with a pile of correspondence. Amelia was a striking, dark-haired girl currently enjoying her first foray into a London social season under Lily's occasionally unsociable care—a situation that suited Amelia, who disliked being the center of too much attention, quite well. She was currently busy sorting Lily's letters and setting aside invitations that would require a response. It was not she who had demanded to know whether Lily was attending.

"Not closely, no," Lily admitted apologetically to the other woman in the room. "At least, I think I must have misheard you. Surely you did not just say that you fear two of the guests at your soiree will come to blows in the middle of the party?"

"I did indeed say so," exclaimed Ofelia, Lady Carroway, slapping her hand down with a dramatic flair that made Lily smile. Ofelia, who had arrived in London from the West Indies two years before as a young heiress, was preparing to host her first society ball since her marriage to an only slightly less young baronet, and she was on edge with nerves at the prospect. Her usual poise had disappeared accordingly, at least when she was among her friends. "Because the Carters were convinced that Mr. Peters was going to offer for Miss Carter—you remember how last year he was seen by her side at nearly every function?"

She rose without seeming to realize it, pacing back and forth in front of the fireplace while Lily and Amelia watched in bemusement. "But then, all of a sudden last fall, his engagement to Miss Evans was announced, and no one missed that it happened right after her uncle died and left her that five thousand pounds, and none of them have spoken since, but Neddy's mother insists that not inviting both families would be inconceivable." She glanced at Amelia, and her tone grew thoughtful. "You know, I believe one of the Carter boys is in the navy—perhaps I should ask your brother his thoughts on the matter. Tell me, is there any chance of Captain Hartley stopping by? I believe he is in London now, is he not?"

"I've not yet heard whether he has arrived," Amelia said. "It will be strange to see him so frequently, now that he has left the navy. He has been aboard ship for most of my life. But in any case, he may not know the gentleman. Carter, did you say?"

"Hmm," Lily put in, still not really attending. Her mind was turning over the letter, unsure why she was so hesitant to open it.

"Well," Ofelia said, dropping back into her chair, "it is worth asking. And I cannot imagine"—there was an almost pointed emphasis to her words—"that he will allow much time to lapse before he calls. His sister is here, after all, and his dearest—" She broke off suddenly, her scattered attention drawing to a point as she frowned at Lily. "Mrs. Adler, what is the matter?"

Lily blinked at her, disoriented by the sudden change of both her friend's conversation and manner. "What do you mean?"

"Usually by now you would be telling me not to work myself up over something that might not even happen. Or saying that you have already predicted the precise moment the captain will call. But instead, you keep glancing at that letter in your hand," Ofelia said shrewdly. "And it is unlike you to divide your attention thusly. Who is it from?"

"It is not from my brother, is it?" Amelia asked eagerly, setting aside the invitations she was sorting. "He was supposed to arrive in town today."

"He did," Lily said, her eyes on the letter once more as she turned it over in her hand.

"You have seen him, then!" Ofelia said, sounding almost triumphant.

Lily shook her head. "No, he sent a note 'round with his boy, Jem. I've no idea who sent this one—I've not opened it yet." She held up the letter so they could both see the direction on its front. "It seems to be from someone seeking my assistance." She squared her shoulders. Now that they were both watching her, her hesitation felt foolish. "Shall we see what it says?"

"Oh," Ofelia breathed, leaning forward. She had been there when an unexpected death had launched Lily's first foray into murder and investigation—and that had not been the last time she had stood by Lily's side through intrigue, in spite of her husband's recurring pleas that she keep herself far away from such dangers. Ofelia could no more refuse a summons from someone in need than Lily could. "Yes, do not keep us in suspense. Open it!"

Lily slid open the wafer with a single, decisive gesture. The silence in the room as she began to read was so absolute, as though the other two were holding their breaths, that she could hear the clock ticking out in the hall.

Lily read the letter through twice, the chill that was half eagerness, half wariness prickling her neck the entire time.

To a Lady of Quality,

Word of your reputation and insight has reached me in a roundabout way, as such things often do. And while I might, at another time, have abhorred the thought of approaching a stranger in such a manner, based on no more than whispered gossip, my circumstances have lately become so dire that any remedy seems preferable to the results that inaction might bring.

If you would be so good as to call at number 6, Walton Place, I will be at home to visitors, beginning at one o'clock this afternoon. I beg you will offer your assistance, or I fear I will be left to face a future of ruin and destitution, and quite possibly the loss of the love of my life.

Yrs. hopefully,
A Young Gentlewoman

Lily glanced up. "I do not suppose either of you knows the family who reside at number six Walton Place?"

"Not I," said Amelia as Lily passed the letter to Ofelia. "Is it in London?"

"Yes, in Hans Town, I think. But I do not know anyone in that neighborhood." The young Lady Carroway scanned the missive eagerly, then made a face as she looked up. "Either the writer has read too many novels, or she is truly in dire trouble. It is difficult to decide which."

"I am inclined to think both things may be true," Lily said, retrieving the letter and glancing at it once more before handing it to Amelia. She didn't sit down again afterward, but instead paced toward the windows. The rain was clearing, though the sun seemed disinclined to emerge, and clouds still hung low and scattered in the sky. "The tone is certainly melodramatic, but the writing itself . . ."

"It is a fine hand," Amelia put in, still studying the letter. "Well schooled. Whoever the writer is, I think she must be telling the truth about being gently raised."

"I agree," Lily said, turning from the gloomy view. "And I think also that she was distressed when she penned it. Distressed and in a hurry. Though whether she was hurrying to avoid detection or so as not to lose her nerve remains to be seen. As for the cause of her distress . . ." She turned from the gloomy view. "That I shall have to see."

"Do you intend to call on her, then?" Ofelia asked, sounding surprised. She took a sip from her cooling tea, then grimaced and reached for the pot to pour a fresh cup. "With no other information to go on and no indication of her identity?"

"No, indeed not," Lily replied slowly, thinking the matter through as she crossed to the table and nudged her own neglected teacup in Ofelia's direction. Her friend obligingly poured for both of them. "I began this whole business of inquiries and investigations without much thought—"

"Hardly that," Amelia interrupted, setting the letter down. Her voice and her expression were both serious. "You caught a murderer, Mrs. Adler. You saved my brother from the gallows."

"Several murderers, in fact," Ofelia put in. "There is no need to diminish your accomplishments. Or," she added with a pert toss of her curly head, "the accomplishments of those who have assisted you in such matters."

If Lily had been the type of person who laughed easily, she would have done so at Ofelia's unsubtle reminder of the role she herself had played in several of Lily's unintentional investigations. Instead, she smiled, the corners of her eyes crinkling up with unvoiced humor. "Be that as it may, the point I intended to make was that it has become somewhat more serious than a matter of being in the right place at the right time—or the wrong time," she added, shaking her head. "And as the seriousness of the matter grows, so too does the potential damage of public exposure. I've no intention of making a spectacle of myself—or of anyone currently in my care." She gave Amelia a stern look when it seemed the girl was about to protest. "Were I to accept this invitation, I should place myself in danger of just such a spectacle if this young gentlewoman is not serious in her request for aid."

"Then what do you intend to do?" Ofelia asked as she handed Lily her teacup.

Lily contemplated the milky-dark swirl. "I believe," she said slowly, "I shall extend an invitation of my own." She glanced toward the window. "With the rain clearing, a stroll in the Green Park would be a welcome diversion." She took a sip of tea before adding, "It is, after all, a place where a young lady might walk or sit apart from her chaperone for some little time should she have need of a private conversation."

Amelia rose from her seat. "I'll fetch your writing portfolio, if you like, Mrs. Adler. There should be time to have a response delivered before the afternoon."

"Well, drat," said Ofelia with a sigh, flopping back into her chair. "I shan't be able to come with you."

★ ★ ★

"Do you think I will not tell you what happens?" Lily asked with no little exasperation as she held Ofelia's hat and gloves so her friend could button up her pelisse.

They were alone together in the front hall as Ofelia prepared to take her leave, and she had given the return missive to *A Young Gentlewoman* an irritated look as Lily handed it over to her maid for delivery. Lily had sent Amelia off to fetch her embroidery. It was the sort of task that she rarely asked her young houseguest to perform, but Lily had wanted a private moment with Ofelia before she left.

"No, but you know I hate to miss any excitement," Ofelia grumbled. "Your afternoon sounds much more promising than mine. Neddy's mother wants to review the guest list. Again. Which is absurd. The invitations have already been sent. Whatever mess we've created, we shall simply have to endure it." She sighed again. "Do you promise you will tell me all about it?"

"Certainly I shall." Lily held up a hand to forestall Ofelia's thanks. "If you tell me why you were so eager for me to have seen the captain now that he is in town once more."

"Oh." Ofelia glanced away, looking suddenly uncomfortable. "I was not . . . that is, I did not mean . . ." She cleared her throat. "Is he well? Captain Hartley, I mean?" The eagerness of her earlier inquiries about Amelia's brother was gone; now there was nothing but concern in her dark eyes. "I've not seen him since before . . ."

She did not finish her sentence. But she did not have to.

"Ah." Lily was not entirely convinced that the question explained Ofelia's earlier enthusiasm—an enthusiasm that, after several months of hints, she was beginning to suspect she understood. But regardless of her suspicions, Ofelia deserved an answer. Lily nodded. "He is well, so far as I know. And . . ." Then she hesitated, wondering if she should say more, while her heart hammered almost painfully against her ribs.

Jack Hartley had been her husband Freddy's closest childhood friend. And after Freddy's death, he had become her confidante and friend in his own right. It had been Jack who had stood by her side as she found her place in London society after her husband's death; Jack who became her co-conspirator as she was drawn into investigating a murder in order to protect a friend; Jack who had first presented Lily with the cards that directed those in need of discreet assistance to write to A Lady of Quality.

It had been Jack who was already planning to leave his naval career behind when an unexpected blizzard had stranded him, Lily, and several others at a country house in Hertfordshire. When the situation had turned deadly, it was not because of the storm, but because of the secrets one neighbor had decided were worth killing to keep.

The storm had ended with a murderer caught, but not before Jack had taken a bullet in one shoulder.

He had escaped the infection that his family feared could end his life. Lily had seen him again on his feet and eager for her to take his sister away to London, wanting Amelia to escape her own brush with scandal and danger. But something had changed between them the night he was injured.

It had been nearly four years since Freddy's death. In that time, Lily had been relieved to discover that losing her husband hadn't meant that she would be alone in the world. It hadn't even meant that she would never again feel the heat of romance or desire.

Yet no one had come to mean to her what her husband had once meant, until the night she had pressed her hands against Jack's injury, trying to stem the bleeding and willing him to hold on until a doctor could be summoned.

But Jack had been Freddy's brother in every way but blood. And no matter what else she thought or felt, she was sure of one thing: she could not risk losing her friend.

"And what, Mrs. Adler?"

Ofelia's gentle query tugged Lily back into the present moment. She pushed aside her thoughts—she didn't like it when they tumbled around themselves in that manner anyway—and smiled. "And I expect him for dinner tonight. I imagine he'll be glad to see his sister and report back to their parents on whether I am caring for her properly."

"And he has recovered, so far as you know?" Ofelia asked, more than a little anxiously. "You saw him over the winter, did you not?"

"He is recovering," Lily said. Ofelia and Jack were not as close as Lily was with either of them. But as children of mixed heritage who had nevertheless been raised within the circle of upper-class English society—Jack with an Indian mother, Ofelia raised by her wealthy English father after the death of her West Indian mother—there was a sympathy and understanding between them that Lily knew she could never quite be part of. There had been a time or two when that had chafed at her. But far more often, she had been relieved that her two friends had decided to like each other. It was infinitely preferable to the distrust and sniping that had characterized their earliest interactions.

And though she knew Jack and Ofelia's husband corresponded on occasion, neither of them had seen the other since Jack's injury. Of course Ofelia would be concerned. "Would you and Sir Edward care to join us?" Lily asked gently.

Ofelia sighed as she pinned on her hat. "I wish we could, but we are engaged to dine with the Prescotts. Neddy's mother believes they have a son who might do for one of the girls."

The girls were Ned Carroway's unmarried sisters, ranging in age from twelve to nineteen. Lily could not help the lift of her eyebrows. "Any of them, or one in particular?"

"I believe she is not picky as to which. The girls, however, might disagree on the matter." A smile played around Ofelia's lips. "Which means that it at least has the potential to be an entertaining dinner." Her expression grew more serious as she drew on her gloves. "But you will give my best to the captain, will you not? And you will *ensure* that he is caring for himself and his injury, and not doing some stupid, manly thing like taking up boxing?"

"If he is, I shan't hesitate to let you loose upon him in all your fury," Lily promised. "He knows a thing or two about injuries, Ofelia—he ought to, after his years at sea and at war. I am sure he is caring for himself."

"And have you—" Ofelia hesitated. "That is, has he—" Lily waited for her to continue, uncharacteristically nervous to know what her friend might be hinting at. But Ofelia seemed to change her mind quickly, giving her head a little shake. "I mustn't dawdle. You will tell me how your appointment goes, will you not? You promised." She smiled eagerly, as though putting Jack and whatever she had been about to say out of her mind. "I am excessively curious to know what this young gentlewoman intends to ask."

Lily's answering smile was wry. "As am I. Curious, and not a little wary. If nothing else, it promises to be an interesting afternoon."

CHAPTER 2

The response had arrived more quickly and with fewer protestations than Lily expected.

I will be there, it ran in the same eager, agitated hand. *Look for me reading on the bench under the stand of sycamores.*

"That bodes well for her sincerity," Amelia said, reading through the letter as Lily prepared to go out. "And also for us actually identifying her."

"Us?" Lily gave her companion a sideways glance. "There will be no *us,* Amelia. I cannot in good conscience allow you to be involved in something that could be dangerous, either to your person or your reputation."

"But I have been involved in such things before!" Amelia protested.

"Those were different circumstances," Lily pointed out. "For now, your parents have entrusted you to me with the intention that I will safeguard your reputation, not imperil it once more."

"Please, Mrs. Adler?" Amelia begged. "I live here; the odds of my not becoming involved somehow are small. Besides which, would it not be helpful to have another set of eyes? In case this lady is indeed trying to deceive you in some manner?"

Lily's pursed lips twisted to the side. She knew she ought to stick to her refusal. It was the responsible thing to do, and what would be expected of any proper chaperone under such circumstances.

On the other hand, a proper chaperone would hardly be making plans to meet with a complete stranger for the purpose of some clandestine inquiry. "Very well, you may come. But you will stay with my maid, and you will watch from a *distance*, do you understand?"

Amelia smiled, looking satisfied with herself. "As you say."

Lily sighed. "Fetch your hat and coat, then, and meet me in the front hall."

★   ★   ★

The Green Park was a short walk south of Half Moon Street, a pretty, pastoral corner of London. Though clouds still gathered on the horizon, plenty of servants and clerks had taken advantage of the brief burst of sunlight to stroll in the park. A governess was chasing a small herd of children who seemed intent on running away from her, and more than one courting couple strolled side by side with an eagle-eyed matron watching them from a few paces back.

But there were not crowds the way there would have been in the popular promenade of Hyde Park. That suited Lily and her plans just fine. A busy day would have meant that they were less likely to stand out or be remembered. But with fewer people, it was less likely that someone would overhear their conversation.

Arm in arm, she and Amelia strolled slowly along the path, with Lily's maid, Anna, keeping several paces behind. Lily, who had done this sort of reconnaissance before, kept up a quiet, innocuous stream of conversation about everyday matters until the stand of sycamore trees, and the young lady sitting on the bench beneath them, came into sight.

Amelia would have stopped in her tracks and turned toward her had Lily not given her arm a gentle tug, drawing her along the path they were already on with barely a pause.

"Do you not think that is she?" Amelia asked in some confusion.

Lily glanced toward the sycamores out of the corner of her eye. "I believe it is. But before we approach, I wish to see what manner of person we are dealing with. It is impossible, in this sort of business, not to share your identity with some people. But we must be careful about choosing who those people are. And," she added, giving Amelia a warning glance, "I remind you that I shall be approaching her alone."

"Of course, ma'am," Amelia said, nodding in agreement. Though growing up she had been the popular, admired daughter of a popular, admired local squire—and though her mother had been an accepted part of their Hertfordshire neighborhood for decades—being the daughter of an Anglo-Indian family had necessarily made Amelia cautious of meeting new people. It was a trait that had only been exacerbated by her own recent brush with scandal and danger. "How will you approach her?"

"In time," Lily said, turning down the path in such a way that they could circle around behind the bench, observing the young lady under the sycamores without her being able to see them in return.

She was sitting alone, which might have meant that she was married and therefore able to venture out without a chaperone. But her mode of dress, though stylish, was demure and unassuming, more like that of an unmarried girl than a young matron. And she glanced frequently toward a couple who was sitting some distance away on another bench, their heads close together as they whispered and laughed. Judging by their clothing, Lily suspected they were a servant and a store clerk.

The girl's maid, then, Lily decided, and her chaperone for the outing—no doubt enticed to leave her young mistress unsupervised for the moment by the promise of a stolen half hour with her own sweetheart.

Satisfied, Lily continued to talk to Amelia about the tea they had been to the previous week while she turned her observation toward the young lady herself.

The girl might have been a gentleman's daughter; judging by her posture and poise, someone had certainly spent time and money on her education. Though that someone could have also been a tradesman who was determined to see his children advance in the world. She sat with a book open on her lap, and her gaze was on its pages.

But Lily could tell that she was not reading. In five minutes, she did not turn a single page. Instead, her attention darted around, her gaze going to every person who strolled nearby, before returning to her lap when they did not pause or meet her eyes. In spite of her elegant comportment, she was clearly as anxious as her letter had conveyed: one of her legs was bouncing under the book's cover, and her fingers fiddled with the folds of her gown.

But she didn't seem to be watching any person in particular other than the maid she was still keeping an eye on. And glancing around, Lily did not see anyone else lingering obviously in the area.

Lily took a deep breath. It would be a risk to approach her. But everything in life was a risk, and she had taken far more dangerous ones in the past. "All right," she murmured to Amelia. "I believe it is time for me to go speak with her. Anna?" She turned, summoning her maid with a glance. "Will you accompany Miss Hartley to sit a way back, please? I must have a private conversation."

"I am eager to hear what has put her in the path of ruin and destitution, and how you may help," Amelia said before she turned away.

"Don't forget the loss of the love of her life," Lily murmured. "I only hope she is not having an affair with a married gentleman. I have seen enough troubles of that sort to last a lifetime." That earned a quiet laugh from her young companion as they parted ways.

Lily observed the young woman under the sycamores for a moment more before taking a deep breath and striding confidently forward. "Excuse me?" She raised her voice as she drew abreast of the bench. "Is the rest of your seat occupied, or may I sit down?"

The young lady jumped at being addressed and looked up at her with a hopeful expression. But it faded into something more like confusion as she looked Lily over. "Oh . . . no. That is, no, it is not occupied. I was waiting for someone, but . . ." Her attention was already drifting out over the park once more as she scanned the small clusters of passersby. "Do make yourself comfortable, I suppose."

Lily couldn't have said at that moment whether she was more amused or exasperated. She had seen that moment of excitement in the young lady's face, the same anxiety that had been reflected in the letters. She was the young gentlewoman, Lily was certain.

But that first excited look had been replaced by something almost like disappointment, though the anxiety had not disappeared.

"A lovely afternoon for an outing, is it not?" Lily asked pleasantly. "At least now it is not raining."

"Mm," the young woman agreed without paying much attention, her eyes half on her book, half glancing about the park.

She truly did want to meet the lady to whom she had written. She just didn't seem to think the woman next to her could be the person she was hoping to see.

Lily took a good look at her seatmate. She was, Lily judged now that they were side by side, a little older than Amelia—old enough that she could have been several years married, but still young enough that it would not be too surprising were she still unwed. She had wide eyes, pale skin that had not quite managed to avoid a dusting of freckles the previous summer, and hair halfway between brown and red: the sort of young lady that many acquaintances would describe as a lovely girl, but not handsome enough to turn heads on the street.

But it was her clothing that caught Lily's eye the most. Her hat and spencer were beautifully and expensively made, and the gown visible below was luxurious in both its fabric and trimming.

It was a lovely ensemble. And it was two years past the height of fashion.

Lily folded her hands atop her reticule and looked the girl up and down. "Surely you are not unaccompanied?" she inquired.

"My maid is with me," the girl said, starting to sound a little irritated, "but she is giving me some privacy. A state I value greatly."

"But no one else?" Lily pressed, imitating the nosy matrons who had so often made such inquiries into her own life and activities. "I would have expected a pretty girl like you to be meeting any number of suitors on an afternoon like this one."

The response came through gritted teeth. "Oh dear, I just remembered: I *am* supposed to meet someone. Do excuse me—"

"No need to depart so quickly, my love," a masculine voice, rich with amusement, put in. "Nor to be put off by her manner. This, I believe, is the lady we hoped to see."

Lily stiffened, the back of her neck prickling with apprehension. At first, her only thought was worry that someone had schemed to create exactly the kind of spectacle she had feared. But it only took a moment for a different kind of unease to hit her.

She knew that voice.

She had not heard it in over a year, but it took her back in time immediately, to an autumn in Hampshire and a family with too many secrets. She turned slowly. The gentleman smiling at her was almost handsome, a little short and a little plump. He was dressed with fashion and elegance, and he regarded her with the sort of confidence that was passed down from one wealthy, well-bred generation to the next.

It was a lie. Not the confidence—Lily had rarely met a man more sure of himself—but the impression that he worked so hard to give of himself and his background. And he was well aware that Lily knew it.

"Mrs. Adler," he said, smooth and polite as ever, "what a charming surprise it is to find you close at hand yet again. I confess, I had wondered whether you might be the lady to whom my dear Sarah had turned in our time of need." He smiled at her. "I did recall what a talent you have for seeking out information."

"Mr. Clive," Lily said, her voice wary and her manner more than a little cold. "What a surprise to see you in London."

"Is it?" he asked pleasantly, though there was an edge to his smile. "I would have thought it was the obvious place for a gentleman of my interests to find himself. I never was suited to country life."

"You? You are she?" The young lady on the bench stared at Lily, not bothering to hide her surprise.

Lily stood. "I think you are mistaken, miss." She glanced at Clive. "Sir. Do excuse me."

But he did not step out of her way. "A moment, Mrs. Adler—just a moment of your time. I would like to introduce you to Miss Sarah Forrest, who is in need of your help. When she proposed writing to this *lady of quality* of whom she had heard, I suspected it might be the same Mrs. Adler who had so adroitly untangled that strange business in Hampshire. And we are asking for nothing so dangerous as unmasking a murderer."

Lily wanted to protest again that they had the wrong person, to insist that he stand aside and let her leave. But there were enough people in the park that she could not risk making a scene, especially not with Amelia nearby and likely to insert herself into any altercation.

Slowly, Lily sat, glancing between Miss Forrest and Clive, wondering what their connection was. "Miss Sarah Forrest, I think it was?"

"Yes, ma'am. And you are Mrs. Adler? You do not look anything like I expected," the young woman said bluntly. "I thought that someone who offers such investigations would be . . . more dramatic, I suppose. But you are very nearly plain. Well, not *plain*," she added apologetically, looking Lily over once more. "Your gown is beautifully made, I must say, and you are very elegant—a tall figure helps with that, I suppose." She sighed, glancing down at her own figure, which was of average height and rather waiflike. "But I thought you would be more glamorous. Is it not a glamorous occupation that you have?"

"Hardly an occupation," Lily said firmly. Miss Forrest was not wrong; with unremarkable coloring and looks only just on the pretty side of average, *elegant* was the best descriptor Lily could hope for from an impartial observer. But it still rankled to be sized up so bluntly. "And not a genteel one, if it were. Besides, I think what you have heard of are *discreet* inquiries for those who need them. A dramatic or imposing appearance would hardly serve that purpose."

"Oh, indeed. That does make sense." The girl's eyes were wide as she nodded along. "That is what Mrs. Mannering said—that you were the soul of discretion. I am so hoping it is true, believe me. My predicament is *dreadful*, and it would become even worse were it to be widely known and discussed."

"That is often the case, especially in town," Lily said, but her eyes narrowed as she spoke. The Mannerings' daughter had disappeared one night, leaving no trace of where she might have gone, and they had been beside themselves when Lily arrived for tea with a mutual friend. She knew Mrs. Mannering to be a loose-tongued woman, so rather than offering to help directly, she had presented them with one of her cards and suggested that her "acquaintance" might track down their daughter.

The daughter had been located—she had become so fed up with her parents' matrimonial ambitions that she had run away to the home of her aunt—and the Mannerings had never known that it was Lily herself who had found her.

"So it was Mrs. Mannering who suggested you contact the lady of quality?" On the one hand, Mrs. Mannering loved to gossip. On the other hand, sharing such a story about her own daughter would hardly reflect well on her, even if that daughter was now well married. And Lily had no interest in assisting someone who began with lying to her.

"Yes," the young woman said, nodding.

Lily waited silently, her brows rising just a hair.

"No . . ." Miss Forrest stretched the word out hesitantly, biting her lip as she looked away. "That is to say, not exactly. Mrs. Mannering mentioned that someone had assisted them with a sort of inquiry— she made it sound dreadfully dramatic, which is why I thought—well, and she showed my cousin, who is my companion, and me the lady of quality's card over tea. And I was already so worried, and in need of help, that I—I took it." The final words came out in a rush, and the girl looked suddenly both deflated and relieved. "I stole it, I suppose. And then I wrote because I so desperately needed someone to help me. Can you?" She raised her eyes hopefully to Lily's.

"Perhaps," Lily said. "Though beginning with a falsehood does not bode well." Miss Forrest's face fell, and she looked like nothing so much as a scolded puppy. Lily sighed. "Tell me what it is you need assistance with." She glanced at Clive and added coldly, "And how you come into it, sir. Then I shall make up my mind."

Miss Sarah Forrest sat up very straight. "I need your assistance to escape my uncle. I fear he has stolen all the money my father intended for me to inherit." Her mouth and hands both trembled, and she clasped her fingers together tightly to keep them still. "He says it is for my own good that he controls my inheritance. But I do not believe my father would do such a thing. And now, because he has kept my independence from me, my uncle is preventing me from marrying in order to keep me dependent on him, perhaps forever."

Lily sat back against the bench. She glanced at Clive. "And that is where you come into it, I suppose?"

He, still standing, bowed. "I have asked Miss Forrest to marry me, yes. We met during the winter and were instantly in sympathy with each other."

"Mr. Clive's family is from Suffolk, and his property is there too, of course." Miss Forrest said, holding out her hand to her suitor. "But he felt so dreadfully isolated that he came to London last winter."

"I had not recalled that your family was from Suffolk," Lily said, her eyes fixed on Clive. Her hands were clenched into fists by her sides; she took a deep breath, trying to relax them. "How forgetful of me."

"No matter," Miss Forrest went on, not noticing Lily's tone. Clive's sideways glance, however, said he had not missed it. "Such a handsome, charming young man is much better suited to life in town, do you not think?"

"My dear Sarah is too kind to me," Clive said gallantly, taking the hand she held out to him, giving her a warm smile as he pressed it between his. "And I am fortunate indeed that she is. She is the love of my life."

"So Miss Forrest said in her letter," Lily said a little more cynically than she intended. But it was impossible to keep a completely straight face as she watched their romantic interlude, or as she remembered the melodramatic turns of phrase the young woman had employed.

"Yes." Miss Forrest smiled at her sweetheart, showing no hesitation or embarrassment over her elevated prose. "He is a most dashing, wonderful young man. Though I hardly need tell you that," she added earnestly, turning back to Lily, "as you are already acquainted."

They were acquainted. And when Lily had met him in her aunt's small Hampshire village, he was a cardsharp and a bookmaker, accepted into more elevated circles than the ones into which he had been born because nearly every young man with pretensions to dissipation owed him money. No one had trusted him, but no one could risk offending him either. He knew it, and he had despised those around him even as he needed them in turn.

Once or twice, Lily had thought she saw a hint of the more admirable man he might have become had he chosen a different path. But if there was, he had not bothered to cultivate it. And he had made no secret of his plan, during that brief week of their acquaintance, to use his ill-gotten income to one day place himself in the role of a gentleman and improve his lot in life.

It seemed he had succeeded. Or would have, if Miss Forrest's inheritance had not disappeared.

"But it seems this dashing, wonderful young man will not marry you without your inheritance?" Lily asked.

That prompted a scowl from Miss Forrest. "I know what you are thinking, ma'am. But you are wrong. My dear Mr. Clive has some money of his own. The problem we face is that my uncle will not give his consent."

"How old are you, Miss Forrest?" Lily asked, glancing sideways at Clive.

"I am not yet two-and-twenty," Miss Forrest said sitting up very straight, as though to look as mature and worldly as possible.

"Then you are legally able to marry, even without your uncle's consent," Lily said pragmatically. "If it is not a question of needing your inheritance, why not simply do so?"

Clive sighed. "Because—"

But Miss Forrest broke in. "Just because he is not marrying me for my money does not mean we've no need of something to live on," she said, the irritation plain in her voice. She gave Lily a look up and down. "You will forgive me for saying, ma'am, but you look like you are no stranger to comfort. Is it so wrong that we might wish for the same in our own lives?"

Lily wanted to argue the point, but it was a reasonable one. Or it would have been, were it not for what she knew of the gentleman in question. "Very well," she said, inclining her head. "I merely wish to know all the facts of the situation."

"And if I had come to you for marriage advice, your interference might be warranted," Miss Forrest snapped, her cheeks going splotchy with irritation. "But I did not."

"Sarah," Clive said before Lily could reply. When she glanced at him, his smile was firmly in place, but there was a cynical edge to it. "It is a mark of her good character that she asks such questions. Mrs. Adler does not know me as you do."

Miss Forrest took a deep breath, reining in her emotions once more. "I suppose. But my uncle's refusing his consent only proves my concern is warranted." She clasped her book tightly against her midsection, as though it were a shield she could hide behind. "Even if my father did change his will, whatever inheritance my uncle is currently steward of would pass from Uncle Forrest's control to that of my husband if I marry. What other reason could he have for refusing his consent if not to keep control of those funds?"

"Skepticism of your suitor, perhaps?" Lily murmured.

"But we have never met," Clive put in. "He has refused to do so."

"Which is also suspicious!" Miss Forrest declared.

Lily glanced around. Miss Forrest's emphatic tones had drawn curious stares from the couples strolling nearby. One of the women glanced at them several times, though she had not stopped talking to the man with her. A feeling of unease settled in Lily's stomach. She thought she recognized the woman, though she could not put a name to the face.

She needed to leave this conversation as soon as possible.

"Well," she said, tapping the tips of her fingers together, "you tell an interesting story."

Miss Forrest met Lily's eyes; her own, for the first time, were wide and sober. "I know it sounds like something out of a novel. But it is the truth. All I want is to reclaim the independence that should be mine."

"Then you would be best served by speaking to your father's solicitor," Lily said briskly. "He would be able to assist you in understanding how your father left things, I've no doubt."

The young lady scowled, her cheeks flushing red. "I do not know who his solicitor was. And for obvious reasons, I cannot ask my uncle for the name."

"Then what is it you are hoping I will do?" Lily said. "I am one woman, Miss Forrest. I cannot retrieve your money for you."

"I know that. But my uncle will have a copy of my father's will in his house, and I think I know where it would be." The girl leaned forward, her breath coming quickly and her hands trembling once more. "I want to hire you to steal it for me so I can prove what he has done."

CHAPTER 3

For a moment, Lily was certain that she had misheard. But Miss Forrest was watching her with an earnest, eager expression. And when she glanced at Clive, certain it must be some sort of prank devised with his assistance, he looked equally somber.

Lily looked back at Miss Forrest. "I am not in the habit of taking on commissions for theft," she said coldly.

Miss Forrest's face fell, and to Lily's surprise, there were tears visible in her eyes. "Please," she begged. "I need help, and I've nowhere else to turn. Look"—she pulled a folded piece of paper from inside the pages of her book—"I have even drawn up a map of each floor of the house. You see, everything is labeled, and I have put a little mark on each of the rooms where I think he is likely to keep his private papers, and—"

"Then you ought to find the will yourself," Lily said pragmatically. "If your uncle is, as you say, your guardian since the death of your father—my condolences—surely you are better placed to find it than anyone else?"

Miss Forrest shook her head while she scrounged around in her reticule for a lacy little handkerchief to wipe her eyes. "He does not permit me to live with him. Nor even to visit his house—which by rights ought to be *my* house."

That was surprising enough to make Lily pause. "You do not live alone?" she demanded.

"No, I am under the care of a cousin, who was my mother's relative. My father brought her to live with us some years ago, when I was still a child. She is a spinster, and now my uncle provides the two of us only a small allowance, which is why we must live at such an unfashionable address. When my father was alive, I lived on Queen Anne Street," she added, her voice growing louder with defensive pride.

"Speak more quietly, if you please," Lily said, trying not to sound snappish as she glanced around. "What is your uncle's name?"

The girl scowled but dropped her voice. "Martin Forrest. My cousin is Miss Mary Waverly. Uncle Forrest lives at my father's house now, but I am certain it was supposed to come to me. Along with all the rest of it. My cousin is not permitted to visit either, and all the servants are new since my father's death, so they will not defy his edict that we are to be kept away." Her mouth trembled, and she sniffed back tears once more.

"We believe it is all a design to keep Miss Forrest from finding her father's will and discovering her uncle's villainy," Clive put in, taking a step closer.

Lily sighed. She wished she was standing as well, so she would not have to look up at him. The whole conversation was beginning to feel like a scene from a novel, and not the sort that had a happy ending. "If you, as his niece, cannot gain entry, how do you expect me to?"

"Mr. Clive says you are an eminently resourceful woman," Miss Forrest said eagerly. "He was certain you would be able find a way. If you need a few days to consider, I understand. But I beg you will decide quickly. My uncle just wrote to my cousin that he intends to shut up his house and depart for Bath within the week. Please." Miss Forrest lifted her chin. Her eyes, still shining with tears, regarded Lily with a discomfiting degree of hope. "All I want is to regain the independence that should be mine. Surely that is not so terrible a wish?"

It was not, and it was one Lily could not help feeling sympathy toward, even as she remained skeptical of Miss Forrest herself. But to be asked to rob someone . . .

If Miss Forrest was correct, her uncle was the one stealing from her. In that case, though the legality of the situation might be questionable, the morality was quite clear. And Lily, as she had to admit to herself, had not scrupled in the past to steal from those she suspected of nefarious behavior.

But however much sympathy she might feel, there was the man standing beside her to consider. He was already lying to Miss Forrest about himself. How else might he have deceived her? Lily did not trust him to be acting in anyone's best interests but his own. And knowing that, she couldn't risk helping Miss Forrest, whatever she might otherwise have wished to do.

Lily stood. "I am sorry to disappoint you, Miss Forrest. But I cannot in good conscience do as you ask."

The young woman sprang up from the bench, reaching for Lily's arm, though she stopped herself before she grabbed it. Instead, she clutched her suitor's arm. "But—you must, please. I've no idea what—"

"Mrs. Adler," Clive broke in, laying a soothing hand on top of Miss Forrest's. "Might I have a word with you?" He gave his intended a gentle smile, then carefully removed her hand from his arm. "A slightly more private word?"

Lily gave him a cool look. "I do not think that is necessary. As much as I sympathize with your plight, Miss Forrest, I—"

"I think it may be." He held out his hand to her. "Miss Forrest's maid is at liberty again and will be coming over here in a moment. Pray, take a turn around the sycamores with me, Mrs. Adler."

Lily stared at him, equally irritated by his interruption and unnerved by his words, which clearly had the air of an order, not a request. She wanted to walk away. But she suspected that if she did, she would risk some sort of scene, which she had already worked hard to avoid. Perhaps agreeing would be the fastest way to remove herself from the situation. "Very well, if you wish."

"You honor me," he said before turning to favor Miss Forrest with a smile. "A moment only, my love. I shall return to say farewell."

"Of course. I will go speak with my maid in the meantime."

Lily waited until they were some distance away before she spoke. "You know, it is customary for a fortune hunter to seek another object for his gallantry if the first object proves to be insufficiently wealthy," she said conversationally.

"What makes you think I am a fortune hunter?" he asked as he led them onto the path around the sycamore grove.

"You stated your intention very clearly, the last time we spoke, to take on the mantle of a gentleman through whatever means necessary. And given that Miss Forrest has no inkling as to your background, I can only assume that she is your newest means to do so." Lily gave him a sideways glance.

"Would you believe me if I said I wish to marry her because I care for her?" Clive asked. His voice was calm, hardly passionate, and he watched her closely as he spoke.

"I would believe you if you said that you asked her to marry you when you thought she was to be wealthy, and now that you have discovered otherwise, you cannot back out of your own scheme without causing a scandal that would thwart your purposes in town," Lily said, a polite smile fixed on her own face. Others could see them, after all. She did not want to draw too much curious attention. "Can you not make her jilt you herself?"

"Are you so arrogant that you believe the lower orders to be incapable of true feeling?" he asked, his empty smile matching her own.

"Your parents being shopkeepers has nothing to do with it except that your disowning their memories is further proof of your dishonesty," Lily said through gritted teeth. "You are not from Suffolk; your family has never owned property there; and you made whatever money you have through bookmaking, gambling, and bribery."

"You were born to money and position, Mrs. Adler," he said. "I was not. Is it so wrong to wish for a change of circumstances, to create for myself what you were given through nothing but an accident of birth?"

"It is if you resort to fraud and deception in order to achieve it."

"Your kind leave precious few other means of entrée into their elevated ranks." The smile had not left his face the entire time they were walking, but he did not disguise the disgust in his voice.

"I will not deny that, nor will I argue with your comments on the accident of birth," Lily said, earning her a surprised look from him. Clearly, an argument was exactly what he had expected. "I could even find something to admire in your industriousness, or at least in your respect for your parents' memory and your housekeeping, both of which I recall being quite admirable." He snorted, looking almost amused. But Lily was not done. Her voice grew sharper. "But anything of good that I might have said about you pales in comparison to the villainy of entering into a marriage under false pretenses."

"I do own property in Suffolk now," he put in. "That was not a lie."

"You are deceiving that young woman as to who you are, and you are doing it for your good, not hers. Was it you who put the idea in her head that her uncle was stealing her inheritance? Would she have even thought of it on her own?"

"Well, as to that, she would and she did, for I had nothing to do with it," Clive replied, a little smugly. "My dear Sarah needs no help in looking after her own interests. It is one of the reasons we are so suited for each other."

"You are an unscrupulous charlatan," Lily snapped, forgetting her polite facade.

"Even a charlatan may fall in love."

"Then shall we tell her the truth?" Lily suggested, fixing her smile in place once more. "If it is love, as you say, then would you not want her to accept you for who you truly are?"

For a moment, his steps slowed, and Lily wondered if he would say yes. When they had first met in Hampshire, she had seen glimpses of humanity under his immoral exterior. There was always a chance that would be the side of him that won out.

But he had been playing the scoundrel for a long time. And in Lily's experience, people rarely changed unless something that they could not ignore made them do it. So she was unsurprised when he turned and led her onward, almost forcefully, the expression in his eyes grown cold. His arm was tense under her hand. "You will tell her nothing."

Lily shook her head. "I thought as much. Now, if you will excuse me——"

"I am not finished," he said, laying a hand over hers. It was not a gentle gesture; it would have taken some force to dislodge him. "We're not strolling so that you may tell me the defects of my character. I'm well aware of those, thank you."

"Then why?"

He slowed to a stop. They were behind the sycamores now, in a more secluded part of the park. No one could have said they were improperly alone. But for the moment, neither was anyone close by. "To ask you to change your mind, of course."

"I will not," Lily said.

"Because of the request itself or because of my connection to it?" When Lily hesitated before replying, he smiled cynically. "And here I thought Sarah's plight would be enough to prompt your sympathy."

"I have a great deal of sympathy for her. If what she suspects is true, it is appalling. But I will not embroil myself in it." She yanked her hand off his arm and gave a polite bow. "Please tell Miss Forrest I wish her all success. Good day, Mr. Clive."

"You will change your mind."

Lily, already turning away from him, stopped. As much as she wanted to keep walking, there was a certainty in his voice that sent a shiver down her spine. She turned back. "I beg your pardon?"

"You will change your mind," he repeated softly, stepping toward her. "Take my arm and I will tell you why."

"No." She did not try to leave. But she would not play his games either.

His jaw tightened. "You will walk back there, and you will tell Miss Forrest that have decided to help her locate her father's will. Because if you do not, Mrs. Adler, I shall have a few choice things to say about you. Not just to Miss Forrest, you understand—no indeed. Far more publicly than that. About your creeping around, in

Hampshire and in London, prying into other people's homes and lives. About your discreet inquiries and confidential investigations. About who this *lady of quality* truly is."

Lily's expression did not change as he spoke. But inside, she felt as though she were standing at the edge of a precipice. His voice was too steady for her to think it was an idle threat. And if he followed through on his words, it would be disastrous for her.

There had been curious gossip about her before, but it had been nothing more than speculation and happenstance. No one who repeated it had ever truly believed she had been involved in anything scandalous or nefarious. But if Clive did what he was threatening, people would start putting the pieces together. They would remember where she had been, who she had known. What had been uncovered and discovered. They would know he was telling the truth.

It did not matter that she had only done good. That she had helped people who needed help, assisted the police, uncovered the plans of more than one murderer.

She would be completely ostracized. She would have to avoid her friends or risk tainting them by association. And in scandal-loving London, such gossip would follow her for years. She would have to leave the place that had become her home.

Lily took a deep breath. She refused to be cowed by such a man, to give in to his threats and blackmail. "You do not scare me," she said, lifting her chin. She had started over once. She could do so again.

But Clive only smiled. "And of course those discreet investigations were not just yours, were they? What was your friend's name, the one who came to see me when we were all in Hampshire?" Clive looked thoughtful, though Lily had no doubt it was all for show. "Lady Carroway, I believe? She was so quick with a bribe. Such a surprising trait in a ladyship. Though perhaps less surprising in someone of her background."

In spite of her plan to stay calm in the face of his threats, Lily drew in a sharp breath. "You would ruin your own chances of making your way into London society," she bit off, wishing she could slap him.

"Unlike you, madam, I have neither family nor friends to whom I wish to stay connected. I could easily start over in another town. When you are a resourceful man with some money and property, a great many doors will open to you, no matter where you go. But it would be far more difficult for you to start over, would it not? And even more difficult for Lady Carroway. She is a charming woman, but her husband's family is so very proud. I hate to imagine her shut away in one of their country properties, unable to rejoin good society without risking a terrible scandal."

For a moment, Lily could think of nothing to say in response. It was exactly the sort of thing that could happen to a woman like Ofelia. Ned Carroway would never condone it—but his mother was a cousin to the Earl of Portland, an old and rigid family. As the scion of a junior branch of the family, he might not have much say if the senior members decided that his young wife should be sent away to the country in order to protect the reputations of his sisters and cousins.

Lily stared at Clive, her mouth tight and eyes snapping with fury, saying nothing. She had never hated anyone before, but she did in that moment. She was willing to gamble with her own reputation and well-being.

She could not take such a chance with Ofelia's.

Clive smiled. "As you said, Mrs. Adler, I am unscrupulous. So, what is it to be?"

Lily gritted her teeth. She did not want to tell him yes, but she could not risk telling him no. "Give me two days to decide," she said, glad when her words came out firm and calm. She would not give him the satisfaction of knowing how his threats had rattled her. "If Mr. Forrest is not leaving London until the end of the week, you can wait that long, can you not?"

Clive eyed her for an unnerving moment, then nodded once. "Very well. You have two days. And after that, we shall see what happens." He took a step back, tipping his hat in a mockery of politesse. "I bid you a good day, madam."

CHAPTER 4

Amelia waited to speak until they had left the park and its troublesome visitors some blocks behind, when it was clear that they were not immediately returning to Half Moon Street. "Is everything all right, Mrs. Adler? What happened?"

Lily started a little. She had been distracted with trying to decide the best way to proceed—and how much to tell her young companion. "The conversation did not go as I expected," she said at last.

"There was a gentleman," Amelia said, her curiosity plain. But she spoke quietly; Lily's maid, Anna, followed a few sedate steps behind them. Anna knew better than to try to eavesdrop, but unless they kept their voices low, she would have no trouble overhearing what they were saying.

The thought made Lily smile a little in spite of her worry. Anna had been a housemaid in her home when Lily was still Miss Pierce, and she had elected to come along as lady's maid through Lily's marriage and widowhood. There was little about Lily's life that she did not know.

But that was yet another consideration on Lily's shoulders, in light of Clive's threats. Her countenance grew serious again as they paused at a street corner, waiting for several carriages and delivery carts to pass by. Her servants depended on her for employment and care, and she took that responsibility seriously. Were she to end up embroiled in a scandal, it could impact their lives and livelihoods as well. They would have to choose between staying with her through public

disgrace or seeking new employment—if they could even find someone new to hire them when a character reference from her would be
worth very little.

"Mrs. Adler?" Amelia was watching her with concern.

"The man was our young gentlewoman's suitor," Lily said,
answering Amelia's question at last. "Her name is Miss Sarah Forrest.
And I"—she took a deep breath—"I need more information about
her. Would you prefer to return home while I make my inquiries?"

"Indeed not," Amelia replied firmly. "Do we proceed on foot, or
shall we require a conveyance?"

"It is not far," Lily said. She turned, catching her maid's attention.
"Anna, you may return to Half Moon Street. Let Mrs. Carstairs know
we will still be dining at home tonight."

Once she was gone, Lily turned her steps toward Grosvenor
Square, Amelia at her side. "We are in need of a reliable source of
gossip," she said by way of explanation. "Which means it is time to
pay a visit to Lady Walter."

★ ★ ★

Serena, the Viscountess Walter, was covered in children. The two
elder boys climbed over the chaise on which she was reclining while
their harried nursemaid attempted to herd them toward the door and
they evaded her with delighted shrieks. Mary Walter, only seventeen
months old, was building towers of wooden blocks, clapping her
hands and yelling with ferocious pleasure each time she knocked them
over. Through it all, Serena's fourth child, just two months old, lay at
her mother's breast, seeming as unbothered by the chaos as Serena
herself was.

"I am so sorry, my lady," the nursemaid said yet again as
she scooped up five-year-old Francis in one arm and attempted—
unsuccessfully—to get hold of his older brother with the other. "I
told them they were not to disturb you—"

"No need to fret," Lady Walter replied, rolling her eyes toward
her guests with an imitation of a long-suffering sigh that fooled no
one in the room. "They are just so smitten with our little Louisa.

And who can blame them?" she added as the boys escaped their nurse once more and crowded around the new baby. "She is a charming little thing, though she does still somewhat resemble a wrinkled old man."

"Wrinkled old man!" shrieked seven-year-old John, draping himself over one of his mother's arms while Francis climbed the back of the chaise and laughed uproariously.

"Oh, indeed, my lady," the nurse agreed, even as she glanced askance at the chaotic tableau. "But perhaps your ladyship would like me to take Miss Louisa away so that you are not . . ." She cleared her throat delicately. "That is, so you might entertain your guests without any distractions?"

"You mean so I might close my gown and stop baring myself to the world like a peasant woman?" Serena asked too innocently while the nurse blushed and stammered that she had meant no such commentary on my lady's care of her infant. But Serena was already fastening her bodice. "A little space, if you please, my loves," she admonished her boys. They scooted obligingly away from her as she handed the baby, now close to falling asleep, over to the nurse, who already had Mary by the hand. "Mama must entertain her guests now, so off you go. And if I hear you've been disobeying Nurse, there shall be no pudding after supper, so mind you are on best behavior."

Serena leaned back against her chaise as the children and their noise disappeared into the hall. "At last, some peace and quiet."

"I see you've not given into her entreaties that you hire a wet nurse," Lily said as she took a seat on a comfortably upholstered chair.

The Gilbert Street house had been recently rented so Serena might have a more stylish London address than the family's larger but less fashionable property in Marylebone. The little upstairs sitting room, its windows streaming with sunlight and its furnishings a riot of fashionable color, was reserved exclusively for family use, or Serena would not have been nursing her infant there. But Lily was a family friend of long standing, having gone to school with Serena. They had seen each other through marriages, births, and deaths, and it was the discovery of an unknown gentleman's body in Serena's own garden that had first caught Lily up in the investigation of murder.

And so on this occasion, Lily had been shown up to the private parlor almost immediately, with Amelia granted the same privilege as her companion. Now Lily smiled at her friend's pretense of fashionably unconcerned motherhood, which she knew could not be further from the truth. "Has Lord Walter come around, at least?"

"He grew accustomed to it with Mary, I believe," Serena said, gesturing for Amelia to take a seat as well, before closing her eyes for a moment, as though to better savor the silence. "And as Dr. Cowper has advised that it is better for Louisa, and for my own health, if I am the one to nurse her, Lord Walter has voiced very few objections."

"Well, Louisa is clearly thriving," Lily said. "And I am glad to see that you are as well."

"She *is* thriving, the dear thing," Serena said, opening her eyes and fixing Lily with a curious stare. "But you did not drag your charge over here to discuss the feeding of infants."

"No, indeed," Lily agreed. "I came for gossip."

"My favorite thing, as you well know," Serena said. "What is it you need to know? Has Miss Hartley found a suitor that needs vetting?" She glanced at Amelia. "They are not all to be trusted, as I hope you know."

"I do, my lady," Amelia agreed with a sideways glance at Lily. Suitors who were not to be trusted were one of the reasons Amelia had been so eager to leave Hertfordshire, though Lady Walter did not know that. "But it is not a man about whom Mrs. Adler needs information."

"A lady then?" Serena asked, sitting forward. "How intriguing."

"Do you know the name Miss Sarah Forrest?" Lily asked, watching her friend carefully. "Or anything about her family?"

She preferred to give no other details at first, waiting to see what information might be lurking in the encyclopedic depths of Serena's mental catalogue. Judging by what Miss Forrest had said, her family had not seemed quite like the sort of people with whom Serena, the well-connected wife of a viscount, would be likely to socialize. But it was not impossible that their circles could overlap. And if there had been any scandal or interest in the late Mr. Forrest's will, it might have spread beyond their immediate circle of acquaintance.

Lily was not disappointed.

It took only a moment for Serena's expression to brighten. "Someone died, and he was rumored to be quite wealthy. Or was it that he was not as wealthy as he should have been? I cannot recall precisely." She fixed her eye sternly on Lily. "Has yet another unnatural death crossed your path?"

That made Lily laugh. "Fortunately not. This time it is a question of inheritance. The Mr. Forrest who died recently—I do not know quite how recently, but perhaps you do—left behind a daughter. I am curious if you know of anything odd about the disposition of his will or the situation of the daughter."

"And how did you come to be so curious about the late Mr. Forrest's estate?" Serena asked, eyeing Lily over her steepled fingers. "And do not say you are interested in gossip for gossip's sake. I know you well enough not to believe that, Lily."

"I am as entertained by gossip as the next person might be," Lily said, smiling a little as a maid entered with the tea tray. "Anyone who claims otherwise is lying."

"Yes, but this time you are seeking it out," Serena said as she sat forward to pour a cup for each of them. "Allow me to venture a guess: you heard of a young lady who might be in a precarious financial situation, and you wish to involve yourself as her protector."

Lily sighed as the maid left the room. "I shall tell you, but this part must not be repeated about." Concisely, and with far less melodrama than Miss Sarah Forrest had employed, Lily laid out what she knew. She left out the details of Clive's involvement; for the moment, she wanted to know only about the members of the Forrest family. Amelia, who had not yet heard the story, listened with rapt attention. "Miss Forrest has sought my aid," Lily concluded as she accepted her tea from Serena and took a sip.

"And you are trying to determine whether there is any merit to her suspicions, or if someone has, shall we say, advised her poorly?"

Serena guessed. "Or, I suppose, whether she is deceiving herself into unnecessary alarm?"

"Precisely." Lily nodded. "Miss Forrest's story could be true, but she could also be mistaken about how her father intended to leave things. Or perhaps he once intended to leave her inheritance to her outright but grew concerned for one reason or another. If he thought she was not ready to be mistress of her own affairs, he might have appointed her uncle to exactly the position he now occupies."

"A shrewd observation," Serena said, looking pleased with herself, "considering what I know of the uncle—if it is indeed the same man. Is his name Mr. Martin Forrest?"

Lily sat forward. "You have heard of him?"

"Yes, and for quite a peculiar reason." Serena set her own tea down and went to the writing table in the corner of the room, where she kept her correspondence. It took her only a moment to locate the letter she was searching for; when she returned, she handed it to Lily. "I would not know his name at all, except I received that invitation from him two days ago."

Lily read through it quickly. It was predictable enough: Mr. Martin Forrest requested the pleasure of Lord and Lady Walter's presence at an evening soiree, et cetera. The address was Queen Anne Street—just as Miss Forrest had said. When Lily looked up, Serena's eyes were on her, brows raised.

"An odd coincidence, do you not think?" Lady Walter asked, retrieving her teacup.

"But you do not know him?" Lily demanded, handing the invitation to Amelia.

"No, indeed. I hadn't the slightest idea who he was when I received it," Serena said, shaking her head. "I was utterly baffled, and not a little offended, as we had never been introduced. It was dreadfully forward of him, do you not agree?"

"He must have a great deal of social ambition," Amelia observed, passing the invitation back to Lady Walter.

"That was what I thought," Serena agreed, sniffing a little. "I still think it. I would have thrown such a thing out, but Sally Windermere was visiting when it arrived, and she said she had received one as well."

"I thought you disliked Sally?" Lily murmured, amused.

"I can never decide if I do or not," Serena admitted, shrugging a little, then stretching out her back in an unladylike manner. "But how I feel about her is beside the point. She is an old acquaintance, and most importantly, she knows everything that happens in London. I swear it is impossible for a cat to have kittens in town without her hearing of it."

"And she knew something of Mr. Forrest?"

"Apparently so. Her mother knew the late Mr. Forrest a little, so it was not so odd for Sally to be invited, though she has no intention of attending. But the only reason she could think that Mr. Martin Forrest would be brazen enough to send an invitation to Lord Walter and me was that we have been introduced to Miss Crawley, and perhaps he thought that was enough of an acquaintance."

"Who is Miss Crawley?" Lily demanded.

"Julia Crawley. Her mother is a very distant cousin of Lord Jersey. Her family lives in Berkeley Square, but they absolutely live on credit, so they intend to marry her off to this Mr. Martin Forrest. Sally told me all about it."

"And?" Amelia demanded, leaning forward.

That made Serena laugh. "Very well, I shan't keep you in suspense any longer. Either of you," she added, giving Amelia an indulgent smile. "According to Sally Windermere—which you know really means according to her mother, who remembers absolutely every—"

"Serena," Lily said sternly, warning her to stay on topic.

Serena laughed again. "The father of your Miss Sarah Forrest was considered quite an eligible bachelor in his day. Drove four matched grays and had young ladies absolutely swooning at his feet. But he was nearly disinherited by his family when he married the late Mrs. Forrest, just over twenty years ago. Sally says it was quite the scandal, which is why her mother had so much to say about it all these years later."

"What was the objection to the lady?" Amelia asked.

"She was a tradesman's daughter, so it was considered quite a comedown for him. But they could not cast him off completely, because she brought a tidy little fortune with her to the marriage, and the family estate was entailed and in dire straits." Serena glanced at the tea tray, as if noticing the cake on it for the first time. "They needed the money," she added as she leaned forward to cut each of her guests a slice.

Lily waited until Serena had passed the plates of cake around. "And did Sally Windermere know anything of the uncle and daughter today?"

"Indeed, yes. According to Sally's mother, the birth of Miss Sarah Forrest produced a rift between the brothers. Apparently, the elder Mr. Forrest and his bride declared their intention that their daughter should inherit the bulk of their money should no son be forthcoming—which none was, as Mrs. Forrest died soon after. No one knew whether it was the parents' stubbornness or the terms of the marriage settlement, but in either case, the younger Mr. Forrest was to be left with a once-more impoverished estate to support."

"God bless London gossip," Lily murmured, taking a bite of her cake. "This is excellent, Serena. You must be pleased with the new cook. So it seems likely that the uncle is—" She broke off as she caught sight of Serena's face. "Good heavens, did Sally have even more gossip than that?"

"A great deal more," Serena said, beaming with her eagerness to share what she knew. "The elder Mr. Forrest stayed in London, but the younger joined the army and left the country. According to the story, he did not set foot on English soil again until last year, when he returned at his brother's behest."

"Was that just before the brother died?" Lily asked, her eyes narrowing.

Serena shook her head. "It was meant to be, and I know what you are thinking, madam, but not everything is about murder, thank you."

"I did not say it was," Lily said mildly.

Serena rolled her eyes. "You did not have to," she said, prompting Amelia to muffle a laugh. "The elder had been ill for some time, and with his wife gone and his daughter in need of a male guardian, he wrote to his brother and asked him to come home."

"But he did not make it in time?" Lily asked.

"Whether he did or not, I suppose they must have been reconciled." Serena sniffed a little, as if affected by the pathos of the situation, then quickly covered a yawn. "Do excuse me. According to Sally, the general understanding of those who know the family seems to be that his final illness recalled the elder Mr. Forrest to a sense of what he owed to his family. He decided to make sure that his family estate was provided for." Serena let out a breath, looking pleased with herself. "And that is everything I know, which I think should satisfy even your thirst for knowledge."

Lily settled back in her chair, thinking. For a moment, she stared at the fire crackling on the hearth without really seeing it.

Serena's gossip, she knew, was highly reliable—as far as such things could be. She was excellent at discovering what was whispered among certain circles of London residents. But just because something was frequently repeated and generally accepted did not make it true.

When she looked back at her friends, Lily found them both watching her.

"What do you think, Mrs. Adler?" Amelia asked quietly. "How does that strike you after your conversation with Miss Forrest?"

"On the surface, it seems plausible," Lily said as she set down her plate. "Miss Forrest seemed to think that her father intended all along for her to be the sole heir of his wealth. But he could have changed his mind. That would mean there is nothing nefarious in the conduct of her uncle. But . . ."

"But?" Serena asked, looking excited, though the expression was somewhat ruined as she tried to hide another yawn.

Lily did not fidget or drum her fingers on the arms of her chair while she thought. She did not rise to pace about the room, as she often liked to do while she turned over a problem. Instead, she sat very still, thinking through everything Serena had said. "But there is an oddity to the whole affair," she said at last.

Amelia thought for a moment. "The house?"

Lily nodded. "For Miss Forrest's uncle to have, in effect, banished her from her childhood home, rather than simply installing himself as her guardian, and to provide her and her cousin with very little to live on . . . It is not the act of a well-intentioned guardian, however her father might have left things."

"How terribly intriguing," Serena said. "I cannot wait to hear what you—" She broke off, looking embarrassed as she had to cover yet another yawn. "Dear me."

Lily, smiling apologetically, stood. Amelia quickly followed suit. "We have imposed ourselves on you for long enough, I think. You ought to take advantage of the quiet and rest."

"Temporary as it is," Serena laughed. "I suppose you are right, though it is invigorating to be able to receive visitors once more. Dr. Cowper says I shall be ready to go about regularly very soon. I cannot wait."

"Well, all your friends will be delighted to have you up and about once more. But do not overtax yourself," Lily said, fixing Serena with a stern eye before bending to brush a quick kiss against her friend's cheek. "And I am glad to see you doing so well."

"Thriving, as always," Serena said, beaming. "Thank you for stopping by. And for giving me such interesting things to think over."

"Just be careful you do not repeat them around," Lily said. She hesitated, then gestured at the invitation that sat on the table next to Serena. "What are you planning to do with that?"

"This?" Serena plucked the paper up with two fingers, eyeing it somewhat askance. "I had intended to throw it away. Even if I could manage a ball—which I sadly cannot yet—neither Lord Walter nor I would dream of attending a ball thrown by a man we have never met. What if his guests are licentious? Or tradespeople?" Seeing Lily's disapproving expression, Serena rolled her eyes. "Do not look at me like that, thank you. You have nearly eight hundred pounds a year, Lily; you are no more a woman of the people than I am."

Lily shook her head, not wanting to argue. "Would you mind if I took it with me?"

Serena's brows lifted, and she was smiling as she handed the invitation over. "By all means. But whatever do you plan to do with it?"

"I've not decided yet," Lily murmured, tucking the card into the reticule she carried. "But it pays to be prepared."

"Well, so long as you promise eventually to tell me what you get up to, I've no objection at all. Oh, and Miss Hartley?" Serena gave them an impish smile. "I hear that charming brother of yours is back in town. Do give him my greetings, and tell him I expect him to dance with me at least twice this spring. Now, shoo, both of you, and let a poor mother rest."

CHAPTER 5

"Captain Hartley has arrived, madam," Lily's butler announced from the doorway of the drawing room. "Shall I show him in?"

"You know you may, Carstairs, and don't pretend you are not glad to see him as well," Lily said, rising from her chair. The evening had grown chilled, and fire crackled in the hearth, casting dancing shadows around the candlelit walls.

Though he normally wore the unreadable expression that was so useful in his profession, Lily's butler could not keep a smile from his face. "I should never dream of dissembling with you, madam," he said with grave humor as he bowed his way out of the room.

Lily smiled to herself, listening with half an ear to the conversation in the hall.

"And Mrs. Carstairs is well?" That was Jack's thoughtful inquiry after Lily's housekeeper-cook, currently busy in the kitchen.

"She is very well, sir. And she will be honored to know you asked after her," Carstairs rumbled, and Lily could hear the pleasure in his voice. "And your boy, Jem? Is the little scamp behaving himself?"

"Not so little these days," Jack chuckled. Lily had forgotten how comfortable Jack was with those he encountered, no matter their rank—a trait that set him apart from most men she knew. His manners were as easy with servants or clerks as they were with other gentlemen, a legacy, no doubt, of his twenty years in navy service, where midshipmen and officers from every walk of life lived in close quarters, depending on one another for safety and support. "I swear he grew half a foot over the winter. I fear I may beggar myself with the cost of his clothing alone. If I am not careful, he shall be outgrowing my service along with his coats."

Carstairs was smiling as they appeared in the drawing room. "Captain Hartley to see you, madam."

"Mrs. Adler." Jack bowed, polite as always in his address when they were not alone.

Lily held out her hands, grateful for the buffer of her butler's presence as she looked him over. "You are looking well, my friend. Is life ashore suiting you?"

Tall and broad-shouldered, with the easy, loose-limbed movement of a man long accustomed to the roll of a ship's deck, Jack filled the doorway with presence as much as with size. His dark hair, always a little disheveled despite his attempts to adhere to the latest fashions, was in need of a trim, and it curled around the nape of his neck. He had the same luminous eyes as Amelia, inherited from their mother, but his sparkled with the roguish humor that was always at the edge of his expression.

He did look well. He looked like himself, she was relieved to see, neither his strength nor his good humor diminished by his injury and recovery. She could not help noticing that, as he took her hands in his, the movement of his left arm was stiffer than that of his right. But she did not say anything about it as he smiled wryly.

"After recuperating in Yorkshire with Amal and her numerous offspring, I find myself longing for the measured calm of a sea battle."

"Your sister only has three children," Lily pointed out. She refused to be distracted by the touch. She had never been a romantic soul, and she had no intention of becoming one now. Still, the heat of his palms warmed her even through their gloves. "That hardly counts as numerous."

His smile grew. "I challenge you to repeat those words after spending a month with them."

"And how does the recuperating progress?" she asked, not bothering this time to hide her glance at his left arm.

He dropped her hands to rotate the shoulder in question. "Splendidly. I feel almost as good as new. Now," he said, waiting for her to sit before he did as well, "tell me what news I have missed while I was rusticating up north . . ."

Lily had caught the edge of a grimace when he moved his shoulder. And she had not missed how quick he had been to steer the conversation away from his injury. She almost reached out to touch his shoulder and had to press her palm flat against a fold of her gown to keep it still. She didn't want to risk causing him pain. Besides which, they had not touched since the night he was shot, and the memory of holding her hands against his wound still made her breath catch.

She wondered whether he was putting on a positive face for her or whether he had grown accustomed to such pretenses for the benefit of his family and had forgotten to drop them.

There had never used to be pretenses between them. From the very beginning of their friendship, they had been their honest selves, even when—perhaps especially when—those selves clashed. But even as they fell into an exchange of news about their mutual friends, there was something not quite easy in their conversation. Each brief pause felt strained rather than comfortable, and one or the other of them hurried to fill the silences, as though they were new acquaintances worried the other might find them dull.

She was not the only one who sensed that something had changed between them the night he was shot. But what that change meant to him, she couldn't say with any degree of confidence.

Lily squared her shoulders. This was absurd. They had known each other for years, and there was no reason anything should have changed between them. The best way to defeat awkwardness with an old friend was to call it what it was and laugh at it.

But she had only just parted her lips to speak when a delighted squeal cut her off.

"Raffi!"

Amelia burst through the drawing room door in an unladylike rush to throw her arms around her brother just as he rose from his seat. Lily was close enough to hear a grunt escape him from the impact, but he still caught his sister with no difficulty, even taken by surprise. Lily was relieved to see it; perhaps his injury did not bother him too much after all.

"Happy to see me then, Noor?" he asked, beaming down at her eager face.

Their habit of calling each other by their middle names, the ones given to them by their Indian mother, made Lily smile. All of the Hartley siblings did so, Jack had once told her. Their parents had encouraged it as a way for the four of them to feel close to one another in spite of the large gaps in their ages.

"More than you can imagine," she said. Jack was more than a decade Amelia's senior, but that didn't stop her from looking him over with a critical eye from head to toe. "You seem remarkably well for a man who almost died a few months ago."

"Amelia!" Lily exclaimed. It sounded like a scolding for rudeness, and judging by their laughter, that was how the two Hartleys took it. But for a moment, Amelia's words had made Lily feel as though she couldn't breathe.

"I hope you've better manners than that when Mrs. Adler takes you out," Jack said, gently pulling on a curl that had escaped the thick coronet of hair twined around his sister's head. "I'll not have you embarrassing my friend from one end of London to the other. How are you enjoying town, by the way? Our parents will expect a full report, you know."

"Oh, we've far more exciting things than teas and dances to tell you about," Amelia said, her eyes sliding over to Lily. "Though you should perhaps not share them with Papa and *Ammi*."

Jack glanced at Lily as well. "What sort of nefarious business have you dragged my sister into?" he asked with pretend disapproval, though he was grinning as he said it.

It was the sort of teasing that had been absent between them before Amelia's arrival; Lily was glad to see it return. She leaned forward in her chair, handing over the card that she had tucked in the edge of her glove.

Jack looked at it, his brows rising in surprise. "Are these still making their way into the world? I would have thought your services had no need of advertising these days. You've uncovered how many miscreants and criminals now?"

"I much prefer the miscreants," Lily said lightly, standing to cross to the sideboard. She gestured Jack back into his seat when he would have risen as well, and she was relieved that he didn't argue. Had he insisted on observing such polite conventions when they were not in public, things would have been strained between them indeed. "But you are correct—I've no need to be handing out cards these days. They seem to make their own way into the hands of those who need them. This time it was the hands of a young lady seeking aid."

"And which do you think is the cause of her distress?" Jack asked, stretching his legs comfortably out in front of him as Lily poured sherry into three glasses. "Miscreant or criminal?"

"Miscreant, I hope," Lily said at the same time as Amelia replied, "Criminal."

Jack's eyebrows climbed toward his hairline. "Are we placing wagers, then? I shall need more information if I am to join in."

For the second time that day, Lily shared Miss Sarah Forrest's story. Jack listened silently, though his expression grew more and more incredulous, and Lily could see his fingers tightening around the stem of his sherry glass.

"And so the general understanding, as Lady Walter put it, is that all must be as the late Mr. Forrest intended," Lily concluded. "It is a touching tale, is it not, of two brothers reunited, their quarrel set aside at the last?"

Jack downed the last of his sherry, then set down his glass. "And how much of Lady Walter's gossip do you believe?"

"I believe that her report is accurate. If she has heard that gossip claims all is well, then that is what is being said. But"—Lily shook her head—"what is said and what is true are often not the same. And it strikes me as a rather convenient story for the younger Mr. Forrest, especially as Serena had heard nothing of the daughter to explain her father's change of heart."

"Well then, Raffi," Amelia said, "what is your guess? Criminal or miscreant?"

"What makes you think criminal?" he asked, rather than answering her question.

"Prior experience," Amelia replied. She smiled as she said it, but there was a dark edge to her humor, and it made Lily shiver.

"It does seem that there is at least the potential for something nefarious at work," Jack said slowly. He had placed his glass on a side table, and now he turned it in absent-minded circles with one hand, his brows pulled together in a thoughtful frown.

"The business with the house does seem odd. As does the uncle's coldness toward his niece," Lily agreed. "Though it does not necessarily have to be criminal in nature. Perhaps he had held onto more animosity toward the brother who had cut him off than he had let on while the other Mr. Forrest was alive. And perhaps that animosity is now being directed toward Miss Forrest in her father's place."

"You do not necessarily believe so, though," Jack said, watching her. "Do you?"

"I feel a great deal of sympathy for her circumstances," Lily said, not quite answering the question. "It is a hard situation for any young woman to be in. And her uncle's behavior is suspicious, if nothing else. Under other circumstances, I would not hesitate to do as she asked." She glanced at Jack. "It is not unheard of for a man to take advantage of his access to a young lady's inheritance when that young lady is in his care."

"True," he said, nodding, his expression grim. They had both seen such things before, and it had not ended well for anyone involved.

"But it would be even more dastardly if he was not supposed to have that access in the first place. She is correct that if we could find the late Mr. Forrest's will, we would know whether that is the case."

"But would you steal it, as she asked?" Amelia asked, eyes wide. "Surely you could not bring yourself to do such a thing."

"Again, I think you mean," Jack chuckled. "Surely Mrs. Adler could not bring herself to do such a thing *again*."

"We, I think you mean," Lily countered, a little archly. "Surely *we* could not bring *ourselves* to do such a thing again."

Amelia's eyes narrowed as she glanced between them. "Well," she said slowly, "then it appears that concern is not a stumbling block to your decision."

"In this case it is," Lily said. "Had I decided to assist her, I should be more likely to help her find the name of her father's solicitor rather than try to steal from her uncle. But she seems a melodramatic young woman, so I am not surprised she settled on theft as the best course of action. Especially given—"

Lily broke off. She had nearly mentioned Clive's involvement, and she had been careful to keep any information about him from being shared where Amelia was present.

Jack's eyes had narrowed. "Especially given?" he prompted.

"Her age," Lily said calmly, as though it were what she had intended to say all along. "She is young enough to be impulsive still."

"She could just marry her suitor," Amelia pointed out. "What-ever her uncle's plans, criminal or otherwise, he cannot stop her from doing that."

"True," Jack said. "But if you knew you were entitled to a dowry, and someone was keeping it from you—for spite or worse—would you simply say 'devil take them' and walk away without what was rightfully yours?"

Amelia wrinkled her nose in distaste. "Likely not," she admitted.

But before anyone could reply further, Carstairs entered to announce that their meal was ready. After that, the conversation turned to more innocuous topics, the sort that could be discussed with Lily's servants coming in and out of the dining room at unexpected moments. They were aware of the sort of affairs she had previously been swept up in—they had, from time to time, been swept right along with her. But she did not want to worry them without cause. Half Moon Street was their home as well, and she wanted everyone who lived under her roof to feel safe there. So they discussed Jack's time with his other sister, Amal; news from their mutual friends; and the visit that Lily was expecting from her aunt and aunt's companion that spring.

"I hope it will be soon," Jack said cheerfully as the final course of fruit and syllabub was set before them. "I've not had the pleasure of seeing Miss Pierce or Miss Clarke in years, but I feel as though I know them well after all you've told me of them."

"I think I will have to forbid you from leaving London until they do arrive," Lily replied. "They shall be most put out if their paths do not cross yours while they are in town, and I shall be the one who never hears the end of it, even if the absence is entirely your fault."

"Forbid away, Mrs. Adler," Jack said, smiling at her over the edge of his wineglass. "I am at your service, as always."

Lily wanted to laugh the statement away as one of his gallant quips, but there was something in his gaze that made her suddenly doubt whether that was the correct way to respond. Unsure what to say, she was relieved when Amelia spoke up, though her relief was short-lived.

"I hope you will forgive me, but I think the excitement of the day has finally caught up to me," Amelia said as she stood. "I've the most dreadful headache beginning, and I think I must excuse myself from the rest of the evening."

"Do you need anything?" Lily asked, standing quickly, Jack rising only a moment behind her as he frowned in concern at his sister.

"No, I shall be quite all right," Amelia said, smiling at them, though she winced a little, one hand rising to her temple. "I think rest is all I require. Is there anything else I can do for you this evening, ma'am?"

"Of course not." Lily shook her head as she turned to Carstairs, who was waiting by the sideboard. "Will you tell Anna or Mrs. Carstairs to look in on Miss Hartley once she is upstairs? One of them may have a remedy for a headache that could be of use."

"Of course, madam." He bowed his way out of the room.

Amelia gave a wan smile. "Good night, then, Mrs. Adler." As she passed her brother, she stopped to give him a kiss on the cheek, but he caught her arm before she could step back.

"Are you sure you are well?" he asked, giving her a head-to-toe look much like the one she had given him when he arrived.

"Raffi, please do not be overbearing," she said, rolling her eyes. "It is a headache, nothing more. And Mrs. Adler has you to keep her company, so I do not even need to worry that I am shirking my duties as a companion." Her pat on his cheek was dripping with the sort of condescension that only a younger sibling could manage. "Did you not write once that you and Mrs. Adler often used to sit in her book-room in the evening? Now you may do so with no younger sister as interloper."

"But—"

"I have grown accustomed to not being fussed over," Amelia said as she pulled away to head for the door. "So I shall take my leave before you do any more of that. Good night, Raffi. Good night, Mrs. Adler."

Jack turned to Lily as soon as the door was closed behind her, his mouth twisting in wry humor. "Accustomed to not being fussed over?"

"She did have to put up with rather a lot of fussing at home last winter," Lily pointed out. "And you know I am not the sort of person to hover in the slightest."

"But you are looking after her?" he asked a little anxiously, looking toward the door once more. "Do you think anything is really wrong?"

"Jack." Lily did not bother to keep the exasperation from her voice.

He held up his hands. "Very well, very well. I will endeavor not to fuss. But it is hard not to be concerned for her, after . . ."

"I believe she feels the same about you," Lily said, giving his arm a pointed look.

"Ah." Jack's wry smile returned, and he rotated his shoulder once more, this time not bothering to hide his slight wince. "I am making do."

"Brave and stoic as always," Lily said, shaking her head. More quietly, she added, "Would you tell me if it were otherwise?"

He raised a brow. "Does this mean that my sister is not the only one concerned for my well-being? Have you spent the winter fretting about my health, Lily?"

Lily wanted to say yes. Instead, she narrowed her eyes at him. "I do not fret any more than I hover. As you well know."

That made him laugh, and he turned to survey the table. "You know, now that we are alone, I have an idea that we ought to be a little bit naughty." Lily stared at him in surprise, but he was already continuing before she could think of anything to say. "I see three bowls of syllabub on the table. Shall we take ours to the book-room and eat in comfort there?"

Whatever Lily had been expecting, it had not been that. "How truly scandalous," she said dryly.

That made Jack laugh again. "You know I like to be shocking," he said, catching up two glasses with one hand and spoons with the other. He bowed. "Shall we?"

There was a fire already lit and waiting in the book-room, and Lily curled up on one chair while Jack took the other. It was such a familiar ritual that she sank back in her seat without thinking, happily pulling her feet under her as she took a spoonful of her pudding. Only then did she noticed Jack watching her, his expression not entirely sanguine.

"Is something wrong?" she asked, suddenly nervous and glad he had already provided her with something to occupy her hands.

"The whole business with this Miss Forrest," he said, turning from her to frown at the dancing shadows thrown by the fire. He set his bowl aside. "What was it you did not wish to say in front of my sister?"

Lily sighed. Trust him to remember that brief stumble in her explanation. "There is something I left out, both tonight and when I spoke with Lady Walter. Unfortunately . . ." She hesitated. But it was best just to say it plainly. "Unfortunately, it seems I am being blackmailed."

"What?" Jack bolted from his seat, anger and disbelief warring in his expression as he stared at her.

Lily winced. "Please, keep your voice down," she said sternly. "There is no need to make a scene over it."

"I beg your pardon, but this is exactly the sort of thing worth making a scene over," he snapped. "Who is it? This Miss Forrest? What on earth could she have to blackmail you with?"

"Not her, her suitor. A man named Mr. Clive, whom I have had the misfortune to meet once before, in Hampshire." She didn't take her eyes from Jack while she spoke. "During that business with the Wright family."

"Ah." Jack had not been in Hampshire that particular autumn, but she had written to him of what had happened. "So he knows about . . ."

"Yes." Lily sighed. "But that is not the worst of it. He is also threatening Lady Carroway."

Jack sat down slowly. "Tell me everything."

Lily did. It did not take her long; her thoughts had been in a riot earlier that day as she tried to think through her options, but she was calmer now—at least outwardly. "He agreed to give me the two days, but he also insisted that I take the map she had made with me."

Jack had been listening in grave silence; at that, he looked thoughtful. "May I see it?"

Lily could not tell from his tone whether he was simply curious or if some other thought was brewing in his mind. She nodded at the table to his left. "It is tucked into that book of Hertfordshire maps. I did not want to leave it lying around where your sister might find it. I think Mr. Clive assumed that I would use it to begin planning my burglary. Horrid man," she added as Jack studied the drawing, his brows pulled into a frown. She sighed. "I suppose one must admire his confidence, if nothing else. Now, not only do I have to decide whether to do as he demands but also how to tell Ofelia and Sir Edward about it," Lily concluded, staring down at her bowl, forgotten until that moment. She set it aside and looked up to meet Jack's eyes. "Her position is more precarious than mine."

"To say the least," Jack replied, sliding the map back into the pages of the book. "And Carroway is not at his most reasonable when he thinks she is in danger."

"Or even if he thinks someone has insulted her," Lily agreed. "Telling them would be a tricky business. But it would not be right to tell her and keep it from him."

"No . . ." Jack looked grim but a little distant, as though his mind was too busy sorting through the possible choices to focus properly on the room in front of him. It made Lily smile to see him thus, in spite of the circumstances. She and Jack had spent many hours planning and plotting together, and she missed it whenever he was away.

His eyes returned to her at last. "If you wish to avoid sharing what happened, could we simply encourage them to leave London? If they returned to Somerset, they would be away from this Clive and his threats."

"But if a scandal does break, it would be worse for Ofelia if neither she nor her husband were here to defend her," Lily pointed out. "Besides which, I could not keep something so important from her. She is not a child to be protected; she is a woman grown who deserves to be allowed to make her own decisions."

"She is barely past being a child," Jack grumbled. Lily shook her head. The young Lady Carroway was only a little older than Amelia, and he had an elder brother's turn of mind. "If a scandal breaks, Carroway's family will take those decisions from her control—and his—before you can blink an eye," he added.

"Which is all the more reason that she should make them now," Lily said firmly. "On that point at least, I can decide with confidence. It is just a question of how to approach the matter."

"Bluntly," Jack advised. He smiled, though it was not an entirely cheerful expression. "It is what you do best. And knowing Lady Carroway, she will appreciate it."

Lily nodded. "Yes. Best to be straightforward, and then we can move on to the business of deciding what to do." She sighed, sinking back into her chair. She felt better for having talked it over with him, even though nothing had truly changed. "Thank you, my friend. I know I could count on you."

"And *I* ought to have known it was only a matter of time before you found some trouble," he said, one elbow on the arm of his chair and his chin resting against his fingertips. He regarded her through narrowed eyes. "What would you do if Lady Carroway were not involved?"

"I think . . ." Lily considered the question. "Were it only me that he were threatening, I would take the risk. I would lose friends, certainly, and I might lose London. But better that than give in to blackmail."

Jack shook his head, rubbing at his temples as though she were giving him a headache. "You would," he muttered. "Reckless woman that you are."

His irritation made her smile. "Are you still so worried about me, after all these years?" she asked a little teasingly, hoping to lighten the grim mood.

"Two years is not so many," he replied, his thumb sweeping back and forth against his jaw, as though he were too restless to stay completely still. Lily forced herself not to watch the movement; she had been courted, even offered marriage, since Freddy's death. She had not acted like a girl just out of school then, and she refused to act like one now. "If you hadn't spent so much of those two years courting one danger after another—and were not doing so again now—I'd not need to worry so much."

"But you will not try to stop me?" Lily asked, brows rising.

He shook his head at her, but he was grinning, a playful expression that had caught the eyes of no fewer than half a dozen ladies of Lily's acquaintance. Most of them had eagerly asked her for an introduction to her handsome friend.

"I have learned better than that," he replied, settling back into his own chair. "In fact, I will offer my assistance. Knowing you as I do"—he fixed her with a stern look—"I suspect that if this Mr. Clive were not involved, you would be inclined to help Miss Forrest."

Lily pursed her lips against a smile. It was warming that he knew her so well. "Her uncle's actions do seem suspicious."

"Lady Walter gave you some information, but you clearly need more in order to decide what to do. What if I were to try to learn something about the uncle?"

Lily sat forward, curiosity rising like soap bubbles in her chest. Dreadful though the whole situation had ended up being—perhaps downright dangerous, if she choose poorly—she couldn't help being excited by the prospect of learning more. "How?"

"There is a club in Saint James that many men of the army and navy are members of, particularly those who have left their years of service behind. I could see if this Mr. Martin Forrest is a member, or if anyone there knows anything about him."

"Why, Captain," Lily said, not bothering to hide either her relief or her pleasure at the suggestion, "you do know how to pique a woman's interest."

He raised his brows, smiling. "I am known for it. Though I must say, it does seem unfair that I should spend so much time concerned for your well-being when you have made it so clear that you do not worry about me in return." He sighed in an exaggerated fashion, his right hand rising to clasp his left shoulder pitifully.

"Oh, is that how far you have come in your recovery?" Lily asked, though she felt a little shocked. She was not quite ready to be so flippant about his injury. And she had worried about him a great deal. "Will you now be using it to gain sympathy from all the ladies you encounter?"

"Not all," he said. "Just the ones who refuse to fret over my well-being."

"Well, if it makes you feel better, I might not have been fretting, but I did think of you. Often." She didn't realize, until the last words had left her lips, that her tone was no longer as playful as it had been a moment before. Feeling suddenly too exposed, she wanted to look away. But she kept her eyes on his. The hesitation in their earlier conversation had made it clear that they both had felt some kind of change between them. Perhaps . . .

Lily made up her mind in a rush, and she took a deep breath. "More than often."

Jack, no longer teasing, reached forward, and she let him take her hand. "I was not in any real danger, Lily," he said gently.

"Liar," she whispered, the memory of that night rushing over her. The warmth of his hand soothed away some of the remembered fear, but not all. She hesitated, then slowly threaded her fingers through his before looking up to meet his eyes. "And I do not know what I would have done without you, Jack."

It was not quite a declaration, but it was nearly one. Lily did not look away, waiting for his reply. Neither of them spoke. His fingers tightened on hers, and for a moment she didn't dare breathe.

But then his smile returned, a little embarrassed this time, and he pulled his hand abruptly from hers. "Well, someone has to keep an eye on you, after all, with all the trouble you manage to stir up. Freddy would never have forgiven me if I shirked that duty."

Lily felt as though a knot had been pulled tight inside her chest. She took another deep breath to clear it. She could have let the matter go. But she suddenly found that she wanted the certainty of knowing, one way or another, whether she was alone in how she felt. "Is that the only reason you do it?"

For a moment Jack stared at her. Then he stood so quickly that Lily nearly jumped. "I had not realized how late it was growing," he said, his chair wobbling a little from the abruptness of his movement. He cleared his throat. "My apologies, Mrs. Adler. I ought to be going."

Lily stood slowly, trying to wish away the heat rising to her cheeks. "Of course, you must have other engagements for the evening," she said, pleased by how even her voice sounded. Even her hands were calm at her sides, though her stomach was twisting with mortification. "I should not have kept you so long."

"No. That is . . ." He cleared his throat again and smiled. "It is never a hardship to pass an evening in your company, my friend. I believe I will call tomorrow to take Amelia for a drive. I can tell you then if I met with any success tonight."

There, at least, she was on steady and familiar ground. Lily nodded. "Thank you. I hope you know I am always grateful for your assistance." She couldn't help a glance at his arm, then. Judging by the look on his face when she met his eyes again, he had not missed it. "If you are sure you wish to help, that is?"

"I am hurt you would even ask the question," he said as she walked him into the hall. "After all, what else am I to do with my time now that I have no profession? I shudder to think what misdeeds I would get up to did I not have you and your investigations to keep me occupied."

Lily shook her head as he retrieved his hat and gloves from the stand in the hall, determined that no matter how mortified she might be, she would not be the reason things grew awkward between them. Jack was too important a part of her life to let that happen. "Good night, Jack," she said, holding out her hand.

When he bowed over it, to her surprise, he brushed a quick kiss against her knuckles. Lily, feeling her face heating again, was torn between wanting him to linger and wishing he would depart immediately. "Will you do me one favor?"

"Of course," she replied, surprised.

"Will you check on my sister before you retire for the night?"

Lily had almost forgotten Amelia, her sudden headache and even more sudden departure, in the conflict of her own feelings. "I certainly shall," she said, touched by his care for his sister, unnecessary though she suspected it was.

Jack smiled, looking relieved. "Good night, Lily."

CHAPTER 6

Dear God in heaven, could he have behaved like any more of a bounder?

Jack would have swung his cane at the stone walls of the houses he walked past had he not known it would splinter the polished wood. Instead, he settled for berating himself silently.

Lily Adler—Lily, who more than one person had accused of having ice in her veins instead of blood, who could sit down to tea with a criminal and not let her feelings show; Lily, who kept her herself on so tight a rein that she could look at the body of a murdered man and not turn a hair—Lily Adler had told him she did not know what she would do without him.

And he, like a nervous boy, had leaped up and run from the room.

Jack groaned as he turned his steps toward St. James, where the gentlemen's clubs of London were clustered. He could remember clearly, half-conscious though he had been at the time as Lily stood over him, a pistol in her own hand as she faced down his assailant. *"If you have killed him, I will shoot you dead,"* she had said without hesitation. He could remember the look in her eyes when she had seen him at last, unsure if he would ever be able to use his arm again but standing on his own two feet once more as he faced her.

And he, who prided himself on his fearlessness in war, his ability to charm any woman or man who crossed his path—he had run away. He had stayed nearly two months in Yorkshire—in the middle of winter!—claiming that he needed the recovery time. But really, he had wanted to prepare to face Lily again.

And now . . .

"You look thoughtful this evening, Captain, if you will forgive me for saying so. Is there anything I might assist you with?"

The polite voice pulled Jack from his thoughts. He had stepped into the front hall of his club without realizing it and was unthinkingly in the middle of handing his overcoat to one of the footmen.

The man who had spoken to him was Mr. Hawes, the majordomo. He was in his usual place by the front door, ready to greet each member as they arrived and, with a quick glance or a snap of his fingers, summon whatever assistance they might require.

"Hawes, my good man." Jack greeted him with a respectful nod, pushing his other thoughts aside. They would keep—and he didn't mind the chance to think of something other than his embarrassing conduct. "How goes your evening thus far?"

"Well indeed, Captain Hartley. You are kind to inquire," Mr. Hawes said with a bow. Tall and thin, with round spectacles on his nose and an impressive mental catalog of names and faces, he always put Jack in mind of a heron, perched above a pond to better survey the fish below him. "A pleasure indeed to have you with us tonight. Is there anything I might arrange for you?"

"As a matter of fact, I was hoping to run into someone tonight," Jack said. "Name of Forrest. An army fellow, or at least he was until recently. Do you know if he is here this evening?"

"Forrest, you say?" Mr. Hawes frowned. "I'm afraid, sir, I don't recall anyone of that name. Nor any pending memberships. Are you certain the gentleman applied for membership?"

"Not certain, no," Jack said, trying to appear unconcerned. "Perhaps he's not got around to it yet. No matter, Hawes." He handed over a tip to the majordomo, who bowed once more as he slid it into his pocket.

Jack didn't want to leave right away. Someone would be likely to notice him walking out the door almost as soon as he had arrived and wonder at it. And Jack didn't want Hawes, with his impeccable memory, to grow too curious about his interest in Mr. Forrest. So he continued strolling into the club as though he had no other plans for the evening, smiling at the men that he knew and joining a game of vingt-et-un.

Inside, though, he was puzzled. The club was hardly secretive, and many officers of the army or navy who settled in London when they left His Majesty's service became members, at least for a time. It was a comfortable thing, to be surrounded by those who could understand one's experiences in battle. Jack's own patron, one Admiral Folks, had encouraged Jack to apply for membership. And Jack couldn't think of a single man of his acquaintance, married or not, who didn't appreciate having a place to retreat to that was not his own home.

It was not impossible, of course, that Mr. Forrest had no interest in membership. He could even, as Jack had glibly suggested to the majordomo, be planning to apply and simply not have done so yet. But it was strange to Jack that a man so recently returned to civilian life, especially one who, it seemed, had been gone from the country for so long, should be absent from the membership rolls.

But just because he was not a member did not mean he would be unknown there. Jack spent the next hour at various card tables, greeting those he knew and making a point of chatting with any army officers he encountered. He didn't know what regiment Mr. Forrest had been in, so he cast a wide net, dropping the man's name into the cheerful, rowdy conversation every so often and waiting to see if anyone might know him.

"Martin Forrest, do you mean?" one former major asked at last, his words a little fuzzy as he contemplated his cards. "I think we came up together. I've not seen him in . . . must be near twenty years. Is it the same Forrest, do you think? Surprised he's not around here. The only thing I remember about him was that he liked to gamble."

But the former major knew nothing beyond that—he hadn't even known, Jack discovered, that Mr. Forrest had returned to London. Jack, after another hand of cards, was about to give up and go home. In a last, half-hearted attempt at learning something, he mentioned the name one more time over a brandy with an old naval acquaintance.

"I met a Forrest the other evening."

Jack, who had barely been attending, took a long drink from his glass to cover his surprise. "Oh?" he asked, trying to hide his excitement.

The speaker, a junior naval officer who had served under Jack once but left the navy after an injury, shrugged. His smile pulled at the long scar that curved around one side of his face, which would have given him a villainous look had he not had such a cheerful nature. "Can't say for certain that it was the same man, but I'd not be surprised if he was an army fellow. No head for strategy."

Jack chuckled. "What makes you say that, Vane?"

"Ran into him at a faro hall. I would say I was impressed with the boldness of his wagers. But mostly I was astonished by how bad they were." He shook his head, still grinning. "Hope that wasn't your Forrest, sir."

Jack was still turning the comment over in his mind when he finally left his club. Martin Forrest was a gambler, the major had said. Which made it possible that the Forrest in the faro hall was the man he was looking for.

They could, of course, be completely unconnected. But Jack was accustomed to trusting his instincts. And as he currently had nothing else to go on . . .

Well, the only other choice was to admit defeat and head home. And Jack had never been one to admit defeat easily.

There were too many faro houses in London to count, of varying degrees of respectability. But Vane was from a well-to-do family, and Jack thought it unlikely that he would play at a gaming hall that was anything less than genteel.

Fortunately, Jack was an old acquaintance of the proprietor of a very elegant faro house near Covent Garden. Even if she did not know Mr. Forrest herself, she might be able to point him in the direction of someone who did.

★ ★ ★

"Martin Forrest, you say?" Constance du Varnier murmured, giving Jack a considering look as she passed him a glass of sherry. "What makes you think I know anything about a Martin Forrest?"

Jack did not visit her establishment often. But she hadn't blinked an eye when he asked for a quick word in private, taking charge of him from the steward who guarded the door and escorting him to her small, pretty office off the front hall. They had known each other for years, after all, though it had been some time since their paths had crossed.

Madame du Varnier was a former courtesan who had boasted a number of wealthy, well-connected protectors in her younger years. They had first met when Jack was still a lieutenant, and he had served on the ship sent to bring her to meet a certain admiral in Portsmouth. It had been Jack's role to entertain Madame du Varnier on the voyage. He had expected the task to be a tedious one, but the two of them got on splendidly, playing piquet and trading stories. She had even, after several days, begun to drop her remarkably good French accent in his presence, confessing that she had actually grown up in Lyme Regis before embarking on her career.

Jack took an appreciative drink. "Well, in the first place, Madame, because you boast a wealth of knowledge and insight that few can match."

She laughed at his flattery. She was a remarkably beautiful woman, the frothy good looks that had made her first career such a success having hardened into elegant steel as she aged. Jack suspected that nature had been given a helping hand in the chestnut sweep of her brows and the deep pink of her lips, but that sort of thing didn't matter when it was done well. Madame du Varnier could have had her pick of protectors still, but she seemed content to have given up living on her charms in favor of living on her connections and business acumen. "And in the second?"

"In the second place, because I've been told he enjoys passing an evening at a faro hall or two. I do not know if he has been fortunate enough to be admitted to your lovely establishment." Jack gave her a half bow from his seated position as he spoke, earning himself another indulgent chuckle. "But I thought you might be able to point me in the correct direction."

"Now, Captain, you know it would be bad for business were I to speak indiscreetly about my guests," Madame said, giving him a stern look.

Jack leaned forward, undeterred. "So he has been here, then?"

She pursed her lips, looking irritated. "Naughty boy," she murmured. "Catching my slip of the tongue like that." Jack simply grinned at her, and she sighed. "Very well, then. Yes, he has been a guest here."

"Can you tell me anything about him?" Jack asked. With anyone else, he might have offered a bribe to sweeten the question. But that was not the way to treat an old friend. He did not try to flatter her again either, only regarded her patiently, letting her see the seriousness of his inquiry. "You have discussed your guests with me before, if you recall."

"That was some years ago, and you were assisting a gentleman from Bow Street then," she said. "I presume that you would have already said so, were that the case now."

Jack didn't argue that point, only waited silently as she regarded him, one finger tapping against her lips. At last, she stood. "Come with me. And do bring your drink. It is always best to have something to do with your hands when you are up to no good."

"What makes you think I am up to no good?" Jack murmured as he followed her out of the room and up the stairs.

Madame du Varnier gave him a sideways glance. "You are always up to no good, Captain Hartley," she said as she led him into the faro hall.

It was lit with dozens of candles and set with four green baize tables, each with a pert young woman in the center seat as banker. Gentlemen, and a few daring ladies, crowded around the tables while other guests disported themselves at the sideboard, sampling the house's excellent supply of spirits and wines.

Madame did not go much farther than the door, and Jack stayed by her side, waiting to find out what she wanted him to see. He did not have to wait long.

"I believe the gentleman you seek is the one in the burgundy coat by the farthest table." Madame du Varnier nodded discreetly toward the corner table. She kept her gaze demurely toward the glass in her hand, but under her lashes, her eyes gleamed at Jack. Her voice, when she spoke, was pitched so that he could barely hear it, even from only a step away. "He is a reckless bettor, and I suspect he would cheat if given the chance. So I know why *I* wish to keep an eye on him. Why do you?"

Jack hesitated. Had they been in private still, he might have told her more. But the faro room was hardly the place for a protracted discussion. "There is a young woman in his care, a niece," he said at last, his voice as quiet as hers. "A friend of mine suspects that he might be mistreating her. I wish to see what kind of man he is, and if my friend may be right."

"Do you indeed," Madame du Varnier said slowly, her gaze drifting back to where Mr. Forrest was just placing a new bet on the table. The pleasant smile never left her face, but her eyes had grown cold. "Well, I will not stop you, then. I hope for the niece's sake that you are wrong. But if you are not . . ."

Jack downed his glass in a single gulp. It felt good to have a purpose, to be chasing something again after months of convalescing. He bowed. "If you will excuse me, madame?"

She raised her glass in a toast. "Good hunting to you, sir," she said, casting one more considering look toward Mr. Forrest before strolling away to check on her other guests.

The faro game was already in progress at the far table, a crowd of men cheering or groaning in turn as the pretty banker drew each pair of cards. As Jack approached, the man in the burgundy coat looked up quickly.

He was a tall, dark-haired man, likely close to fifty, with the alert bearing and broad shoulders so common in men who had spent years in military service. He was good-looking enough, or perhaps just not bad-looking, and dressed with luxurious flair, his coat expertly tailored and his waistcoat beautifully embroidered.

His eyes lingered on Jack for a moment before sliding past him to the door, where a few other gamblers were just entering. When he caught Jack's eye—by accident, it seemed—he lifted his glass in a quick toast.

"Joining the game, sir?" he asked. "There is room yet at the table."

Jack nodded politely as he stepped up, but he did not yet reach for his purse. He would watch only at first. The other men were frowning or laughing or boasting as they laid their own bets. Mr. Martin Forrest, after scowling down at the table for some time, placed his wager. It was not a small one.

"Careful, Forrest," one player warned, grinning. "You may have only two dependents now, but who's to say you won't collect more in the future? I had a third cousin land in my lap last year. Damned unpleasant surprise, let me tell you."

The dealer turned over two cards, and Forrest let out an unhappy grumble as his bet proved to be poorly placed. "One of them has to be a winning hand, does it not?" he said as the banker swept his money off the table. "But you're right about dependents, the devil take them."

"Are yours unpleasant?" Jack asked, leaning over the table to examine the bets already made.

Forrest shrugged. "I don't bother with them any more than I have to. How many tens have there been?"

"One of them's young, right?" another player demanded, slurring his words a little. "Tell me she's a pretty girl, maybe I can take her off your hands." He laughed at his own joke as the dealer turned over another set of cards. "Well, look at that! Well placed, if I do say so myself."

"Devil take it," Forrest snapped, having lost yet another hand. "The luck's not in tonight. And don't talk nonsense. No one wishes to marry Sarah. Not without a dowry, at least, and I can assure you *that* is not in her future."

"At least she need not be an expensive burden," the first player said, clapping Mr. Forrest on the shoulder. "An unmarried girl—even two spinsters—need very little to live on. Ask me how I know." He laughed.

"Any new bets, gentlemen?" the faro dealer asked, smiling up at them so they could all see her dimples. Several of the men hurried to place new wagers, beaming back at her as they did so. Jack decided to join in, smiling to himself as he leaned forward to place his own bet on the table. *Sarah,* Mr. Forrest had said. He had the right fellow.

Forrest grimaced as he placed a new bet on the five. Jack could tell it was a poor one; the dealer had already turned over three fives, and the deck was only half drawn. The odds weren't in Forrest's favor. Jack wanted to roll his eyes. The man clearly had no business playing faro.

Jack took a deep breath, hoping that Madame du Varnier was not in the room to see him disturbing her faro bank. And that the dealer was distracted by the number of gentlemen currently crowding around her table.

"Are you not going to bet this time?" he asked loudly, slapping the slurring player on the back. "Go on—your luck was in earlier. Perhaps it still is!"

The others shouted their own encouragement, and the pretty dealer added her smiles. The man, who was young enough to smile back, asked her to advise him on where to place his bet.

"Why, how can you ask such a thing, sir, when you know I must play the bank?" she said coyly, fluttering her fan. The smiles she lavished on him had the air of a young woman looking for a new benefactor, and the young man's blushes made the other players chuckle. "You will have to judge for yourself."

The young man finally slid his counters across the table, and the others leaned over to see where he would put them. While all eyes were on the king where he at last placed his bet, Jack nudged Forrest's counters off the five and onto the six.

The king turned up that round as the dealer's card, and the young player was good-natured enough about losing. But the next draw, the player's card was a six, and Mr. Forrest hesitated only a moment before claiming his winnings.

"Luck had to turn at some point, did it not?" he said cheerfully. He glanced at Jack. "I think I shall sit the next one out. Would you care to join me for a drink?"

"Certainly, sir," Jack said.

As they crossed the room, they passed Madame du Varnier standing by a different faro table than the one where they had been. But instead of watching the gameplay, she was watching Jack, her eyes narrowed. Her banker might not have seen his sleight of hand, but she had.

He slowed as they walked past her, holding his breath, and she fell in with him. She would be within her rights to throw them out or accuse him publicly of cheating. But she did neither. "Trying to break my faro bank, sir?" she murmured as Mr. Forrest went to the sideboard.

"When pursuing a potentially dangerous quarry, devious methods are sometimes needed," he replied, barely above a whisper. "I shall repay you, of course."

"You had better," she muttered, but her eyes were alight with curiosity as she said it. "Gentlemen," she added, in a louder voice. "I hope you are enjoying your evening. Is there anything else I might do to see to your comfort?"

Her eyes lingered on Jack a moment longer, and he bowed politely. "Your hospitality is all that a man could desire," he said gallantly, taking her hand and pressing a kiss against her gloved knuckles.

Madame du Varnier's lips pursed as though she were trying not to laugh; she lost the battle. "I wish you luck in the rest of your evening, you charmer," she chuckled, patting his cheek. "I am sure I will see you again—and your friend, of course," she added, turning her brilliant smile on Mr. Forrest, who bowed politely. "Gentlemen."

The look Mr. Forrest gave Jack as he handed him a glass of liquor had the air of a man trying not to seem too impressed. "Adroitly done, sir," he said. "I was worried, for a moment, when she took an interest in you."

"And why was there need to worry?" Jack asked as he accepted the drink, a knowing smile on his lips.

Mr. Forrest chuckled. "Oh indeed. I know better than to comment overmuch on such assistance as you have provided, sir," he said as he raised his glass in a toast. "At least, not within these walls, which doubtless have ears. But may I at least know your name?"

Jack hesitated only a moment. "Hartley. And I am happy to do a good turn to a deserving fellow."

"And what makes you think I am—" Forrest broke off, his eyes at a point over Jack's shoulder. He was looking at the door again, Jack realized, as he half turned himself to see what had caught the man's attention. But it was nothing more extraordinary than two young men arriving, swaying against each other for support and trying their best to look dignified about it.

Mr. Forrest cleared his throat. "What makes you think I am so deserving? Not that I am complaining," he added, smiling broadly, though the expression did not quite reach his eyes.

"A man with a dependent niece?" Jack snorted. "I have a sister yet unwed, and a great deal of sympathy for you, you may be sure." It made his skin crawl a little to say it. Though he knew more than one man who thought thusly, Jack had never considered either of his sisters a burden. But now was not the time to be inflexible with the truth.

Forrest chuckled, and it was not an entirely pleasant sound. "Better do something about her if you can. My niece has a spinster cousin who has become mine to support as well, and they do not grow more pleasant with time. But at least my friend at the faro table was right: they can indeed be maintained on remarkably little."

He laughed again, and the self-satisfied sound made Jack long to hit the man in the face. But he forced himself to chuckle along. "I suppose you could always pay someone to take the girl off your hands?"

Forrest shrugged. "I might settle a small dowry on her if I get desperate enough. But I doubt that will come soon, as she has dreadful taste in men—even her father thought so, devil take him. I mean,

God rest his soul." He winked, downing the rest of his drink and smacking his lips. "Well, the night is yet young, my friend. And entertainments await. Will you join me?"

Jack set down his own drink. "What entertainments do you have in mind?"

CHAPTER 7

"What a smart little rig, Captain," Lily said as Jack handed first her and then his sister up into his new curricle.

He had called, as promised, first thing in the morning, arriving just as Lily and Amelia were finishing breakfast. As Jack strode into the dining room, offering a polite greeting and helping himself to a plate of sausages, Lily had seen Carstairs hovering in the hallway before he shook his head and walked away. She had smiled to herself at his resignation, though she could not help wondering what her rather stoic butler, who, in spite of his own slightly checkered past, was now a model of propriety, made of Jack's easy comings and goings these days.

A simple explanation was sitting beside her, holding her hat against the wind. And that, Lily reminded herself, trying not to think of her embarrassment the night before, was all there was to it.

Except this morning. She could tell from Jack's expression that he had something to share. But first they had to deliver Amelia to the circulating library, where she was planning to meet a young lady she had made friends with since coming to London.

Lily was making pleasant conversation for the benefit of any neighbors close enough to hear, but her admiration of the curricle was genuine. She had recently had a suitor with a fondness for horses and their vehicles, and she had learned a great deal in the time she had spent in his company. Jack's vehicle was elegant and light, pulled by a pair of well-matched grays whose cost she didn't want to guess at. It was normally the sort of vehicle that would have carried two passengers, but there was enough room for three with Amelia perched between them.

"My brother is clearly intending to become a man about town," Amelia said a little dryly as they set off. "I shall have to write to our parents and let them know how he is frittering his money away now that he has no profession to keep him occupied."

"Write away, little sister," Jack said, grinning at her. "You know as well as I do that our father is as likely to try to buy it off me as scold me for my lack of economy."

"Yes, but our mother will be happy to scold, and that will be satisfying for me," Amelia said. But she settled back against the seat as she spoke, looking pleased to be driven behind such beautiful horses.

Lily shook her head at their comfortable squabbling. "Do you intend to pass the entirety of the drive arguing?"

"No indeed." Amelia sat back up. "For Raffi has news to share with you, and I wish to hear what it is as well."

Lily saw Jack dart a sideways glance at his sister. "What makes you think I have news?" he asked as he turned to avoid a broken-down dairy cart in the road ahead of them. Lily tried not to glance at his hands. He was handling the ribbons with ease, but she could not help wondering about his arm. Driving a pair was taxing work.

"You have given Mrs. Adler no fewer than three very secretive looks since you greeted us in the breakfast room," Amelia said, sounding a little smug. "Yet each time you have restrained yourself from saying anything. Either the two of you are having an affair, or Raffi has some news to share."

"Amelia," Lily said sharply, hoping her mortification did not show, while the girl giggled at her joke. Lily could not bring herself to look at Jack, who was still facing straight ahead, his eyes on his horses. She should not have felt so embarrassed; Amelia was hardly the first to tease or speculate about Lily and Jack's friendship being of a less than platonic nature, and they had both easily shrugged off such comments in the past. But after their conversation last night—and Jack's abrupt departure—the jest landed differently.

"Since I know it is not the first," Amelia continued, uncowed by the reprimand, "it must be the second. And since Raffi has brought us driving rather than simply sharing his news when we were more private at your house, Mrs. Adler, I am forced to conclude that it is news you wish to keep from me. Which means I insist on knowing what it is," she finished triumphantly, giving her brother a very satisfied look. Then she dropped her voice. "Is it something to do with Miss Forrest?"

Jack said nothing, only glanced at Lily, raising one eyebrow as he waited for her decision. It lessened her mortification somewhat that he was so willing to defer to her preference, even as concerned his own sister. Though perhaps it was because that sister was currently living under her roof, and Lily would be the one to bear the brunt of Amelia's displeasure if she felt something important was being kept from her.

But the girl knew some of what had passed, and her occasionally cynical outlook often made her a shrewd judge of people. So long as there was no mention of blackmail, they might well benefit from her knowing what Jack had discovered.

"Very well," Lily said at last. "Last night, your brother went in pursuit of some information about Mr. Martin Forrest, who is Miss Forrest's uncle."

Amelia turned toward her brother eagerly. "And what did you discover about him?"

Jack spoke quietly. They were mostly private, but there were carriages enough nearby that he did not want to risk being overheard. "That he does not make a very favorable impression."

Lily sat forward, her earlier embarrassment entirely forgotten in her eagerness to hear more. "Oh?"

"I had the fortune—I cannot say if it was good fortune or ill—to meet Mr. Martin Forrest last night," Jack said, his eyes on his horses' ears. "And he did not strike me as a pleasant or trustworthy man."

"Explain," Lily ordered, her heart speeding up with excitement and no small amount of worry for her friend. "How did you discover him? Were you in any danger?"

"Of being accused of cheating and thrown out of a faro house, yes."

But before he could say more, they passed close to another carriage. This one was full of young people out for a drive, two gentlemen and two ladies, and they hailed Jack with waves and happy shouts. The two vehicles slowed as they drew abreast, and Lily hid her impatience while smiling through a round of introductions and pleasant inquiries about the weather and London engagements.

At last the other carriage drove on, and Lily gave Jack a stern look. "Explain," she repeated. Her eyes grew wider as he did, though she allowed herself no other outward sign of emotion.

Amelia was not so restrained. "You cheated?" she interrupted him as soon as he described the faro game, though she had the good sense to do so in a whisper. "Raffi, I have never known you to do something so dishonorable. I shall have to write to Papa immediately. The horses he may excuse, but—"

"Don't you dare," Jack said sharply. "I repaid the proprietress before I left. I'd not have done it for a lesser cause, and I took no pleasure in the dishonesty. So I do not care to have it more widely discussed. Reputation is everything in London, Noor. You ought to know that by now."

His expression grew even more serious as soon as the words were out of his mouth, and he gave Lily a sideways glance. She could guess that he was thinking of Clive and the current threat to her own reputation. She shivered a little and pulled the driving blanket more closely across her lap.

"I did not need London to teach me that, Raffi," Amelia said, but she sounded chastened. "And I was merely teasing."

"Well, tease about something else," Jack said, the words coming out short and grumpy.

"But he did not object," Lily pointed out thoughtfully. "Mr. Forrest. He thanked you for your assistance."

"You noticed?" Jack said, nodding. "An honorable man would have repaid the house himself. Or called me out for cheating. But he pocketed the money and toasted me for it." The disgust in his voice was clear as he spoke. "In fact, he was so pleased with my assistance that he invited me to join him in further carousing."

"Did you accept or decline?" Lily asked.

"I declined," Jack said. His mouth twisted as though he had tasted something unpleasant. "The invitation was for a sojourn to South-wark House."

"Oh, for heaven's sake," Lily grumbled, not bothering to hide her disgust. "Can he not be at least a little creative in his vices? At this rate, he will soon be transformed into a villain on the stage at Drury Lane."

"What is Southwark House?" Amelia demanded.

Jack growled and shook his head, which made Lily want to laugh. "A brothel," she said, glancing at Amelia. "It calls itself a gentleman's tea parlor, but it is a brothel with a rather unsavory reputation."

"Unsavory how?" Amelia asked curiously.

Jack growled again, and even Lily hesitated to answer. "Unpleas-ant management," she said at last. Amelia, who looked as though she had been about to ask more, fell silent instead, a thoughtful frown pulling at her brows. "If you ever hear a young man mention a visit there," Lily continued, "stay far away from him."

"No need to worry on that score, ma'am," Amelia said, making a face. "You know well I am not in London to husband hunt."

"*Any* young man," Jack said sharply. "Whether you have a matri-monial interest in him or not."

Amelia rolled her eyes. "Yes, brother. May I drive your horses?"

Jack eyed her. "Have you ever driven a pair before?"

"No, but how difficult can it be?"

"Very difficult," he said firmly. "Especially in London traffic. I shall teach you the next time we take a drive to the country."

"Oh, very well," Amelia grumbled. "So you are saying that Mr. Forrest thought to take you there as . . . what? A show of thanks?"

"Or he was already planning to visit and thought I might like to accompany him," Jack said. "I declined, by the by. But given that, and the manner in which he spoke of his niece and his disinclination to provide her a dowry, he seemed altogether an untrustworthy, unpleas-ant fellow."

Amelia glanced between them. "But does that necessarily make him a thief?"

"It does not," Lily said, folding her hands demurely in her lap while her mind raced through her options. "But it does make him suspicious."

★ ★ ★

Amelia grumbled at the thought of the conversation continuing without her when she alighted at the circulating library. But her friend was waiting, with the young lady's mother a step behind to chaperone them. All Amelia could do was attempt to extract a promise that they would let her know if they learned anything else.

"I do not expect to discover anything today," Lily demurred, not wanting to promise anything. "All we intend to do is call on Sir Edward and Lady Carroway. You remember how eager she was to see your brother?"

Jack waited until they had left the circulating library behind to ask, "Hanover Square, then?"

"Yes," Lily said, nodding. When she glanced at him, he was watching his pair and the road ahead, and she could not see his expression. But judging by the tension in his arms and shoulders, he knew exactly what Lily's errand was. "Will you come with me?"

He snorted. "I'd have been offended if you expected anything else."

That made her smile in relief, in spite of her nerves. He was still her friend, and he would stand by her through whatever came next.

Ofelia and her husband rented a pretty townhome just off Hanover Square, though he was the owner of a much larger property in Berkeley Square. But his mother and four unmarried sisters still lived there, and Lily could not blame the young couple for wanting their privacy. And as the Carroway family was monstrously wealthy, and Ofelia had brought her own large fortune—made by her father in the West Indies—to the marriage, the added expense of a second house troubled them very little.

Lily was relieved to discover that they were both at home and happy to receive visitors. While the tea tray was brought in and Ofelia asked Lily to pour, they discussed Jack's travel to London and the Carroways' dinner from the night before, with Ned shaking his head over his mother's blatant matchmaking attempts. But as soon as they were private once more, Ofelia set her glass of cordial aside.

"What is it, Mrs. Adler?" she asked. "Entertaining as the machinations of Neddy's mother might be, I am certain you did not call to ask about the marriage prospects of his sisters. Did you meet with the letter writer? Is it good news or bad?"

Lily took a fortifying breath. "Bad," she admitted. She would not attempt to soften the blow. "I met with the young gentlewoman yesterday in the Green Park, as planned. But she was not there alone." She glanced at Ned, who was standing by the mantlepiece, one hand tapping nervously while he watched her. "Do you recall, from our time in Hampshire two autumns ago, a man by the name of Clive?"

Ned's chin jerked up in surprise, and on her other side, Lily heard Ofelia draw in a sharp breath. "The bookmaker?" she demanded. "The one I bribed to tell us what he knew?"

Lily winced at the reminder. "The very same. He remembered us, I am afraid, all too well. And he will not scruple to use that knowledge to get what he wants."

"What does that mean?" Ned demanded.

"It means, Carroway," Jack said, his voice surprisingly gentle, "that Lady Carroway and Mrs. Adler are being blackmailed."

"What?" Ofelia half rose from her seat, her lips parted in shock. "How . . . what could he . . . what does he want? Why was he even there?"

"He wants to set himself up as a gentleman. It seems he has decided his path to do so is to marry Miss Forrest."

"He wants her money," Ofelia said flatly. Ned, his normally cheerful face wreathed in concern, crossed the room to set a hand on his wife's shoulder. She reached up her own hand to press against his, but she did not look at him, her gaze fixed on Lily. "And he seeks to persuade you to get it for him. That must mean you refused to help her. What made you do so?"

Lily sighed. "His being there did." Quietly, in as straightforward a manner as possible, she told them what had happened in the park, and what she had since learned of Sarah and Martin Forrest.

"Well, there is only one course of action to take," Ned said, looking grim, when she had finished.

"Of course there is," Ofelia said. She had sunk into her chair as Lily spoke, as though the weight of each word was pushing her down. But now she sat up straight and gave Lily a stern look. "And that is not to give in to his demands."

"What?" Ned stared at her.

"Well, of course we cannot, Neddy!" Ofelia exclaimed before remembering to lower her voice. Even if the servants were not in the room, there was no knowing who was close enough to overhear their conversation. "He will simply come back with another demand in the future, and then another, and it will never end. He can hold the threat of exposure over our heads forever."

"Which is why you should never have—"

"But they did," Jack said quietly. "We all did. Forgive me for saying so, Carroway, but you hardly held yourself aloof from such matters. We did what we thought was right at the time."

"And we *were* right," Ofelia protested. "Anyone who thinks of the facts impartially can hardly deny it."

"Unfortunately, impartial observers are not thick on the ground in London society," Lily said quietly, rising and crossing to the window. It overlooked the square, and she stared out at the traffic and passersby without really seeing them. "And I am sorry, Ofelia, that I put you in this situation."

"You do not need to be," Ofelia insisted. "I stand by what I have done. And you should too, ma'am. So there, Neddy."

Lily could not help smiling at that, and she heard Jack chuckle quietly behind her.

Ned Carroway sighed. "Very well, then. But we still have to decide what to do now. If we say devil take the lot of them and keep our distance, we must be prepared for what we are risking."

"Mrs. Adler, forgive me, but . . ." Ofelia hesitated. "But why not help Miss Forrest anyway? You seem to believe her, or at least to think there is some merit to her concerns. Normally, that would be enough for you to already be plotting."

"And under other circumstances I would be," Lily said, turned from the window. "I think I would be inclined to help the girl, to find her father's solicitor and learn the truth of the matter, if nothing more. But I know you understand why Mr. Clive's presence makes me wish to stay far away. While I can hardly be surprised by a mercenary marriage"—she shook her head—"this seems rather more than that. I worry that he is using her to arrange all for his own benefit, with no thought of her safety or well-being."

"And he clearly has no thought for yours or Lady Carroway's," muttered Ned.

Lily smiled grimly. "Too true. Which may make it impossible for me to keep my distance, no matter how much I might wish to."

"If he is manipulating her, all the more reason to help," Ofelia said firmly. "A girl with more financial options is also one with more matrimonial freedom. She might feel less dependent on him and his advice if you discover that her uncle *is* cheating her."

"I thought you said just a moment ago that you would never give in to blackmail?" Jack pointed out.

"And I stand by that," Ofelia declared. "But he gave Mrs. Adler two days in which to make up her mind."

"You mean, I ought to do what I wish with those two days and see what there is to be uncovered?" Lily said. "I have the invitation he sent to Lady Walter . . ."

"There you are!" Ofelia said triumphantly. "Use it without telling Mr. Clive or Miss Forrest what you intend to do. Slipping away from a party where no one knows you will be an easy matter."

"All I need to do, really, is discover the name of the father's solicitor," Lily said slowly, a hint of excitement growing inside her. She always felt better when she had a plan of action.

"Once you have that, Miss Forrest should be able to handle matters herself. And then you've stolen nothing," Ofelia said, almost triumphantly. "Really, you'll have done nothing except attend a ball to which you had an invitation."

"I think this Mr. Forrest might feel otherwise should he discover Mrs. Adler sneaking about his house," Ned said, scowling. "And remember, we do not want our names being drawn into anything."

"Well, then we shall have to be careful not to be caught."

Three pairs of eyes turned to regard her. "We?" Jack asked.

"Well, of course," Ofelia said primly, sitting up straight and folding her hands in her lap. She looked the picture of a demure young matron, but her eyes gleamed ruthlessly. "My reputation and well-being are equally at stake. Of course I shall attend as well."

"They are," Lily said, going to sit next to her friend. "I've no wish to dismiss your interest in the matter—it is rightfully earned, to be sure—but I think the fewer people who are snooping around Mr. Forrest's home, the safer we shall all be."

"But you do not intend to go alone?" Jack said, taking a half step toward her. "That would be ridiculous."

Lily could not help the lift of her brows. "Ridiculous?"

"To try to search all by yourself?" he replied, uncowed by her stern look. "Yes, it would be ridiculous."

"Ever the protector," Ofelia murmured, smiling a little.

Lily hid a wince, remembering Jack's words about Freddy the night before. But for all they had become friends in their own right, she had long known that Jack saw his role in her life as an extension of his friendship with her husband. She could hardly start holding that against him now just because she had begun to imagine something different.

Jack either hadn't heard Ofelia or had decided to ignore her. "If I come with you, there will be two people searching, which means less time away from the ballroom in which to be caught. Besides which, the invitation is for two people. It would look odd if you arrived by yourself."

"Well, if the captain is going, then I certainly shall," Ofelia declared. "Neddy and I both will. We can keep watch over Mr. Forrest while you are searching and make sure that he does not leave the ballroom. And if he tries to, we can distract him."

"We haven't got an invitation," Ned pointed out. But even he didn't sound as though he truly objected anymore. Lily was starting to suspect that even if she told them not to come, they would simply show up anyway.

Ofelia made a dismissive noise while she poured a fresh cup of tea, added a splash of milk, and slid it across the low table in front of her, toward Lily. "If he is as much of a social climber as Lady Walter says, he'll not object to a baronet and his lady attending, even if we arrive without an invitation. He is far more likely to welcome us with open arms and ask us to begin the dancing."

That made Jack chuckle, and even Lily felt a smile pulling at the corners of her mouth. Ofelia's determination was catching.

"And in any case, you cannot afford to keep me away, you know," she added, giving her head a pleased toss. "I've a better head for legal affairs than you, after spending so long involved in my father's business. If you do find the will, and there is anything odd or confusing in how it is written, you may need me to interpret it."

Lily reached for the delicate, steaming teacup. "I will not argue that point. But let us hope it is not the case. The time it takes to untangle legal complexities might be more than we can afford. The quicker we can conduct our search and be done, the better." More quietly, she added, "It could be a terrible scandal you know—perhaps worse than a scandal—if we are discovered."

"Well, then we shall do our best not to be discovered," Ofelia said with cheerful optimism, reaching forward to claim Lily's untouched cake. "Besides, it has been ages since you got me mixed up in some sort of intrigue. I was missing it dreadfully."

Lily smiled grimly. "Let us hope you feel the same way tomorrow."

Ned looked pained at his wife's statement, but a moment later he brightened. "Well, fortunately Clive won't know you are attending tonight. Ought to be well protected from his machinations, at least."

"I do not know if I will feel safe from his machinations until he is gone from London," Lily said, sighing a little. "But it would certainly be safer than attempting to steal something at his behest, with him fully knowing where and when it is happening."

"Is it decided then?" Jack said, leaning back in his chair and crossing his ankles. "Are we on the prowl tonight?"

With one of Ofelia's delicate teacups in one hand and his legs stretched out before him, he looked perfectly relaxed, as though they were discussing plans for a typical evening soiree. But there was the same look in his eye that had been in Ofelia's a moment before: steely, determined, and even a little eager.

Lily wondered if she looked the same. She certainly felt it. "It seems so. And in that case, Captain, I will need to ask your young Jem for a lesson this afternoon. Could you perhaps bring him by?"

"Certainly, madam," Jack said, though he looked a little surprised by the request. "But what kind of lesson will it be?"

Lily smiled. "If we are to conduct a thorough search tonight," she said, lifting her cup to her lips, "I believe I need to learn how to pick locks."

CHAPTER 8

"Are you sure about this, mum?" Jem eyed Lily nervously—an easier task than it had been when they had first met. The gangly urchin that Jack had taken on as a body servant two years before could now look Lily in the eye. With his tousled, curly hair and newly deep voice, he was more young man than boy these days.

"Very sure, Jem," Lily said calmly, trying not to smile at his nervousness. "And I know for a fact that you *can* teach me, because you taught the captain."

The young servant glanced nervously at Jack, who was leaning against one wall with his arms crossed. "Well, you did," Jack pointed out, grinning.

"But that's very different from teaching a *lady*," Jem said, his voice cracking a little on the word. He cleared his throat, looking embarrassed. "Since the captain already knows, why can't he just take care of it?"

Lily shook her head. "The less you know, young man, the better."

That made Jem's expression grow alarmed. "You ain't thinking of doing nothing illegal, are you?" he demanded.

"No, I wish to learn how to pick locks for highly respectable reasons," Lily said with a straight face. That earned her a sour look from Jem, which made her smile. "Come now," she said briskly. "I know boys who grow up in the Seven Dials pick up all sorts of interesting skills. This is one I need to learn, and I have every confidence you will be an excellent teacher."

Jem sighed, though he still looked unhappy. "All right, mum. But if'n you gets in trouble for it, don't you go ratting me out."

"I'd never dream of it," Lily said, matching his seriousness. She gestured to the desk in her sitting room. "Would this suffice to begin the lesson, or would a door be better?"

Jem bent down to examine the desk drawer, putting his eye very close to the lock. "Well, it's a pretty silly lock, if'n you ask me. No one in the Dials would dream of putting anything valuable behind that. You could just smash the daft thing with a hammer."

"But if I want to see what was behind it *without* letting the owner know I had done so—"

Jem sighed again. "Then you would begin with these." He gave his employer a wary look, and when Jack nodded, pulled out a roll of black cloth. When he unrolled it on top of the desk, it proved to contain several thin metal rods and a ring of oddly shaped keys. Jem picked up the ring, the keys chiming gently against one another. "Now, pay attention, mum, if'n you please. These is called skeleton keys . . ."

Lily was perspiring and her fingers were achy by the time Jem had her move on to a door lock. She shifted Jem's rough, homemade picks to one hand, wiped her forehead, and glanced at Jack, who was watching her with an amused smile. "How am I comparing to the captain?" she asked Jem.

His mouth pulled to one side as he thought about it. "You've got a good hand, mum," he said. "Maybe from needlework or summat. But you're worrying too much. Captain just wanted to learn for fun, so he weren't so tense about it."

"Are you saying he progressed faster than I?" Lily asked, feeling indignant.

"Well, you did all right with the desk," Jem said, sounding uncomfortable. "But skeleton keys is easier than picks, so . . ." He shrugged.

"Just tell her I was better," Jack suggested.

"No, thank you, sir," Jem said firmly. "I ain't foolish enough to do so."

Jack chuckled, and Lily smiled ruefully. "All right, I shall endeavor to relax somewhat. And," she added, with an arch look at Jack, "to be grateful, I suppose, that criminal activity does not come naturally to me."

"Nonsense. You enjoy being a natural at anything. I doubt that excludes criminal activity," Jack said, still sounding amused.

Lily sighed, shifting the pick and the tension rod so that she was holding one in each hand once more. "Well, I'll not get any better standing around. Shall we—" She broke off as the sound of someone knocking echoed up the stairs.

"Are you anticipating visitors?" Jack asked.

"No." Lily frowned. But she had given Carstairs instructions that she did not wish to be disturbed. "Luckily, your sister is downstairs, and she is well able to handle any callers." She glanced down the hall, then turned back to the door. "Now, Jem, what do I need to do differently?"

She had just triumphantly, and with Jem coaxing her through the process, succeeded in opening the lock when Amelia appeared at the top of the stairs.

"Mrs. Adler?" She looked surprised, even a little alarmed, to see Lily kneeling before a door, lockpicks in hand, with Jack nearby and Jem peering over her shoulder.

Lily stood, dusting off the knees of her gown. "What is it?"

"There is a girl asking for you downstairs. Mr. Carstairs attempted to deny you, but she was most insistent." Amelia hesitated, then added, "She says it is a matter of murder."

Even Lily could not keep the surprise from her face. "It is not Miss Forrest, is it?"

"No." Amelia shook her head. "She said her name is Andrews, and I had the impression from what she said that you might have met before. But she would not say more about her business to anyone but you. Should I tell her to leave?"

"No." Lily glanced at Jack and her young tutor. "Wait here, if you please. I think I should see what she wants."

"Of course."

"Yes'm."

As Lily made her way down the stairs, she heard Amelia asking, "Can you teach me to pick locks too?"

"Certainly, miss," Jem replied, at the same time as Jack declared, "Absolutely not."

Carstairs had put the girl in the front parlor. In dress, she could have been the daughter of a well-off, but not wealthy, tradesman. Her golden-red hair and dark eyes set off pale skin, and a dusting of freckles across her nose spoke to either absent-mindedness or stubbornness in not wearing a bonnet outside. She was young, likely not yet sixteen.

And Amelia had been correct in her deduction: Lily did know her.

"Miss Andrews," she said in some surprise. "Fanny Andrews, I believe? You are Mr. Simon Page's niece."

"Mrs. Adler." The girl bowed, a little stiffly and very precisely. "And your full name is Lily Adler. I remember because you told it to me when I said I liked botany. The genus *Lilium*."

"I recall," Lily said, nodding. "And I said I wished I had been half so well educated when I was your age." She glanced around the room. "Are you alone, Miss Andrews? Did a maid come with you?"

"We do not have any maids, just a girl who comes in once a day to clean," Fanny said, a simple, unembarrassed statement of fact.

It gave Lily a little pang in her chest that felt almost like affection, though she had met Fanny Andrews only once before. Her uncle, Simon Page, was a constable in the new Bow Street force—not so new now, but everyone still called it that. Lily had come to know Mr. Page when she had first returned to London and had realized, when she met his niece, that Miss Andrews did not live in the world in quite the same way as most people did.

There was an uncompromising honesty about her, a straightforwardness in the way she understood and interpreted the world. Though Mr. Page had told Lily that Fanny worked hard to temper it and remember the unspoken rules that governed how she was supposed to act and speak, it clearly slipped out from time to time.

Most young ladies, when faced with the difference between their own position and that of a woman like Lily's, would have done their best to conceal such circumstances as not having a maid at home. But Fanny said it plainly because it was a fact.

There was something both endearing and heartbreaking about that. The world was not always patient with children like Fanny Andrews, or with the adults they became.

"I brought my brother with me. One of Aunt Judith's rules is that a young lady should not walk through the city alone," Fanny continued. "George is not very useful, but at least I was not alone. I think your housekeeper is giving him biscuits in the kitchen. I would have also liked some biscuits, but your butler brought me here instead."

Lily smiled. "Well, I can remedy that." She crossed to the bellpull and gave it a quick tug. "Will you sit down, Miss Andrews, and tell me why you've come?"

"Yes, thank you." Fanny perched on the edge of a chair, her expression serious. She sat almost unnaturally still, her hands in her lap and her back ramrod straight, but Lily had the impression that her stillness concealed deep discomfort, perhaps even nervousness. "I am in need of a particular kind of assistance. I'm afraid there is a person living near me who has killed someone, or perhaps who is planning to do so."

Whatever Lily might have been expecting, it was not that. For a moment, she did not respond, the patient expression with which she had been regarding her young visitor fixed in place, as though Fanny were a timid kitten and might bolt if startled.

"You don't believe me," Fanny said as calmly as if she were commenting on the weather. "Is that because I am a child or because I am a strange child?"

"I did not say I do not believe you," Lily replied slowly. "I have been in the position of having my words dismissed without consideration far too many times to wish to do so to anyone else, child or not." She felt a little cowardly for not saying something about the strange child comment as well, but she was unsure how to respond to that without giving offense. "But you must know it is a surprising thing to say."

"It is a surprising thing to observe," Fanny agreed. Her gaze had been fixed on a point past Lily's shoulder, but she lifted her chin and met Lily's eyes with great deliberateness.

"You observed this person killing someone?" Lily asked, and even she could not keep the disbelief from her voice.

"I have observed her murder weapon," Fanny said. "And I believe possessing such a weapon can indicate only ill intent. I suppose now you are wondering why I have not told my uncle, who is a constable."

"The thought had crossed my mind," Lily said faintly, feeling out of her depth. She was not used to dealing with children, never mind children who were accusing their neighbors of murder. She nearly sighed out loud in relief when Carstairs arrived in response to her earlier summons. "Some of Mrs. Carstairs biscuits for Miss Andrews," she said in response to his inquiry. "I trust Master George is in good hands downstairs?"

"Indeed, ma'am." Carstairs bowed again.

"And when there is a moment, I would like someone to step out and summon a hack carriage," Lily added in a quieter voice. "I will need to take the children back to their home when Miss Andrews has concluded her business."

Clouds had been threatening all morning; now, outside the drawing room's windows, rain began to fall. The watery light that drifted through the windows cast wavering shadows across the room. Lily rose to light a taper and stir up the fire.

When she turned back, Fanny Andrews was watching her closely. "You disapprove of my being here."

"I've not yet decided," Lily replied, deciding to be straightforward as well. "You had best start at the beginning."

Fanny gave a single nod. "My uncle Simon is a constable." Lily wanted to interrupt and say that she knew that part, but she held her tongue. "He must handle all sorts of strange incidents, and his work often distracts him from matters at home. I have been observing my neighbor for some time, but when I tried to speak to Uncle Simon about my suspicions, he was just departing for the Old Bailey and was too distracted to attend. Besides which, I think he believes that a girl would not know more about such things than the constables."

Lily nodded, a little overwhelmed by the flow of information, carefully delivered though it had been. "And what are the things he believes you do not know about?"

"One of my neighbors has either killed someone or is planning to."

"And you said you did not see this person—"

"Mrs. Carver."

"You did not see Mrs. Carver commit these murders, but you saw her with the murder weapon, is that correct?"

Fanny nodded eagerly. "Yes, that is it exactly. In her window boxes."

"In her . . ." Lily stared at the girl. "Miss Andrews, are you talking about a plant?"

"Yes," Fanny replied, still very serious. "She's growing wolfsbane plants. *Aconitum napellus*, if you are familiar with the Latin name."

"I'm afraid I am not," Lily replied, still too taken aback to formulate a real response. "But you know a great deal more about botany than I."

"It is part of the genus *Aconitum*, which contains over two hundred species belonging to the family Ranunculaceae," Fanny said. She sounded a bit as if she was reading from a textbook; indeed, her gaze had settled over Lily's shoulder once more, as if she were seeing a page from one of her books in her mind's eye. "It has a great many other names, but in his *Natural History*, Pliny the Elder called it wolfsbane because he said it came from the saliva of Cerberus." Fanny hesitated, then added in a serious whisper, "My Aunt Judith would not approve of my saying *saliva*."

"Well, I promise not to tell," Lily replied, not knowing what else to say.

"Thank you. In any case, he was correct that it is quite toxic. I already knew a little about *aconitum*, and I looked up more once I realized what Mrs. Carver was up to."

"I've no doubt you were very thorough," Lily replied just as Carstairs entered with a plate of biscuits and a decanter of cordial water.

"Oh, is that for me?" Fanny asked in surprise as he set the tray down.

"Indeed, miss," Carstairs said, giving her a formal bow. Fanny looked pleased, and even more pleased when Lily served her, munching happily on the biscuits.

The interlude gave Lily a welcome moment to get a hold of herself. Fanny might be a child still, but she was hardly fragile. She deserved to be dealt with as Lily would deal with any other person who came asking for assistance, rather than dismissed with indulgent agreement or vague platitudes. That meant taking her concerns seriously enough to meet them with a heavy dose of realism.

"Fanny," she said as the girl sipped her drink. "Can you think of a reason other than murder that one might wish to grow wolfsbane?"

Fanny considered the question. "The flowers are pretty," she said at last. "The ones Mrs. Carver is growing have a lovely purple color, which isn't uncommon. It is happiest growing in woodlands and meadows with plenty of rain, but I suppose people do grow it in gardens."

"Could that be why Mrs. Carver is growing it?"

Fanny frowned. "There is always a chance. But it is an odd choice for a window box, as it can grow quite tall. And anyone who knows anything about plants knows it is poisonous, sometimes even if you only touch it. There was a time in ancient Rome when cultivating it was illegal, and anyone who did could be sentenced to death." She leaned forward eagerly. "So you see, just growing it could clearly be evidence of murderous intent."

"*Could* be," Lily repeated. "Is there a chance Mrs. Carver does not know much about plants and simply chose it because it is pretty?"

Fanny considered her a moment, as though silently sorting through the implications of Lily's words, before she set aside her glass. She sat back in her chair, her gaze dropping to the carpet. "You think

I am imagining things," she said. Her words were calm enough, but she was clearly disappointed.

"I think you perhaps have not imagined quite enough," Lily said, trying to ignore the sting of that disappointment. "Before I investigate anything, I consider every possible explanation for strange circumstances."

Fanny perked up. "Then you will investigate," she said, and it was not quite a question. "I felt certain that you would not be the sort to dismiss the concerns of someone simply because she is young and female."

Lily hesitated. That hadn't been what she meant; she had simply wanted to encourage Fanny to realize that there could be many explanations for what she had seen. And with Clive's threats looming over her, Lily had no desire to take on the worries of another fearful young girl.

But young girls so often had no one to take their worries seriously. And what harm could there be in asking a few questions?

"I shall look into the matter, though I make no promises as to what I will find," Lily said at last. "The situation may be entirely innocent, which means I would discover nothing of note."

"I understand," Fanny said, her hand hovering over the biscuits, passing several by before she settled on just the right one. Once that was selected, she looked back at Lily, making very careful eye contact once more. "And I thank you."

"Then come along," Lily said, standing. "I have no wish for your aunt and uncle to be concerned over your absence."

★ ★ ★

Judith Page had indeed begun to grow worried over the children's stroll, which had lasted far longer than such outings usually did. When Lily arrived at the Pages' home in Clerkenwell with Fanny and George in tow—George with his pockets stuffed full of biscuits, as Lily had discovered in the carriage—Judith went from relieved to irate in an impressively short span of time. Simon Page, recently arrived home from the offices on Bow Street to find his niece and nephew missing, glowered at them from over her shoulder. Once both children had been chastened and sent upstairs to wash for tea, Judith turned to Lily, offering a rueful smile of apology.

"I do beg your pardon, Mrs. Adler," she said. "I had no idea what they intended, and I cannot imagine what possessed them to trouble you. It was terribly kind of you to bring them home."

"It was no trouble at all," Lily said politely. "But Fanny . . ." She hesitated. "Might I have a word with Mr. Page in private?"

Judith looked surprised by the request but was clearly too well-bred to say so out loud. "Of course," she said instead. "If you will excuse me, I shall go check on the children."

Lily waited until she had closed the door to the house's only sitting room—small and a little threadbare, but scrupulously clean and with a cozy fire already warming it for the evening—before taking a seat. Mr. Page followed her lead a moment later.

"Is Fanny well?" he asked. He was clearly uneasy; he sat with his feet planted wide and his hands clasped between his knees. But Lily could not say whether his discomfort was from worry about his niece and nephew or simply from having her in his home.

She felt suddenly unsure of how much to tell him. Mr. Page's unremarkably average appearance meant those who did not know him often underestimated his shrewd intelligence, and she thought he would not dismiss Fanny's concerns out of hand. But she had, more than once over the course of their acquaintance, bumped up against his firm expectations for how people should behave. Those expectations might have relaxed somewhat, but she suspected that might not be the case when it came to the behavior of a young girl in his care.

"Fanny is concerned about the conduct of one of your neighbors," she said at last. "A Mrs. Carver." She waited for a flash of recognition; Fanny had said she had mentioned the wolfsbane to her uncle. But apparently, she had also been correct when she said he had been distracted during the conversation, as Mr. Page only stared at Lily blankly.

"What could possibly worry her about Adelaide Carver?" he asked, sounding perplexed. "She's a widow who sells lace."

Lily sighed. "That is not all Fanny suspects her of doing." Briefly, she told Mr. Page what Fanny had reported. As she spoke, the briefly incredulous look on his face shifted into something more unreadable. His mouth drew into a straight line, and his forehead and eyes gave no hint of his thoughts.

"I did try to speak to you about it, Uncle," Fanny's voice came from the doorway, where she stood watching them calmly. "But you were busy with work. So I asked Mrs. Adler for help, since it seems it is not yet a matter for the police."

"Fanny." Mr. Page beckoned her forward, and she hesitated only a moment before obeying, stopping just in front of him. He did not reach out to her; Lily remembered he had mentioned once that Fanny disliked being touched. He took a deep breath. "How did you get to Mrs. Adler's home?"

"George and I walked," she said calmly. "You and Aunt Judith always say it is unseemly for a young lady to go about unaccompanied. So I took company."

A muscle twitched in Mr. Page's temple. "That is nearly three miles."

She considered that information. "My feet are a little sore," she said at last, looking surprised by the fact but still unbothered.

"Fanny." Mr. Page's voice was remarkably steady, but that muscle in his temple jumped again. "You have no possible reason to be spreading such slanderous allegations against Mrs. Carver, who—"

"I have every reason when she is growing poisons."

"—who was herself the victim of an attack just last night," Mr. Page finished, his voice growing louder. When Fanny flinched away, he took a deep breath.

"You are angry with me," Fanny said softly, and it was almost a question.

"Your aunt and I were worried about you," he said more calmly. "Mrs. Carver was set upon by a man when she was coming home last night, not half a mile from this very house. She was lucky to escape with her life. So we will have no more wandering about from you, Fanny, not when there are cutpurses and footpads at large."

"There have always been cutpurses and footpads in London," the girl pointed out.

"*Fanny.*"

There was a clear warning in her uncle's voice, and she sighed. "I am not supposed to argue," she said, as though reciting a lesson. "Even if I think I am right. I am supposed to say 'yes, Uncle,' and do as you say."

"Because it's my responsibility to keep you *safe*," he said sternly. "No more wandering about. I will have your word on it."

"Yes, Uncle."

"Then go take your tea."

As soon as she was gone, Mr. Page turned to Lily. "I thank you for bringing them home safely, ma'am."

"Of course," she said, her mind still turning over what he had said. "Was Mrs. Carver all right after the attack?"

Simon Page sighed. "Shaken, and I think she got a cut on her arm, but otherwise unharmed. The man attacked her on her way home from the market. She sells lace at a stall there once a week," he added. "Luckily, a group of laborers one street over heard her shouting for help and chased him off."

"So the man is still at large?"

Mr. Page smiled without humor. "Hence my dislike of having my very young niece and even younger nephew wandering about alone."

Lily hesitated. "And what do you think of what Fanny told me? About her distrust of your neighbor? Surely her being the victim of one crime does not prevent her from being the perpetrator of another."

Mr. Page's brows rose as she spoke. "What I think is that we need to convince Fanny to read something other than books on botany. Surely you cannot believe such wild speculation? Why would someone grow poisons in their window box, where anyone can see?"

"Well, it is unlikely," Lily agreed, smiling a little. "But you must admit, were a person to do so, the very boldness of it would be an excellent misdirection."

That made him chuckle a little as he stood. "It was kind of you to treat her concerns seriously, however outlandish they might be. She admires you greatly."

"Does she?" Lily shook her head, standing as well. "Gracious, I'd no idea a meeting so brief would make such an impression."

"Yes, well." Mr. Page cleared his throat. "That business with the ghost in Hampshire got back to us here. Fanny and George were fascinated. Children occasionally have a gruesome turn of mind," he added, a little apologetically.

"Well, I am glad the impression was favorable and that she harbors no suspicions about any murderous intent of mine. Would it . . ." Lily hesitated. "I told her I would look into the matter, and I do not want to go back on my word."

Mr. Page looked amused. "By all means, poke and pry away, ma'am. I know nothing I might say would stop you in any case."

"No, it would not," she admitted.

"Mrs. Carver lives around the corner on Aylesbury Street. I only ask that you not go about unaccompanied either." He shook his head. "The constables don't need you making any more work for them."

"I shall endeavor not to fall afoul of your local cutpurse. Or if I do, I shall be sure to have my pistol with me. Now, if you will excuse me?" She stood. "I've no wish to keep you from your tea, and I've an evening engagement of my own."

"Hobnobbing with the rich and insipid?" he asked, though there was humor in the question where once there would have been bitterness. "Or getting into mischief of your own?"

Lily smiled. "Only a ball. Though perhaps I shall add in a little light burglary to liven up the evening."

He laughed, as if at a good joke. Lily did not contradict him as she took her leave.

CHAPTER 9

The ball was far more elegant than Lily had expected, given that the host was a military bachelor who had not set foot in the capital in two decades. The house itself was not in the most fashionable part of town. But it was not the least fashionable either, and Mr. Forrest had clearly decided to make up for whatever his address lacked through the beauty of his gathering.

Stands of candles gleamed from every surface, and mirrored sconces caught the light and bounced it dramatically around. The paper in the ballroom looked freshly hung, and a quartet of musicians in livery played from one corner while the guests waited for the dancing to begin. Peeking through one of the doorways off the ballroom, Lily could see the supper room at the end of the hall, its half-dozen windows hung with long sweeps of brocade.

Mr. Forrest, luckily, had not been at the door when they arrived, presenting Serena's invitation and leaving their wraps with the servants. Lily suspected that much of the help had been hired temporarily for the evening. A man in Mr. Forrest's position, even if he did have an elegant townhouse, was unlikely to have such a large staff.

But that was useful for their purposes. Temporary staff would not know the house as well, and they would have no need to go anywhere other than the kitchen, the servants' hall, and the rooms that were in use for the party.

"Do you see him?" Lily murmured to Jack and Ned as the four of them made their careful way around the ballroom. They nodded to anyone who caught their eyes, though Lily recognized barely anyone; Mr. Forrest's guests, for the most part, were a different set than she was acquainted with, perhaps drawn from his military acquaintances or neighbors. There were a few whom she knew, though not well. She suspected that, like Serena, they were acquaintances of Miss Crawley's family who had been included to raise the profile of the gathering. It did not, however, look as though many of Mr. Forrest's aspirational guests had accepted his invitation.

That was fine with Lily. The less chance of anyone recognizing them, the better.

"He is the gentleman speaking with the musicians, in the bottle-green coat," Jack replied as they paused by the refreshment table. He occupied himself with procuring glasses of Madeira wine for the ladies, keeping his back to Mr. Forrest. When Ned turned to look, Jack took his arm and turned him firmly away as well. "We should not risk drawing his attention too closely."

"Ah yes, of course," Ned said, looking a little embarrassed. He dropped his voice. "Forgot we were not strictly invited."

"When will you attempt to slip away?" Ofelia murmured as she took a sip of her wine. "Later in the night might be less conspicuous, but we would need to avoid his notice for longer."

The map Sarah had eagerly handed over was tucked into the beaded reticule that Lily carried. Three locations were marked on it, on three different floors. The upper floors would be the easiest; the servants would be busy downstairs. But the thought of the library on the first floor was daunting.

"As soon as we feel we can, the captain and I will go," she decided. "I would rather not delay and risk his being recognized, and earlier in the night, the servants will be busier with the arrivals and preparing the supper room. If we can choose a moment when Mr. Forrest is sufficiently occupied, we should be able to depart without attracting the notice of him or any of the other guests."

"It looks like the musicians are preparing," Ofelia pointed out as they continued on from the refreshment table. "Mr. Forrest will have to lead off the dancing, will he not? And the others will be busy watching the floor."

Lily glanced sideways at Jack, and he nodded. "Very well." They strolled almost aimlessly toward the nearest doorway. "And if you two can keep watch on—"

A commotion at the doorway to the ballroom interrupted her. Lily glanced over without much interest, expecting the sort of disruption that was common at this sort of gathering: the hem torn on a lady's frock from a careless step, or perhaps a gentleman arriving a trifle indisposed after drinking too deeply at his club.

Instead, she spotted two familiar figures, pursued by a servant who was clearly remonstrating with them in spite of his low voice and polite posture. Another footman hovered by the door, anxiously wringing his hands.

"Good heavens, it *is* Mr. Clive," Ofelia whispered as all the heads in the ballroom turned toward the new arrivals. "And that must be Miss Forrest with him?"

Lily glanced at Mr. Forrest. He had turned, along with his guests, to see what the interruption was. For a moment, she thought she saw a look of wide-eyed panic on his face, but it was gone so quickly she might have imagined it, replaced with indignation, then almost as speedily smoothed into an unruffled smile. He bent to whisper to the musicians, who, though they looked confused, immediately began playing the first dance of the evening. Mr. Forrest, his smile still in place but his eyes flinty, strode across the room.

There was a brief, puzzled murmur around the room, but there were enough young people present who were eager to dance. Couples began to claim their partners, though half of them still craned their necks to see what was happening, while the onlookers seemed torn between watching the dancers and watching whatever polite drama was unfolding near the ballroom's main doors.

"What are they doing here?" Ofelia demanded. "Did you know they would be attending tonight?"

"I had no idea," Lily said, trying to watch the argument between Miss Forrest and her uncle while keeping her face averted so she would not be recognized. Mr. Forrest was clearly attempting to keep his voice down and not cause a scene, but it seemed his excitable niece had no such delicacy. Either she wanted to garner the attention of his guests, or she was too distressed to care. "He cannot have invited her unless she misled me greatly as to their relationship."

Jack frowned. "And if they were planning to come, why—"

"—intending to announce an engagement?" Miss Forrest's outrage cut through the ballroom in spite of the musicians' valiant attempts to play loudly.

"Ah, it seems we have Miss Crawley to blame for their presence," Lily murmured as Miss Forrest continued loudly.

"I would have expected that, as your niece—"

Her uncle grabbed her arm and shook it, cutting her off, his voice still low but his fury clear on his face. Clive, looking equally outraged, threw off Mr. Forrest's hands and interposed his body between them.

"Never a better time to sneak away," Jack suggested, raising his eyebrows at Lily.

He was right. The musicians continued to play, and the dancers to dance, but around the room, all eyes were turned toward the arguing trio, and Lily could see no fewer than three other servants had joined the hovering footman, all of them clearly at a loss as to how to help their employer without making more of a scene.

Lily glanced at Ofelia and Ned. "You will be able to manage here?"

They nodded. "No doubt we can invent some excuse to detain him if we need to," Ned said staunchly.

"I can always faint in the middle of the ballroom," Ofelia suggested impishly, though her smile looked a little strained. "Hurry. The sooner you go, the sooner we can leave before something dreadful happens."

It was a melodramatic comment, but Lily could not blame her for it. She laid a hand on her friend's shoulder, giving it a quick squeeze. Then Lily took Jack's arm. Trying to look as innocent and unhurried as possible, they walked calmly out of the ballroom.

The door took them into the passage toward the supper room, which, Lily was pleased to see, was currently devoid of servants or guests, all of whom were presumably riveted by the drama in the ballroom. She and Jack did not linger. Lily had fixed the layout of the first floor in her mind, and she led them quickly toward the house's main rooms.

The library was just behind the main staircase. They paused outside its door, listening for the sound of anyone in the hall.

"I shall take this one," Jack said in a low voice that clearly brooked no argument.

Lily had no intention of arguing, however. The first floor was the one most likely to have servants moving around it during the ball, and Jack would have an easier time explaining his presence if he was discovered there. "I will start on the third floor, then head to the sitting room on the second. When you come upstairs, turn . . ." She consulted the sketch. "Left. You will have more to search down here than I, so we can meet there and return downstairs together."

"Lily." Jack caught her arm as she was about to turn away. His customary levity was missing, and his brow was furrowed. For a moment, she thought he was about to suggest that she return to the ballroom and leave the search to him. But in the end, he gave her a tight smile. "Be careful."

"You as well." She gave the hand that rested on her arm a quick pat, then, turning away, lifted the hem of her gown and hurried up the steps.

The noise of the music and guests faded behind her as she climbed swiftly to the third floor. It made her shiver a little, to be in a strange house with no one about and no good explanation for why she was wandering around, should she be discovered. But that was all the more reason to keep her wits about her and move quickly. Lily consulted the map again, then turned down the hall toward Mr. Forrest's bedroom.

She had the lockpicks from Jem tucked into her reticule as well, but she heaved a sigh of relief to discover she would not need them yet; the door to Mr. Forrest's bedroom was unlocked. Clearly, he had not anticipated the possibility of burglary during his soiree.

Inside, the room was dim, with its curtains drawn and the fire banked low, but Lily was able to find a candle and light it at the embers. Looking around, she saw all the tidiness she would expect from a military man, and none of the ostentation she would expect from one suddenly come into a large and unexpected fortune. The furniture was elegant but a little worn, and the bed linens and curtains had been the height of fashion several years before. He had not redecorated since taking over his brother's house, then. That either spoke to a great deal of affection—which struck Lily as unlikely, given the strain between Mr. Forrest and his brother's only child—or he was simply awaiting the preferences of his bride-to-be.

But that restraint made Lily's task easier. There were few changes from what Miss Forrest had indicated on her map. Lily decided to go through the furniture one piece at a time, starting with the least likely.

The tallboy and washstand were devoid of papers, legal or otherwise, and the dressing room off the bedroom held only what a man would need to bathe and shave. Lily, being somewhat familiar with the process of searching a stranger's room, also checked for things concealed beneath the pillows, on the underside of the bed, and behind the paintings on the walls.

She stopped by the fireplace as well, intending to check the inside edge of the lintel. There was nothing there—Lily was not surprised, it was an unlikely spot for papers to be concealed—but glancing at the ashes from the day's fire, she paused. It was hard to tell, but she thought she could see the remains of several papers, all burnt beyond the chance of seeing what they had once contained.

Lily frowned. But there were many reasons someone might want to dispose of letters; no one could keep everything they were sent. If Mr. Forrest had burned his brother's legal papers—a significant *if*, as far as she was concerned—that was a suspicious but not insurmountable obstacle. Whoever had been the brother's solicitor would have a copy. All she needed was to find that solicitor's name.

And then decide whether or not she wanted to provide it to Miss Forrest and her blackmailing suitor.

At last, she turned her attention to the writing desk beneath the windows, a handsome, stately old piece of heavy furniture with a promising number of drawers and cubbyholes. Again, she was grateful for the military discipline that clearly still governed Mr. Forrest's habits. Everything was neatly organized, with bills for tradesmen and deliveries—all intended for the ball currently happening downstairs— marked as paid or outstanding and tucked neatly away. There were several unremarkable letters from Miss Crawley's father. Scanning them, Lily found a straightforward outline of a betrothal agreement, including only a token dowry. But Mr. Forrest did not need money, from what Miss Forrest had said. What he craved was status. There was nothing from Miss Crawley herself.

It was not until she tried the drawer on the lower part of the desk that her heartbeat picked up. It was locked. Glancing at the door, hoping she had not already taken too long, Lily knelt by the desk and pulled out her lockpicks.

Either Jem had taught her well or the lock on the desk drawer was not as sturdy as Mr. Forrest might have hoped. It took her less than a minute to hear it pop open. Lily slid the drawer out and began to go through the papers there, eager to see what had been important enough to keep behind lock and key.

A bundle of correspondence tied with a string, all addressed to *Captain Martin Forrest, 12th Light Dragoons.* Papers detailing the sale of Captain Forrest's army commission in anticipation of his return to London, and a glowing letter of introduction from his commanding officer for him to take into his new, civilian life. Letters from soldiers still in France, wishing Mr. Forrest well in his new life and lamenting the loss to their company that his departure would bring. A handful of notes from old acquaintances scattered across England, expressing surprise upon hearing that Mr. Forrest had at last returned to the country and condolences for the death of his brother.

There was nothing incriminating there. If anything, it painted Mr. Forrest in a distinctly admirable light. Apparently, he had been well liked by his fellow officers. Even a few enlisted men had written to thank him or wish him well. And in spite of his long absence, he had been remembered kindly enough by old friends for them to reach out.

But at the bottom of the drawer, she found a bundle of letters whose hand she recognized. Each one had been penned by Miss Forrest. And all of them had been left unopened and unread.

Lily sat back on her heels. There were, it seemed, a number of contradictions in Mr. Forrest's character. She would have liked to spend more time puzzling over them, but now was not the moment for such ruminations. There were no legal papers in the desk, not even a note or a scrap of paper to indicate who the late Mr. Forrest's solicitor might have been. She closed the drawer, holding her breath for a nervous moment while she attempted to relock it. At last, the pins clicked back into place, and she stood, scanning the room to make sure nothing had been left disturbed.

The hall was still silent and empty when she peeked cautiously out. She hesitated, then took the candle with her; it was unlikely anyone would have laid a fire in an unused room when a party was happening downstairs. Lily checked her map one more time to be certain of her destination, then hurried down to the sitting room on the second floor.

★ ★ ★

Jack didn't linger near the library once he had finished searching. He didn't sneak either—a man could get away with a great deal so long as he walked with confidence. But he did move as quietly as possible as he climbed the steps to the second floor. There was no sense attracting attention that was better avoided.

Lily's directions had been to turn left, and the sitting room on her map had been the third door off the upper hall. His steps slowed as he approached. The door was cracked just the barest inch, and he could see a thin, weak flicker of candlelight from the other side. Anyone who was supposed to be there would have more light, so he assumed Lily had arrived first. But just to be safe, he paused in the hall and whistled softly.

He wouldn't have heard the quiet snort from the other side of the door if he hadn't been listening for it, and it made him smile in spite of the tense circumstances. He had whistled the opening of a bawdy sailor's ditty that he had been uproariously entertained to hear Lily humming when it was popular a few years before.

Now, she whistled the next few bars in response, letting him know that it was indeed she on the other side of the door. A moment later Jack was in the room, closing the door softly behind him and turning to give his friend an encouraging smile.

"Anything of interest?" he asked, glancing around.

There were two writing desks in the room, likely intended for guests who had correspondence to manage. There was no banked fire in the hearth, but Lily had left lit tapers on each one. She was at the one just before the windows; the other was beside a crowded wall of bookshelves.

"A great deal of interest upstairs, but nothing to our purposes," Lily replied, just barely above a whisper. "Anything from downstairs?"

"It was mostly the brother's papers downstairs—a great deal concerning the estate, letters that I can imagine his daughter would like to have, things of that nature. But I did find this." Jack couldn't hold back a pleased smile as he offered her a folded sheet of paper.

Lily let out a sigh of relief as she read it. "The solicitor. Thank goodness. I was afraid we would be risking all this for nothing." She glanced at the two desks. "We still ought to finish our search, though. Just to be thorough."

"Agreed." Jack waved her off when she would have handed the paper back to him—it was for her use, not his—then went to the desk by the bookcase, where she had left the candle burning for him. It made him nervous to have it lit, knowing it could be seen around the doorframe by someone who was looking for such a thing. But there was no help for it. With its heavy curtains drawn, the room would be near completely dark without the tapers. And it had been a cloudy enough night that Jack did not want to rely on moonlight for their search.

The desk was a small affair, likely intended just for writing letters. There was nothing of note on its surface, but it did have a drawer. Jack cursed softly when he discovered it was locked, then pulled out his lockpicking tools with a sigh.

When he discovered what was inside, he nearly laughed aloud.

"Any luck?" he asked after examining the drawer for anything else.

"Nothing," Lily replied just as quietly. "A few periodicals, some old correspondence from Miss Forrest's father. What about yours?"

"Paper and wafers for guests who wish to write letters," he said. He couldn't hide the note of amusement in his voice as he added, "And a rather scandalous novel tucked into the locked drawer. I wonder who put it there."

"Which one?" Lily demanded, closing the drawers she had been searching. Taking up her candle, she came over to see what he had found.

Jack had already closed the drawer in question, and he laid one hand on it, as though keeping it teasingly out of her reach. "Are you so versed in salacious literature that you know all the entries in the genre?" he asked, grinning at her.

But before Lily could reply, they heard the sound of footsteps on the stairs, moving so quickly as to be almost running. They were some distance down the hall, but both Lily and Jack instantly blew out their candles, settling into stillness as they waited to see which direction the footsteps would go.

"—stairs, you say?" they heard a quick, irritated voice ask in the hall. "Where do you think she's gone?"

"I certainly don't know," a second, nervous voice replied. "I just saw her in the hall, and I came to get you, like I was told I ought when they brought us in for the night, because we're not supposed to bother Mr. Forrest with it, and I'm sure I'm not the one—"

"All right, all right." The irritated voice sighed, getting quieter again as the speaker moved farther away. "I'll start looking. You go find Bennet and tell him . . ."

Jack didn't let out the breath he was holding until the voices faded away and he heard footsteps on the stairs once more. They were in darkness now that their candles were blown out, but he could feel Lily close beside him. She didn't tremble—she was not the sort of woman who would, even if she was afraid—but he could feel the tension thrumming through her. His hand brushed her arm, then traveled down until he could give her fingers a gentle squeeze.

"Come on," he whispered, his mouth close to her ear. "We should get back downstairs before they bring more searchers."

"How did someone see me?" Lily demanded, her voice no louder than his. "I was careful to—"

He squeezed her fingers again, and she fell silent. There was a time to wonder and a time to be quiet and make their way back to the party as quickly as possible. They both knew which one this was.

They left the candles behind them, moving to the door by touch and memory. Jack did not let go of Lily's hand, and he walked with the other outstretched, feeling with his toes as they went. Beside him, he could hear her doing the same, and he fell back to let her go first, as her daintily slippered feet were better suited to the task. They made it to the door without too much noise or mishap. In the darkness, Jack was all too aware of Lily next to him as they both leaned their ears against the wood.

There was no sound from the other side, and a moment later they had the door open and were slipping quietly down the hall. It wasn't until they were almost to the stairs that Jack realized he still held her hand. He wondered briefly if she had noticed, but then there wasn't time to think about it for more than a moment.

There were footsteps coming up the stairs, blocking their path back down.

Jack cast around quickly. They had only moments before whoever it was came around the curve in the staircase and discovered them there. But Lily was ahead of him; she yanked open the closest door and pulled him in after her. He stumbled, caught off guard, and knocked the door from her hand. He managed to catch it just before it swung closed and eased it shut.

They both stood still, trying to listen to the voices in the hall.

"—call a constable?"

"There are guests downstairs—we can't make a scene, even if someone is sneaking around." Both voices were unfamiliar. Other servants, Jack could guess, fetched to help with the search. "Find her first, and then I'll decide whether or not to summon a constable. You head upstairs, I'll take this floor. Go on, what are you waiting for?"

"I thought I heard—"

"What?" A pause. "Over . . . One of those rooms, you think?"

They could hear the footsteps coming down the hall, and the sound of a door being yanked open. A careless servant had forgotten to draw the curtains in the room. In the fitful moonlight that slunk through the windows, Jack could see Lily holding very still. Her gaze darted around the room, as though searching for another way out, but her wide eyes and quick breathing gave away her distress.

There wasn't another way out. Jack clenched his jaw, hoping he was not about to make a terrible mistake. The footsteps stopped outside the door.

"Lily," he whispered, "I hope you will forgive me for this."

Her head snapped toward him. "What—"

Jack didn't let her finish. He tossed off his coat, then yanked Lily toward him, toppling them both onto the bed and kissing her soundly just as the door opened.

CHAPTER 10

For a moment, Lily felt frozen in shock. One instant she had been standing, the next she was lying on top of Jack, surrounded by the scent and heat of him. His arms were wrapped around her, and his mouth—

Lily had been kissed in the years since she had become a widow—kissed, romanced, and on occasion, a great deal more. There should have been nothing extraordinary in the moment that Jack pulled her onto that bed, a moment that the logical part of her mind knew at once wasn't even real.

But there was. She could feel it in every inch of her body. And when she kissed him back without hesitating, it wasn't truly because she knew she needed to follow his lead. She couldn't seem to help herself.

It was a deception, nothing more, and any second they would be discovered. But some dazed corner of Lily's mind was still drinking the moment in, knowing it would likely never happen again.

She cupped his face in her hands, then let her mouth travel down his jaw and neck. There was a hitch in Jack's breathing, and he pulled her more tightly against him, his hands splaying across her hips.

The door slammed open behind them, and Jack suddenly sat up, making her squeak in surprise at the rapid change. He pressed her against his chest so that her face wasn't visible to the people standing in the doorway. Lily was fairly certain her petticoat had bunched up around her stockings, and his hands were in unseemly places, but that was all the better. They would make a convincing picture of a couple who had snuck away for an illicit tryst.

"I beg your pardon," Jack said, managing to sound both flustered and indignant. She could feel his heart pounding, and it was some comfort that its beat was as rapid as her own. "I would prefer a little privacy, if it's not too much trouble?"

"Sir, you cannot . . . that is . . . I must ask you to . . ."

Lily could hear how distressed the servant was. Her own face felt as though it was on fire, and it was a struggle to slow her breathing to a normal pace.

"Very well, very well, if you insist. I should have locked the door," Jack said, chuckling a little hoarsely. "Give us a moment, and we will be happy to make our way back to the ballroom."

"That would be for the best, sir." The servant's voice was stiff and uncomfortable. "Madam."

Lily didn't say anything, and she kept her face averted. She and Jack stayed frozen as the door closed, both of them breathing heavily and neither one speaking. Lily didn't know if Jack was looking at her; she kept her eyes fixed on his chest, not yet ready to look up. She wondered if his silence was to keep the servants from overhearing them or because he, like her, was still trying to gather his scrambled thoughts.

Likely the first. Jack had been in control from the moment the door had opened, his manner just the right mixture of debauched and commanding. It had all been pretend. She couldn't afford to think of it as any more than that.

And they weren't out of danger yet.

She rolled off him so suddenly that he grunted, sliding to the ground and hurriedly shaking her petticoat and gown back into their proper place. "Do you think they've gone?" she demanded in a whisper, raising her gaze to his at last.

The clouds had cleared somewhat, and in the moonlight she could see that Jack's jaw was tight and his cheeks flushed. He stared at her for a heartbeat before he answered. "Give it a moment to be sure. But we ought to be quick. If they say anything to Forrest, he is bound to come see what the trouble is."

"And we cannot have him recognizing you," Lily said, nodding, almost grateful for the urgency of the task at hand. There was no time to be embarrassed; they had to decide quickly what to do. "Will you listen at the door for—" She broke off.

They were in what she presumed was a guest room. It was furnished well enough, if not elaborately. The large bed that they had so recently occupied was directly in the middle of it, and as she averted her eyes from it, they landed on the old-fashioned desk that occupied the corner nearest the fireplace.

Jack had already followed both her gaze and her thoughts. "Is there time?"

Lily hesitated. They needed to get back downstairs. But . . . "If Miss Forrest's suspicions are correct, what better place to keep things out of the way than a room that is never used?"

There was enough moonlight now that, even without candles, Lily could see the lock on the drawer. She checked it, then gestured Jack forward and passed him the lockpicks she had already pulled from her reticule. "You are faster at this than I."

"Very noble of you to admit it," he said, pausing just long enough to grin at her, though the expression was more tense than usual.

"Very practical of me," Lily countered in an impatient whisper. "Can you get it?"

A quiet, triumphant, "Ha!" was her only answer. Lily could see Jack's pleased expression as he bent to search the drawer.

Lily was standing close enough to see the stillness that settled over him. "What is it?" she whispered.

"There *is* something in here."

It was a letter, Lily saw when he handed it to her, addressed to *Captain Martin Forrest, 12th Light Dragoons* and with the wafer already broken. She didn't hesitate to slide it open and scan its contents as quickly as possible. There was still just enough light to make it out.

> *The doctor tells me, brother, that he does not expect I will have long to live. And so I must beg you to sell your commission even more speedily than we planned and make your way to England once more. It will pain my girl, I know, to lose out on the fortune that her companion, being her mother's cousin, has told her for so long should be hers and hers alone. But I cannot be reconciled with you and yet remain so cruel as to leave you without the means to support our ancestral property. And I am relieved, as you will surely understand, that my Sarah will not be left solely to the care of Miss Waverly when I am gone. I expect that she will be only a short time in your care—she is a girl who longs to marry, and she will be well suited to it, and with marriage she will receive, if not the entirely of what Miss Waverly has led her to expect, at least a great deal of it. I know you, dear brother, will not withhold your consent unreasonably. There is no need to be too cruel or too particular—any reasonably young fellow of good family and decent prospects will do. But it is a great comfort to me that we were reconciled in time for you to take on her guardianship, as I—*

"What does it say?" Jack broke in. "We should not linger overlong."

"Here." Lily held out the letter. Jack pulled it so quickly from her fingers that Lily almost thought he might have been trying his best not to touch her. She scowled at him. Did he think she was as timid and missish as that? She understood exactly what had just happened, and he should know her well enough to know she would not be offended.

But he was looking at the paper and did not see her scowl. He blew out a heavy breath. "If it is real, her uncle was indeed summoned back by her father. And he did wish to protect the family property through a new arrangement of inheritance."

Lily nodded. "But—"

The sudden thumping of hurrying feet from the floor above them made Lily and Jack both jump, glancing toward the ceiling as they recalled where they were. Lily hastily tucked the letter back into the drawer and slid it closed. Jack still had her lockpicks, and it was only a moment more before he had jiggled the pins back into place.

They could still hear the music drifting up from the ballroom. Lily took a deep breath as she returned the picks to her reticule. Jack echoed her.

"We ought to go back down," he said, one hand on the doorknob. At Lily's nod, he swung it open and stepped into the hall.

"Hartley."

The sharp voice made them both freeze, Lily only halfway out the door. In front of her, she could see Jack's entire body tense; he gave a small motion of his hand, gesturing for her to stay where she was.

"Forrest," he said, his voice cheerful and breezy, with just a hint of fuzziness to it. He put one hand against the doorjamb to steady himself, giving an excellent impression of a man who, while not quite foxed, had certainly imbibed more than was wise. "Good to see you, man. Splendid party."

"Hmm. Thank you, sir." Mr. Forrest did not bother to disguise his displeasure. Anyone would be unhappy to find guests—uninvited ones, at that—traipsing around his house. But there was a hardness to his tone that made Lily shiver. "Though I'm surprised to see you at it, as we only met yesterday, and my invitations went out some time ago."

"Oh, as to that," Jack said carelessly, "my friend had an invitation, and when I recognized your name I thought, well, why indeed not?"

"I see." Mr. Forrest suddenly came into Lily's view as he stepped to one side of Jack, looking her up and down. "And do I know your friend?"

There was an emphasis on the word that made Lily's skin crawl, but she did not let it show. He was not an unattractive man, but his eyes were hard as he stared at her. For a moment, she was all too aware of his broad shoulders and big fists, and of Jack's still-injured shoulder. There was an edge of roughness in Mr. Forrest's words, a reminder that he had spent many years on the battlefield, surrounded by soldiers and far away from the polish of London society. He looked and sounded like the sort of man who would not hesitate to grow violent, though she hoped that her presence—and that of the servant standing behind him, who had clearly fetched him to deal with his rowdy guests—would make that unlikely. Even though she wanted nothing more than to run in the opposite direction, she smiled at him, a languid, amused expression that she hoped gave away neither her thoughts nor her racing heart. If Mr. Forrest had concealed that letter on purpose, and if he was indeed trying to keep his niece's money from her, then his suspicions would be instantly aroused by seeing them emerge from the spare room. She had to give him the impression that they were nothing more than dissipated partygoers seeking a little privacy, even at the risk of provoking gossip about her and Jack should Mr. Forrest discover who she was. That, at least, her reputation had withstood before and could again.

"I must confess, sir, that my invitation was obtained at secondhand," she said playfully. "My dear friends, Lord and Lady Walter, were unable to attend." She dropped her voice to a gossiping whisper. "Lady Walter was so recently delivered of her fourth child, you see. But they asked me to pass on their greetings and their hope of a future meeting."

"The viscount and his wife?" Mr. Forrest could not hide his surprise as he glanced back at Jack. "You keep distinguished company."

Jack grinned, wobbling a little and catching himself on the door once more. "Full of surprises."

"So it seems." Mr. Forrest looked between them, and Lily drew a little closer to Jack without entirely meaning to, unnerved by that cold gaze. "Well, you're welcome to stay, but I hope you'll remember that the party is happening downstairs." He gave them a sour smile. "Not on the upper floors."

Jack chuckled, and Lily smiled as though embarrassed. "Of course, sir," she said demurely, relieved that he had not insisted on knowing her name. Perhaps they had fooled him after all.

Mr. Forrest gestured to the servant, who was still standing at the top of the stairs, trying to look anywhere but at the scene in front of him. "Bennet, please escort Mr. Hartley and his companion back downstairs."

"Of course, sir."

"Are you not coming?" Lily asked brightly. "You will not want to miss the dancing, I am sure."

"I'll rejoin my guests in a moment," he said. "If you'll go ahead?"

He gestured toward the stairs, and they had no choice but to do as he bid. Jack bowed, then offered Lily his arm as they turned to follow the servant down the stairs. Lily could feel Mr. Forrest watching them, and the sensation made her neck prickle with nerves. Just before they turned at the landing, she glanced back.

She was just in time to see Mr. Forrest walk into the spare room, closing the door sharply behind him.

★ ★ ★

However flustered the servants upstairs had been by their search, and by the uncomfortable situation that search had uncovered, they had not let it spill into the party downstairs. As they entered the ballroom—Bennet the servant giving them a stiff bow and leaving them there quickly—the musicians were playing a lively reel.

"Do you see the Carroways?" Jack asked as they paused at the edge of the room, lowering his head so his mouth was close to Lily's ear.

The feel of his breath against her neck made Lily shiver, but she managed to nod calmly as she looked around for their friends. "There," she said after a moment, nodding toward one side of the dance floor, where Ofelia and Ned were engaged in a heated, whispered conversation. "They do not look happy."

"Likely because they lost sight of Mr. Forrest," Jack said. "We should depart quickly, I think."

"Yes." Lily pictured Mr. Forrest heading into the spare room and shivered. "Can you catch Ned's eye?"

"Did you find anything?" Ofelia asked in a breathless whisper when all four of them had met at last in an alcove by the ballroom doors.

"We found something," Lily replied, glancing back at the dance floor. Mr. Forrest had just returned, and she was worried he would be keeping an eye on them. But fortunately, he was immediately greeted by a brunette beauty whose pert little shake of her dance card indicated that she was supposed to be his partner for the gavotte just beginning. Lily wondered if it was Miss Crawley, though the lady looked a little older than the just-out-of-the-schoolroom debutante of rumor. "What happened here?"

"He sent Miss Forrest and Mr. Clive on their way with impressive discretion," Ofelia said. "I think they must have given up, for I've not seen them in some time. Have you, Neddy?"

"Pair of footmen escorted them out," Ned replied, shaking his head vigorously. "Don't think the uncle was taking any chances."

"It might have been more of a scene, but the whispers are much more concerned with Miss Crawley," Ofelia said. "She has yet to make an appearance, it seems, despite her arrival being predicted at any moment."

Lily glanced again at the dark-haired beauty on the dance floor. Not Miss Crawley, then. "Well, as charming as the announcement of their betrothal would be, I do not think it would be wise for us to await it," she said. "I've no wish to test our luck any further."

"Any further?" Ofelia's eyes grew wide. "What happened?" Beside her Ned looked ill with nerves.

Lily almost glanced at Jack but stopped herself before she did; she didn't want to risk another blush with her friends looking on. "We can tell you more once we have departed," she said quietly, already turning toward the door. "Let us make haste."

Lily did not breathe easily until they were ensconced in the Carroways' comfortable carriage once more. She heard her sigh of relief echoed from Jack and Ned.

Ofelia, however, was looking at Jack, and in the swinging light of the carriage lamps, Lily could see a narrow-eyed look on her face. "Captain, why was that fellow who fetched our wraps smirking at you as we walked out the door?"

CHAPTER 11

It took some time to quell Ofelia's excitement. To Lily's relief, she accepted Jack's quick explanation that he had run into the servant while he was searching and convinced the fellow he was avoiding a jealous husband who suspected Jack of flirting with his wife. He didn't look at Lily as he said it, and she kept her face as straight as possible when Ofelia and Ned glanced at her for confirmation.

"We split up while we were looking," she said, dry as ever. "Whatever mischief the captain got up to does not concern me."

She regretted the words the instant they were out of her mouth, worried Jack would take more meaning from them than she had intended. But there was no opportunity to take them back, and as the carriage rattled through the streets of London, she decided it was better that way. Far more mortifying, after their conversation in her book-room the other night, for him to think she placed too much importance on what had happened in Mr. Forrest's spare room. It had been quick thinking on his part, nothing more. She had no intention of being the one to make things uncomfortable between them as a result.

And there were more important things to worry about.

"But that was not what I was referring to," she said quietly. "When Mr. Forrest left the ballroom, he found us upstairs."

"Dear God." Ned gulped. "What happened? Does he suspect anything?"

"I hope not," Lily said. They had left the letter where it was, after all, and locked the desk once more. He would have found nothing out of the ordinary in the room, and they had certainly left the bed rumpled behind them. "He recognized the captain, but he seemed distracted enough when I mentioned that my invitation came from Lord and Lady Walter."

"Did you give him your name?" Ofelia demanded.

Lily shook her head. "He did not ask, thank goodness. But he seemed . . ."

"He was on edge," Jack put in. "He was jumpy when I met him last night too. He gives the impression of a fellow up to no good and waiting for someone to discover it."

"And did you discover anything?" Ofelia asked, the swinging carriage lights catching her worried expression.

Lily glanced at Jack. "We did," she said quietly, describing what they had learned.

"What do you intend to do about Clive now?" Ned demanded once Lily finished. He placed a protective hand on his wife's arm as he spoke. "Will he accept that there was no will to be found?"

Lily glanced at Ofelia, who was biting her lip and frowning. For all her friend's pretense of confidence, Lily knew she had been worried from the beginning. "I do not know," Lily admitted reluctantly. "My hope is that if I can deal with Miss Forrest directly, when he is not present, I can give her the name of her father's solicitor. Without him there to encourage her, she might accept that. And if she does, she can report back to Mr. Clive that I've done as they asked." Lily looked at Ofelia again. "Are you comfortable with that as a solution?"

Ofelia sighed but nodded. "It is a risk either way, but this seems the best option if we do not want to directly give in to his demands. Which I still do not," she added, lifting her chin. "If he realizes there is nothing you can do that he cannot do himself, perhaps he will leave us alone."

"And if he does resort to underhanded tactics, to rumor and gossip, your friends and family will stand by you, Lady Carroway," Jack said warmly. He glanced at Lily. "And by Mrs. Adler. Your characters are well-known. I've no doubt that both of you will be able to weather whatever storm he might produce."

"I hope so," Lily said, sighing. "But I would much prefer sunshine."

"As would I," Ofelia agreed as the carriage slowed to a halt on Half Moon Street. She smiled at Jack, though the expression was not as sunny as it usually would have been. "But I thank you, sir, for the reassurance. Now, shall we take you home as well?"

Jack shook his head. "I will see Mrs. Adler to her door, thank you. It is not so long a walk for me from here."

"Are you certain?" Ned asked, frowning, before seeming to start a little, as though he had been on the receiving end of a discreet pinch. "Well, of course, whatever you like," he said, shrugging as the groom swung the carriage door open.

Lily tried not to feel embarrassed. No doubt Ofelia had meant to remind her husband only that Lily and Jack were friends of long standing who did not require chaperoning the way another unmarried couple might. She did not like the thought of anyone speculating about her life behind her back.

"And you will let us know, I hope, Mrs. Adler, what happens when you speak with Miss Forrest?" Ofelia tried to ask the question carelessly but did not quite succeed. As Jack stepped down from the carriage and turned to offer his hand—on the uninjured side—to Lily, she saw Ned pat his wife's arm.

"Of course I will," Lily said, giving her friend what she hoped was a reassuring smile. "I am sure all will be well."

As they watched the carriage roll away, Lily murmured to Jack, standing beside her, "I am not at all sure, you know."

She could not see his face clearly, but she could hear the smile in his voice. "That is because you are too much of a realist for your own good."

That made her smile in return, in spite of her nerves. "Perhaps. Are you seeing me to the door?"

"Yes." But he hesitated as she opened it. She still held his arm; he laid his hand on hers, drawing her to a halt in the doorway, the lamplight from the hall spilling over both of them. "Lily, we ought to talk about what hap—"

"Good evening, Mrs. Adler."

The cool voice made them both start, but Lily recognized it instantly and swung toward the street.

"I didn't have the pleasure of seeing you tonight at the ball thrown by my dear Sarah's uncle," Clive continued, stopping halfway up the steps. Beside him, Miss Forrest looked up at them expectantly, her hand clutching his arm. "Did you not wish to greet us? I'm quite certain you knew we were there." His smile grew a little self-deprecating. "You might have noticed that we weren't as subtle in our arrival as we'd intended."

Lily regarded him, her face impassive. "What makes you think I was there?" she asked. Under her fingers, she could feel the muscles in Jack's arm tense, but he did not interrupt, content to follow her lead. "I've not given you an answer yet."

"Mr. Clive saw your friend there," Miss Forrest put in eagerly. "He says it was your friend. Lady Carroway, I think her name was?"

"She and that redheaded husband of hers were watching Mr. Forrest," Clive said, still smiling. "I may not be the smartest man in England, but I've wits enough to guess that if she was there, it means you were not far away."

"Will you let us in and tell us what you found?" Miss Forrest asked. "Please? Oh, please do. I know it is not polite to turn up here uninvited, but you've no idea how I've longed for answers."

Lily wanted to ask how they had known where she lived, but she could guess well enough. If Clive had seen Ofelia and Ned, it would have been easy enough to wait near Mr. Forrest's home until they left, then follow the carriage to Half Moon Street. And now that they were there, if she tried to send them packing, she risked the sort of scene that her gossip-loving neighbors—was there any other kind of neighbor? Certainly not in London—would be all too eager to watch if they were still awake.

Lily held back a grimace, nodding as coolly as if she had intended nothing else all evening. "Very well. You may come in."

None of her servants were up. She had instructed them, at the beginning of the night, to turn in without waiting for her. It had been as much for their benefit as for hers, not knowing what the night would bring and how long it would keep her from home. And it was a request she made frequently enough that none of them had found it odd.

Now, she was doubly glad for the precaution. Whatever Clive might say, whatever she might have to admit to having done, none of her servants would be there to witness it.

Carstairs had left a lantern for her in the hall. Lily used it to light several tapers in the drawing room, which was cold and unwelcoming at this time of night. Lily hoped the chill would encourage her guests to be on their way quickly. They took seats as though everything about the situation were normal, but Lily and Jack stayed standing, Lily by the fireplace, Jack by the door.

Miss Forrest glanced between them a little nervously before her gaze settled on Lily. "Did you find anything? I was ever so surprised when my dear Mr. Clive said you were there. However did you manage it?"

Lily sighed. "We had an invitation. It was unwise, Miss Forrest, to attempt to attend yourself when you did not. Irritating your uncle now will not help your case."

"But he was planning to announce an engagement!" she protested. "I could scarcely believe it when my cousin told me the news. You do realize what this means, do you not? If he is married, he will have even more cause to continue cutting me off from my property. I had to know if it was true."

When Lily glanced at Clive, she was surprised to see a tight, resigned smile on his face. "It was, perhaps, unwise. But it's hard to gainsay a woman when she is so distressed. And also so determined."

Lily paused, considering that. It was not quite the dynamic she had expected. She wondered whether to believe it. "And what did you learn?"

Miss Forrest sighed, slumping back in her seat. "Nothing we did not already know. What about you?" She sat forward again, eager and nervous. "Did you find my father's will? What did it say? What has my uncle done?"

Lily shook her head. "Miss Forrest, it is very late, and you had an upsetting evening. Perhaps it would be better to have this conversation when you have had time to restore your spirits—"

Sarah Forrest had been looking Lily up and down, growing a little frantic as she seemed to realize that Lily could not be carrying anything so large as a will with her. "What happened? Did you not find it? Dear God, has he destroyed it entirely? I was worried something like this would—"

"No, nothing of that sort," Lily said quickly, cutting her off as the girl's voice began to rise. Clive reached out to lay a hand over Miss Forrest's. Lily caught Jack's eye over their shoulders, and his expression was grim. "That is, I do not know. I was unable to locate your father's will. But I also found a letter that your father wrote regarding your uncle's return to England. And he seemed to have some concerns . . ." She hesitated.

Miss Forrest's mouth trembled. "I was wrong, wasn't I?" she asked in a small voice. "My father did disinherit me."

"It seems he did change his plans for your inheritance, in the interest of allowing his brother to maintain the family estate," Lily said gently. "However, you were not—"

"But how could he do such a thing?" Miss Forrest demanded in a disbelieving whisper. "My cousin says that he promised my mother—on her deathbed!—he *promised* her—"

"Sarah, you must not distress yourself so," Clive said, squeezing her hand. He shot a glare at Lily. "This was not what we had hoped for from the estimable Mrs. Adler," he said, a sarcastic edge to his voice that set Lily's shoulders on edge.

Miss Forrest was still protesting. "But how could he have—"

"However," Lily said more loudly. To her relief, both of her unwanted guests fell silent. She lowered her voice to a more gentle tone and kept her eyes on Miss Forrest, though she could feel Clive's gaze boring into her. But she had read what was there, and she couldn't make it otherwise just to please him. "You were right to think there are some oddities as well. In the letter to your uncle, your father described his conviction that his brother would serve as your guardian only for a short time, expecting that you would wish to marry soon. And he seemed to expect that your uncle would quickly approve your marriage and dower you generously. The fact that he has not and instead has sent you away from your home . . ."

Miss Forrest's hands had tightened on Clive's arm as Lily spoke, her cheeks growing pale and her breathing agitated. Now, eyes wide, she broke in. "It could mean exactly what I suspected, then. That if I do not marry, he can retain control of my money." She glanced at Clive. "I was right."

"I never doubted you, my dear one," he said gallantly.

To Lily's ear the endearments felt heavy-handed and made her regard him suspiciously. But Miss Forrest seemed to take it in stride. She smiled in relief, turning back to Lily. "Let me see the letter."

Lily sighed. "I certainly did not take it. I never agreed to such a thing."

"But—"

"And even if I had promised to help you—which you may recall, I did not—I could not risk it. Not when he had so clearly set it aside to prevent its being discovered."

"I shall risk it," Clive declared.

"By yourself?" Lily asked, her brows rising. "Or do you mean that you would like me to risk it?"

She could see Clive clench his jaw. "Determined to think the worst of me, I see?" he asked, though he seemed to regret the words as soon as they were out of his mouth. He darted a look at Miss Forrest, as though hoping she had not heard him.

She frowned. "Why should Mrs. Adler think the worse of you?"

"Oh, because I am a scoundrel," he said lightly, though the smile he gave her looked a little forced. And a moment later, it had faded completely as he turned back to Lily. "But that doesn't mean I'm wrong. If the letter is what gave you pause, then we must have it. Where will I find it?"

Lily regarded him impassively. "I shan't be revealing that."

Miss Forrest glanced back and forth between them once more. "But—"

"*But*," Lily continued, "I also found the name of your father's solicitor, the one who drew up the will."

"What is his name?"

Lily glanced again at Clive. She still didn't want to have this conversation with him there, but it seemed there was no help for it. And it was information that Miss Forrest deserved to have. She pulled the piece of paper Jack had given her from her reticule. "The solicitor was a Mr. Christopher Sloane, with offices on Theobald's Road. He should have a copy of your father's will, and no doubt he will also have been privy to any discussion regarding your dowry, prospects, or any other expectations your father may have had of your uncle." Lily sighed. "I am afraid that is all the information I was able to uncover for you. If your uncle is hiding something, he has been thorough about it."

Miss Forrest took the paper with trembling hands. She read it through several times. "Is there nothing else?" she asked in a small voice. "What if this Mr. Sloane will not speak to me?"

Lily's heart went out to the girl. She hated the answer she had to give. "Then I am afraid you have very little recourse, Miss Forrest. Legally, your father's property seems likely to be your uncle's concern. And unfortunately, you are as well. Unless and until you marry."

"That is not fair," Miss Forrest whispered.

Lily shook her head. "No. But it is the way it is."

"That is nonsense," Clive declared, loudly and suddenly enough that both women started. "Mrs. Adler, by your own discovery and admission, Mr. Forrest is doing his damnedest to keep Sarah's rightful property from her, in the form of her dowry if nothing else. It's a travesty, and I'm sure you cannot help feeling some sympathy for her situation."

Lily regarded him coldly. What would he do if she threw him out? "I do, Mr. Clive. But even if that is the case—"

"And I'm sure, resourceful woman that you are, you can think of some way that you can help us to prove it." He leaned forward. "You do wish to help her, do you not?"

Lily stood. "I feel for you, Miss Forrest," she said, speaking directly to the girl, who looked up at her, hope and confusion warring in her expression. "Truly, I do. It is an appalling reality, that a man may exert such control over the life and fortunes of a woman, especially one for whom he has so little regard or care. But I have done what I can to assist you. I am sorry that your father's will was not to be found, but I cannot do anything more." She glanced at Clive, her voice growing cold. "Not even under threat of blackmail."

"Don't—"

He had started to his feet as soon as he realized what she was about to say, but he was not quick enough. The words hung in the air as soon as they were past Lily's lips. Out of the corner of her eye, she could see Jack shift so that he was no longer lounging against the doorframe, but alert and ready for whatever the other man might do.

Sarah Forrest stared at Lily for a long moment, her initial puzzlement fading into horror as she realized who Lily was looking at. She turned, slowly standing and taking a step away from him. "What does Mrs. Adler mean by that?"

His appalled expression matching Miss Forrest's own, Clive shook his head. "It's not what you think."

"What does she mean, *blackmail*?" Miss Forrest insisted, her voice growing louder. "Tell me now. Tell me this instant!"

"It's not . . . I wasn't . . . I was only trying to help you," he said, starting to sound a little desperate. "I was worried she wouldn't want to risk helping, and you needed help. We need help. Surely you can see that?"

"What . . ." Miss Forrest glanced between Clive and Lily. "What did he threaten you with?" she asked in a very small voice.

"Exposure," Jack said from his place by the door, making both Miss Forrest and Clive jump, as though they had forgotten he was still there. "However noble the actions undertaken by Mrs. Adler, and however much good they may have done, Mayfair society would not look kindly on the blatant exposure of such an adventuress in their midst."

"But that is . . ." Miss Forrest shook her head, her eyes wide and shocked. "That is *dreadful*. You must believe me, Mrs. Adler, I was not . . . I had no intention of . . . How could you *do* such a thing?" she demanded, rounding on her suitor.

He was staring at her with equal parts horror and pleading. "For you, Sarah. You must believe me."

"You lied to me," she whispered.

"No—" He broke off, his eyes darting to Lily and back. "Not about that. Not about wanting to help you."

"Then about what?" Sarah demanded. "If not that, then what?" When he hesitated, she shook her head, taking a step back. "It does not matter, does it? You deceived me. You threatened to blackmail someone who *was* helping me." Lily could hear the tears in the girl's voice as she choked out, "Was it truly just about the money all along?"

"*No*. Sarah—"

She turned away, even as he reached for her. Then, to Lily's surprise, she turned back, straightening her shoulders and lifting her chin. "I think you should leave."

"Sarah—"

"You no longer have permission to call me that, sir."

He stared at her, the hand that had been outstretched toward her falling to his side. "You don't mean that," he said. There was a trembling emotion in his voice, but Lily could not tell what it was. Anger, perhaps? Disappointment?

Or was it genuine sorrow? He was putting on a convincing enough show of regret and horror, but she did not know how much of it to believe.

"Good night, sir," Miss Forrest said, not flinching away from his gaze.

He stared at her for a long moment, then turned a venomous stare on Lily. "You did this."

She didn't look away either. "You should have taken no for an answer." She looked over to Jack. "Perhaps you can escort Mr. Clive to the door?"

Jack looked only too happy to do so. But as soon as his hand landed on Clive's shoulder, the younger man shook it off. He pushed his way past but paused in the doorway, squaring his shoulders as he faced the three of them. He took a deep breath. "I only want to help you, Miss Forrest," he said. "And if Mrs. Adler will not resolve this situation with your uncle, then I will."

Her expression did not change. "Good night, sir," she said again, turning away.

He left.

Lily did not let out the breath she was holding until she heard the front door slam behind him. Apparently Miss Forrest felt the same. As soon as her erstwhile suitor was gone, she slumped into a chair, burying her face in her hands as sobs shook her.

Lily and Jack stared at each other over the girl's head, neither of them sure, at first, what to do. At last Jack cleared his throat.

"Shall I go outside and look for a carriage to summon?" he asked.

"I have a hired one waiting outside, and a servant to accompany me," said Miss Forrest, stiffly dignified. "I thank you for your assistance tonight, sir, but it is no longer needed."

Lily glanced at Jack. It was clear from the young woman's tone that she wanted him to leave, and Lily could guess that Miss Forrest wanted to speak to her in private. Jack raised his brows in a silent question.

As much as Lily did not want him to go, she felt bound to do as Miss Forrest clearly wished. She was not the one whose hopes for the future had been thoroughly dashed—for the second time that night. "I will bid you good night," Lily said, crossing the room to him and holding out her hand.

His fingers tightened on hers as he took it. "You will be all right?" he asked in an undertone.

"I shall." Lily glanced at Miss Forrest, who stood with her face turned resolutely toward the window, only a flickering edge of candlelight illuminating it. She turned back to Jack. "I think I have taken greater risks tonight than being alone with a distressed young woman," she added wryly.

Jack chuckled, though the sound was a little forced. "I cannot argue with that. I shall return to my own home, then, but . . ." He cleared his throat. "May I call tomorrow? I think we should—that is, if we need to discuss—"

"There is no need, is there?" Lily asked, hoping she had not cut him off too quickly. But she did not want to hear him apologize for his conduct in the spare room. "We are not schoolchildren, Captain. We both understand the exigencies of such circumstances. There is no need for a fuss."

He was silent for a moment. "Of course," he said at last, giving her fingers another squeeze.

In spite of everything that had happened that night, Lily could feel the warmth of his hand all the way up her arm. She pulled away quickly. "Good night, my friend."

He stepped back, bowing. "Good night, Miss Forrest, Mrs. Adler."

Miss Forrest did not speak until they heard the front door close behind him. "How did you really know him?" she asked, still staring out the window.

Lily did not need to ask whom she meant. "Mr. Clive was a card-sharp and a moneylender in the Hampshire village where I met him," she replied. "His parents, as far as I could gather, were respectable tradespeople. But he made no pretense, even during our brief interaction then, that he did not have ambitions beyond that."

"So he was courting me only for my money."

A day before, Lily might have said yes with very little hesitation. But as soon as she parted her lips to reply, she remembered Clive's face. His anguish had looked like more than the regret of watching his schemes for advancement fall apart. Or perhaps he was simply a very good actor. He would have to be, after all, to be as successful a gambler as she knew him to be.

"I can tell you only his actions, not his motivations," she said at last. "For those, you will have to ask him yourself."

"I've no intention of ever seeing him again," Miss Forrest said fiercely. "Tell me, Mrs. Adler, do you know what it is like to discover in one night that both the father you loved and the man you thought loved you have betrayed your trust? Have lied to you, have manipulated you, all while pretending to be concerned with your well-being and your future?"

Lily sighed. "I can only recommend, Miss Forrest, that you talk to the solicitor, Mr. Sloane. I know learning of your father's conduct has hurt you, but you do not yet know the full story."

The look Miss Forrest gave her was painful in its bitterness as she turned toward the door.

"There may be more to it than you think," Lily added gently. "And if there is not, well, at least then you know you have the whole truth, not just the parts of it you have uncovered and pieced together on your own."

Miss Forrest walked to the drawing room door, her shoulders stiff. "Thank you, I suppose, for what you attempted. And . . ." She hesitated, half turning. Lily could see the line of her profile, the drawn furrow of her brows. "If I have not said it, I am sorry for what you endured. With Mr. Clive."

"You did not know," Lily said calmly as she followed the girl into the hall. She had yet to decide how much of the couple's scheming could be blamed on Clive, and for how much Miss Forrest herself had been responsible. But she was quite certain, after watching their interaction that night, that Miss Forrest had not known the truth about her suitor's unethical past or present.

Miss Forrest laughed bitterly, her hand on the front door. "No, it seems there was a great deal I did not know." She yanked it open. "Good night, Mrs. Adler."

Lily watched as a groom hopped down from the carriage that waited outside, then climbed onto the seat with the driver after he had helped Miss Forrest in. She waited until they were driving away before pulling the front door shut and locking it. Suddenly exhausted, she leaned her back against it and closed her eyes.

"At least," she said out loud, her voice sounding strange in the quiet of the hall, "that will be the end of it."

CHAPTER 12

When Lily first heard the frantic knocking, she thought she was still dreaming. The sound was distant, and she was just awake enough to know that dawn was only beginning to creep around the edges of the curtains. It was far too early for callers. Muffling a groan—it had been a later night than she had expected—Lily rolled over, tugging the blankets over her head.

But the sound continued until it was joined by the quick footsteps of someone running to the door. And by then Lily was awake enough to know that something was wrong. She threw off the bedclothes and began hunting around for her dressing gown.

By the time she made it downstairs, her three servants were already there. Since Lily was the only resident, they did not need to start their duties as early as some households would require, and all of them were still in their nightclothes. Mrs. Carstairs's hair was held back with a large scarf, while Anna had a shawl wrapped around her shoulders and a long braid hanging down her back. Carstairs, in the scarlet dressing gown that usually made Lily smile, was talking to a stranger in the front hall.

But even her butler's sartorial splendor couldn't distract Lily. The man who had been pounding at her door wore the uniform of the Bow Street constables.

Whatever he had been saying, he broke off as Lily appeared in the hall. "Mrs. Adler, do you remember me?"

It took a moment for Lily, her mind still fuzzy with sleep, to recognize the young man. "Mr. Hurst," she said at last, nodding. "It has been some time since we met in Hampshire."

Mr. Hurst bowed. "You are kind to remember, madam. I apologize for intruding on your household so early. But the matter is of some urgency."

He was less gangly than Lily remembered from the last time she had seen him, as though he had grown into the length of his arms and legs some, and there was a little more polish to his manners. He was also breathing heavily, as though he had been hurrying.

"Is Simon Page well?" Lily asked. It was the only thing she could think of that would bring a Bow Street officer to her doorstep before the sun had fully risen.

"He is. And it was he that sent me to fetch you." The look Mr. Hurst gave her was intense in its directness, but there was a curiosity to it as well, as though she were a puzzle he was trying to solve. "Will you come with me to meet him?"

"Certainly, if you will give me a few minutes to dress. Anna," Lily said, turning back to her maid, "will you go upstairs and begin getting my things ready?"

"Yes, Mrs. Adler."

Lily turned back in time to see Mr. Hurst fidgeting with his hat, looking uncomfortable. "I will endeavor not to delay for too long," she said. "But I will not be leaving the house in my dressing gown."

"Of course, ma'am," he said, seeming to notice for the first time that she was not dressed for the day and looking a little embarrassed by the realization. "That is . . . please do not take long. It is a matter of some urgency."

"I assumed as much." About to turn away, Lily paused. "May I ask where we are going? Should I bring my maid with me so I am not unaccompanied?"

"We will not be the only ones where we are going, ma'am. There are maids and a housekeeper in residence. And it is not far. Mr. Page is waiting for you at a house on Queen Anne Street."

Lily felt a shiver make its way down her spine. "Queen Anne Street, you said?"

"Yes, number twenty-seven." Mr. Hurst nodded, his Adam's apple bobbing nervously. "It is the home of a man named Mr. Martin Forrest."

"Martin Forrest," Lily repeated, staring at the constable as she tried to think of something else to say that would not give away her sudden fear. "Did this Mr. Forrest send for me?" she managed at last.

"I'm afraid Mr. Martin Forrest was unable to send for anyone," Mr. Hurst said, looking more uncomfortable yet. "As it seems that the gentleman is dead."

"Oh." Lily took a deep breath, wondering if she had been right the first time, and this was indeed a dream. But she could feel the all-too-real chill of the floor through her slippers. And Mr. Hurst was still watching her, as though wondering whether she might faint or go into hysterics at the mention of a dead man.

"Oh," she said again, pulling herself together. She gave the Bow Street constable a brisk nod. "Well, in that case, I suppose I ought to move quickly indeed."

★　★　★

Simon Page met them at the front door, looking surprised. "That was faster than I expected."

"When I am told that a man has died, I am not likely to linger," Lily said. She suppressed a shiver as she stepped over the threshold. There were signs in the hall of the party the night before: a glove dropped in one corner, furniture that had been jostled out of place as the guests left, a few paintings crooked on the walls. It was early enough that the servants had not yet set them to rights.

Mr. Page glanced sharply at his colleague. "How much did you tell her, George?"

"Just that, sir," Mr. Hurst said with enough polite diffidence that Lily thought Mr. Page must have risen in rank. Or perhaps simply risen in his colleagues' estimation, and deservedly so. He could be a difficult man from time to time, impatient of social niceties and of Lily's class in particular, but he was excellent at his work.

"Is there more to tell than that?" Lily asked, trying not to show the way her stomach was twisting with nerves. She did not hide her glances around the house—curiosity was only to be expected—but she did not move farther into it. Without knowing what had happened or why she had been summoned, she did not yet want to reveal that she had been there before.

Mr. Page regarded her silently for a moment, as though trying to read her thoughts. She met his assessing gaze with as calm a one as she could manage, though she let her puzzlement show. That was only to be expected too.

"Somewhat more," he said at last, turning toward the sweeping staircase. His footsteps rang against the polished stone of the hall as he gestured for her to follow him. "Come with me."

The silence as they climbed the stairs made the back of Lily's neck prickle with unease. The house felt unnaturally still, especially after the music and bustle of the night before. Even at dawn, a house like this one should have had some movement of servants. But it was silent, as though everyone there—she wondered how many that was when it was just the regular staff—were waiting to learn more, just as she was.

Lily followed a few careful paces behind Simon. As they began to climb toward the third floor, she suspected they were heading to Mr. Forrest's bedroom. She began to think hopefully that perhaps he had simply died in his sleep and been found by his servants. There might be nothing for her to be worried about; Mr. Page had, in the past, asked her for her perspective on matters pertaining to her class. Perhaps he simply wanted her help in a quick survey of Mr. Forrest's situation, to confirm that indeed there was nothing odd or suspicious to be concerned about. He had not, after all, asked her whether she had been there before, or even whether she knew the gentleman.

Mr. Page paused at the door to Mr. Forrest's bedroom. His expression was grim but otherwise inscrutable as he regarded her. Lily met his eyes without difficulty, though she knew some of her uneasiness was apparent. "What is it, Mr. Page?"

He seemed about to speak, then shook his head. "I would rather show you first. And then I will say more."

Mr. Hurst had followed them up the steps. Now he cleared his throat. "Sir, are you sure we ought to—"

Mr. Page held up a hand to forestall him. "I value Mrs. Adler's insight," he said. It was a flattering enough statement, but it did not quell Lily's unease. There was still a flatness to the way he was regarding her that was unlike the respectful camaraderie they had developed over the years. "I would like to see what she makes of the situation."

"But sir, a lady—" Mr. Hurst looked a little shocked.

For the first time, something like a smile lightened Mr. Page's expression, though it was only a flicker. "I am sure you recall what she saw in Hampshire, George," he said, glancing at Lily out of the corner of his eye. "She can handle it."

She inclined her head. He would not be surprised by her equanimity; she was known for it. But neither would he be surprised by the cautious way she regarded him. He had to know she would pick up on the oddness of his manner. "I do not shock easily, it is true. What is it you wish me to see?"

He glanced at Mr. Hurst. "Go down to the kitchen, if you please. Make sure all is well there. I'll join you soon."

"Yes, sir."

The young constable did not go back in the direction they had come, but turned instead to go farther down the hall. Lily assumed there was a servants' stair there, which would be the most direct route to the lowest floor and the kitchen. She did not miss the uneasy glance that Mr. Hurst sent over his shoulder, though he quickly turned away when he saw that she was looking at him.

When she turned back to Mr. Page, she found that he was watching her closely. "Is the gentleman who has expired in there?" she asked, gesturing at the door before them.

Mr. Page's expression gave nothing away. "He is."

As he turned the key in the lock, Lily told herself again that perhaps Mr. Forrest had suffered a tragic but natural death. But she braced herself none the less as the door swung open.

Mr. Forrest lay on his bed, his feet over the side and still resting on the carpet, one hand outstretched in the direction of the door. His eyes were wide, a look of stupid shock on his handsome face, and his mouth hung open at an awkward angle where it was pressed against the bedclothes.

The hilt of a knife was sticking out of his back.

Lily took a deep breath. There was very little out of place from what she remembered of the room. Judging by the bowl of water on the washstand and the coat and waistcoat tossed on the floor, Mr. Forrest had been in the middle of preparing for bed when he was . . . interrupted? Surprised? Lily held back a shudder as she glanced around the room.

The fire was still banked from the night. Whoever had come to tend to it that morning must have found him and summoned the constables.

Her eyes drifted back to Mr. Forrest's still body. Someone would have needed to get close to attack him in such a manner. If he had been undressing for bed but still let them into the room, that had to mean it was someone he knew. Someone he did not see as a threat until it was too late.

It took only a moment for Lily's mind to leap to Miss Forrest's face the night before, devastated and furious. But her fury had been directed at her suitor, her devastation at her father. She had barely said a word about her uncle.

Lily pushed the image of Miss Forrest from her mind. She had no desire to leap to conclusions. Especially not when Mr. Page was standing there watching her, and when she had no idea why he had summoned her in the first place. Did he know that she had stood in this exact spot only hours before?

She turned to the constable. It had only been a moment since they had stepped into the room. "What a dreadful thing," she said, letting some—but not too much—of her distress show. "Have you any idea what happened?"

"Do you know the gentleman?" Mr. Page asked, his voice a little softer than it had been when they were in the hall. She suspected it was by accident; he was too accustomed to thinking of her sex as having gentler feelings. Even as well as he had grown to know her, it was difficult not to fall back into old habits.

Lily's mind sifted rapidly through the possible answers she could give. She did not want to be dishonest—and, as Ofelia had pointed out when they were making their plans, she had not truly done anything wrong. Questionable, certainly. Unethical in the likely judgment of many, including that of the upstanding constable beside her. But it was not a crime to attend a party, even with someone else's invitation, so long as the invitation had been freely given. It was not a crime to walk about a man's house during that party, nor even to snoop through his things, especially as she had taken nothing with her when she left.

A crime, though, had undeniably occurred. And until she knew why she was there, she did not want to say too much.

"I would recognize Mr. Forrest even had your colleague not named him to me," she said after only a moment's pause. She spoke calmly enough, but she had to remind herself to breathe slowly and carefully. It did not matter that she had seen death before. The scene before her was still shocking. "Our paths have crossed at other times, though I cannot say we were truly acquainted." She met Mr. Page's eyes steadily. "So you can imagine my curiosity as to why I have been summoned."

"Well, as to that—" Mr. Page gestured for her to proceed him out of the room. Lily, after one final, morbidly curious look at Mr. Forrest's body—it was hard to look away, almost as hard as it was to look at him—did so. Once they were in the hall, Mr. Page locked the door behind them. "I wasn't, in fact, the one who summoned you."

Lily narrowed her eyes at him. "I distinctly recall being told that you had."

"If you'll turn to your right, Mrs. Adler, we shall follow Mr. Hurst down to the kitchen," Mr. Page said, his hands clasped behind his back as he watched her closely. "Hopefully, all will make sense then."

Lily's brows rose. "And if I am still confused?"

Mr. Page surprised her with a small smile. "Then I'll be utterly baffled myself. Shall we?"

It was three flights of narrow stairs down to the kitchen. When they emerged, Lily could see the servants' hall to her left. There were only a few people there, watched over by a third constable she did not know. She wondered if some of them were still abed or if that was the whole of Mr. Forrest's staff. To her right were several other doors that would lead to storerooms or even some of the servants' quarters. It was in that direction that Mr. Page indicated. A few doors down, Mr. Hurst stood waiting for them.

"Are you sure, sir?" he asked, looking uneasy as they approached.

Mr. Page shrugged. "It's why she's here, George. We might as well see what we can learn."

"But if—"

Mr. Page held up a hand to forestall him. Mr. Hurst sighed and pulled a key from his pocket, handing it to Mr. Page with a small bow before leaving them alone. Lily did not hide her curiosity, stepping forward to stand beside Mr. Page as the door swung open.

She suspected it was the housekeeper's office, which would connect to the woman's bedroom. But the housekeeper wasn't present. Instead, a man in wrinkled evening clothes sat at the small wooden table. His hair was disheveled, and his jacket had been tossed over the back of another chair. He sat with shoulders slumped, his head in his hands. But he looked up quickly as the door opened.

Lily managed not to gasp, but she felt her eyes grow wide with shock.

The man sitting before her was Mr. Clive.

CHAPTER 13

"**M**rs. Adler." Clive stood slowly, glancing at the constable, who was watching his every move. But his gaze fixed on Lily with a desperate relief. "You came."

Lily wanted to walk out of the room immediately. Instead, she turned to Simon Page. "Explain, if you please."

"I was hoping that you would," he said, and there was some trace of humor to his voice. "When Mr. Forrest was discovered this morning by the housemaid, this man was also discovered, hiding in Mr. Forrest's dressing room. The servants imprisoned him in the larder and sent a messenger for us. And when we arrived, this man"—the narrow-eyed look that he turned on Clive did not pretend to be anything but suspicious—"begged us to send for Mrs. Lily Adler of Half Moon Street, saying that you would vouch for him."

Lily looked at Clive, who was staring at her, wary and hopeful at the same time. "Rather a large assumption, sir," she said coldly.

"You do know him, then," Mr. Page remarked.

"I do. Whether I will vouch for him is another matter."

"I did not kill him," Clive replied, his voice shaking. "You have to know I did not."

"He has been staunch in his claim that he was simply trying to steal from Mr. Forrest, not murder him," Mr. Page said dryly. "We are deciding how much credence to give his word."

Lily frowned. Clive had said he wanted to retrieve the letter. She had assumed that with his true colors revealed to Miss Forrest, he would abandon his pretenses, even leave London entirely. But perhaps he had decided to prove himself to her rather than beginning his schemes anew with another young woman. It was perfectly possible that he had returned to Queen Anne Street, made his way inside using the bustle of the party ending as a distraction, and attempted only to search the rooms that Miss Forrest had described.

"Well, Mrs. Adler?" Mr. Page asked. He stood just behind her in the doorway. "What do you have to tell me?"

"A question first, if you will indulge me," Lily said, not looking away from Clive. "What was Mr. Forrest killed with?"

Simon Page was silent for a long moment. She wanted to turn to look at him, but she kept her eyes on Clive, wanting to see how he felt about the question. To her relief, Mr. Page answered at last. "It seems to have been a letter opener from his desk." She could hear the distaste in his voice. Before her, Clive flinched, looking ill. "An unpleasant thought," Mr. Page added.

Lily shuddered. It was also perfectly possible that Mr. Forrest had interrupted Clive while he was searching, and that the would-be thief had grabbed the nearest object to hand to deal with the situation.

"I did not kill him," Clive said again, sounding yet more desperate.

"Then what were you doing in his dressing room while he bled to death only a few feet away?" Lily asked coldly.

Clive shook his head. "He was dead when I found him. It took me some time, after you turned Sarah against me—" He caught the tightening of Lily's expression and broke off, taking a deep breath. "Very well, after Miss Forrest found out the truth about me. We can debate who was at fault another time."

"It will not be much of a debate," Lily pointed out. "You are not doing a good job of convincing me to plead your case, Mr. Clive."

"Clive?" Simon Page asked. "Is that his name? He had refused to give it to us."

Lily pursed her lips, regarding the haggard man before her. "How very innocent-seeming of you."

He let out a sad, short laugh. "I panicked. Please, madam." Clive took a deep breath, holding his hands out like a supplicant. "I know, at this point you have every reason to think ill of me. But I think more highly of you than you might suspect. So I beg you will hear me out before you walk away."

She did not want to. But she was curious enough to find out what he would say that she turned to Mr. Page. "Will you allow me to speak with him in private? Only for a moment. I give you my word that I will tell you what he says afterward."

The constable drummed his fingers briefly against the doorjamb. "First, you will tell me what is going on here. How do you know this man? And how does he know the man upstairs?"

Lily did not take her eyes from Clive as she spoke, describing only Miss Forrest's suspicions about her uncle, her request that Lily assist her, and Lily's hesitation to do so. She could see Clive's shoulders grow tense as she came to his involvement, as though waiting for her to denounce him as a blackmailer. But she was hesitant to reveal that she had been at the party the night before until she knew more of what had happened, and even more hesitant to risk dragging Ofelia's name into a matter that now concerned murder. So she described Clive only as Miss Forrest's suitor.

She did not stint, though, in explaining how she had come to know him, and she was more than a little pleased to see him flinch at her description of his unsavory background and questionable intentions toward Miss Forrest's missing fortune.

"So you claim that you snuck into the house merely to find some proof of Mr. Forrest's supposed wrongdoing?" Mr. Page said. When Lily turned to watch him, he was glowering at Clive in an unsettling manner.

"Yes, sir," Clive said firmly, though Lily could see his throat bob in a nervous swallow as he faced the constable.

Mr. Page glanced at Lily. "Your tale does not make me feel any easier in leaving you alone with him," he began, but at that moment there was a knock at the door.

"Excuse me." George Hurst looked between them and cleared his throat a little nervously. "Sir, the coroner has arrived."

Mr. Page shook his head. "And yet it seems I will anyway. Mrs. Adler, do you give me your word you will report truthfully to me whatever you learn in my absence?"

"I do, sir."

"Then you have five minutes. Come along, George." He fixed Clive with an intimidating stare, then gestured for Mr. Hurst to follow as he strode abruptly from the room.

The latch closed behind them. It should have been an ominous sound—to be trapped in a room with a man suspected of murder, the corpse of the man he had most likely killed only a few floors above them. But Clive now had none of his typical bravado or cynicism. There was no sneer or unkind humor in his look as he met her eyes.

"Thank you," he said simply. "I know I've no right to ask anything of you, but will you do me the kindness of taking a seat?"

He swayed a little on his feet, catching the edge of the table to steady himself. There were dark circles of exhaustion under his eyes, and she could see his hands trembling, with fatigue or nerves or perhaps both.

"Surely you need not stand on polite ceremony with the woman you have so recently threatened to blackmail?" she asked.

A muscle clenched in his jaw. "I suppose I brought that on myself," he said, shaking his head. He remained standing.

He still looked like he might fall over at any moment. Lily sighed and sat. "What is your full name? I do not know it."

"Henry. Henry Francis Clive. And thank you," he added gratefully, taking his own seat once more. He dropped his head into his hands, then ran them up over his face and across his head, his fingers catching his hair and making it stand on end. When he raised his head again, Lily thought he looked very young, though she knew he could not be much younger than she was, perhaps even a little older. "And thank you for coming."

"Had I known it was you that summoned me, and not Mr. Page, I rather doubt I would have," Lily said bluntly. "You have proved yourself criminal in every possible way. What makes you think I will help you? Do you intend to blackmail me again?"

"No," he said in a quiet voice. "I will not. And I wouldn't have, even before. I never intended to do as I threatened. A blackguard I may be, but I am not a monster."

"A convenient claim to make now."

His smile was bitter. "It is, to be sure. But you are not an unfair woman, Mrs. Adler. You even found, I think, a thing or two to admire in my character, though you rightly disapprove of the rest. I have not been in the habit of being an upstanding man." His expression became more serious as he regarded her. "But I ask you: Have I ever, to your knowledge, taken from anyone who didn't walk into the situation willingly? Have I ever truly harmed those who couldn't afford to make up the loss?"

"Right or wrong does not depend on the ability of your victims to recover from your misdeeds."

"Misdeeds." He shook his head. "What a villain you make me sound. But in truth, what victims were there? Rich, bored young men who could find nothing else to do with their time but gamble and wager? I didn't force them to place their bets or borrow what they owed me. I merely accepted the money they were careless enough to spend. In the end, what harm came of it wasn't due to me."

"Again, a convenient argument. There was a great deal of harm done. Even if you did not intend your part in it, you helped create the circumstances." Lily regarded him impassively. "There is a reason usury and wagering are considered vices."

The smile he gave her was almost sympathetic in its helplessness. "And if I say that you're right, that I left Hampshire because I did regret my part in it, will that soften you toward me?"

"I cannot say that it does."

He sighed. "I suppose I admire your honesty. But if you won't help me for my own sake, then I beg you will do so on the principle of the matter."

"Which is?"

"That everyone deserves a chance to be proven innocent." His bitter humor faded, his expression and voice growing more serious than she had ever yet seen. "You're a shrewd judge of character, madam. I'm a scoundrel, we both know that. But that doesn't make me a murderer. If I intended to kill the man, why would I not have done so from the first? My Sarah would inherit then, and all our problems would be solved. Instead, I came to you."

"In the first place, you might not have intended to kill him when you came here. And in the second, you were not the one who came to me. Miss Forrest was."

"Who do you think gave her the idea? As soon as she told me the story of Mrs. Whatshername and the lady of quality, I was sure it had to be you. I'm a fairly good judge of character myself."

"I suppose one must be, to swindle so many people."

To her surprise, that made him smile, though the expression was strained. "Precisely. So then: Will you help me?"

Lily wanted to stand up and walk out. But she could not deny the truth of what he had said. She *did* believe that he had a right to prove his innocence, if innocent he was. "Let me see your coat," she said abruptly.

He frowned at her, but stood once more without asking why. The coat was on the back of his chair; he offered it to her.

"Lay it on the table, if you please." Once he had done as she asked, Lily stood as well and bent over it, glaring him to silence when he started to ask what she was doing. Inch by inch, she studied the wool. It was well-made, stylish without being extravagant, and new enough not to have any patches or fraying. "Did you have a new wardrobe made when you came to London?" she asked as she studied the cuffs and collar.

"Not an entire wardrobe," he said, sounding surprised by the question. "I'm not always an extravagant man. But I did buy new coats and waistcoats, boots, cravats, things of that nature. I had a part to play, after all," he added, a mocking lilt in his voice. "Does that make you think even more poorly of me?"

"No," Lily murmured, her attention still focused on the pale brown coat. "It was the wise thing to do if you wished to make a good impression."

"Mrs. Adler, I might almost think that was a compliment."

Lily lifted her head at last, handing the coat back to him. "Very well, then, Mr. Clive." She sat so that he might as well, and she did not miss his grateful sigh as he sank into the chair once more. "Tell me your version of what happened after you left my home last night."

Clive contemplated his hands for a moment, which were pressed flat against the table in front of him. "I went home after I left. I had some thought of leaving London as soon as possible, but a part of me also wanted to follow Sarah home and throw myself on her mercy." He looked up. "She does care for me," he said quietly. "And I know you don't believe me, but I care for her as well. I admit I stared out playing a part, but that did change."

Lily regarded him without speaking, then gave a single nod. "Continue."

He sighed. "Instead of doing either of those things, I went out and had too much to drink. And after a few hours of that, I decided the best way to win Sarah back was to do as I said I would: go to Queen Anne Street, gain entrance to the house, and search the places that I remembered from her map."

"When did you arrive?" Lily asked, lacing her fingers together and resting her elbows on the table as she watched him.

"Around two in the morning, I believe," he said. "It was easy enough to slip in, with the noise and confusion of all the guests leaving. I was still foxed and feeling quite bold with it, so I started my search right away. I had the presence of mind to look in Mr. Forrest's bedroom first because I knew that he would make his way there soon. But I found nothing."

"How long did it take you to grow sober enough to realize what you had gotten yourself into?"

His bitter smile returned. "Not long. By that point, the servants were cleaning up, and I couldn't sneak away. But I could hide in one of the back rooms that didn't seem to be in use—the hearth was quite cold—and wait until everyone had either departed or gone to bed."

"But you did not leave?"

He shrugged. "I probably should have. But by then, the house was silent, and I decided I could in fact search without too much risk. So I lit a taper and started again, beginning on the first floor and working my way up."

"And did you find the letter?"

He let out a short, sharp laugh. "No. All that trouble and I found nothing. I spent hours on it too, going back over all the rooms Sarah had mentioned, and every parlor and drawing room besides, even the ones that looked like they'd been shut up for months. It's too big a house for him," Clive added, a hint of a sneer to his voice. "He doesn't know what to do with it. Sarah and I would make grand use of it."

"A statement which does not argue for your innocence," Lily pointed out.

Clive sighed. "I suppose not. In any case, I found nothing. Except . . ." She saw his throat move as he swallowed, looking suddenly ill.

"And now we come to it." Lily leaned forward. "Why were you in Mr. Forrest's dressing room if you were not the one who killed him?"

"If I were the one who'd killed him, I'd have been a damned fool to stick around until dawn," Clive said, his voice growing heated. "You saw the man, did you not? He was killed as he was readying himself for bed. Do you think he did that at six o'clock in the morning?"

It was a point Lily had already considered in his favor, but she did not want to tell him that. Not yet. "How did you come to be there, then?"

Clive sighed, slouching down in his seat once more. "I didn't want to search that room a second time because I didn't want to risk waking him. But eventually, I had to admit that I needed to. And that was when I found . . ." He swallowed again, his eyes fixed on the table, though Lily did not think he was seeing it. "I think I just stood there staring at him for . . ." He shook his head. "I don't know how long—likely only minutes. But then I heard someone coming. I couldn't leave through the door, so I hid in the dressing room." He lifted his hands in a helpless shrug. "And thus I was discovered."

It was a ridiculous story, from start to finish. There was absolutely no reason to believe he was telling the truth, especially given what she knew of his history. And yet . . .

Lily took a deep breath. And yet, it was also perfectly plausible that a young man, drunk and angry and, perhaps, grieving, would come up with just such a ridiculous scheme to prove himself to the lady he wished to marry.

Was it any less ridiculous than what she herself had done?

And if he was telling the truth about being there to steal the letter, he might be telling the truth about the rest of it as well. As he had pointed out, it was a long way from gambling and bookmaking to murder.

Clive was watching her, his nervousness clear in the rigid set of his shoulders, the way he clenched and unclenched his jaw. His hands, where they lay on the table, trembled a little. Lily could not help remembering with some sympathy that, according to his story, he had not slept in over a day.

In spite of that, he did not take his eyes from her.

Lily stood, and after only a moment's delay, he did the same.

"Well?" he asked, his voice shaking a little. "Have I convinced you, madam?"

"Of your innocence?" She shook her head. "Not entirely. Not yet. But"—she held up a hand to forestall his protests—"you have convinced me that there is reason to be curious, and reason to look further. While I make no promises, I will speak to the Bow Street constables on your behalf."

He let out a heavy breath and sank into a chair, his hands covering his face. She could hear his shuddering breaths as he tried to compose himself. At last he looked up. "Thank you, Mrs. Adler."

"You may wish to hold your thanks until I actually accomplish something," she said. "There is no knowing yet whether they will heed anything I say."

He shook his head. "The fact of your saying it at all is worthy of thanks. I know you have no reason to trust me, or even to think well of me." Again, that bleak, cynical smile. "I know I'm not a good man. It would have served me right had you said no, I suppose."

"Laying it on with a heavy hand, Henry Clive," Lily said dryly. "Your sincerity convinces me less than your irony."

He stood, bowing a little. "I'll endeavor to be more flippant, then, if only to please you." His expression was serious once more as he straightened. "But no matter what happens, I do thank you."

Lily nodded, turning to leave. But she paused at the door and glanced back at him. "Was Henry your father's name?" she asked curiously.

He looked surprised by the question, but he nodded. "And Frances my mother's. I was named for both of them, as they thought it unlikely that they'd have more children. Which was proved correct." He hesitated, then added, "They'd have admired you, I think. They always admired clever people."

"And would they have admired you?"

"Not in the slightest," he said, his smile growing bitter. "They'd have been terribly disappointed by the man I've become. Which is why I took pains not to become him until they were gone."

CHAPTER 14

"So you trust him, then?" Mr. Page asked.

They were sitting in the upstairs drawing room, where the butler had reluctantly shown them and where a trembling housemaid had delivered a tray of tea. Mr. Hurst, having finished with the coroner and seen Mr. Forrest's body removed from the house, paced restlessly from one end of the room to the other, a teacup held precariously in one hand.

Mr. Page, by contrast, sat across the tea table from Lily, feet planted wide and firmly on the ground, his hands clasped loosely in his lap as Lily finished relating her conversation with Clive to the two constables.

"Not at all," she said in response to his question, turning her own teacup in her hands. She had poured for the two men as soon as they sat down, and even stoic Mr. Page had not completely hidden his surprise at the gesture. It was a service few women of Lily's class would have performed for them.

Mr. Hurst took a gulp from his teacup and scowled. "Knew I recognized him from somewhere," he said, shaking his head. "Thought he just had one of those faces you see about London. I should have remembered him from Hampshire."

"You should have," Mr. Page agreed, while Mr. Hurst flushed at the calm rebuke. "You made a mistake. Now you'll be less likely to make it again." He turned back to Lily. "If you do not trust him, then what are you doing here?"

"He is not a trustworthy man. But there are reasons to think that this time, he might be telling the truth."

Mr. Hurst paused his pacing by the mantlepiece and gave her a narrow-eyed look. "And those reasons are?" He had grown into himself somewhat since Lily had first met him, but there was still a certain gangliness to his movements that emphasized his young age. Still, Mr. Page seemed to take him seriously, so Lily did as well.

"His coat, to begin with. There was no blood on it," Lily said, adding a splash of milk to her tea. "And I think there would have been had he stabbed someone."

"Perhaps you missed it," Mr. Hurst suggested.

Lily shook her head. "That sort of pale fawn color is terribly impractical. Would you wear a coat like that in London?"

A cynical smile played around the corners of Mr. Page's mouth. "I think I can safely say, Mrs. Adler, that neither Mr. Hurst nor myself has ever owned such a garment."

He meant it as a comment on the cost of the coat as much as the color, but Lily did not let that distract her. "Anyone who has lived in London for more than a few months knows not to purchase a coat in that particular hue, lovely though it is. London is a terribly grimy city, and that shade of fawn hides nothing. Had there been any blood, it would have easily shown up against the wool. And there was a great deal of blood—" She had to pause for a moment to gather her composure. It had been a gruesome scene upstairs. "There was a great deal of blood, if I recall, on Mr. Forrest's bedspread. I think if Mr. Clive had been anywhere near him, and especially if he had been the one to stab him, there would have been blood on his clothes."

"He might've worn a driving coat to cover it," Mr. Page pointed out. His tone was not argumentative, or even disbelieving. But it was challenging, inviting her to prove her point. Lily had always appreciated that about him. "We've not searched through Mr. Forrest's own wardrobe yet. Mr. Clive could have worn something large to cover his clothes, then taken it off and hidden it in the room."

"But that would speak to there being forethought involved in the scheme," Lily pointed out. "And were that the case, why would he not bring a better weapon with him? Why go confront a man you intend to kill and simply hope that there is a letter opener close at hand when the time is right? It is hardly a practical way to plan a murder."

Mr. Page nodded slowly, taking a drink of tea while he considered her words. "It doesn't prove his innocence."

"No," Lily agreed, setting down her cup and clasping her hands in front of her. "But it does call into question his guilt."

Both constables looked at each other without speaking. Mr. Page's eyebrows lifted a fraction, and at last Mr. Hurst nodded. "She has a point," he said, a little reluctantly.

"I agree." Mr. Page turned to Lily. "What is it you're asking us to do?"

She sighed. "In truth, I am not sure. I understand that to release him would be unwise—it would be all too easy for him to disappear into the City, or to another part of the country, or even to France. And if you then discovered he was the one who killed Mr. Forrest . . ." She shook her head. "I suppose I am asking you not to assume that it was he. To look into all the possibilities rather than allowing his presence—which I agree, does not help his case—to be your proof."

Simon Page sighed, a remarkably human expression from the normally stoic constable. "We can't spare a guard for him, so he must go to Newgate," he said, turning to Mr. Hurst. "But you and Davies can take him to retrieve his clothes and other necessities from home first. Tell him that if he has money, as he says, he'll be able to purchase a room on the State Side and pass his time there in some degree of comfort."

"Yes, sir," the younger constable said, nodding.

"His being discovered in the dead man's dressing room would be enough for nearly any jury in the land to declare him a murderer," Mr. Page said, turning to Lily. She did not protest; they all knew it was true. "But in consideration of the points you have made"—his smile grew a little ironic—"and out of respect for your insights in such circumstances, I'll continue to examine the matter and see if another possibility arises."

"You are generous to do so," Lily said, feeling more relieved than she had expected. It was a puzzling feeling. She had no love for Henry Clive, and she still was not entirely convinced of his innocence. But neither was she entirely convinced of his guilt. She was glad the constables were not either.

"I am." He turned to his colleague. "Will you see to the arrangements for Newgate?"

"Yes, sir." Mr. Hurst set down his teacup and bowed to Lily. "Madam. My thanks again, for your cooperation this morning. I know it was not a pleasant thing to be awoken so abruptly."

"I cannot say I am glad of it, Mr. Hurst," Lily replied, nodding politely in farewell. "But I hope I have been of some use."

When Lily would have risen to leave the room as well, assuming her part in things was done, Mr. Page gestured her back to her seat. He waited until Mr. Hurst was gone before speaking.

"George already knows this, but there is something else that calls Mr. Clive's honesty into question," he said, refilling his teacup, though they had been talking long enough for the pot to cool. Lily thought about ringing for a new one but didn't want to trouble servants who were already having such a distressing day.

"What is it?"

Mr. Page sat back in his chair. "When we spoke to several of the servants—there were others hired for the night as well, but all of the ones who are here now were also working—they said there was a disturbance during the party last night. One in addition to Mr. Clive and Miss Forrest's presence."

Lily, about to pour herself another cup as well, fell still. "Oh?" she asked, resuming her task after a moment. She glanced up at Mr. Page briefly before looking back at the teapot, pleased with how steady her voice was. She was fairly certain, though, that she knew what was coming.

"Apparently there were guests wandering through other parts of the house. The servant who was involved in finding them says Mr. Forrest seemed angry about the intrusion, but he did not know any more than that. So there's no way to say for certain what was being attempted during that time, or if it had something to do with Mr. Forrest's death only a few hours later."

"Hmm." Lily added the milk to her cup, buying herself a moment before she had to look up. Part of her wanted to say nothing, but she respected Mr. Page too much to dissemble with him, even through her silence. And if he was to discover what had truly happened to Mr. Forrest, and whether it involved Clive, he needed to know what was and was not a fruitful line of inquiry.

Lily set down her teacup and met his eyes. "Fortunately—or unfortunately—I can shed some light on that particular question."

She could see Mr. Page's shoulders stiffen. "What did you do?" he asked. There was a chill to his voice that made Lily wince, though she did not show her distress. She admired the constable; she did not want him thinking poorly of her.

"First, I must explain the second part of my short acquaintance with Mr. Clive."

"There is more to it?" he asked, his voice too even.

"There is. I am afraid he was blackmailing both me and Lady Carroway." Quietly, Lily told him everything she had left out before, from her conversation with Henry Clive in the park to their decision to see what they could find in Mr. Forrest's home without letting the couple know what they planned to do. She felt her whole body prickling with embarrassed heat as she omitted Jack's quick-thinking deception after the servants discovered them, saying only that she thought that Mr. Forrest had not discovered their true purpose in being there. Through it all, Mr. Page's face remained unreadable.

"I apologize for not sharing all this before," Lily said at last, retrieving her teacup and taking a calm sip, as though she was still entirely composed in the face of what she had just revealed. "I did not what you would make of our conduct, and I was worried that telling you might put you in a difficult situation. And I did not know whether it would even be relevant to the matter at hand."

"I think you could have assumed," Mr. Page said dryly. He eyed his teacup, then drained the entire thing in one gulp. Setting it down, he fixed Lily with a stern gaze. "So you and the captain were the guests wandering about. Did you take this letter from Miss Forrest's father with you?"

"No." Lily shook her head. "We took nothing. I only wanted to find the name of his solicitor so I could give that information to Miss Forrest, which we did. Well . . ." She hesitated a moment, then shrugged. "I suppose we took the paper that the captain wrote Mr. Sloane's direction on. But other than that, no. I was quite decided in *not* taking anything." She added, sighing, "I apologize if I have created more trouble for you."

He barked out a laugh. "Well, as it is, I suppose nothing you did is technically illegal, so I can look the other way. Had you taken anything, it would be a different situation. But tell me," he said, shaking his head, "even after all that, you wish to convince me of this Mr. Clive's innocence?"

"I do not think I can convince you of anything, sir," Lily said quietly, "except to examine all the facts. Including . . ." She hesitated. "Including the possibility that it was Miss Forrest, rather than her intended, who had the most reason to wish her uncle dead."

Mr. Page sighed. "There is that, which I cannot ignore. Though, on that topic . . ." He stood. "Show me where you found this letter. I wish to see for myself what light it casts on Mr. Martin Forrest's actions."

"I think it muddled the matter more than anything else," Lily admitted as she led the way from the room. "Though as I did not have a chance to finish reading it, perhaps the end of it would provide more clarity. But, truly, we would need to talk to the solicitor to know for certain—"

"We?" Mr. Page asked. When Lily glanced at him, his brows were raised, but there was a hint of amusement to the expression.

"Should you wish for my assistance, of course. I have been glad to be of use to you in the past," Lily said with a show of modesty, which made him snort. "Particularly in dealing with those members of my class who are more reluctant to cooperate with Bow Street. And of course there is the matter of my knowing more about the two people most immediately connected to Mr. Forrest."

"A day's knowledge more," Mr. Page pointed out as they climbed the stairs to the second floor, where the spare room was located. "Two days, at most."

"As I said, should you wish my assistance," she said diffidently. "It is up to you, certainly."

"We shall see after you show me this letter."

"Which the captain and I discovered just in here," Lily said as they stopped before the spare room, where Mr. Page politely opened the door for her. "Thank you, sir. Though we may need to ask one of the servants where to find a key," she said, the thought just occurring to her as they faced the desk under the window.

"No lockpicks with you today?"

"Unfortunately not," Lily said, choosing not to acknowledge the disapproval in his voice. "Perhaps I should begin carrying them with me for emergencies."

"I beg you will not," Mr. Page said, shaking his head as he tried the desk drawer. "You cause enough trouble as it is." There was a bellpull in one corner so guests could summon assistance; he went to give it a sharp tug. "No doubt your coiffure contains enough hairpins that you could address the matter yourself, but I vastly prefer to do things correctly and aboveboard."

Lily sat in a chair and folded her hands demurely. "Of course. You may be certain I shan't interfere unless invited."

"I'll believe that when I see it," Mr. Page muttered, but Lily suspected it was not truly a complaint.

It only took a few minutes for the butler to appear. He looked worried to find them so far from where he had left them, but he only inquired how he might be of assistance. He grew even more distressed when Mr. Page requested the key to the desk drawer. "I am afraid Mr. Forrest kept it himself, and I can't say for certain where it might be," he said, wringing his hands a little. "Do you wish us to search through his room?"

Mr. Page sighed. "No, thank you. If you would wait downstairs, however, I'll have a few questions for you when I'm finished here."

"Of course, Constable." The butler looked a little ill, but he bowed politely to them both before leaving the room.

Mr. Page glanced at Lily. "Well, Mrs. Adler, here is your invitation."

"How exciting," she murmured, feeling the twists of curls that Anna had pinned up that morning to find two pins that could be easily removed. She slid them out, carefully straightening both and bending the ends into tiny hooks that she thought resembled Jem's lockpicks closely enough. She took a deep breath, trying to look confident and hoping she was not about to embarrass herself. "If you would be so good as to step aside . . ."

She could not hide her sigh of relief when, a minute later, the lock clicked and the drawer popped open. And she was even more relieved when she discovered that the letter was still in the drawer. "Here you are, sir. And perhaps you will allow me to read the end of it when you have finished?"

Mr. Page's brows drew into a scowl as he read. "A muddle indeed," he said. Lily was relieved when he handed it over to her without protest.

She quickly scanned through the first part to find where she had been interrupted.

There is no need to be too cruel or too particular—any reasonably young fellow of good family and decent prospects will do. But it is a great comfort to me that we were reconciled in time for you to take on her guardianship, as I fear Miss Waverly is not suited to guide her toward a wise choice. Though she is a good-hearted companion, she loves Sarah too well to gainsay her in anything. She would not even speak against Sarah's engagement to that drunkard, though I tried to make them both see that he would not change. I fear Miss Waverly does not have the fortitude to guide so strong-willed a girl as mine. But if you keep Sarah close and guide her well, she will be the better for the influence of your careful discernment. It is a hard thing to be a parent who must leave his child, but I know she will be safe in your care.

Lily could feel the tension spreading through her shoulders. *Sarah's engagement to that drunkard.* Miss Forrest had not mentioned a previous engagement, nor that her father had reason to be worried about her choice of husband. Nor, indeed, that he had been skeptical of her cousin's influence.

But had she known? It was possible the late Mr. Forrest had said nothing to his daughter about his worries. He might have made his plans with no intention at all of discussing them with her, assuming that she either did not need to know what they were or would be better off not knowing. If he had, he would not have been the first man to keep the decisions that would shape a daughter's life from the daughter herself.

But if you keep Sarah close and guide her well . . .

Lily looked up. "It appears that Miss Forrest was not entirely forthcoming about her own history, nor about the reasons her father might have wanted to change the disposition of his will. But it also seems that, whatever the specifics of the legal situation, the late Mr. Forrest had too high an opinion of his brother's good intentions."

Mr. Page shook his head. "I am not looking forward to this one," he muttered. He took a deep breath. "Very well, Mrs. Adler. You get your wish. I'd be grateful for your assistance and your insight, particularly when it comes to this Miss Forrest. I think it will be no easy thing to get the entire truth from her."

"No," Lily murmured, scanning the letter once more. "I think there has been a great deal of untruthfulness from all sides." She looked up at Mr. Page. "And I do not think we will be able to uncover the facts of Mr. Forrest's death until we can wade through it all."

Chapter 15

"There were extra servants hired for the night, is that correct?" Mr. Page asked in his stern, no-nonsense voice.

They were in the drawing room once more, a deliberate choice on Mr. Page's part. A butler might be high in the ranks of servants, but he was still a servant. Sitting down somewhere like the drawing room, even with his employer dead, even with a constable requesting his presence there, clearly made him uncomfortable, even a little distracted. And a man who was uncomfortable and distracted was more likely to accidentally reveal something he wished to hide.

Lily hid a smile as she watched the two men. Mr. Page was admirably good at his work.

"Yes." The butler shifted nervously in his seat as he nodded. He glanced at Lily, not hiding his confusion at her presence, before turning back to the constable. "Mr. Forrest keeps only a small staff in residence. For a party such as the ball he hosted last night, he needed more."

"And where did the other servants come from?"

"Here and there in London." The butler shifted again, his expression eager to please. He had little of the reserve that Lily was accustomed to seeing in men of his profession. Or perhaps his reserve had fled when his employer had been murdered. "Friends and family of the current staff, or those we knew in need of work who had no regular position. A few girls from a nearby tavern."

"I will need a list of those names and where they live," Mr. Page said firmly.

"What? All of—" The butler's swallowed the rest of his exclamation in the face of Mr. Page's stern look. "Yes, sir. I'm sure I can produce such a thing. Will that be all?"

"No, certainly not."

The butler, who had half risen, sank back down into his chair, looking chastened. Mr. Page glanced at Lily.

"You run a very elegant household, Mr. Fleet," Lily said. She was the carrot to Mr. Page's stick, and a quick word with a housemaid in the hallway had allowed her to learn the names of many of the staff. "I myself live in Mayfair, and I have rarely seen such order, especially in the face of so shocking a tragedy. You are to be commended."

He sat up a little straighter, his early confusion at seeing her there vanished in the face of her praise. "Madam is kind to say so. And if I may be so bold, with such a change in our household, if madam is in need of—"

Lily held up her hand, and he fell silent, though he didn't look pleased at having his appeal cut short. "But I noticed that many of the rooms in the house seem untended, even unopened. No fires to speak of, and the furniture and curtains quite dusty." Her voice took on a sharp edge, though she kept the pleasant expression on her face. "Why is that?"

"Ah." The butler shifted once more. "Madam must understand, were it up to me, such economy certainly wouldn't be employed. I've been in service in many elegant houses, and it was always our practice to treat each room, each fine object and bottle of wine and piece of silver, as equally worthy of our care and attention. If madam were to hire—" He broke off as Lily cleared her throat, a flush rising to his cheeks. "Yes. Ahem. Well, Mr. Forrest was only one man, and as I said, he employed a small staff. He instructed us to attend only to the rooms that he used. I had hoped that, with his engagement to Miss Crawley, such a practice would change. But now . . ." He shook his head.

"Their engagement was settled, then?" Lily asked. "Did they make the announcement last night? How dreadful for Miss Crawley when she hears the news today. She will have to go into mourning, of course—hardly a pleasant thing for a young lady who might hope to find another husband. Was there a strong attachment between them?"

"Ah. Well. As to that, madam . . ." The butler shook his head. "Unfortunately, Miss Crawley and her parents never appeared last night, so there was no formal announcement. Or perhaps it was fortunate for the exact reason you so astutely noted." He leaned forward, as though preparing to impart a secret. "I believe the marriage was desired more strongly by Miss Crawley's parents than by the lady herself. I imagine that, for delicacy's sake, she'll need to wait a week or so before resuming her normal social calendar. But other than that, she'll have no need of a formal mourning period."

"Fortunate, indeed, for Miss Crawley, " Lily murmured. She gave the butler a regal nod. "You have a keen attention to detail, Mr. Fleet."

"Madam is kind," he said, flushing an even deeper red but preening a little at the praise. "Indeed, madam is too kind to say so."

"And with such a keen attention to detail, surely you can tell us something of Mr. Forrest himself," Lily said encouragingly. "What sort of gentleman was he?"

"Ah. Hm. Well, as to that . . ." The butler frowned, as though he were thinking hard about how to answer the question. "In point of fact, the gentleman mostly kept to himself, which I can't say we would complain about. He liked his fire laid no later than six each morning, his wash water promptly at seven, and his breakfast ready at eight. Once he had dined, he didn't want to be disturbed until four o'clock for tea. He would sometimes be out during the day, and often at night."

"And where did he go during these outings?" Mr. Page asked, rejoining the conversation.

The butler regarded the constable with raised brows. For a moment, Lily thought he wasn't going to answer. "I'd never have dreamed of asking," he said at last, an edge of condescension in his tone.

"Surely his valet would know," Lily put in. "He would need to have a sense of Mr. Forrest's activities, to judge what clothes to lay out."

"The gentleman preferred to dress himself," the butler said, shaking his head. "He didn't keep a valet on staff. Though, I must admit, he didn't seem to need one," he added, a note of reluctant admiration entering his voice. "I've never seen a gentleman with such skill at tying a cravat before."

Lily glanced at Mr. Page. "He did spend years in the army. No doubt there were many occasions on which he had to dress himself. Perhaps he had grown to prefer it?"

Mr. Page nodded. "And what did you think of him?" he asked the butler. "Remember, no one other than those people present will know what you say. I ask that you be honest."

The butler hesitated, glancing sideways at Lily, as though worried she would disapprove of his offering such an assessment. When she gave him an encouraging nod, his expression grew thoughtful. "I would not say so in any other circumstances, but Mr. Forrest was . . . unpolished. A little coarse in his manner and speech, if I'm to be blunt. Though as madam pointed out"—he gave Lily a small bow— "that perhaps isn't to be wondered at in a gentleman so accustomed to military life. A few years back in good society, and especially a marriage to an elegant young lady, would have smoothed out his rough manners." He shook his head sadly. "A shame it will never happen."

Mr. Page stood, nodding. "Thank you, Mr. Fleet. No doubt you have duties to return to. But when you have a moment, I'll need that list of who was in the house yesterday."

"Of course." The butler stood. He gave the Bow Street constable a polite nod, saving a deep bow for Lily. "A pleasure to be of service, madam. I hope you will remember me."

When Mr. Fleet was gone, Mr. Page gave Lily a sideways look. "Have you need of a new butler?"

"I have not," Lily said, shaking her head. "And if I did, I would choose one with rather fewer pretensions. Mr. Forrest's sending out invitations to those he was unacquainted with speaks to a man who was a social climber. His butler seems to have the same determination to ingratiate himself with those of rank."

"Surely you cannot blame a man for being determined to seek employment."

"I do not," Lily said. "But that does not mean I have to be the one to hire him." She steepled her fingers together, tapping them briefly against her lips before looking back up at Mr. Page. "What did you make of him?"

"I saw no signs that he was being dishonest," Mr. Page said, his hands clasped being his back as he paced around the room. "Grating, but not dishonest."

"If Mr. Forrest had no valet, someone could have easily confronted him in his room while he was preparing for bed," Lily said thoughtfully. "And what he said of Mr. Forrest seems to accord somewhat with his treatment of his niece. And with Captain Hartley's interactions with him." She gave Mr. Page a pointed look as he turned back in her direction. "You know who you need to speak with, do you not?"

"This Miss Crawley," he said, grimacing. "It is curious that she and her parents were expected to attend last night but didn't."

"And even more curious if Mr. Fleet was correct, and the engagement was their wish but not hers," Lily put in.

He nodded. "There are reasons to be suspicious. But there is a good chance they won't make it easy for me. As there was no actual engagement, she had no official connection to him. I've no doubt her parents will refuse to see me, or to allow me to talk with her." He pursed his lips. "I don't suppose you know them?"

"I do not," Lily said. She smiled. "But I have at least one dear friend who does. I shall see what I can arrange. Is there anything else I might do to be of assistance?"

"Yes. I'll also need . . ." He resumed his pacing, scowling. "As a general rule, we at Bow Street still aren't welcomed by the men of the military and navy. As you know."

"Not without reason," Lily pointed out. "They are long accustomed to handling their own affairs, including the pursuit and punishment of criminals."

"True enough, but there are times when it ought to be our responsibility. This is one of them, but I worry . . . I think if I make inquiries of Mr. Forrest's fellow officers, my questions will not be welcome. Or perhaps answered at all." He turned back to Lily. "Will you be the one to write to his former commanding officer?"

"Would Captain Hartley not be better suited to the task?" Lily asked with some surprise. "If it is a question of being well received, certainly he would be the best choice."

"I'm not so certain of that," Mr. Page said. "I imagine it would be hard for an officer to refuse the request of a lady in distress."

"There is that," Lily agreed, nodding. "Especially if I were to write on behalf of the niece of his former compatriot."

"Besides which," Mr. Page continued briskly, "I have other tasks to set the captain about. Will you do it if I can find out his name?"

"Of course," Lily said. "And we've no need to seek far for that, as I saw a letter from him in Mr. Forrest's desk upstairs when I was searching there last night. What am I to ask of him?"

Mr. Page paced slowly about the drawing room. "You were right to point out the weapon that was used to kill Mr. Forrest," he said, not yet answering her question. "It tells us something about the nature of both the crime and of the person who committed it."

"That it was sudden?" Lily suggested. "Perhaps even impulsive."

"Indeed. Likely it began as an argument, with no thought of murder. But when things grew heated . . . ." He shook his head. "I want you to ask whether Mr. Forrest had any enemies. Any officers he might have quarreled with before he left, anyone who might have held a grudge against him. Because if it wasn't this Mr. Clive— and I'm still not convinced of his innocence—then it was someone else who knew Mr. Forrest. And I think whoever it was must have truly despised him, even if they came here with no thought of murder."

Lily nodded calmly, though her heart was thudding in her chest. Someone who had impulsively killed once might do so again, especially if they thought they were close to being discovered. She had seen it before; what Mr. Page was asking her to do was not a safe request. But she knew him, and he wouldn't ask if he didn't truly need her help. "I will see what I can discover."

CHAPTER 16

"Good morning, Captain Hartley," Carstairs said politely, taking Jack's hat and gloves at the door. Jack shrugged off his driving coat as well and handed it to the butler. A light, misting rain filled the air that morning, and the spring air still had a winter chill to it. "Will you be joining your sister for breakfast this morning?"

"If Mrs. Adler would have no objection."

There was a faint smile on the butler's face, but underneath it Jack could sense an edge of worry. "I believe she is expecting you, sir. We had . . ." He hesitated, then said tactfully, "an eventful morning."

"I imagine you did," Jack said, shaking his head. "No need to announce me, Carstairs. I can show myself through to the breakfast room while you return to your duties."

"As you like, sir." Carstairs bowed.

When he had been in London before, Lily's servants had been fastidious in adhering to the proprieties, as though determined to safeguard their employer's reputation. But they seemed to have lowered their guard somewhat this spring. He wondered whether it was because Noor had joined the household, and his sister's presence would make his seem only natural to even the most inquiring busybodies. Or perhaps they had simply decided, as the rest of their London acquaintances seemed to have decided, that there was nothing between Mrs. Adler and the captain and never would be. And thus no need to guard against impropriety.

How ironic that the people they knew should have lost interest in speculating about the two of them, just as . . .

Jack realized his steps had slowed to a halt, and he shook his head to clear it. He wanted to stand there, letting memories of that moment in the spare bedroom last night have free rein in his thoughts. He wanted to think through every surprising sensation, to let his mind wander to what could have happened had it been real, and not a quick-thinking pretense to protect their search from being discovered.

He wanted—

Unbidden, a different memory came to mind, from the summer he was fourteen. He and his parents had already decided he would leave for the navy that autumn. But a glorious summer of freedom had stretched before him and Freddy Adler, with no lessons in sight.

They had tied a rope to a tree by the cow pond, launching themselves from its branches and swinging out over the water, with what they imagined were fearsome battle cries, before plunging into its murky depths. Freddy had carved a doll for Noor one week, and the next had convinced Amal to give him his first kiss. Jack had punched him for that, determined to defend his sister's honor, and Freddy had punched him right back, until they ended up hot and dirty and bruised, too tired to remember why they had been fighting in the first place. They had made a fire in the orchard one evening, skewering pears on sticks to roast them over the coals and accidentally setting the dry grass on fire. Panicked, they had beaten out the smoldering flames with their coats. By the time they were tying both ruined garments around rocks and sinking them in the pond to hide all evidence of their crimes, they were laughing over it, too proud of their success to remember how scared they had been. They had given each other a solemn oath that night to take the secret of that accidental fire to their graves, and for the rest of the year, neither of them had been able to look at a pear with a straight face.

Jack closed his eyes, his uncomfortably lusty thoughts gone in the flood of memories. It had felt more than natural, when Lily had first returned to London, to take on the role of her protector. He had owed Freddy nothing less.

How he felt about her now was a far cry from a duty to his friend. But the memory of Freddy—his oldest friend, her first love—still stood between them. As did the risk that any change between them would feel too painfully close to a betrayal.

He needed to talk to Lily about what had happened, to explain why he had panicked when she told him in that terrible, wonderful way that she had feared to lose him. She more than deserved that consideration from him.

But Mr. Page had visited him that morning. And the grim news that the constable had shared with Jack had shoved the possibility of such a conversation unceremoniously aside.

He took a fortifying breath and kept walking. Perhaps it was for the best that talking with Lily would have to wait until the matter of murder was dealt with. Hopefully, by then he would have decided what he wanted to say.

"Good heavens. In his own bed?" his sister was asking as he came to the breakfast room, her eyes wide with surprise. "Does my brother know of all this?"

"I imagine he does by now," Lily said, lifting her own eyes to the doorway just as Jack came to a halt. "Good morning, Captain. Did the good Mr. Page already pay you a visit?"

"He did." Jack studied Lily's face. There were shadows of fatigue under her eyes, though she looked alert enough as she sipped her tea and studied him back. "Good morning, Mrs. Adler. I had hoped to surprise you both this morning, but I see you have anticipated my arrival. I ought to have known you would be as alert as ever."

"She nearly fell asleep on the kippers a moment ago," Noor put in helpfully, earning her a sideways scowl from Lily.

"I did not. I was thinking, and your sister was worried I was too fatigued after such an early morning." She grimaced. "It was an unpleasant awakening. And an even more unpleasant discovery after that. Won't you sit down? Amelia knows, by the way," she added. "I decided it was best, as the matter has come to our door, so to speak."

"This Mr. Clive does not sound like a gentleman with whom I would wish to be further acquainted," Noor said with a sniff, buttering her toast.

"You should not be," Jack said firmly as he filled a plate at the sideboard. "I assume, Mrs. Adler, that you do not plan to sit idly by with such news filling your mind?"

"Indeed not," Lily said, shaking her head. "I need to write to Ofelia and Ned, to let them know what has happened. And Mr. Page has asked me to write to Mr. Forrest's commanding officer, to see what we might learn of Mr. Forrest. And . . ." She hesitated. "To see if there is a possibility that he had any enemies."

That made them all fall silent for a moment. At last, Noor cleared her throat. "Well, you cannot do either of those things without paper and a pen. Shall I fetch your writing portfolio for you, ma'am?"

"Thank you, Amelia," Lily said, giving her shoulders a little shake, as though to recall herself to the present moment. "That is very kind of you." As soon as Noor was out of the room, she turned to Jack. "Did Mr. Page set you a task as well?"

Jack nodded. "He suggested we accompany Miss Forrest to visit her father's solicitor and see what we can learn about the will."

"Will we be the first ones to tell her what happened?" Lily asked, pouring him a cup of tea and handing it over.

"No, one of the constables will have called on her this morning," Jack said, nodding his thanks. "But they were instructed not to give any indication that we were . . ."

"Working with Bow Street?" Lily said. "That is for the best, I imagine. She will be more forthcoming around us if she does not suspect any sort of ulterior motivation. And that way," she added, her lips curving a little, though there was a grimness to her smile that he did not wonder at, "she will not realize that Bow Street is no doubt as suspicious of her as they are of Mr. Clive."

"Are you?" Jack asked curiously, leaning back in his chair a little. "You would have thought her deserving of your help had Mr. Clive not been involved. Do you still believe so?"

"I am not certain," Lily said, her voice quiet as she turned her teacup in slow, thoughtful circles on its saucer. "I still believe there was something suspicious in her uncle's actions, which merited her concern. Perhaps finding out what is in her father's will shall shed some light on that. But she was not, as it turns out, entirely forthcoming in what she shared with me." She lifted her head to look at him. "I look forward to discovering how purposeful those omissions were and what that might imply about her role in all this."

Her gaze was steely and determined as she spoke, and Jack found himself feeling almost sorry for Miss Forrest. Whatever she sought to conceal, it would not stay hidden long. "Plotting, Mrs. Adler?"

Lily smiled. "Always." She turned at the sound of footsteps. "Thank you, Amelia. Captain, if you will give me a moment to write my letters, we can be off."

★   ★   ★

"You were kind to call," Miss Forrest said, sniffing back tears. She was dressed in full mourning, no doubt in the garments she had worn immediately after her father's death. The dark color made her appear sallow and peaked, except for her wide eyes, which looked immense and almost black in her pale face. The effect was not pretty, but it was very striking. Lily found herself unsurprised that the girl had caught Clive's eye when he first came to London, in spite of the limited social interaction they would have been able to have while she was mourning her father. "Especially after what Mr. Clive and I—what he—and what you had to go through—" She gulped back a sob, her face splotchy with weeping.

Lily wondered how many of the tears were due to her uncle's death and how many to the loss of her engagement. But it would have been indelicate to ask, and for the moment she was maintaining a pretense of delicacy.

There would be time enough, no doubt before too long, to take off the silk gloves.

"I confess I was not certain whether we would be welcome," she said, folding her hands in her lap. "After last night, I would not have blamed you had you wished never to see me again."

"I would not have, but . . . well, circumstances have changed dreadfully, have they not?" Miss Forrest shuddered. Her fingers were twisting a fragile lace handkerchief almost in half in her lap, but her voice was calm as she spoke. "And I am pleased to know you, Captain Hartley, in spite of the dreadful circumstances. You struck me, when we met last night, as a true gentleman."

"You are too kind," Jack said, inclining his head politely.

Miss Forrest gave him a watery smile. "Truly, I cannot say how much it means to me that you would call. So many of my old friends dropped me after my uncle sent me away, and my cousin Miss Waverly has taken to her bed with the shock. And with Mr. Clive gone—" Her voice trembled before she gathered herself together once more. "I have been quite alone since the constable left." She looked between them. "I suppose word has gotten around, then?"

"About Mr. Forrest's death, yes. I am afraid it has," Lily said gently. They had decided to wait until later in the afternoon to call on her, precisely to make such a story believable. It would have strained credulity for them to claim they had heard about Mr. Forrest's death through servants' gossip by ten o'clock in the morning. "Such shocking news does travel quickly."

"We were terribly concerned, after what happened with Mr. Clive last night, that the strain would be too much for you," Jack put in, at his most earnest and charming. He reached forward to take Miss Forrest's hand in his, and Lily had to hold back an unladylike snort of amusement at the performance. "Mrs. Adler asked me to accompany her as soon as she heard."

Miss Forrest took a deep breath. "But it is worse than you know," she said. "The Bow Street constable said that they . . . that they . . ." Her mouth trembled, as though she could barely force the words out. "That they suspect Mr. Clive is the one responsible for my uncle's death," she finished in a rush. A fresh flood of tears took over, and she buried her face once more in the lacy handkerchief.

Lily and Jack exchanged a look. Her distress seemed genuine, but they both knew such appearances could be deceptive.

"How dreadful," Lily murmured, pleased that the young woman had introduced the topic of conversation herself. It would have been tricky to find a polite way to bring it up otherwise. "What did you say to them? Do you believe it?"

"I don't know what to think," Miss Forrest hiccupped, lifting her tear-stained face. "I could never, not in a thousand years, have imagined him capable of such violence. But I also could not have imagined him lying to me about who he is, and it seems he was doing that all along. Besides which, it is unfathomable to me in the first place that my uncle is . . . that my uncle is . . . ." She gulped, unable to say it. "But the constable said they found Mr. Clive in the house. So what am I to think?" She looked between Lily and Jack, her expression almost desperate. "What am I to do? I think I will go mad if I must sit here with my own thoughts all day, waiting for something to happen."

"Well, I cannot answer the question of Mr. Clive's guilt or innocence," Lily said briskly. Out of the corner of her eye, she caught a brief smirk on Jack's face; no doubt he had heard the unspoken *not yet* at the end of her words. "But I can suggest something to occupy your mind while you wait for news. Why not pay a visit to your father's solicitor?"

Miss Forrest recoiled a little. "Isn't that a terribly indelicate thing to do, now of all times?"

"At a time like this, practicalities cannot wait," Jack put in firmly. "You need to understand the financial circumstances in which you find yourself, for your own well-being. And who knows? You may find that a conversation with this Mr. Sloane sheds some light on the situation."

"You are a man of action, I see," Miss Forrest murmured.

"I cannot deny it," Jack replied. He leaned forward to lay his hand on hers once more. "And if you feel hesitant about the matter, I would be honored to accompany you."

Lily pursed her lips. To her mind, he was laying the charm on rather heavily, but she said nothing. And Miss Forrest lapped it up like a cat with a bowl of cream; she sighed in relief and squeezed his hand.

"You are too kind, sir. I should be grateful for your assistance." She hesitated, glancing at Lily. "For both of your assistance, if you are willing. I know I've no right to ask you yet again for help, but . . ."

Lily smiled. Perhaps the charm had not been too heavy, after all. "I would be pleased to offer my aid," she said, standing. "Shall we?"

★ ★ ★

The solicitor, Mr. Sloane, was elderly, with thinning white hair that would have been served better by the powdered wigs of a few decades past than by the styles currently in fashion. But there was an upright, no-nonsense air to him as he looked them over, taking in Miss Forrest's mourning clothes and the fortifying presence of two business-like people accompanying her, standing to either side. He nodded approvingly as he invited them to sit, then turned to the large cabinets that lined his office.

"Yes, your father came to see me early on during his final illness," he said, his tone brisk but gentle as he thumbed a drawer that seemed to be full of ledgers and papers. "My condolences for your loss, Miss Forrest. Please, do sit down. Now, where . . .?"

The solicitor trailed off for a moment as he found the documents he was looking for. He took his seat across the desk from them, setting the papers down in a careful pile. "Mr. Forrest amended his will at that time. The estate in Somerset, as I'm sure you know, was always to go to your uncle, as it was entailed in the male line. But your father decided to . . ." He cleared his throat. "Forgive me if this sounds indelicate. I understand how deeply it must affect you, both the practicalities of your life and your natural sensibilities."

"You may continue," Miss Forrest said, sounding more determined than Lily would have expected.

"Thank you. Your father changed the bequest that left most of his money directly to you. Instead, the bulk was to go to your uncle, his brother, in order to preserve the family estate. You may see the relevant passages here." He shuffled through the papers, pulling several out and, after a quick, uncertain glance between the three people in front of him, handing them to Jack.

The captain read through them, then looked up. "Well, Mr. Forrest might be a bounder, and worse," he said slowly. "But if this document is genuine, he does not seem to be a thief."

Miss Forrest sank back against her chair. "My uncle was telling the truth, then."

Mr. Sloane looked surprise by the turn the conversation had taken. "Were you in doubt of his veracity?"

"Miss Forrest's father had not discussed the new disposition of his estate with her," Lily said carefully, when the young woman herself seemed too overwhelmed to answer. "So it was a great shock to her when her uncle sent her away from her home."

"But that . . ." Mr. Sloane frowned. "Well, that is unexpected. Mr. Forrest clearly stated in his will that he intended his daughter to be maintained in her accustomed style of living. Here, you may see for yourself." He pulled out several more papers, which he also passed to Jack.

Jack did not bother to hide his surprise as he read. "This also states that a substantial dower portion was set aside for Miss Forrest."

"Indeed. I believe the amount was ten thousand pounds?" Mr. Sloane glanced at the paper and nodded. "Subject to her uncle's approval, of course. I believe Mr. Forrest had . . ." He cleared his throat a second time. "Again, not to be indelicate, but I recall that he thought it important for his daughter to be guided in the matter of choosing a husband."

Jack passed the paper to Lily, and her mind worked rapidly as she read it through. Mr. Forrest might not have been an thief in the strictest sense, but combined with the letter they had found in his house, the will painted a damning portrait indeed of his behavior toward his niece. He had not stolen her money outright, but it certainly seemed that he had been determined to keep as much of it for his own use as he could, and to keep her at arm's length so she would not be able to prove his deceit.

"I think you were right to be concerned, Miss Forrest," Lily said, laying a hand on the girl's arm. "You ought to read this." Eyes wide and uncertain, the young woman did as she was bid while Lily turned back to the solicitor. "What happens to the estate now, with Mr. Martin Forrest's death?"

His eyebrows rose. "It comes to Miss Forrest. There is no remaining male issue, so it will be hers, held in trust until she—or her daughters—have a son to inherit it. And the money with it, of course," he added, almost as an afterthought. He took the papers from Jack as he spoke and tapped them into a neat stack.

"Her dowry, you mean?" Lily asked.

"Oh no, all of it," Mr. Sloane said. He laid the will down in front of him and folded his hands on top of it as he regarded them calmly. "Mr. Martin Forrest had not created a will since his return, though I urged him to." He shook his head. "Unwise, certainly. So, as she is his only living relative, his money comes to Miss Forrest in its entirety."

CHAPTER 17

Lily paced around the small drawing room in Half Moon Street, not really seeing anything in it, her mind preoccupied with what they had learned at the solicitor's office.

Miss Forrest had started crying again after finding out that she was to inherit everything from her uncle. Lily had first thought it was with relief, until the girl lifted her tear-blotched face to reveal eyes blazing with anger.

"He did want to marry me only for my money, then," she had whispered. "Well, he won't see a penny of it, ever! I might be forced to profit from my uncle's death, but Henry Clive never will. You may be sure of that."

The poor solicitor had been stunned as she stormed from the room, leaving Lily and Jack to smooth things over. Eventually, he had accepted their reassurance that Miss Forrest was so distraught from grief that she did not know what she was saying. Miss Forrest herself had remained withdrawn and silent all through the return trip to Hans Town, speaking only when they finally delivered her to the door of her house.

"I thank you for your assistance today," she had said, her posture and her voice both stiff. "I hope you will understand, Mrs. Adler, and not take it as a personal offense, when I say that I hope I will never see you again."

Lily stopped in front of her fireplace, which crackled in a friendly fashion, and shook her head, sighing to herself.

"What does such a grim sound portend?"

She turned to find Jack lounging in the doorway, watching her, having returned from tying up his horses. "How long have you been standing there?"

"Only a moment. What are you thinking?" he asked, coming into the room and taking a seat opposite where she was standing.

Lily was relieved by the easy informality. She hadn't had time to worry over whether things would be awkward between them after their accidental interlude the night before, but she was glad to discover they could move on without needing to dredge up anything uncomfortable.

"Lily?"

She realized with a little start that she hadn't answered him. "I was thinking of Miss Forrest. Trying to decide whether . . ."

"Whether the fact of her now substantial inheritance makes her more of a suspect than Mr. Clive?" Jack asked, leaning back in his chair.

"Precisely." Lily nodded. "And regretting that I did not have the opportunity to ask her about her previous engagement. I was hoping I would be able to another time, so I did not press it today. But if I am to take her final words seriously, that chance may have passed."

"For now, perhaps. But Mr. Page may be able to discover more about it." Jack cleared his throat. "And, while we are discussing the good constable . . ."

Lily frowned when he did not continue. "What is it? Something from your conversation with him this morning?"

He gave an uncomfortable chuckle. "Well, more something that was missing from our conversation this morning. How much—" He hesitated again. "When I spoke to him, he already knew that we had been searching the house on Queen Anne Street last night. But he did not seem to know anything about the specifics of that search. I take it you did not tell him about . . ."

Lily felt her entire body growing hot, but she met Jack's eyes calmly, refusing to be embarrassed. They both knew why it had happened, after all. "About what happened in the spare bedroom before we found the letter? No, I saw no reason to share that with him." She stepped toward him as a sudden, horrified thought occurred to her. "You did not say anything, did you?"

"Dear God, no," Jack said quickly, sitting up and reaching for her hand. She gave it to him without thinking. "No, I would never do such a thing."

Lily let out a relieved breath. "Thank you," she said, laughing a little at her panicked reaction. "I would hope that it would not change Mr. Page's opinion of me, but he can be rather stuffy from time to time."

She knew what she needed to say next, just as well as she knew that saying it would hurt. But it would hurt far worse to be the reason that things grew uncomfortable or distant between them. She had risked that once already when she had tried to tell him how her feelings had changed. Better pain that was hers alone now than the loss of the friendship that had become such a cornerstone of both their lives.

Lily forced herself to smile as she shook her head. "I should hate to fall in his estimation because of a meaningless deception we were forced to play."

"I am sure he would not—" Jack broke off. Lily thought she saw his eyes narrow a little. "Meaningless."

Lily suddenly wished she had not let him take her hand. She wanted to pull away, but that felt too pointed. "Surely you know me too well to think that I was offended by what happened? It was quick thinking on your part, and I was most grateful for it."

"Grateful," he repeated.

Awkward or not, Lily tugged her hand from his, trying to wish away the uncomfortable feeling suddenly squeezing her chest. She was not certain what the look Jack was giving her meant, but she was starting to realize that all was not as easy between them as she had hoped. The thought made her want to weep. Instead, she scowled at him. "Jack, what has gotten into you? I understood perfectly why you—"

"It was not meaningless to me."

The words hung in the air between them. Lily stared at him, certain that she could not have heard correctly. "What?"

She could see Jack's throat move. He stood up, and she had to resist the urge to take a step back. "It was not meaningless to me," he repeated more softly.

Lily shook her head, but she couldn't look away from him as she did, from the longing and hesitation in his own eyes. For a moment, the hopeful sensation fluttering in her chest was almost as painful as her certainty of a moment before had been. But she pushed it down. His rejection the other evening had been too decided. Either she was misunderstanding, or he was trying to soothe her feelings in exactly the wrong way.

"You do not mean that," she said as firmly as she could manage, needing to say the words to herself as much as to him.

He gave her an exasperated look. "You may tell me to stop talking if you wish, and I shall obey instantly," he said, irritation making the words snappish. "But you may not tell me what I mean."

"But . . ." Lily stared at him, trying to make sense of what he was saying.

It was the exasperation that convinced her. Had he been charming or soothing or loverlike, she would have suspected he was playing a part, saying what he thought she wanted to hear or doing what he believed was the honorable, gentlemanly thing. But he was as flustered and uncertain as she.

"But I told you . . ." Her mind raced through those moments from the book-room, trying to understand what had happened. What *was* happening. "I said I did not know what I would do without you. I said those *very words*." Her voice had turned accusing without her fully intending it, and she stepped forward, jabbing him in the chest with one finger. "And you positively *fled*. So do not try to tell me, now—"

"Lily!" He caught her hand when she would have poked his chest again.

She yanked her hand away and glared at him. "Now, of *all* times, when we are in the middle of dealing with—"

"Lily, I know!" She thought he might have been laughing, but a moment later she realized his face was flushed with embarrassment. "I know what I said. Or what I didn't say. What I did. I was a fool. Does it make you happy to hear it?"

"Not particularly!" Lily exclaimed, not sure why she was suddenly so angry with him. She felt hot all over, with embarrassment of her own, or confusion, or perhaps just hope. "Why did you leave, then?"

"I panicked," he said through gritted teeth, closing his eyes. He let out a gusty breath. "I had stayed away weeks longer than I should have. I did not want to return to London, to you, because after that night—"

He broke off, and the silence in the room was so absolute Lily thought he must be able to hear the way her heart was pounding. She could see his chest shake as he hauled in a breath. They both knew which night he meant.

"You almost died, Jack." Lily didn't mean for the words to come out as a whisper, but they did anyway.

His eyes snapped open. "I almost died," he agreed, running both hands through his hair so it stood nearly straight up. He paced away from her, his words coming faster. "And it became very clear—I knew then . . ."

"What did you know?" Lily didn't take her eyes away from him.

But he was too worked up, flinging his hands out to the side as he strode across the room. "And then I saw you again, and I still did not know how you felt. But then you told me—you told me directly!"

The fluttering sensation beat against Lily's chest once more, bright and hopeful. "Jack."

He turned back, shaking his head. "And then I, being an utter idiot, had to go and mention Freddy! Of all the things I could have said." He sounded disgusted with himself.

Lily, still half convinced that she was imagining every word, felt a smile pulling at the corners of her lips. "Jack."

"I had to get out of there before I said anything else to—"

"*Jack.*"

He stopped his pacing at last, breathing as heavily as though he had been running. "What?"

Lily lifted her chin toward him. "Kiss me."

"What?" He was utterly still, staring at her as though unable to believe what he had just heard.

"Must I repeat it?" she asked, holding back the laugh that was pressing against her throat.

"No. Dear God, no." A moment later he had his arms around her, a sensation that was disorienting and surprising and comforting all at once. "At least one of us has some sense," he muttered before lowering his mouth to hers.

When he had kissed her in the spare room, they had been afraid and desperate, as aware of the people about to discover them as they were of each other—even Lily, who had been painfully certain that kiss would be the only one they ever shared. Now, the world outside the circle of his arms may as well not have existed. She could feel every ounce of his attention as he brushed his lips gently against hers.

It was not enough. Lily rose up on her toes, curling her hands around his neck and shoulders to pull him more tightly to her. She could feel his breath catch in response—the same way, she realized with delight, that it had caught in the spare room. For a moment, he pulled her flush against him, the press of his mouth growing more urgent before he eased back.

Lily opened her eyes as he laid his forehead against hers, both of them breathing in shaky bursts as they stared at each other.

"Yes?" he murmured against her lips.

Lily smiled. "Oh yes," she whispered, already pulling him back to her.

Her hands didn't stay still after that, and neither did his. Heat pooled under her skin where he touched her, warm as firelight, and she urged him backward until she felt him collide with the settee. He took the hint immediately, letting himself sink down into it and pulling her with him.

It ought to have felt strange. Her mind ought to have been racing in half a dozen directions at once. But for once, Lily did not think of anything but what she was doing right then.

She didn't even stop to think of what it might lead to beyond that moment. She only knew that she was in Jack's arms again, with both of them meaning it this time, and that it was where she wanted to be.

In Jack's arms, in the middle of—

The sudden sound of a door closing in the hall made them both jump, staring at each other in momentary confusion.

"Mrs. Adler?" Lily heard Amelia's voice in the distance, but growing rapidly closer. "Are you home, ma'am?"

Lily sprang up, inordinately pleased by the moment of hesitation she felt before Jack let her go. She shook the layers of her clothing back into place while Jack stood and hastily did the same. "In the drawing room, Amelia. Your brother is here."

Amelia poked her head in. "Raffi, how nice to see you." She frowned. "Or is it? You both look dreadfully serious. What has happened?"

"We spoke with Miss Forrest and the solicitor," Jack said smoothly, no trace of the heat with which he had been embracing Lily only moments before in his voice or his manner. "If you want, I can take you for a drive in my curricle and tell you what we learned." He glanced at Lily. "That is, if Mrs. Adler has no objections?"

It took Lily a moment to find her voice. "No objections at all," she said, hoping she did not look as flushed and disheveled as she felt inside.

"Can you wait just a moment, Raffi, while I fetch a heavier pelisse?" Amelia asked guilelessly. "It will be breezier if we are in your curricle instead of walking."

"Of course."

As soon as she was gone and they heard her footsteps hurrying upstairs, he turned to Lily, smiling ruefully. "A little inconvenient, under the circumstances, to have my sister residing here as well."

"Or very convenient," Lily pointed out, stepping closer and running a finger down the edge of his coat. She watched its path, then glanced up to find Jack's eyes fixed on her. She couldn't hold back her pleased smile at the intensity of his attention. She began to draw her fingers back up. "You may visit as often as we wish without anyone batting an eye at it."

"And how often will you wish me to visit, madam?" he murmured, trapping her fingers against his chest with one hand. Beneath her palm, Lily could feel his heart pounding. It was a relief to know he was not so calm as he seemed.

Lily took a deep breath. "Well . . ." she began before stopping, her face falling into a scowl. "Well, frequently, but not this evening. It is Serena's Vauxhall party tonight."

"We could both send our regrets," he suggested, then sighed when she fixed him with a stern look. "Very well. But I will see you there?"

"You will," Lily said quietly, a happy, fluttery feeling in her chest. But a moment later, the feeling faded as she recalled what they had originally been talking about. "And while you are out with your sister, I ought to write to Mr. Page and tell him what we have learned."

The warmth faded from Jack's expression, replaced by grim determination. He nodded. "A wise idea." By then, they could hear Amelia coming back. Before she appeared in the doorway, Jack caught Lily's fingers once more and pressed a quick kiss against them. "And please be careful, Lily. If someone other than Clive is responsible for what happened to Mr. Forrest, I do not want to risk them finding out that you are involved."

Lily was left alone with that uncomfortable thought as he left to join his sister. Shivering a little, the warmth of Jack's embrace now faded, she went in search of a pen and paper.

CHAPTER 18

They approached Vauxhall Gardens by boat—a silly frivolity, but Jack enjoyed watching his sister smiling as she trailed her fingers in the water. When he had returned to Hertfordshire the previous winter, Noor had been mired in a neighborhood scandal she did not deserve—a scandal which grew to enormous proportions while she was still too scared to tell anyone what had truly happened. It had been a relief when Lily offered to remove her from the neighborhood and bring her to London. And it was even more of a relief to see his little sister thrive outside the strict scrutiny of village life.

"When do the fireworks begin?" Noor asked, shaking water droplets from her fingers.

"At ten o'clock," Lady Walter answered from the next boat, where she sat with her husband while they were rowed at a sedate pace across the Thames to the gardens' water entrance. "But the concert in the rotunda begins at eight o'clock. And the dancing lasts all night."

It had been years since Jack had spent an evening at Vauxhall, and he found himself enjoying the festive assault on his senses. The gardens were open the whole year round but became particularly crowded in the spring, when the residents of Mayfair and St. James joined the throng. Anyone could enter the gardens so long as they paid the entrance fee, and the paths were crowded with young country couples in their best attire, shopkeepers and their wives marveling at the clockwork castle, and laborers and servants enjoying a night of revelry on the dance floor. Around them, thousands of lanterns illuminated the colonnade and hung from the trees, which arched over secluded and winding paths.

Lord and Lady Walter had rented adjoining boxes for the evening, and their guests crowded happily into them, gossiping and flirting while they watched the dancers or called for punch and supper. Lady Walter presided over the tumult with her usual dramatic flair, clearly delighted to be back in her social element once more.

Lily had been correct—it would have hurt her friend terribly had they not attended that evening. But Lily, though she talked and laughed while supper was served and guests moved between boxes or swept each other onto the dance floor, seemed distracted. Jack doubted that anyone else noticed—Lily was long accustomed to concealing how she felt from curious eyes—but he saw the moments when her mind and her gaze wandered away from the conversation, staring at the dancers or at the minstrels who wandered from box to box without truly seeing any of them.

He wanted to know what she was thinking, whether it was about the shocking events of that morning, their visit to Mr. Sloane—or their own surprising interlude that afternoon, which he still could barely believe had happened. But he could not ask, not with so many others around them.

"Come now, Captain, why such a serious countenance on a night that should be entirely festive?" Lady Walter jostled his arm playfully. He had often wondered how thoughtful, reserved Lily Adler had come to be such good friends with the sunny, frivolous Serena Walter. But perhaps the contrast in their personalities was what had drawn them together in the first place. "I have been watching you, sir, and you have yet to set foot on the dance floor this evening, for shame."

"But I have been enjoying your company, Lady Walter," he replied with an easy smile, leaning back against the side of the box and draping his arm over its side, the picture of an indolent gentleman. "Surely you cannot fault me for that?"

Lady Walter beamed at him; she adored being flirted with. "I do indeed fault you for remaining so aloof when there are ladies who, I am sure, are longing to dance. Especially on the arm of a man with your grace and figure."

Out of the corner of his eye, Jack could see Lily watching them. For a moment, he wondered what she thought of the exchange. But then he saw the smile tugging at the corners of her lips. And he found himself wanting to make her smile more.

He leaned forward conspiratorially. "And pray tell, who have you noticed admiring my figure? I long to know." The guests around him laughed at his shamelessness, and Lily's expression grew into a real smile. Jack felt oddly triumphant.

"I am a vault," Lady Walter declared, shaking her head. "You will receive no such encouragement to vanity from me."

"Well, in that case . . ." He stood, bowing. "I shall take to heart your other encouragement and remove myself to the dance floor." He turned, smiling. "Would Mrs. Adler care to accompany me?"

Lily's hesitation was so brief he would have missed it had he not been watching her so closely, and he wondered if he had made a mistake asking her. With so many eyes on them now, it would have looked strange for her to refuse, even if she had wanted to.

She stood. "With pleasure. Though I hope you will recall what Lady Walter told you about me the first night I was back in London."

"That you dislike being flirted with?" When she inclined her head in agreement, he grinned. "I would not dare to forget it, madam. That was the same night you threatened to break an importuning gentleman's nose."

With the laughter of the Walters and their guests following them, Lily took Jack's arm and let him lead her to the dance floor.

The dancers ended their reel just as the two of them arrived. Jack expected them to begin another of the lively dances that had been filling the air all night, but it seemed the musicians had decided a change was in order. The strains of a waltz filled the air.

Beside him, Jack heard Lily catch her breath. He felt momentarily frozen and wondered if she was thinking the same thing he was: the only other time they had waltzed together was when Lily first returned to London after Freddy's death. She had been in half-mourning still and unable to dance in public. But he had seen the longing in her face when she was watching the dancers and had convinced her to sneak away and waltz with him in an empty room, the sounds of the music floating in through an open window.

They had both been missing Freddy that night two years ago, Lily raw with lingering grief, he still wracked with guilt that he had not been able to see his friend before he died. It had been a long time before Jack had been able to admit to himself that their waltz that night had also been the beginning of something else.

At least for him. He wondered if it had been for Lily too. He wondered if she was also thinking of Freddy now, as they waltzed under the thousand lanterns of Vauxhall, dozens of strangers turning around them.

He wanted to place his hand under her chin, to lift her gaze to his. But the venue was too public for such a gesture. Instead, he asked softly, so that none of the other dancers could hear, "What have you been thinking of this evening, Lily? You've been distracted all night."

She hesitated, glancing around them. The dance floor was large enough that it was not crowded, but it was hardly private. "Will you walk with me?"

The gardens were made for wandering as much as for seeing and being seen. Gravel paths wound under the overarching trees, around artificial ruins and between iron colonnades. It didn't take long for them to leave the supper boxes and dance floor behind. There were other parties strolling, but they were far more private than they had been at any other point during the night.

Though they did not go too far. Vauxhall was hardly a rookery, but its paths could be secluded, and more than one pickpocket or thief had thought to try their luck there.

"All right, Mrs. Adler, what has you so distracted?" Jack took a deep breath. "Is it about—"

"Mr. Forrest?" she said quickly. "Of course. It is hard to let anything else occupy my thoughts just now."

That hurt Jack's pride a little, but he could hardly argue the point. Murder had to take precedence over sentiment. "Will you tell me what you are thinking?"

Lily sighed, and he could feel the tension in her arm where it rested on his. "Nothing productive, I fear. I keep thinking of when we encountered Mr. Forrest last night. I was so afraid that he had guessed why we were there."

"As was I," Jack said quietly, remembering the expression on Mr. Forrest's face when he confronted Jack in the hall, Lily still concealed behind him. There hadn't just been fear in the man's eyes, but a kind of fury that had made Jack wish he had a weapon with him. But the expression had been so short-lived he could have almost convinced himself that he had imagined it.

Almost, but not quite.

"And I have been thinking of Mr. Clive," Lily said, sighing. "I worry that I was too quick to believe in his innocence. If our suspicions are to fall on Miss Forrest now, given the state of her inheritance, surely that could equally implicate Mr. Clive?"

"But there was the matter of the coat," Jack reminded her. When she gave him a surprised look, he shrugged one shoulder. "Mr. Page told me about it this morning."

"There is that," Lily said quietly. She glanced at Jack. "At least I am, it seems, safe from blackmail for the time being. If I were wiser, perhaps I would take that as a warning and distance myself from this current matter. But . . ."

"It was not your fault you were brought into it," Jack pointed out. "It is not as though you asked the fellow from Bow Street to bang on your door at sunrise."

Lily shook her head. "There is that too."

"Besides which," he added, glancing down at her as their steps drew to a halt. They were in one of the tree-lined walks, having circled back around toward the dance floor and the supper boxes, but they were still alone. "Besides which, I think you would be bored otherwise. You enjoy being involved in dangerous things."

That made her smile; in the lantern light, her eyes seemed to glow as she looked up at him. "So do you," she said softly, lifting her face toward his. "We have that in common."

Almost involuntarily, Jack leaned back, though he longed to do just the opposite. "We are not private here," he reminded her, trying to ignore how distracting her nearness had suddenly become.

"I know," Lily murmured. "But as we just pointed out, we both enjoy being involved in dangerous things."

Jack gave up; he didn't really want to argue with her, in any case. Unable to hide his smile, he leaned forward, his eyes on her lips.

"I believe they went this way. Mrs. Adler? Are you there?"

They sprang apart as though a fire had suddenly appeared between them, both turning toward the end of the walk, where Lady Walter and several of her guests were just approaching.

That was when Jack saw the man in the trees, the gun in his hand raised and pointed directly at them.

Jack pushed Lily down, his body landing protectively on top of hers, just as the report of a pistol firing echoed through the walk. Chips of wood exploded out from the tree that they had been standing in front of only a moment before.

Screams filled the air. Jack stared at Lily for a single, wide-eyed second, neither of them moving or breathing. Then he leaped up and ran toward the trees.

The man who had fired at them cast aside his pistol and dashed away. But he stumbled over a tree root. Jack threw himself at the man and caught him around the waist, bringing them both crashing to the ground. The man grunted, kicking and swinging his fists wildly in an effort to get away. Jack held grimly on, but one flailing limb landed a solid hit right against his injured shoulder, sending such a shock of pain through him that for a moment his vision went black.

Jack gasped, his hold on the attacker loosening. The man yanked away and sprang up, about to dash away again. Gritting his teeth against the pain in his arm, Jack barely managed to grab one ankle.

The man cursed, kicking out, and Jack had to drop his hold and roll away to protect his head.

But it had been enough. The shouts of the other guests had caught up with them, and before the man could go more than two steps, several pairs of arms grabbed at him, wrestling him at last to his knees.

Panting, Jack climbed to his feet, his shoulder throbbing and half his body bruised.

"Are you all right, Hartley?" Lord Walter demanded, looking him over.

"Fine," Jack grunted, shaking his head to clear it. "Mrs. Adler?"

"Well, thanks to your quick action." The viscount clapped him on the shoulder—luckily, not the injured one, though Jack still had to hold back a wince—and turned to where two of his guests were holding the attacker by his arms. His expression grew grave. "He cannot be a thief, I think. He would not have fired like that if his intent was to rob you or someone else."

"No," Jack agreed. He had already been thinking the same thing. He stepped in front of the man, who was staring sullenly down at the ground, and forced his chin up. He felt cold all over, thinking of that bullet coming so close to where Lily had been standing, and the chill of his rage seeped into his voice. "Who are you?"

The man glared back at him, saying nothing. He could have been a respectable laborer, judging by his clothing, which was plain and worn but well-made. And his face did not show the pinch of poverty. Though Jack could smell a hint of liquor on the man's breath, he did not seem drunk or desperate or anything else that could explain his attack.

"Very well, then." Jack glanced at the men holding the attacker's arms. "Would one of you be so good as to search his pockets? Perhaps there will be some hint there of who he is or what he was intending."

The man, who clearly had enough sense to realize that with four of them and only one of him he was well outmatched, didn't fight the search. But he didn't make it easy on them either. Finally, one of the partygoers discovered a folded piece of paper inside the man's coat and handed it to Lord Walter.

The viscount read it through quickly, and Jack could see him go very still as he did. At last, he lifted his head. "It seems, Captain, that someone hired this fellow. You are mentioned by name, and though there is no specific instruction given"—he glanced at the attacker—"I think we may all guess at what he understood his task to be."

For a moment, Jack could not say anything. "I do not suppose," he managed at last, surprised by how level his voice sounded, "that there is any signature to the letter?"

"There is, in fact," Lord Walter said, holding the paper out toward Jack. "He was hired by a man named Martin Forrest."

CHAPTER 19

Lily passed an anxious, jittery night after the attack at Vauxhall, waiting for news. Jack had insisted on going with the night watchmen who took the unknown attacker into their custody. And he had whispered to Lily—one hand resting comfortingly on the small of her back, where no one else in their party could see it—that he planned to summon Mr. Page to deal with the matter.

He had also insisted that she and Amelia spend the night at the Walters' townhouse rather than alone on Half Moon Street. Lily had been shaken, but she would have nevertheless insisted on refusing the protective gesture, in spite of the Walters adding their own entreaties. But one look at Amelia's face, at the way she clung to her brother, made Lily accept without protest.

In the end, as she lay awake, hearing the sound of that gunshot again and picturing Jack tearing off through the woods after their assailant, she was glad she had accepted.

But she still wanted to return to her own home that morning.

Serena, across the breakfast table from Lily when she announced her intentions, threw two sugar cubes into her tea with undisguised distress. "Too stubborn to let even a little thing like the threat of death curtail your independence?" she asked angrily.

Lily, who knew her friend was only worried for her and shaken from the attack herself, didn't take offense. "He was not after me," she pointed out practically. "The letter indicated that he had been hired to attack the captain."

"And that bullet came no closer to his skull than to yours," Serena bit off, glaring at her. "Why must you insist on putting yourself in danger?"

"If Mrs. Adler is returning to Half Moon Street, I shall go with her," Amelia declared.

Serena threw up her hands in disgust and stormed out of the room.

Lord Walter, accustomed to his wife's showy temper, continued to butter his toast. "Will you allow me to send an extra footman to stay with you?" he asked quietly. "At least until this matter is resolved?"

Though he was more than a decade older than Serena, John Walter was still handsome and energetic, and he had often played the role of a distinguished older brother or uncle in Lily's life. But though he spoke calmly, Lily could see that the lines around his mouth were deeper than usual that morning, and there were dark shadows under his eyes. She was not the only one who had passed a restless, worried night.

"I thank you for the kindness," Lily said quietly, "but I do not think it is necessary. As I said to Lady Walter, the attack was not directed at me."

Lord Walter didn't look pleased, but he nodded. "You have only to say if you wish to change your mind."

When Lily and Amelia at last returned to Half Moon Street, they discovered that Jack had been successful. Mr. Page was waiting in the front hall for them, and he had news about the Vauxhall assailant that left Lily staring at him in disbelief.

"What do you mean he did not know Mr. Forrest was dead? Are you certain?"

"As certain as I can be, given that the fellow refused to open his mouth at all," Mr. Page said, shaking his head as he paced from one end of the drawing room to the other. "He wouldn't even give us his name. But when I mentioned Mr. Forrest's death, he couldn't hide his shock. Looked like he was going to be sick. Or break something."

"So he was probably not the person who . . ." Lily glanced at Amelia, who sat next to her, hands clasped in her lap and eyes wide.

Amelia gulped but lifted her chin. "He was probably not the person who killed Mr. Forrest," she said, her voice deliberate and firm.

"Likely not," Mr. Page agreed. "But the question remains, then, why Mr. Forrest sent him to harm the captain."

"We can certainly guess," Lily said quietly. "If he thought we had discovered that letter . . . He did not know my name, after all, but he knew the name Hartley, and he had run into the captain twice. It might have made him suspicious."

Mr. Page nodded. "He could have sent a message to that man during or after the ball if he suspected his scheme to take Miss Forrest's money had been uncovered. But . . ."

Lily could guess what the skeptical note in his voice meant. "But it seems a shocking step to take," she said. "To have a man, a stranger, killed? On the strength of two chance encounters and a bare suspicion?"

"Even had he known for certain that the captain had discovered his wrongdoing, it hardly seems worth killing over," Mr. Page agreed. "Especially as he had not, technically, done anything illegal. He was his brother's heir, after all."

"Immoral, certainly," Amelia put in. "To keep her dowry from her thusly. But legally, as her guardian, he had every right to do as he wished."

"It's a damned mess," Mr. Page said, shaking his head. "Begging your pardon, ladies." He grimaced, staring at the hat that he held in his hands, then looked up, a stoic constable once more. "But you are both well? Unharmed after last night's altercation?"

"Shaken but unharmed," Lily said firmly, rising.

"I'm glad to hear it." Mr. Page bowed politely. "If you'll both excuse me, I must return to my duties."

Amelia, after bidding him farewell, made her way upstairs. But Lily followed him to the front door. "Where is the man now?" she asked.

"Newgate," Mr. Page said as Lily opened the door for him. "Until we can learn who he is, and more about this matter with Mr. Forrest, that's where he'll stay."

"Well, that is a relief at least," Lily said. "And you will let us know if you learn anything?"

"I suppose I will," Mr. Page said, reluctant but resigned. "Good day, Mrs. Adler. And . . ." He hesitated. "Please be careful."

Lily inclined her head. The memory of that gunshot was too fresh to argue with such a sentiment. "I shall."

She returned to the drawing room once he was gone, pacing restlessly from one side to the other, trying not to think about the fear she had felt the night before and wondering whether Jack would call that morning. She could not go to visit him at his lodging, not without raising too many eyebrows. But she wanted reassurance that he was well. And she had not missed the stiff, pained way that he had been holding his arm when they went their separate ways.

Perhaps he had told Amelia when they would see him again. Lily was about to follow her young houseguest upstairs when she heard voices in the hall. She paused to listen, but it was not someone she recognized. Lily frowned. The post had already come that morning, and she was not expecting other visitors. But there was no better way to find out who it was than to go see for herself.

When Lily stepped into the hall, she saw a young man in a dusty traveling coat, with a small valise at his feet. He was talking to Carstairs, about to hand over what looked like a little package, but at the sound of Lily's footsteps, they both fell silent and turned. The young man snatched the hat off his head and bowed politely.

"Mrs. Adler," he said as he straightened. "Do you remember me?"

There was something familiar about him, but it took Lily a moment to place the memory. "You are the youngest Mitford boy, are you not?" The Mitfords were Hertfordshire neighbors who moved in the same circles as the Adlers but lived some distance from them, and she had not seen them in several years. "I apologize, I have forgotten your name."

"Fitzwilliam," he said, bowing again, his ears red. He was very young, Lily saw now, likely not yet twenty, and still moved like a boy unaccustomed to the new length of his limbs.

Lily felt a flutter of worry in her stomach. "Did Lady Adler or Sir John send you? Is everyone well?"

"Everyone is exceedingly well, Mrs. Adler," he said earnestly. "They heard I was coming to London to execute a commission for my parents, and Lady Adler asked that I make a delivery to you as well." He offered her the package that he had been about to give to Carstairs. When she took it, a little bemused, he pulled a letter from his pocket and handed that to her as well. "And they send their regards, of course."

"Thank you." Lily turned the letter over, frowning a little. But it was hardly uncommon for deliveries to be made in such a manner. There was no reason it should set her on edge, except that she did not want to think of Freddy and his family just then. But that was not Fitzwilliam Mitford's fault. She gave him a polite smile. "I think you must have just arrived in London, Mr. Mitford. Have you dined yet? May I offer you breakfast?"

"You are very kind, ma'am," he said with another bow. "But my aunt expects me in Bedford Square this morning, and I've no wish to keep her waiting. I will be in London until Tuesday next. May I call before I depart, to see if there is any return that I may convey to the Adlers for you?"

"Yes, I thank you. That would be most appreciated."

A few more polite words and he was on his way to Bloomsbury, and Carstairs had returned to his wife and his silver in the kitchen. Lily walked slowly up to her room, where she settled at her dressing table, turning the small package in her hand and feeling unaccountably nervous to open it. She set it aside and opened the letter instead.

The first half was only news from her former mother-in-law. Since she knew Lily would not have to pay the postage for it, Lady Adler had not stinted in her writing, and the letter filled several sheets. It was not until the very end that she came to the matter of the delivery.

> *I have been holding onto this for some time, dearest Lily, as I was unsure what to do with it. Freddy commissioned it for you before he fell ill, but it was not delivered until after his death, and—forgive me for saying so—I thought your equilibrium too fragile to present it to you at the time. And truth be told, it was too hard for me to look at it either. I put it away, but of course that meant I forgot about it. By the time I remembered, you had left us for London, and I was hesitant yet again to disturb you with it. You have built such a lovely new life for yourself, my dear, though I sometimes worry at the dangers you have encountered, and I do not want you to think that we begrudge you that at all. But in the end, it was always meant to be yours, and I have delayed long enough. I know you will treasure it as you should.*
>
> *With love, &ct . . .*

Lily read the letter twice, feeling a little ill. She had no idea what Freddy's mother might have sent. Had he mentioned a gift before he fell ill? She could not remember; there was a great deal from their last years together that was etched into her memory, but even more that had faded with time.

Once, that had made her feel disloyal to her husband. She had since come to believe that was how it ought to be—neither her mind nor her heart were made to live always in the past. But at the moment, that sense of disloyalty was rearing its head once more.

Lily stared at the package. But there was no point delaying or avoiding what she knew she would eventually do. Before she could talk herself out of it, she pulled off the paper and stared at the small object in her palm.

It was a miniature portrait of Freddy.

Lily sank to the floor as she stared at it. It was not the work of a master, but there was a liveliness and care to it that made Lily suspect the painter had known Freddy well. Perhaps one of his friends from university had done it? No wonder Lady Adler had hesitated to send it to her for so long. It was only in the last year, Lily knew, that she could have looked at such a thing with some degree of composure.

Even now, it was hard to swallow back the emotion that rose like a lump in her throat. Too many of her memories of Freddy were of the time after he had fallen ill, when he was worn down by two years of sickness and the knowledge that he did not have long to live. But he smiled up at her from the miniature, brimming with health and good humor, the young man she had fallen in love with and married when she could see their life together, full of order and purpose and ease, stretched out pleasantly and predictably before her.

She had been a different person then. And for a moment, as she had not in years, she felt a wave of guilt that she had changed.

It almost felt as if Freddy's mother had sent the portrait because she knew what had happened between Lily and Jack. It was absurd, she knew—Lady Adler had, just the winter before, made it clear that she thought Lily was on the verge of being engaged again, and she had been unequivocal in her approval of the possibility.

But the man they had expected her to marry, the man she had eventually refused, had been nearly a stranger to them—charming, personable, but ultimately unknown. Jack the Adlers knew, and had known from boyhood. He and Freddy had been raised almost like brothers. It would be different for them to contemplate . . .

Contemplate what? Lily had no idea what Jack intended, nor even what she intended. They had both been acting on impulse the day before—and the night before that—with no thought of what would come after.

She had no idea what Jack imagined would happen next for them. And she was not sure she wanted to risk asking. At least, not until the matter of Mr. Forrest's death had been dealt with and they were both safe. Then she could give her full attention to whatever the answer might be, good or bad.

Lily sighed and then, before she could second-guess herself, shoved the letter into a drawer. She would have put the portrait there too, but she hesitated at the last moment, running one finger over the delicately painted lines of her husband's face.

She was a different person now, but surely Freddy would have understood that.

Sighing, Lily propped the miniature up against her dressing table mirror. She would decide what to do with it later—what to do about all of it—but for now, it felt wrong to hide Freddy's portrait away, even for a little while.

"Amelia!" she called out, rising. When she stepped out the door, Jack's sister was just poking her head out of her own bedroom.

"Do you need something, Mrs. Adler?"

"A distraction," Lily admitted. "Would you like to accompany me to Clerkenwell? I think it is time I turned my attention to young Miss Andrews's concerns."

★　★　★

"I am hoping to call on your Mrs. Carver," Lily said, moving a stack of books off the parlor chair and taking a seat. "Can you tell me more about her?"

Judith Page, who had first welcomed them into the Pages' home, had been flattered but flustered by their visit; it had not taken Lily longer than the time needed for the teakettle to boil to realize that Fanny's aunt had been in the middle of schooling her young nephew, George. But when Lily and Amelia tried to depart, Judith Page insisted they stay, deputizing Fanny to entertain the visitors while she returned to George and geography.

"At his age, there are only about ninety minutes in a day when I can convince him to attend to his lessons, so I must take advantage of them," Miss Page had said with an apologetic smile. "You are kind to be so understanding."

"We shall be well entertained by Miss Andrews," Lily had reassured her, feeling somewhat humbled. Most of the families she knew sent their children away to school, if they did not employ a governess or tutor. She hadn't considered what a disruption she might be bringing into the Pages' routine before deciding to make her visit. "I do apologize for interrupting your day."

"Not at all, Mrs. Adler. We are honored by your visit." Miss Page glanced around the room once more. "At least the cleaning girl already came," Lily heard her murmur to herself as she left, shaking her head.

Lily waited until she was gone before posing her question. Fanny, pouring the tea with careful precision—Lily noticed that the liquid reached the exact same point in each cup—thought for a moment before answering.

"I thought my uncle didn't want us bothering her."

"I've no intention of bothering her," Lily said as she accepted her cup. "But if you are still concerned, I did give you my word that I would look into it. Are you?"

Fanny nodded. "I am curious, at least."

"Then tell me a bit about her. I think your uncle said she was a widow?"

Fanny dropped a lump of sugar into her cup and stirred it three brisk times before setting her spoon aside. "Her husband died in France, though I can't remember when word came about it. He'd been away for years, so I don't think I ever met him, but our neighbor Mrs. Williams remembered him, and so did Aunt Judith. I don't think she approved of him, though she never said so. But she used to make this face"—Fanny pursed her lips, eyes going wide and glancing to the side—"whenever a neighbor mentioned him. Though she does not make it since he died. I think it wouldn't be polite."

Lily hid a smile behind her cup. "He was a soldier?"

Fanny frowned. "I think perhaps he was a servant to a general, or something like that. Or a soldier who served an officer? I am not certain how that works. I know Mrs. Carver was in service before she married, because Mrs. Williams said so."

"How does Mrs. Carver manage now?" Amelia asked curiously, setting her cup down. "Does she get a widow's pension from the army?"

"I don't know," admitted Fanny. "Aunt Judith says it's rude to talk about money, so I've stopped asking those sorts of questions. Which is a shame, I think. How else am I to learn what I might expect when I'm grown?" Fanny sighed. "But I have to remember what Aunt Judith says. There are many things to remember for young ladies."

"Too many," Amelia murmured.

Fanny gave her a serious nod of agreement. "I know she does sell lace. Mrs. Carver, I mean. Not my aunt."

"From her home?" Lily asked. "Or only at market?"

"Both. And I think she sells to dress shops too. It's pretty lace, and she sells it for two shillings a yard for a band two inches wide, three shillings a yard for a band four inches wide, and custom orders at one shilling every quarter yard."

Lily kept another smile from her face. Fanny always knew the price of fabrics and trimmings, though her aunt and uncle had to remind her from time to time not to size up the cost of strangers' clothing—at least, not where they could hear her assessments.

Lily set aside her cup and stood. "In that case, Fanny, might you escort us to Mrs. Carver's home? My maid is making over one of my gowns for the summer, and I think some new lace to trim it would be just the thing."

★ ★ ★

Mrs. Carver was sitting on her front stairs when they arrived, beneath the blue-flowered window boxes. A shawl was wrapped tightly around her shoulders, and she was too busy staring at something in her hands to notice them approach.

Fanny paused a few steps away. "Mrs. Carver?"

The woman shrieked, leaping to her feet, the object clattering from her hands onto the stones of the road. Lily had just time to see that it was a miniature portrait before Mrs. Carver snatched it back up and tucked it under her shawl.

"What do you want, you dreadful girl?" she said, wiping her eyes.

"Was that Mr. Carver's picture?" Fanny asked.

"And what business is it of yours if it was?" Mrs. Carver scowled.

Fanny sighed. "I suppose it is not, but I thought that was how one makes conversation. In any case, this is Mrs. Adler, who knows my uncle, and Miss Hartley, and they are interested in purchasing some lace. I told them you make very fine lace and that it's generally two shillings a yard, and they asked me to bring them here."

"Oh!" Mrs. Carver finally noticed the two women standing there; her round, ruddy face turned even redder and she dropped a quick curtsy. She wasn't an elegant woman, but she was finely dressed, with beautiful trimming on her day gown that Lily suspected was her own work. "Oh, excuse me, indeed, please do excuse me—I didn't see you standing there. I do indeed make lace, very fine lace, if you'll pardon my saying so myself, but you'll see that it's true. Won't you come inside?"

She hurried up the steps to throw open the door to her narrow house, stepping aside so they might precede her in. She followed behind them, and she talked the entire time, an almost frantic note to her voice that Lily thought she was trying to hide.

"You're a good girl, Fanny Andrews, indeed you are, to be recommending my wares around," she said, giving Fanny what she clearly thought was a friendly pinch on the arm, which Fanny endured with a clenched jaw, stepping to Lily's other side as soon as she could get away. "An odd girl, to be sure, but I never believe the things people say about you, to be sure I don't, I always knew you were a considerate little thing." She beamed at Lily and Amelia, dropping another curtsy and rubbing her hands against her shawl eagerly. "What might you be looking for, madam? Or perhaps your . . ." She paused, eyeing Amelia's fashionable pelisse and hat. Her manner of dress made it clear that she was not a servant, and Fanny had made a point of introducing her when they arrived. Mrs. Carver hesitated, looking worried about offending. "Your companion can help me pick it out?"

"Miss Hartley does indeed have a keen eye for trimmings," Lily said. "I am sure I will benefit from her opinions, and we may wish to select something for her as well, as Miss Andrews has assured us you have a lovely selection of patterns. Would you be so good as to show us what you have available?"

Mrs. Carver hurried to reassure them that she had whatever madam and the young lady might want. She eagerly invited them to take a seat in the parlor while she went to fetch her stock. "Fanny, be a good girl and come help me."

Fanny obeyed, her face set in resignation, while Lily and Amelia took the offered seats. While they waited, Lily looked about the room.

It was similar to the Pages' home, but less well tended. Only half the curtains had been drawn back for the day, and the fire had clearly been made on top of yesterday's ashes. There was a layer of dust on the room's one bookshelf, as though the volumes on it had not been disturbed in months, or perhaps years. And every surface was cluttered and crowded with periodicals, fabrics, baskets, sewing notions, bottles, tinctures, and the morning's breakfast dishes that had not yet been cleared away.

Lily swallowed down a sneeze. It was a far cry from Judith Page's careful housekeeping. But if Mrs. Carver had to work for her own maintenance—respectable enough work, to be sure, and even somewhat genteel—her time to tend to her house would be far more limited. Lily held her breath against another sneeze.

Amelia was not so lucky. "I think if she tried to murder anyone, she would leave a trail of dust behind her," she whispered when she had finally recovered.

Lily pursed her lips against a laugh. "That is hardly kind," she murmured.

Amelia sneezed again. "Tell that to my nose," she said as she fished around in her reticule for her handkerchief.

"Adelaide? Adelaide, are you in?" There was a knock at the door, which had been left propped open to allow daylight in, and a face topped by an enormous and fashionable hat poked inside. "Oh, goodness, you gave me a fright!" the woman exclaimed as she realized that there were people staring back at her. "Is Adelaide in this morning?"

"If you mean Mrs. Carver, she is about to show us some lace," Lily said, caught off guard by the intrusion.

The woman stepped into the room, blinking as her eyes adjusted from the light outside. Then she blinked again as she took in Mrs. Carver's visitors. "Gracious, and we don't see two such finely dressed ladies here every day. Pray excuse me, madam, miss, whoever you are. I won't be a minute. Adelaide, are you there?" she called again, raising her voice. "I need a tonic for Mr. Williams's stomach, if you have such a thing."

Mrs. Carver and Fanny Andrews came out of the back room, Fanny carrying a large basket and Mrs. Carver carrying a beautiful blue cloth, which she began to spread on the table. "A moment please, Mrs. Williams, as you can see, I'm in the middle of helping these ladies. Yes, Fanny, just lay the laces out on the cloth—there's a good girl—so our visitors can see what's what. And mind you don't mangle or tear any of them!" Mrs. Carver turned to give Lily and Amelia a nervous smile. Her hands were shaking, and she tucked them quickly under her apron. "Will you come and take a look, or would you prefer to stay seated while I bring them to you to examine?"

Lily stood. "We are happy to examine them ourselves while you help your neighbor, thank you, Mrs. Carver. It is a beautiful selection."

She wasn't flattering the woman, though she would have if it hadn't been true. But Adelaide Carver did indeed make beautiful lace, and the rolls made a pretty picture set against the blue cloth. Clearly, she knew a thing or two about selling her wares as well as making them.

"You're very kind. I won't be a minute."

Lily kept her head turned toward the selection of laces, but she watched Mrs. Carver and her neighbor closely while she pretended to browse. Amelia did the same, but Fanny simply took a seat and watched the two women while they talked. Neither one seemed to notice her.

"A tonic for his stomach, you said?" Mrs. Carver asked, going to the shelf that was crowded with bottles. "I have a little left from the last batch. But he should go see a real doctor."

Mrs. Williams took the bottle gratefully. "Well, and that's what I tell him, but he won't hear of it. He says he always got his medicine from your grandfather, and so now that the poor gentleman is no more, God rest him, he'll get his from you until the day he dies too."

"Or until I move away from London," Mrs. Carver said a little waspishly, but the sound of tears was back in her voice.

Mrs. Williams stared at her. "Whatever does that mean? You aren't thinking of any such thing, are you?"

Mrs. Carver shrugged unhappily, glancing around the room. "Too many memories here," she muttered. "Mayhap I'll start over in the country. I could open a shop there instead of trudging from modiste to market and back again all week long."

"Don't talk nonsense, Adelaide. All your neighbors are here. You were raised here! And look how well you're doing." Mrs. Williams glanced over her shoulder at Lily and Amelia and gave a little cackle of a laugh. "Such a fine lady at your doorstep, and perhaps more commissions from Mayfair to follow, and won't that be a good thing for you? Poor dear, there's no call to leave London."

"And the gentleman would miss you," Fanny put in calmly.

That made both women snap their heads around. "What gentleman?" Mrs. Williams demanded at the same time as Mrs. Carver said in a trembling whisper, "What do you mean, Fanny?"

"The gentleman who calls here," Fanny put in with wide-eyed innocence. "I saw him one morning when Aunt Judith sent me to the market. Surely he'd be sad if you left?"

"Oh!" Mrs. Williams cackled. "Selling lace is it, Adelaide?"

"Hold your tongue, Nan Williams," Mrs. Carver hissed. "And you," she added, her voice quiet and desperate as she glared at Fanny. "You hush your mouth, you dreadful girl. I'll not have you spreading such vicious rumors about me, no, I won't. How dare you say such a thing?"

Lily, still with her head down as though she were examining the lace, watched the exchange from the corner of her eye. All Mrs. Carver's morose discomfort of a moment before had suddenly transformed into anger. And, Lily suspected, no little bit of fear. That was not hard to understand; in a close neighborhood, like this one seemed to be, neighbors would be constantly privy to one another's business. Any suspicion that a woman was engaging in anything even remotely similar to prostitution, even if it was just rumor, could see her ostracized by her community. And if word of such a thing got back to the shops where Mrs. Carver sold her laces, they might stop buying from her to prevent any hint of salacious behavior attaching to themselves.

Mrs. Williams shook her head at Fanny, though she was smirking as she did so. "Fanny Andrews, don't you go repeating such things around. Your aunt would be horrified if she heard you gossiping about a poor widow. Now, no need to fret, Adelaide. Your secret is safe with me."

"In the first place, there's not a secret this side of the Channel that's safe with you," Mrs. Carver said, her face red and her voice shaking. "And in the second, it's all absolute nonsense. I never entertained a gentleman in such a manner in my life. I have my pride and my morals, even if I don't have much money, thank you very much. I interviewed some potential lodgers a while back, but that was all. All, I say!" She was shaking as she finished speaking, and her voice had grown choked, as though she were trying not to cry.

"Well, well, and don't get so worked up about it," Mrs. Williams said, patting Mrs. Carver's shoulder as she popped the bottle into her basket. "I was only teasing, I was. And I don't know what you mean by saying a secret isn't safe with me. I'm as silent as the grave, as the saying goes. Why, just last week Miss Ainsley told me the reason I haven't seen her father about is that he's been tossed in prison for unpaid debts, and I haven't told a soul about it, so there you are!"

Mrs. Carver turned her gaze up as though praying for patience. "You have your tonic, Nan, now be off if you please. I have customers to attend to. And don't you go spreading any rumors!" she added in a whispered shout. Mrs. Williams only shook her head, smiling as she flounced out the door.

Mrs. Carver took a deep breath, a pained smile fixed on her face as she turned back into the room. "I apologize for my neighbor."

"No need to apologize, Mrs. Carver," Amelia said politely. Lily said nothing, watching Mrs. Carver's face closely. "We all have a busybody or two in our lives, I'm sure."

"You're very kind," Mrs. Carver said, her voice strained. She glanced over her shoulder nervously, then pulled her shawl more tightly around herself and took a deep breath. She gestured toward the table. "Did you find anything to your liking? I do make deliveries, if you've no footman or maid to carry your packages for you."

CHAPTER 20

"Well, I have to say, Fanny, I did not see any indication that she is plotting to kill anyone," Lily said as they made their way back to St. John's Square, packages in hand. She and Amelia had each bought something; it was only polite, and besides which, the laces had been very beautifully made.

"Except, perhaps, that Mrs. Williams," Amelia said, her voice and her expression both dark. "For which I would not blame her. What a dreadful woman."

"Do you think she would?" Fanny asked, eyes wide.

Amelia shook her head. "No, I was not being serious. She seemed more sad to me than anything else."

Lily nodded slowly. "She did seem sad. Do you know what Mrs. Williams meant about her grandfather?"

"He was an apothecary, I think." Fanny said. "Which could make her well suited to poisoning someone, could it not? She might know exactly how to do it. And she does prepare tonics and tinctures for neighbors from time to time."

"Has anyone she made a tonic for ever been ill?" Lily asked. "Or died afterward?"

Fanny sighed. "No," she said, shaking her head. "They tend to get better. I suppose my uncle was right." She sighed again. "He often is. Well, at least you got some pretty lace."

* * *

Amelia spotted the curricle waiting outside number thirteen before their carriage had drawn to a halt.

"That is my brother's," she said, sounding relieved. "Thank goodness. He ought to know better than to take his time calling after what happened last night, the wretch. Hello, Jem," she added as their carriage drew to a halt and she swung the door open. "How is your young lady these days? Is the captain inside?"

Jem, who was perched in the curricle's seat, reading a periodical, had stood up to bow when he heard Amelia's voice. At her question, however, he scowled. "Yes, he is. And I ain't got a young lady," he added in a mutter.

"Oh, I beg your pardon. My mistake," Amelia said politely. "How is your mother then?"

Jem looked like he wanted to continue scowling at her, but he didn't quite manage it. "Mum's good," he said a little reluctantly. "Head's not troubling her quite so much. Yer kind to ask, miss. Do y'need help carrying all those packages inside?"

Jack was waiting for them in the drawing room, pacing in front of the fire. His relief when they walked in was palpable.

Lily was no less glad to have the chance to look him over and reassure herself that he was well after the Vauxhall attack. For a moment, none of them said anything. Then Amelia, trembling a little, went to embrace her brother.

He wrapped his arms around her. "No need to fret, Noor. All is well."

"All is not well," she insisted, her voice muffled by his coat. "Not when such things can happen. And you should not have waited so long to call today."

"I do apologize," he said, looking at Lily over the top of his sister's head as he spoke. Lily, who hadn't yet moved from the doorway, nodded. He smiled, looking a little embarrassed. "I did not return home until late last night, after making sure that blackguard was locked away. And I slept far past my normal hour as a result. But Mr. Page said he would call on you this morning. Did he?"

Lily found her voice at last. "He did. And he told us what he learned from that man. Or rather, what he did not learn."

Jack sighed as he released his sister. "And where have the two of you been passing your time?"

"Visiting with Fanny Andrews," Lily said. "She took us to see her neighbor, Mrs. Carver. We bought some lace."

Jack looked surprised for a moment, then chuckled, though the sound was a little forced. "From the woman growing poison?"

Lily smiled faintly. "The same. Fortunately, her lace was far away from her window boxes."

"And quite pretty," Amelia chimed in, clearly trying to act as though all was normal, in spite of the way her voice still trembled. "I purchased some to send to *Ammi* for her birthday."

"That reminds me, Noor, I have something that should cheer you up." Jack pulled a thick letter from his inside his coat and offered it to her. "This arrived in the post yesterday. Full of news from Papa and *Ammi*, and absolutely no talk of murder or danger. They are eager to hear more about your time in London. And I thought perhaps I might take you to the library, in case the book you were looking for last time has finally arrived."

Amelia perked up as she took the letter from him. "I would like that, Raffi, thank you. Would you mind if I take this upstairs to read it first, though? Do you need anything, Mrs. Adler?"

"Nothing at all," Lily said briskly, giving the girl as normal a smile as she could manage. "You should go enjoy your letter."

Lily and Jack stared at each other without speaking as the door closed behind Amelia.

"People need to stop shooting at you," Lily said at last, crossing the room to him. He didn't pull away as she laid one hand gently against his injured arm. It was a relief to touch him, to reassure herself that he was safe and well. "Does it hurt today?"

"A little sore," he admitted, laying his hand over hers. "And how are you?"

"A little sore," Lily echoed. "Getting thrown to the ground leaves one rather bruised."

"I would apologize for it, but . . ." When Lily scowled at him, Jack smiled. "So Mrs. Carver was not a poisoner?"

"There were at least no signs of nefarious intent from our brief visit," Lily said, grateful for the change of subject. "Thank goodness one young lady's problem could be so swiftly resolved." She turned to stare out the window, not really seeing the dusty street laid out before her. Instead, she saw Henry Clive watching her as she left him awaiting his trip to Newgate. She saw the world lurching around her as Jack threw her to the ground, the crack of a pistol echoing through the air. She shook her head before she saw Martin Forrest as well. That, especially, she did not want to think about. "The other has proved far more complicated."

She heard Jack step up behind her and fell still, not sure what he was going to do. She jumped a little when his arm slid around her waist. It should have felt strange: they had known each other for years without more intimacy than the occasional touch of their hands, perhaps a dance from time to time. But Lily discovered it was easy to lean her back against his chest and let him hold her. Not just easy but comforting, to know that whatever thoughts were in her head, they were in his as well. It helped to know that her worries were shared. And it helped to feel that warm arm encircling her waist.

Jack sighed, setting his chin on the top of her head, which made Lily want to giggle, and then made her appalled that she wanted to do something so girlish. What had gotten into her?

"What does Mr. Page make of it?" he asked. "Did he share any news?"

"He said—" Lily broke off as Jack ducked his head, brushing a featherlight kiss against the side of her neck. She could feel the shock of it all the way to the base of her spine, and she nearly pulled away. "Captain, that is not at all conducive to answering your question," she said sternly. "I cannot think clearly when you are doing that."

"My apologies," he murmured, and she could feel his smile against her skin. He did not stop. "What were you going to say?"

Lily gave up. She would rather not think about Mr. Forrest or any of the rest of it anyway. Turning in Jack's arms, she lifted her face for a kiss, hoping that Amelia took a long time with her letter.

"No need to trouble yourself to announce me," a voice said clearly from the hallway. "I am perfectly able to show myself in."

Lily froze. How had she let herself get so distracted that she hadn't heard the front door opening? She and Jack stared at each other for a single, panicked moment, then stepped apart.

They were not quick enough. Lily was still half in his arms when the door to the drawing room opened. Ofelia, equally frozen in the doorway, stared at them in shock.

Lily yanked away from Jack, who hastily turned toward the fireplace so that he was no longer facing the doorway. Lily could feel her own face flame with embarrassment as she stepped forward, trying to give him what privacy she could to compose himself. But her voice was cool as she greeted her unexpected visitor. "Good morning, Ofelia. Did you get my letter?"

"Did I—" Ofelia stared from Lily to Jack and back again. "Your letter? Yes, I came to—When did—" She trailed off, her expression a riot of disbelief, shock, and delight.

Jack cleared his throat, turning around at last and bowing. "A pleasure to see you, as always, Lady Carroway. I think you must have heard, then, that the matter of blackmail has become somewhat more complicated."

"That is . . . that is putting it mildly," Ofelia said, gathering her composure, though her eyes lingered appraisingly on both of them as she spoke. Lily could guess that her reprieve from questions would last only as long as Jack was in the room. But for the moment, Ofelia seemed content to follow their lead. "Thank goodness whoever this killer was struck later in the night, and not when the two of you were wandering about." Her eyes narrowed. "When you were wandering about together," she repeated, a note of suspicion entering her voice.

"I think that is Miss Hartley I hear coming down the stairs now," Lily said quickly, giving Ofelia a pointed look. She was relieved when her friend nodded her understanding, though she looked a trifle resigned as she did. Whatever Ofelia might be wondering, it was not something that Amelia needed to know just yet.

"Captain Hartley was just about to accompany his sister to the circulating library."

It was not an idle comment; they could all hear the patter of Amelia's footsteps approaching. She was surprised to find another person had arrived but delighted to see Lady Carroway once more, and Lily was grateful for the distraction of five minutes' conversation about the timing of the daily post and the selection at Hookham's Library. But when, at last, Amelia asked whether Lady Carroway would be so kind as to join them on their excursion, Ofelia demurred.

"I thank you, but I must steal Mrs. Adler away from you," she said, sending Lily a sideways glance, even as the smile for Amelia never left her face. "She owes me a great deal of detail about what has been happening these past few days."

"What a tangle it has all become," Amelia said, shaking her head. "At least that dreadful Mr. Clive can blackmail no one from inside Newgate's walls."

"Small mercies," Ofelia agreed, sounding as though she meant it.

In the flurry of departure, Lily barely had a chance to say goodbye to Jack. But that might have been for the best; as soon as the Hartley siblings were gone, Ofelia rounded on her.

"Lily Adler," she said in a stern tone.

Lily sighed. "Come back into the drawing room, please. We can be more comfortable there, at least."

"Oh yes, by all means, let us be comfortable," Ofelia declared. "Cozy, even. You did look dreadfully cozy when I arrived."

"Stop that," Lily said, flustered but refusing to show it. "Shall I ring for tea? Or would you prefer a glass of cordial again?"

That earned her a sharp look of a different variety from her friend, who didn't answer immediately. "Cordial," she said at last. "Thank you."

"Of course," Lily said, tugging the bellpull. Anna appeared only a moment later, having anticipated what the arrival of a guest would mean. As soon as Lily had made her request and they were alone again, she turned back to Ofelia. "Very well," she said as calmly as possible. She sat, folding her hands in her lap, and gave her friend an even look. "You may begin your interrogation."

Ofelia scowled. "Well, it is no fun if you are going to be so calm about it," she grumbled. "You and the captain, Mrs. Adler! Certainly you can spare some heat for that topic." A sly smile pulled at her lips. "You were certainly sparing it when I arrived."

"Stop that," Lily said again. "If you cannot be serious, I shan't answer your questions."

"I cannot," Ofelia said, a laugh bursting out. "You must know how long I've been hoping for just such a development."

"Ofelia," Lily protested.

"Oh, very well," Ofelia sighed, slouching down in her chair and blowing out a resigned breath. She would not have been so informal had anyone else been in the room. "I shall be serious." She sat up straight again. "However did it happen?"

"I think it began the night he was shot," Lily said quietly.

That made Ofelia grow sober for a moment, but she shook her head. "I think it began long before that, Mrs. Adler."

"Well, it was realized then, in any case," Lily said, her eyes fixed on her hands as she tried without success not to remember that night. "Or at least it was for me. But I thought nothing would come of it. The captain and I have been such firm friends. Risking that seemed . . ." She lifted her shoulders in a helpless shrug. "And we might still be risking it. He still sees me as a duty in some ways, I believe. That watching out for me is the last service he can provide for his friend." She shook her head. "It complicates things."

"It does not have to," Ofelia said quietly. "Do you love him?"

Lily swallowed. It took some effort to meet her friend's eyes. "I am trying not to think about it."

"Whyever not?" Ofelia demanded. "Has he not said that he loves you?"

"Ofelia, it has been a matter of *days* since we first acted on this impulse. Day, even. I do not know what you suspect has been happening—" Lily caught the smirk pulling at Ofelia's lips and, knowing exactly what her friend suspected had been happening, hurried to continue. "But no such conversation has been even hinted at, much less attempted."

That was the moment Anna entered with two glasses on a tray, along with a decanter of cordial and a plate of cake. Ofelia looked at it in surprise. "You did not want tea for yourself?"

Lily raised her brows. "It has rather a strong scent, does it not? I am content without it."

That earned her another narrow-eyed look from Ofelia, though the young Lady Carroway said nothing in response. Lily, smiling a little and feeling like they were on somewhat more equal footing, took a sip of her drink and served herself a slice of cake. Ofelia refrained from eating anything, watching carefully until the door had closed behind Anna.

"Do you want such a conversation to happen?" she asked quietly, once they were alone again.

The question made Lily feel as though her skin was prickling all over; she was both hesitant and embarrassed by her own hesitation. But at the same time, she was grateful for it. If she was honest with herself, she had known for years that Ofelia had been hopeful of there one day being a match between Lily and Jack. She had never said so out loud, and Lily had always been grateful for her restraint. Now, it was a relief to talk over the matter with someone who knew them both so well, even if part of her would have preferred not to discuss it at all.

"I am not certain," she said, answering Ofelia's question at last. "It is a difficult thing to find the right way to discuss."

"Because of Mr. Adler?" Ofelia asked shrewdly. When Lily nodded, she hesitated, then asked, "Because you are still in love with him?"

"No," Lily said firmly. "Not the way you mean. I will always love him after some fashion, and I hope I always would have, but it is not the same thing."

Ofelia frowned. "What do you mean? From what your friends say of your marriage, you and Mr. Adler were the stuff of poetry."

"I like to think so," Lily said. "But love at nineteen does not always last. Nor at nine-and-twenty, nor nine-and-fifty. From what I can tell, it is far easier to fall in love than to remain that way. The latter seems more a matter of good fortune and determination than anything else."

"Do you believe, then, that you and Mr. Adler would have fallen out of love?" Ofelia asked quietly. She watched Lily with serious, curious eyes, and Lily remembered that the young Lady Carroway had been only nineteen when she herself had wed.

The memory made Lily smile. "I'm sure we would have, from time to time. It would be impossible not to, over the course of one's entire life. But I like to think we would have been determined enough to fall in love again as well, as many times and in as many different ways as we needed to."

"And what of you and the captain?"

"That is . . . complicated," Lily said, turning away. *Complicated* did not begin to describe her feelings about Jack, or her uncertainties about his own feelings for her.

"No, it's not," Ofelia said quietly. "The captain is in love with you."

Lily felt a lump pressing against her throat, and she swallowed rapidly, trying to push it down. "You do not know that."

"Yes, I do." Ofelia said. "Why do you not?"

"Has he told you so?" Lily asked a little waspishly.

"He has not needed to," Ofelia said, looking amused. "I have eyes, you know. And so do you, if you would care to believe the evidence they have presented you with."

Lily wished she had asked for tea after all. Or perhaps something stronger. "Well, whatever anyone's thoughts on the matter, it is hardly the time for us to discuss it. There are somewhat more pressing concerns at hand."

For a moment, Ofelia stared at her. Then her eyes grew wide as she remembered why she had called in the first place. "Oh goodness, yes. Mr. Forrest. I could barely believe my eyes when I read your letter." She leaned forward. "Do you truly think Mr. Clive had nothing to do with his death? As wretched a man as he has proved himself to be?"

"I think there is reason to doubt his guilt," Lily said, glad for the change of subject. "And that is enough to make me curious."

Ofelia let out a slow a breath. "Indeed. If Mr. Clive is innocent, I wish to know it. I remember too well the fear of being thought guilty of a crime that was not mine." Lily nodded; though Ofelia had never ended up in Bow Street's sights in the same way that Henry Clive had, she had once been afraid of just such an outcome. "And if he is guilty," Ofelia added, her expression growing a little grim, like a hunter setting out on the chase. "After what he put us through, I wish to know *that* as well."

"But you are behind the times, Lady Carroway," Lily said. "You've not yet heard what happened last night."

Ofelia leaned forward. "Tell me everything."

★ ★ ★

As much of a relief as it had been to talk about Jack, it was even more of a relief to talk through her thoughts about Mr. Forrest's death and the attack at Vauxhall. Ofelia listened, wide-eyed, to it all.

"Dear God," she breathed, settling back in her chair once Lily had finished. "An attack from beyond the grave. How horrid."

"If it was indeed Mr. Forrest who set it in motion," Lily said grimly. "For all we know, that letter could have been a misdirection."

"We need to know more of Mr. Forrest," Ofelia said, nodding. "You wrote to his commanding officer, did you not?"

"I did. The letter that he sent Mr. Forrest indicated that he took leave from his regiment not long after Mr. Forrest departed. And his family home is not far from London, thank goodness. I am hopeful that he is still there."

"But while you wait to hear from him—and who knows how long that may take—we ought to do what we can here in London," Ofelia insisted. "What are you planning?"

Lily took a sip of her drink. Ofelia was right. She would feel better taking action. "Would you care to stroll to Hyde Park, Lady Carroway? It is not far, I think, from the Albert Gate to Hans Town."

"Do you know, I would love just such a walk," Ofelia said, a gleam of interest entering her eye. "Having heard so much about your new acquaintance there, I find I am desperately eager to meet her."

CHAPTER 21

Miss Forrest, it turned out, had meant what she said the day before. She would not come down once Lily was announced.

The house in Hans Town was undeniably small. But the parlor that Lily and Ofelia were shown into was pretty and filled with light, and if the paper on the walls was old and the curtains a little frayed, they were at least scrupulously clean. It was the sort of home that would have made any number of people feel very fortunate. But it was a far cry from the elegant house on Queen Anne Street in which Miss Forrest had grown up.

"I tell her every day that she deserves better than a shabby little place like this," said Miss Waverly in a confidential tone, sitting across from them in the parlor and pouring tea from a pretty china pot painted with forget-me-nots and ivy. Sarah Forrest had not wanted to receive any visitors, but her cousin and companion had shown no such disinclination. Indeed, when she found out that the wife of a baronet stood on her doorstep, she had practically fallen over herself to show them inside.

"Milk or sugar, Lady Carroway? Both, both—yes, of course—so happy to oblige." Miss Waverly passed Ofelia her cup and saucer. She was a wiry, fidgety woman some decades older than her young charge, elegant to the point of ostentation in her dress and ingratiating in her manner. "I never want Sarah to underrate her own worth, you understand. If there were any justice in the world, a young lady of her beauty and wit would be married into the peerage by now. Milk or sugar, Mrs. Adler? Milk? Sarah should have been an heiress, you know." Miss Waverly paused, brightening suddenly. "And now she is!"

"Though perhaps not under the best of circumstances?" Lily pointed out. Lily was beginning to understand why the late Mr. Forrest had been so determined to summon his brother back to England to serve as guardian for his unwed daughter. Miss Waverly did not seem to have the temperament for guiding her young charge during trying times.

"Oh, to be sure, to be sure," Mrs. Waverly said immediately, nodding in agreement. "God rest him, villain though he was. But now Sarah shall have the best there is." She sighed contentedly. "And I shall have it with her, you know. She is such a dear, affectionate thing."

Lily exchanged a quick glance with Ofelia. It was just the sort of opening they needed.

Ofelia held her cup in her lap—she had yet to take a single sip— and gave her brightest smile. "She certainly does seem so, and it is to her credit. Though I must confess I have heard a rumor or two," she added, lowering her voice to the same confidential level that Miss Waverly had used, "that she is so generous in her affection that she has not always bestowed it wisely. And not only as concerns this scoundrel, Mr. Clive."

Miss Waverly sighed, shaking her head and stirring her tea with a morose air. "Too true, too true, Lady Carroway. I suppose you heard about that good-for-nothing Mr. Faversham? Well, and I will always say he was terribly handsome, and no wonder poor dear Sarah falling in love with him and saying yes when he proposed, but her father would not give his consent on account of Mr. Faversham being in his cups too much for Mr. Forrest's liking. Dear me, that man was a drunkard, I cannot deny it, and such a shame, for he was so well-looking you would not believe, but her father did say he could not countenance his daughter marrying a drunkard."

Miss Waverly paused for breath at last, but Lily was too caught off guard by the outpouring of personal information—to two strangers, no less—to think of anything to say in response. Luckily, Ofelia was quicker to reply.

"How terrible for poor Miss Forrest. She must have suffered dreadfully."

"Thank you, yes, indeed she did, my lady. How she did suffer! She is such a sensitive soul. She loved her father too well to gainsay him, but she loved Mr. Faversham too well to give him up." Miss Waverly shook her head, her fingers tapping restlessly against her teacup. "I was near to encouraging her to elope with him, for what could her father do, once they were married? They would have made a lovely couple, for you've seen my dear Sarah—or at least you have, Mrs. Adler—and I'm sure but what you've told Lady Carroway so. And as I've said Mr. Faversham was so handsome, and he had such a pretty little property in Sussex that I was all aflutter to see. Poor Sarah, it was such a hard time for her!"

By this point, even Ofelia looked a little dazed. "How did it come to an end?"

"Oh, well." Miss Waverly sighed, eagerly refilling their cups, though Ofelia's was still untouched and Lily had drunk only a few sips. "Her father at last convinced them that he would never give his consent, and Miss Forrest was too young then to marry without it. So Mr. Faversham said they would need to part, and I did cry so to see him leave that last day, for it was I who introduced them, you know, after my dear friend Mary Hopper introduced him to me. He said he was looking for a wife, and dear Sarah has always so longed to marry and set up her own household, so I thought, what could be better? But alas, it was not to be."

Lily found herself wondering how Mr. Forrest had allowed such a terrible influence as Miss Waverly to remain in his daughter's life. But perhaps he thought her merely silly and indiscreet, and hoped that his daughter would outgrow her influence. No doubt, the business with Mr. Faversham had taught him otherwise. She longed to see his correspondence to know if that was when he had at last attempted a reconciliation with his brother.

Miss Waverly, not noticing or not understanding the flabbergasted regard of her audience, sighed. "Dear Sarah was so melancholy after he left, I was terribly worried for her."

"Did she meet Mr. Clive before or after she lost her father?" Lily asked curiously.

"After." Miss Waverly plucked absently at the layers of ruffles on her gown and sighed. "He was ever so smitten with her. Sarah was a little cool with him at first—well, and no wonder, of course, after how things ended with Mr. Faversham. But he was such a comfort to her, eventually they became inseparable."

Miss Waverly fell silent at last, glancing upward to where, presumably, Miss Forrest had sequestered herself in her bedroom. Lily found she couldn't blame the girl for that. Miss Waverly was not the sort of companion she would have chosen were she the one nursing a broken heart.

Or if she had a significant secret to keep from her talkative cousin's notice.

Miss Waverly shook her head. "Poor thing, she does take things so to heart. After she ended things with Mr. Clive—such a charming man I thought him—I could hear her sobbing all night long. I wonder if she will ever recover or if this is the start of her decline."

Lily downed the rest of her tea in a single fortifying gulp. At her side, Ofelia stared into her untouched cup as though wishing it were something stronger.

Miss Waverly sighed dreamily. "An heiress in decline is such a romantic thing, is it not?" she said. She looked almost enchanted by the prospect.

It took some doing to extract themselves from Miss Waverly's solicitous insistence that they stay for another cup of tea or some cake, but at last they were outside once more. Without needing to exchange a word, they set off briskly, eager to put several blocks between themselves and Miss Forrest's garrulous cousin.

"Dear God," Ofelia muttered at last, when they were nearly back to Hyde Park. The late afternoon promenade hour was at hand, and the streets were as thronged with carriages as the paths were with pedestrians, all out in their finest to see and be seen. They had to nod at half a dozen acquaintances between them before they reached the park's gate.

"Indeed," Lily said.

"Perhaps Miss Forrest was a party to her uncle's death because she decided Newgate was the only way to escape her companion's company."

"Ofelia, that is a dreadful thing to say," Lily chided her while she tried not to laugh. "But heaven above, have you ever met such a woman before? Miss Forrest is not what I would consider the most discerning or intelligent of young ladies, but even she does not deserve that."

"No one does," Ofelia said fervently. "Can you imagine saying such things to strangers?"

Lily looped her arm through Ofelia's, gently reminding her friend to restrain her indignation. It was entirely understandable, but they did not want to attract any undue attention from the other promenaders.

"It was lucky for us, at least, that she was so indiscreet," she pointed out.

"Really?" Ofelia gave her a skeptical look. "Did you gather anything useful from that flood of gossip?"

"Two things," Lily said. "The first is that Mr. Clive was likely telling the truth when he said the suspicions about Mr. Forrest's conduct came from Miss Forrest herself, not from him. No doubt she was encouraged in such thinking by her cousin."

"And the second?"

"It seems likely that the business with Mr. Faversham was what made the late Mr. Forrest ask his brother to come home and serve as his daughter's guardian. And it occurs to me that changing his will might have been the price of such an arrangement." Lily paused, considering. "Or it could be the reason that Mr. Martin Forrest refused his consent to his niece's next engagement, having heard in great detail about her poor choice the first time."

"But neither of those explains why he would hire someone to attack Captain Hartley."

Lily sighed as they left the park. The bustle of Mayfair passed around her: the drivers of delivery carts navigating the narrow streets, giving way to a lady's elegant landeau and a gentleman on horseback; a governess herding a set of mischievous-looking twins toward the park for their daily exercise; servants with baskets and parcels going in and out of the houses; a young lady and a gentleman walking side by side with a decorous distance still between them—not engaged, then, Lily noted in the back of her mind—while their chaperone followed a few steps behind, a satisfied smile on her face.

"No," she said quietly. "It does not. Nor do they explain how Mr. Forrest himself ended up dead."

★ ★ ★

Lily was still thinking about Miss Waverly, and everything she had shared about Miss Forrest's unwise past, as she and Anna returned from the linen draper's on Bond Street the next day. With the lace that Lily had bought from Mrs. Carver and a few yards of fabric, Anna planned to alter one of Lily's day dresses from two seasons before.

The post was waiting on the hall table as Lily laid off her coat and hat. One letter, in particular, caught her eye. The bold, messy hand was the only one on the table that she didn't recognize. A prickle of anticipation made its way down her spine.

Upstairs, having tossed her hat and gloves aside on the counterpane, that letter was the one she opened first, looking immediately to the signature to see who had sent it.

Her hope had been correct: it was from Colonel Richard Halliday, formerly the commanding officer of the Twelfth Light Dragoons and now, it seemed, on half-pay leave from the army.

The first two paragraphs from the colonel were all politeness, expressing his regret at hearing of the death of Mr. Forrest and his eagerness to be of service in any inquiries that needed to be made.

The third paragraph, however, was what made Lily's quick-moving eye slow, and she sat up straighter as she read it through.

I received Mr. Forrest here at Highwood a short time ago, and the thought that less than a month later some blackguard ended his life defies my comprehension. But saddened though I am by the loss, I confess I am not so shocked as I should be. It seems the men of my regiment were, much to my sorrow, better served in war than in peace. Mr. Forrest's is the second such death I have heard of in as many months—though the only one, I hasten to add, that has been an act of foul play rather than tragic accident.

Your concern in the matter, though, does you credit, and I would be honored to answer any questions you may have. But I must ask your indulgence, having recently been ill. If you would be so kind as to take the exertion of travel upon yourself, it would be my pleasure to welcome you to my home in Gravesend any day you might wish to visit, and it is my hope that the rigors of a journey from London would not be too arduous to prevent you from coming hence and returning to your home within the day.

I am, yours etc.,
R. Halliday, Col.

Lily had to read it through twice to make sure she had not mistaken its meaning. Then she stood and went to the bellpull to ring for Anna.

If she was to travel to Gravesend tomorrow, she had preparations to make.

Chapter 22

The village of Gravesend was a dispiriting place on a rainy spring day, especially after an early morning and four hours traveling post. But the proprietor of the coaching inn where they alighted was more than happy to send a servant to the colonel's home just outside town while Lily and Jack warmed themselves before the fire in a private room, with a glass of wine each. Gravesend was one of the coaching stops between London and a handful of destinations, so he was well accustomed to such travelers and assured them that they would have no trouble making the return journey to London that afternoon.

"Most days there are five coaches or more that pass through here to London, whether coming from Canterbury or Dover or some such. But I'll advise you to leave no later than four in the evening, else it'll be dark when you're crossing Blackheath."

"Are there still highwaymen prowling the area, then?" Jack asked, handing Lily her glass. He tried not to frown when his fingers brushed against hers and she pulled her hand away quickly. Likely she was worried about what impression they might give.

Her eyes were on the innkeeper, after all. "I thought they were only found in romantic poems these days," she said, smiling a little.

The innkeeper shook his head. "Not highwaymen no more, thanks be. But I've heard tell of robbers, from time to time, though usually they trouble folks traveling alone and not those going by post. Too many common soldiers, I think, returned from France with families to feed and no trade to rely on other than soldiering." He shook his head. "You never know what you might find on the Heath. But if'n you find yourselves in need of lodging, I can certainly accommodate."

"Do you think he is telling the truth?" Lily asked once the innkeeper had stirred up the fire and left them to themselves. "Or is he simply trying to fill his empty rooms for the night?"

Jack had instantly offered his escort when she told him she needed to travel to Gravesend, knowing that Lily did not keep her own horses and that his curricle would make quick work of the drive, which could stretch over three hours in a heavier vehicle. But as soon as the words were spoken, he had wondered if it was a good idea. The man who had attacked him was locked up, and Martin Forrest was dead. Likely, being alone and in the open with him would not be dangerous. But he could not be certain, and he hated being uncertain when it came to the safety of those he cared for.

And then there were all the things currently left unsaid between them. With so much else to worry and puzzle over, it was not the time for either of them to be distracted or discomfited by the intimacy of a long drive alone.

But Lily had accepted, which meant he could not take the offer back. Fortunately, the day proved rainy, forcing them to travel post instead of taking his curricle. It had been crowded with sleepy passengers, all with hot bricks wrapped in toweling at their feet, and there had been neither awkwardness nor danger in the ride.

Now, Jack sipped his drink, frowning a little. "Could be the latter," he replied in answer to her question. "But I would not discount the tale entirely. It is a nearly impossible thing to support a family on half pay. An officer might sell his commission and regain the money he spent to buy it."

"As Mr. Forrest did," Lily put in, nodding.

"Indeed. But an infantryman has no such funds with which to begin anew." Jack shook his head. Officers in the navy did not purchase their commission in the same way as those in the army, instead joining in their youth, as he had, and rising in rank over time. But the problem of money once you left was the same, especially for those who had not come from families of means. During his captaincy, Jack had amassed a respectable fortune from the capture of enemy ships, giving him plenty to live on after leaving His Majesty's service. But many, even among his fellow officers, were not so lucky. "And," he added, staring into the fire, "it can be a hard thing for a man to return from war and be confronted with the reality of the life he left behind. Especially if that life includes a wife or children he's not seen in years."

"Or a niece?" Lily suggested.

"Or perhaps a niece," Jack agreed.

Lily looked as though she wanted to say something but hesitated for a long moment before she spoke. "Was it hard for you?" she asked at last. "To come home?"

Jack considered his words. It had been hard, and it still was, to leave behind the life he had known since he was fourteen. But he did not want her to think he regretted his choice. "It has been an adjustment and will continue to be for some time, I've no doubt. But I had the advantage, in the navy, of not spending so many months at a time engaged in France. We are sent all over in a way that the army is not. And I had been ashore from time to time, these past years, particularly when my ship was in need of repairs." He shook his head. "I do miss it. It was my life for so long that in some ways I must discover anew who I am without it."

"I know the sensation," Lily said quietly.

He nodded, though the words made his chest tighten a little. She was talking about Freddy, he knew, and the struggle it had been to rebuild her life after his death. And it was hard, now, to look at her and think of his friend without a ripple of guilt and unease.

Lily, her eyes on the fire, did not seem to notice his discomfort. Instead, she turned to him and said gently, "I've no doubt you will discover that you are much the same person you have always been. Though you may need some new pursuit to keep you occupied."

"A pursuit other than assisting with searching the houses of strangers or the unraveling of crimes?" he asked wryly, pushing aside thoughts of Freddy. Lily smiled and shook her head, though clearly not in disagreement. "Fortunately," Jack added, "I also happen to be very fond of the people I have come home to. It makes a great deal of difference."

He had not meant it to be a declaration, but as soon as the words had been uttered, he realized that they very nearly were. Lily stared at him, her lips parting as her smile faded into an uncertain, hopeful look. But she did not speak, and Jack's own smile grew.

"It is not every day I have the opportunity to render you speechless," he murmured. When she scowled at him and opened her mouth to reply, he laughed. "No, pray, do not spoil it. Who knows if it will ever happen again."

"You are a dreadful man," Lily managed at last, narrowing her eyes.

"I am," he agreed, turning back to the fire. "But I believe you like me anyway."

Lily took a deep breath. "I do," she whispered.

He would have reached for her then, but the door opened, and he had to keep his hands in his lap. Anna, who had accompanied them for propriety's sake—and in case they had to stay overnight—poked her head in.

"Begging your pardon for interrupting, Mrs. Adler, sir, but Colonel Halliday sent back his own carriage for you with the inn's servant. Are you ready to depart?"

★ ★ ★

Highwood, the colonel's home, was an elegant stone house some way out of the village. It was not overly large, but it was well built and situated on top of a pretty hill where it could command an impressive view of the country on one side and the River Thames in the distance on the other. As they were shown in, Lily could hear the barking of hounds and the shriek of children in the distance.

"Pray excuse the noise," Colonel Halliday said as they were shown into the parlor. "My son and his family are visiting, and the children have discovered that my best pointer just had puppies. You can, I am sure, imagine their delight. A pleasure to meet you, Mrs. Adler."

"You are kind to receive us, sir," Lily said, once she had introduced Jack and they had both been offered sherry and tea. "I know you wrote that you had been unwell of late."

Though he was a broad man, with well-muscled shoulders and a scar above his eye that attested to his career, his cheeks were pale and even a little gaunt, and he had a heavy blanket around his shoulders. But he looked like he was in good spirits, and he had risen to greet them without any sign of difficulty.

"You are generous in your concern, but it was a short affliction."

His hands shook a little as he lifted his glass, and Lily wondered if the illness had been more serious than he wanted to say. But it would have been rude to inquire further or to insist that the colonel was in fact not well enough to receive visitors.

"Well, fortunately, our inquiries are of a limited nature, so I think we will not take up too much of your time," Jack said pleasantly.

And fortunately, though Lily did not say so out loud, she had instructed Anna to discreetly find out what she could in the servants' hall about the visit that Colonel Halliday had mentioned in his letter. If there was anything odd about Martin Forrest or his behavior, the servants in the house would have noticed and remembered.

Lily took a sip of her tea, glancing at Jack to let him know that he should begin. He nodded and leaned forward. "I understand you knew Mr. Forrest for some years. You have our condolences, sir, on the loss of your young officer."

"He served under me for half a decade," Colonel Halliday said, shaking his head. "A terrible loss. I am glad to know these new constables are taking the death seriously. Though I confess some surprise that you are the one asking me questions, sir, and not they. And that your charming companion"—he nodded his head politely toward Lily—"was the one who wrote me." His voice was polite but firm, and his meaning was clear: he would not continue until he understood on whose behalf they were asking questions, and why.

Lily had anticipated just such a hesitation, and she had been deliberately vague in the letter in the letter she had written him, to allow her time to decide how much she wanted to tell him.

Now that she was sitting face to face with him, his skeptical tone when he mentioned the new constables made her think that Mr. Page had been correct. Leading with her connection to Bow Street was not the wisest choice.

"I knew Mr. Forrest through his niece," Lily said, stirring her tea. "By any chance, did Mr. Forrest make you acquainted with the circumstances of his selling his commission and returning to England?"

"His brother's death, you mean?"

"Exactly that," Lily said briskly as she set down her spoon. "Miss Forrest did not know her uncle well, having never met him until he returned to England. But given the manner of his death, she . . ." Lily paused to consider her words carefully. "She naturally has concerns. I thought learning more about him could help lay those concerns to rest."

Out of the corner of her eye, Lily saw Jack's lips press tightly together, holding back a smile at her careful deployment of the truth. Strictly speaking, nothing she had said was a lie. But it was entirely misleading. She didn't like deceiving a man who, so far as she could tell, was perfectly good-natured and deserved no such dishonestly from her. But she needed answers.

For more than one reason, now. She kept her eyes firmly on the colonel, not wanting to look at Jack or remember the shock of the attack at Vauxhall.

"Captain Hartley is an old friend and was kind enough to bear me company today," she finished, inclining her head toward Jack. "Is there anything you can tell us about Mr. Forrest that might help us understand what happened to him? Did he have any . . ." Lily lifted her shoulders in the pretense of a helpless shrug. "Any enemies?"

"If Miss Forrest is worried the same thing might happen to her, you may assure her she is in no danger from that quarter," the colonel said firmly, pouring himself another glass of sherry. "A top-off, Captain? Very good, very good. No, indeed, Mrs. Adler, I cannot say he had a single enemy, aside from the Frenchies, of course." He chuckled a little at his joke, then grimaced, as though realizing it was not entirely in good taste. "Beg pardon. But no, I can only think that what happened to him must have been the veriest chance. A burglar perhaps, discovered at the wrong moment? There is no one I can think of who would wish Martin Forrest harm."

"Miss Forrest will be relieved to hear it, I am sure," Lily said.

"And what did you think of Mr. Martin Forrest?" Jack asked curiously, turning his glass in his fingers, where it rested on the arm of his chair. His posture was easy, but Lily could tell he was watching the colonel closely. "Not as a soldier, you understand, but as a person. Did you enjoy his company?"

"Forrest?" Colonel Halliday smiled, looking a little sad. "I never met a more pleasing man. Well-liked by all, so far as I know. Always had a good word for his fellows, and willing to swap a tale with any man, no matter his rank." He nodded to Jack. "I am sure you know the sort I mean, sir. It can be rare in an officer, to be so easy with the men. But it is a quality I greatly admire when I see it."

Lily felt a small stirring of pride at the colonel's words; it was a quality that Jack had as well. She wondered a little at the description of Mr. Forrest as a pleasing man; she would not have described the man she had encountered—nor the man happy to cheat in Madame du Varnier's faro house—in such terms. But perhaps what was pleasing in a soldier's camp was different.

Or perhaps he had shown a different side when he was in the company of his commanding officer.

"I think you wrote in your letter that you saw him recently?" Lily asked.

"Oh, indeed." The colonel smiled a little sheepishly. "Well, he visited, you understand. But I was actually from home when he called. He left a very kind note saying he would come again another day, along with a bottle of French brandy, which all my men knew I have a weakness for—though between us, it had gone off, and my butler had to pour most of it out." He chuckled. "But I appreciated the thought. He was always a friendly fellow."

By then, Jack was frowning too. "A gentleman in all respects?"

"Oh, indeed. And he was well respected by his fellow officers, temperate and moral—almost too much, sometimes. I suppose that if

I were to name any fault in his character, it would be his moralizing streak. He had a such strong sense of what was right and what was owed that it could grate when he got in one of his moods. No doubt that contributed to his estrangement from his brother," he added. "He could hold a grudge, could our captain."

"He shared the story of his family troubles, then?" Lily asked.

"That he did. With a great many people." Halliday chuckled, an almost mischievous gleam in his eyes. There was color in his cheeks now, as though the discussion were doing him some good. "I know what you are thinking: hardly the discretion one would expect of a gentleman, eh? But everyone must be allowed a flaw, I suppose." He chuckled again. "Forrest made no secret of the circumstances. Most of the other officers were eager to get home when they could, you see. But he always declared he should never set foot on English soil again until his brother invited him. Well, and his brother did invite him in the end, did he not?" The colonel sighed, and his shoulders slumped a little, making him look like an invalid once again. "Though that ended badly for him, as it turned out. It would have been better, perhaps, had he stayed in France."

Lily set down her cup. "Forgive me if this is an indelicate inquiry, but you mentioned in your letter that Mr. Forrest's was not the only death among the men in your regiment after returning to England. Will you tell us what has happened?"

The colonel's heavy, bushy brows drew into a frown, and he fidgeted with the fringe of the blanket that was wrapped round him. "Well, dear lady, it is the oddest, saddest thing. But I would almost fear that my regiment had been cursed, were I a man who believed in such things."

Jack and Lily exchanged a look, and Lily felt her heart speeding up. The colonel had said he believed Mr. Forrest's death to be a random misfortune. But if other men to whom he was connected had also recently died . . .

Perhaps there was something else going on.

The colonel, not noticing the silent interplay between his two guests, was still talking. "The rest of my men are on the Continent, you see—I was home for a short duration when I fell ill, so I've not been able to rejoin them. But Forrest was not the only one who left entirely in recent months. There was one other man who returned to England, and he"—the colonel shook his head—"he has also died. Two of my men, dead where they should have been safe. My son says that I nearly did too, though I do not think this indisposition has been so bad as all that. Just a damned—begging your pardon, Mrs. Adler—a dashed inconvenience."

He said it with a chuckle. But Lily, glancing at the tremor in his hands, wondered again if he had been in more danger than he wanted to admit.

"Was the other man's death at all similar to Mr. Forrest's?" Jack asked gravely.

The colonel shook his head emphatically. "No indeed. No burglaries or stabbing. Just a natural tragedy that befell our regiment's doctor." He sighed and took a sip of his tea. "I've been doing what I can to help out his widow and children," he added with a sad smile. "Though to my regret, I've not been able to visit in person since I fell ill."

"I am sure they are grateful for it," Jack said in a quiet voice. "It is a hard thing when a wife and children are left behind and must find a way to support themselves. And a tragedy, indeed, any time a man makes it back from the battlefield only to die in his own home."

"That it is, my boy." Colonel Halliday sighed again. "We all survived the war, but life back in England seems determined to get some of us."

"Well, we are grateful that it did not get you," Lily said, rising. Jack, following her lead, did as well. "And grateful that you were willing to share a few moments of your time with us. But we've no wish to keep you from your family any longer."

She had been listening to the echo of small feet tromping down the stairs as the colonel spoke, and now they could all hear them rushing by in the hallway. The sound made Halliday smile. "Well, curse or bad luck or whatever it is, it will have to work harder to get me, to be sure. I've spent too long away from these little ones as it is." He levered himself out of his chair. "Can I persuade you to stay for a little luncheon, at least? It is not a short trip back to town."

"You are very kind," Lily replied. "We will not trespass upon your hospitality any longer, but I wonder if I might trouble you for one more thing?"

"Name it," he replied gallantly, bowing.

"Would you write down the name and direction of the doctor who died? I think perhaps Miss Forrest will rest easier once I can show her that all this terrible business is just a string of unfortunate coincidences."

"Of course, of course. Anything to set the heart of a young lady at ease." The colonel went to the writing table under the windows, where pen and ink rested on the blotter next to a crisp stack of writing paper. He was silent for a moment as he jotted down the information she had asked for. When he straightened up to hand her the paper, he shook his head. "I feel for her, truly. What a pity. What a waste of a promising man's life. Well and well. A moment, if you will, and I shall have the carriage brought round to convey you back to the village."

★ ★ ★

Jack waited until they had said their farewells and were in the carriage once more, with Anna perched outside with the driver, to voice what was on both their minds.

"It is hard to make more than a coincidence out of only two deaths," he said. "Particularly if, as the colonel says, there was nothing out of the ordinary about the first."

Lily nodded, staring out the window as the watery landscape swayed past, the scattered houses clustering slowly closer together as they drew nearer to the village and the coaching inn. "No, the odder thing was the colonel's description of Mr. Forrest himself. I find it hard to believe that the man we encountered could be described either as moral or temperate."

"But the description of his holding a grudge felt all too apt," Jack pointed out. "He concealed it from his brother, it seems, but he forced his niece to bear the brunt of it." He shook his head. "But people often show a different face when their circumstances change. He could have easily behaved one way on the battlefield—presenting his most virtuous, heroic self—but given into his baser instincts once he had the means and opportunity to do so."

Lily nodded. "Many men have done as much."

"And women?" Jack asked good-humoredly.

That made her smile, though the expression was grim. "And women. God knows my sex holds no monopoly on virtue." She glanced down at the paper held in her gloved hands. "A captain and the regiment's doctor. They do not have much, other than their time in France, to link them together, do they?"

Jack shrugged. "The doctor would have seen everyone, no doubt, at one time or another. But if the colonel himself sees no connection between the deaths . . ." He sighed.

"Well, there is one other thing," Lily said, once more looking over the note. "Colonel Halliday was kind enough to write down the direction for this Dr. Ivey. And it seems both men—Ivey and Forrest—were living in London when they died." Lily looked up. "Do you suppose it is worth looking into the matter? Just to be certain?"

Jack tapped his fingers against the window in a slow rhythm, looking thoughtful. "Anything may be worth an inquiry. And if there is a connection, I am confident"—a small smile accompanying his words—"that we are determined enough to find it out."

CHAPTER 23

They had time enough, before the next post chaise arrived, to dine at the inn, a meal in which they discussed very little of consequence, as they were seated in the public room. Lily had spent the whole day waiting for a feeling of awkwardness to arise when they were together, now that things between them had changed so drastically but uncertainly. But it was a comfortable break from the thoughts of murder and blackmail that had occupied her for the past days.

When the post chaise arrived, it was crowded with passengers. Lily and Anna were able to ride inside, but Jack sighed and joined those riding on the outer seats while the postboys mounted their new lead horses. After the next change, enough passengers disembarked that Jack was able to join them inside, but there were still too many others for them to discuss what they had learned—or to say much of anything at all, as one gentleman in the corner fell asleep and snored so loudly that he drowned out all other conversations.

By the time they returned to London, Lily was exhausted from bouncing around in the post coach for half the day, and Jack had an evening engagement that he could not beg off.

"It is dinner with my old patron, Admiral Folks," he said with a grimace as they clattered in a hack carriage back to Half Moon Street. "He is still not easy with my decision to leave His Majesty's Navy, and requires some placating."

Lily nodded, swallowing back a yawn. Beside her, Anna swayed against the window, her eyes half closed with fatigue, even though it was only seven o'clock in the evening. "Of course you must see him," Lily said. "And do give him my regards."

Once home, she asked for hot baths for both herself and Anna, and nearly fell asleep in hers. She had her supper before the fire in her room, drowsing while her hair dried until Anna came to help her prepare for bed. It was not until she was seated at her dressing table and Anna was pulling out the curling rags to set her hair for the night that Lily had a chance to ask whether her maid had learned anything of interest while they were at Highwood.

"The footman who answered the door when Mr. Forrest called said he looked a very well-to-do gentleman," Anna said as she brushed out Lily's damp hair. "He told Mr. Forrest he'd just missed the colonel, as his son had taken him on a drive for some fresh air only a few minutes before. But when he heard the colonel had been sick, Mr. Forrest said he'd visit another time."

"And did they say whether he did anything while he was there?"

Anna wrapped a lock of hair neatly around a strip of muslin and tied it in place, her fingers moving quickly through the familiar motions. "Nothing particular. He only spoke to the footman, who didn't think too highly of him."

That caught Lily by surprise. "Did he say why? Colonel Halliday seemed to consider Mr. Forrest a personable sort of gentleman." But perhaps that indicated that he did, indeed, behave differently around his fellow officers than around those he considered his inferiors.

"Because of the wine. Mr. Forrest had brought some kind of wine the colonel likes, though I can't remember what it was, as a gift. But apparently it had gone sour or some such, and it made the colonel even sicker when he had some." Anna shook her head as she brushed out another section of hair. "The footman thought it a terribly poor gift, and I must say I agree. Though I suppose you can't know what condition a bottle of wine is in before you uncork it."

Lily nodded slowly, turning that over in her mind. "Did they say anything about the colonel himself?" she asked. "He seemed a genial sort of man, but one never knows."

"Those in service do," Anna said firmly, winding Lily's hair around another curling rag as she spoke. "They had only good things to say about him. Near everyone I talked to said how liberal a gentleman he is, and they were all glad he's on the mend."

"What was the nature of his illness?" Lily asked curiously.

"An indisposition of the stomach," Anna said delicately, tying off the strip of muslin. Lily grimaced at her reflection; sleeping with the curling rags in was never comfortable. "He'd been unwell since Mr. Halliday and the children arrived a month ago. The head housemaid thinks the children carried some infection into the household, as they often do, because the colonel wasn't the only one who was indisposed. But he was the worst—she told me the night he was most ill, they were sure he was going to die. After that he did begin to mend, though it's been a slow thing." She shook her head. "And they said he was always such a hale, vigorous man before."

"A strange thing, then," Lily said thoughtfully.

On the surface, Colonel Halliday's health didn't seem to have anything to do with her—her business began and ended with Mr. Forrest. But it was curious, and she had learned to pay attention to curious things.

★ ★ ★

Simon Page had been reassigned, in the past few years, to the magistrate's court at Bow Street. But as a senior constable, he was still entitled to his own office, and it was the same tidy, book-filled sort of space as the one where Lily had first stood across from him to insist that he take her seriously.

He had, eventually. And she hadn't needed to convince him since. When she handed over the name and direction of the doctor from the Twelfth Light Dragoons who had died, he had taken it without question.

"I think you were right to ask that I handle the colonel," Lily said, seated across the desk from him as she watched him read. "He did not say as much, but I had the impression that he was not enamored of London's constabulary. But he was terribly eager to soothe what he assumed were the worries of Miss Forrest."

Simon Page snorted. "I hope you did not lie to him too egregiously."

Lily smile serenely. "Strictly speaking, I did not lie to him at all." She grew quiet then, her mind back on the conversation with the colonel and what Anna had learned from his servants.

Mr. Page was silent and thoughtful as well, staring out the window in a distracted manner. But at last he seemed to rouse himself and asked whether it was Forrest or Ivey who was occupying her thoughts.

Lily shook her head. "I am thinking of Colonel Halliday," she said with some reluctance. "And of Mr. Forrest's gift to him. It seems . . ." She shrugged, feeling a little foolish. "The coincidence is too odd for my liking."

"You think there was something wrong with the brandy," Mr. Page said quietly. It was not quite a question.

"Could there not have been? My maid said that, according to the servants, he was dreadfully ill after having some."

"But by all accounts, Mr. Forrest got on well with his commanding officer, and Colonel Halliday spoke glowingly of him to you," Mr. Page pointed out. "Why would he then try to harm the colonel?"

"I cannot help recalling," Lily said slowly, "that Colonel Halliday said that he never saw the person who paid him the visit. Which means we have no way of knowing whether it was indeed Mr. Forrest who gave him the brandy. It could have been someone else entirely who wished the colonel harm."

"You think it was the same person who killed Mr. Forrest himself?"

Lily glanced at him. "I know it sounds farfetched. The colonel had been sick for some time before the brandy arrived. His illness could have been a coincidence that had nothing to do with anything he ate or drank."

Simon sighed. "Would that there was a way to detect a poison hiding in a bottle or meal. But alas, our scientists have not yet gained such insight."

"Do you think they could?" Lily asked in disbelief, distracted for a moment from her thoughts about the colonel.

Mr. Page regarded her in equal surprise. "There are doctors on the Continent who are investigating that very possibility. They've already begun looking for a means to test for dangerous substances, such as arsenic, within the human body after death. I'd have thought," he added, "that a woman of your interests would have kept abreast of such developments."

"I had no idea," Lily said, shaking her head. "It sounds rather gruesome. I cannot imagine that, whatever method they are devising, it would be pleasant." When the constable only stared down at the paper in his hand, not replying, she cleared her throat. "Mr. Page?"

He jumped a little, blinking at her. "My apologies. You were saying?"

"Only that I cannot imagine that developing a method for detecting poisons in a human body would be pleasant."

"It isn't. And yes, it does sound fantastical. But I'm convinced that one day it will be a reality." Mr. Page shook his head. "What a remarkable day that will be."

"Well, until then, you and your fellow constables will continue as you can," Lily said briskly. "Will we need to pay Dr. Ivey's family a visit, do you think?" When he didn't answer right away, she frowned. "Mr. Page?"

He jumped again. "Yes? My apologies, what were you saying?"

"What is occupying your thoughts today, sir?" Lily asked, worried. "You've not been your usual self."

"Nothing at all," he said a little defensively, drawing himself up, though the effect was spoiled as his elbow knocked into a stack of books with unwonted clumsiness and sent them tumbling to the floor. He sighed as he righted them, then met her eyes. "It's the children."

Lily felt a flare of worry in her chest. "Did something happen to them?"

"They've both been unwell," he said, grimacing. "I know children can fall ill suddenly, and they often recover just as quickly. But their parents' last illness was so sudden, and, well . . ." It was a surprising admission from the stoic constable, and he looked embarrassed to have told it to her.

But Lily only nodded. "It is hard not to worry," she said quietly. "No matter how you tell yourself otherwise. For a year after Mr. Adler died, I thought my heart would give out any time someone I knew took ill. I always expected the worst." She hesitated a moment, then reached out to give his hand a brisk pat.

He looked surprised by the touch but did not draw away. "Thank you, Mrs. Adler. I am sure all will be well. We hope the infection will run its course in a few days. Likely they just had too many sweets and made themselves ill."

"I hope you will let me know if they need anything," she said. "And in the meantime, I hope you will allow me to be the one to call on Dr. Ivey's widow so you can concentrate on your family."

He shook his head. "There is no need to trouble yourself. I can send Mr. Hurst to the War Office to make inquiries. They should have records of his death there. And if something nefarious is going on, I've no wish for you to put yourself in its path accidentally." The look he gave her was displeased. "Again. I'm already uneasy that you went to Gravesend without telling me. You were supposed to write a letter only."

"As you like," Lily said diffidently. She let the silence settle for a moment, then asked offhandedly, "Would you have the desk clerk be good enough to summon a carriage for me? I must call on Lady Carroway this afternoon, and the weather is not fine enough for walking."

Mr. Page's gaze had already returned to the window, and he looked a little startled by the request. But he still nodded. "Certainly. I hope you will give my regards to her ladyship?"

"Of course," Lily said demurely, folding her hands in her lap, grateful, for the moment, for his distraction. If he had been thinking clearly, he would have been more firm in telling her not to visit Mrs. Ivey.

And he would have remembered that Ofelia Carroway was exactly the person she would call on if she wanted to take matters into her own hands.

CHAPTER 24

Dr. Ivey's address in Hans Town was only a few blocks from Sarah Forrest's new home. Lily frowned over the coincidence as she climbed down from the Carroways' comfortable carriage.

Ofelia regarded the black muslin on the door warily. "How long has it been since he . . ."

Lily shook her head. "I do not know. But perhaps she will be receiving visitors."

Mrs. Ivey was surprised by her unexpected guests, but when they mentioned conveying the regards of Colonel Halliday, she was impeccably gracious about inviting them in. Lily took some liberty with the message, which she had not been charged with in the first place, expanding on the colonel's regret that he had been unable to visit in person and his hope that he could assist Mrs. Ivey and her children in whatever way they needed.

"He is too good," Mrs. Ivey murmured, her voice deep with sorrow, though her eyes remained dry. "And he has been so kind these past months. It is thanks to his generosity that I was able to hire a governess to teach my younger children this spring, rather than sending them away to school." She sighed. "I could not bear for them to be away from London since . . ."

"It must have been a terrible shock," Lily said gently. "Colonel Halliday spoke so highly of your husband."

In spite of her grief, that made Mrs. Ivey smile. "I think most people could hardly help speaking well of George. He was a terribly kind man. Always had sweets in his pockets for the children in the neighborhood. And once a mouse as well." When she saw the curious looks that prompted, her smile grew. "He found a cat menacing it and adopted it. He used to let it sit on his shoulder, and he would feed it corn to make his patients laugh so they wouldn't be so nervous about whatever brought them to see him."

"He sounds like a tender-hearted person," Ofelia put in.

"He was." Mrs. Ivey's face fell. "Too tender-hearted, I think, to be a battlefield surgeon. Not that he was not competent. He did whatever he needed to do—even got a commendation," she added proudly, pointing to a framed letter that hung on the chimney breast. "He wanted to serve his king and his country, but he was never the same after he returned."

Lily waited until the widow found her handkerchief and wiped her eyes to continue. "In what way was he not the same?"

"He suffered from a complaint of the nerves after he returned from France," Mrs. Ivey said. "He would get nervous attacks—tremors and sweats mostly, but sometimes he said he felt like he was dying, even though he was sitting in our drawing room, looking perfectly well." Her voice dropped. "I think some men get like that after a war. The strain is so hard on them. But they don't like to talk about it."

"That sounds terribly difficult," Ofelia said, her voice trembling a little, and Lily could see tears in her eyes. Ofelia, too, was tender-hearted. "For him, of course, but for you as well."

The look Mrs. Ivey gave her was wide-eyed in its astonishment. "It was," she said, sounding almost grateful to have the chance to say it. "It was hard for me to see him suffer and know I could do nothing for him. And I was angry too, though I did not want to be. Sometimes I wished he had never—" She broke off, swallowing down her words.

"That he had never gone to war?" Lily asked. "It is only natural to feel so, and to say it, Mrs. Ivey. War may be heroic in broadsheet ballads, but it is hell on those who live through it."

Mrs. Ivey nodded, blowing her nose inelegantly into her handkerchief. "Well, and we were luckier than most, I suppose. He was a doctor; he had some sense of what was happening. Mr. Blunt—our apothecary, he lives just up the street—would prepare him a tincture every week, according to George's instructions, to help quiet his nerves when he felt them overpowering him." She fell silent for a moment. "I suppose it stopped working at last, though."

"Can you tell us what happened?" Lily asked gently.

Mrs. Ivey blew her nose again. "He had one of his attacks. But instead of getting better, it got worse. He said his heart was pounding, and his chest hurt, and he couldn't breathe. And he . . ." She gulped, pressing the handkerchief against her mouth and closing her eyes. Her body shuddered with quiet sobs.

Ofelia stood and, crossing the room, sat next to the woman, pressing her hand gently until her tears had passed.

"Your ladyship is too kind," Mrs. Ivey said quietly when she opened her eyes at last, taking a deep breath. She seemed to pull back into herself, and Ofelia politely withdrew to the other side of the settee while Mrs. Ivey regained her composure. "He died that evening," Mrs. Ivey finished quietly. "I miss him dreadfully, as you can see."

"You have our sympathies, ma'am," Lily said. "It is a hard thing, to lose those we love so dearly, and with such suffering in their last days."

Her voice caught a little on the words, and Mrs. Ivey looked up a little sharply. "You know," she said quietly.

Lily nodded. "I do."

For a moment, neither of them spoke; Ofelia sat with her eyes cast down to give them a moment of privacy.

"We've no wish to impose any longer on you," Lily said, trying not to sound too brisk, though she was itching to leave. Mrs. Ivey's grief was too familiar, and she did not want to dredge up the painful emotions that it recalled. And even more than that, Mrs. Ivey was starting to look fatigued. Talking with strangers could be exhausting at the best of times, and these certainly were not the best of times for the new widow. "But if you will permit a final question?"

"Of course," Mrs. Ivey said, nodding, though she looked nervous.

"Did Dr. Ivey ever talk about anyone from his regiment? Anyone he served with, other than Colonel Halliday?"

Mrs. Ivey frowned. "Not that I can recall. He did not like to talk about his time in France at all, once he had returned home. I think he tried his best to forget about it. And even when he wrote, he said very little about the other men."

"He never mentioned a Captain Martin Forrest?" Ofelia added.

"Forrest?" Mrs. Ivey shook her head. "No, that name is not familiar at all." Lily tried to hide her disappointment; Ofelia was less successful. She slumped visibly in her seat next. Mrs. Ivey looked between them, clearly perplexed. "May I ask who the gentleman is?"

Lily hesitated. "He sold out his commission and returned to England some months ago, but unfortunately died this week. His niece is an acquaintance."

"Oh." Mrs. Ivey deflated, tears in her eyes once more. "My condolences to her as well."

They murmured a few more polite words, but it was clearly time to leave. Mrs. Ivey, worn out from the conversation, did not bother to hide her readiness for them to depart. But she still pressed their hands as she escorted them into the hall, thanking them for coming and for letting her speak of her husband.

"He was a good, dear man," she said, her voice thick with emotion. "I am glad to have the chance to say so, even though you will never know him yourselves."

"Which is clearly our loss, ma'am," Ofelia said effusively as she joined them. She had asked for one of Lily's visiting cards and had been writing on the back of it with a stump of pencil at the hall table. Now she handed it to Mrs. Ivey. "Mrs. Adler's direction is on there, as is my own. I hope you will let us know if there is anything we may do for you, now or in the future."

Mrs. Ivey took it with trembling fingers. "Your ladyship is too kind."

"Thank you for speaking with us," Lily said as they reached the door. "Again, our deepest sympathies for your loss."

"Thank you," Mrs. Ivey said, her smile sad. "At least I have so many good memories to think on. We were married more than twenty years, you know. There are many have lost someone and didn't have nearly so long together."

The words hit Lily like a blow to the chest, a sensation she had not felt in over a year. She had, she thought, made peace with Freddy's death and the abrupt, painful end of their marriage. But for a moment all she could think of was the years of memories they had never made together—and how different a person she had become from the woman he had known.

"I pray they are of good comfort to you," Ofelia said, giving Lily a puzzled, sideways glance.

Lily murmured something else polite, still feeling a little dazed. Once they were back in the carriage, Ofelia fixed her with a concerned look. "What is it? You had the oddest expression on your face at the end there."

"Nothing. Nothing at all. Just . . ." Lily stared out the window, not wanting to meet her friend's eyes. "What she said made me think of Mr. Adler. And those thoughts were hard in a way they have not been in some time."

"Why do you think that was?" Ofelia asked quietly as the carriage rumbled through the crowded streets around Hyde Park.

Lily's lips drew into a thin line. They both knew there was an obvious answer. "I think it was for the same reason that you think," she said a little tartly.

"Have you and the captain talked at all about Mr. Adler?"

"Not in the way you mean." Lily sighed. "We shall need to. But if I must be honest, I dread that conversation. Is there not some unwritten masculine code about such things?"

"I do not know," Ofelia said. "And I would ask Neddy, but I suspect he does not know either, dear man. He is frightfully oblivious to such things." She hesitated. "Do you wish for advice or a distraction?"

The delicately phrased question made Lily want to smile in spite of her uncomfortable thoughts. "Is your advice something other than *'You and the captain should talk to each other'* ?"

"No, that is generally the substance of it."

"Then I would prefer a distraction, if you have one."

Ofelia nodded. "Are you engaged for the evening? Neddy's sister and her husband are hosting a card party this evening, and she is panicking because her tables have ended up uneven. Would you and Miss Hartley care to join us? Neddy and I can fetch you in our carriage at half-past seven."

"Of course," Lily said. "We are happy to provide extra numbers."

"Excellent." Ofelia smiled. "She mentioned that three additional guests would be best, so I shall invite the captain as well."

"You are a terrible schemer," Lily said, shaking her head.

Ofelia looked pleased with herself. "I am indeed."

CHAPTER 25

A half an hour after their arrival at the card party, Jack had not appeared, and Lily found herself battling worry and trying not to show it. There was no reason to think that any harm had befallen him, except that only days before it very nearly had. Lily told herself she was worrying over nothing—perhaps he had already had other plans for the evening. But she couldn't shake the uneasy feeling. And when she glanced in Amelia's direction, she saw that she was not the only one.

When Jack strolled through the door—hardly late, after all, as they had only sat down to the tables ten minutes before—Lily saw Amelia slump with relief in her chair, though she quickly righted herself. Lily, for her part, kept her eyes studiously on her cards while Jack went to greet their hostess and the other guests.

"And how goes the play?" he asked, stopping at last across the table from Lily and looking over Ofelia's cards.

"Barely begun," the young Lady Carroway said, smiling brightly at him. "Shall we deal you in, sir?"

"I shall wait until the next hand, thank you. May I fetch anyone a drink while I am unoccupied?"

By the time he had returned, Lily had managed to lose the round. Setting her cards down, she smiled at the commiseration from the other players. "One cannot avoid being out of luck from time to time," she said calmly. "Perhaps I shall fare better with the next hand."

"Perhaps the captain can keep you entertained until we deal again," Ofelia said blithely. Lily fixed a stern look on her friend, but Ofelia deliberately did not look up from her cards.

Jack handed her a glass of wine and gestured toward the window. Lily, her expression as bland as possible, preceded him there.

"Why did you look ready to skin me alive when I arrived?" he asked in a murmur as soon as they were enough apart from the card tables.

Lily's first impulse was to deny that any such thing was true. "I was worried," she said softly, keeping her gaze turned toward the window. "Since Vauxhall, I cannot help feeling that we—that you—are in danger."

"I hardly can be," he pointed out, laying a hand on her arm. "Mr. Forrest cannot recruit any more villains from beyond the grave, and Mr. Page has assured me that his first one is still well locked up."

"Still." Lily took a sip of her wine. "I would be easier in my mind if they had managed to pry somewhat more information out of him. It still seems entirely unbelievable that Mr. Forrest should have sent him after you on such a vague suspicion. And that he should have done so such a short time before his own death."

"It's a tangle, to be sure," Jack agreed. "And it feels we are no closer to unraveling it." He sighed. "I had hoped the visit with Colonel Halliday would illuminate things more. But . . ." He noticed the expression on her face and frowned. "What is it? Did you learn something new?"

"Perhaps," Lily said, her voice low as she glanced back toward the card tables to check that they were still alone. "There was something strange in Anna's report from Highwood . . ."

It did not take her long to explain, nor to describe her conversation with Mr. Page and visit to Mrs. Ivey that afternoon. When she finished, Jack did not have to ask what bent her mind had taken.

"The brandy," he said quietly. "And the tincture from the apothecary."

"Precisely." Lily nodded. "It seems too great a coincidence that they should both be taken ill, and they should both have received some sort of . . ." Lily shrugged. "A delivery? I do not know what to call it. But it *is* odd."

"But Martin Forrest was stabbed," Jack pointed out.

"I know," Lily said, grimacing. "But still."

"Mr. Page could handle the matter," Jack suggested. "Why not tell him your suspicions?"

Lily lifted her chin. "I think it best I not say anything to him until I have some solid information to share. He's terribly worried about his niece and nephew right now, and wild speculations will only distract him."

"Besides which, you were not supposed to be speaking with Mrs. Ivey in the first place?" Jack guessed.

Lily shrugged, unrepentant. "There is that as well. But I was hardly going to sit at home."

"No, you were not, were you?" Jack said, shaking his head. "Very well. What if I send Jem to see what he can learn of this Mr. Blunt? If he has an unsavory reputation, or if there is any sort of suspicion about his work, Jem will be able to unearth it. And he'll be able to talk to the local urchins as well as shopkeepers—they are a good deal like servants, according to him," Jack added. "They see and hear all, apparently. But they would not give us the time of day."

"Would it be safe for him?" Lily asked, looking concerned.

Jack took her head. "He's a smart young fellow; he will know to keep his head down and be careful. Besides which, he is not a child anymore, as he reminds me near daily."

"But you will tell him to be careful, if he agrees, will you not? And let him know he does not have to do it—it does fall rather outside the bounds of his ordinary duties."

"Do you think he will mind that?"

Lily sighed. "No, he will jump at the chance. That boy has always enjoyed getting involved in risky things, from the first time we met him."

"Mrs. Adler! Captain!" The cheerful call made them both jump a little, turning back toward the rest of the party. Ned Carroway's sister smiled at them both. "We are just about to deal again. Would either of you care to join?"

Jack pressed Lily's hand. "We will find something more," he whispered as they made their way back toward the tables. "I promise."

★ ★ ★

Lily was not disappointed when Anna came into the breakfast room the next morning to say that Amelia would be taking her tea and toast in bed. Though she enjoyed her young friend's company, Lily had grown accustomed to solitude in her home before the youngest Hartley's arrival. It had been a strange adjustment to once more have the presence and schedule of another person to consider at all hours of the day.

And that morning, the solitude was especially needed as she turned over her conversation with Jack from the night before, trying to sort through what they knew of Mr. Forrest and the possible reasons for his death.

She wanted to agree with Jack that there was no continuing danger to them now that Mr. Forrest was gone. But it was hard to believe it without knowing who had killed him and why. And then there was her lingering, unwanted obligation to Henry Clive. Without another suspect in the matter of Mr. Forrest's death, the Bow Street magistrate might well decide that Clive was the most likely culprit—and much as she disliked the man, she could not countenance him being convicted of a murder when she did not believe he was guilty.

Lily sighed, staring down at her plate, her appetite gone. She had the prickling, uneasy sensation that she was missing something she should have noticed. But it was like glimpsing a movement out of the corner of her eye—as soon as she turned her mind to try to catch the thought, it was gone.

"Mrs. Adler?"

"Yes?" Lily looked up to find Carstairs hovering at the door to the breakfast room, a small paper-wrapped package under one arm.

"My apologies for intruding, madam, but a parcel arrived for you. Would you like to open it now, or shall I have Anna take it up to your room?"

"I will open it now," Lily said, holding out her hands for it. Perhaps her muddled thoughts would be better for the distraction.

She found a slim, bound book when she pulled off the paper—the sort for keeping one's own notes, not for reading, as she discovered when she opened it and found dozens of densely written pages. Lily frowned as she opened the letter that accompanied it, not at all certain who would have sent her such a thing or why. She glanced first at the signature.

It was from Mrs. Ivey.

The letter began conventionally enough, repeating her thanks for their kind visit and the message from Colonel Halliday. But by the second paragraph, Lily was sitting up straighter, her fingers tightening on the paper as she read.

> *Your visit made me curious, and I found myself last night reading through some of my husband's battlefield journals for the first time. His writing is not extensive—I think there was not a great deal of time for it, and small wonder—but a name or two caught my eye. One of them, I believe, was the uncle of your friend, Mr. Forrest (I am afraid I do not recall his Christian name). If you wanted to show it to her, perhaps the mention of her uncle would bring the young lady some comfort in a difficult time. And perhaps, after that, I will show it to my own children. I think it may help them come to understand what their father experienced.*
>
> *I am, yours &ct,*
> *Harriet Ivey*

Lily turned back to the diary with far more interest than she had shown it in her first glance. It was not, as Mrs. Ivey had warned, a detailed description of the doctor's time at war. But she could read in the brief entries an account of a heart-wrenching time—cold days of guiding their horses through frozen mud and colder nights camping with only the thin walls of a canvas tent between them and the autumn chill, a bombardment of artillery that left a dozen men dead in a single hour. The relief of the weeks spent away from the battlefield, put up in the houses of a village, and grateful for hot water and a real bed.

Then there were the glimpses of the kindness his wife had described shining through even in the short notes that he left behind: the account of helping an injured young officer write a letter to his sweetheart in Devon; his celebratory entry when a soldier whose arm he had to amputate did not succumb to infection; an account of sharing a meal with half a dozen young officers as they toasted to news that the wife of one had been safely delivered of a child back home.

And then Lily saw *Captain Forrest* in one entry and nearly forgot the rest. She abruptly set aside the teacup she was holding, wanting nothing at hand to distract her.

The entry was dated some months before Martin Forrest would have returned to England, in the sparse prose that characterized most of Dr. Ivey's notes.

> *Summoned to Captain Forrest's tent by his body servant, Louis, last night; the good captain had taken a bullet to the hand in today's skirmish and hid it from his companions until all were safely returned to camp. Would have scolded him for such noble idiocy but did not have the heart, as he was near to fainting when I arrived, and I could see immediately that the use of it would never be the same. Told Private Carver to fetch his master's brandy and went for my bone saw, though in the end he kept both fingers and hand. Forrest rests as well as can be expected—we wait to see whether the coming days will bring infection or not.*

Lily stared at the passage, only her shock at the name preventing her from feeling ill at the gruesome story. *Carver.*

★ ★ ★

Lily was glad it was a cloudy, cool day; the veil she wore on her hat to hide her face from curious eyes would have drawn more stares had it been either sunny or raining heavily. She was still wary of letting anyone see her walking into the Bow Street offices. But she might as well not have bothered. As soon as she asked the young man perched at the desk to speak to Mr. Page, he shook his head mournfully.

"At home, he is," the clerk said. "Something the matter with the young 'uns."

Lily felt cold all over. "They are still unwell?" she demanded. "Has anything been done for them?"

The young man looked nervous. "I don't rightly know, mum. Mr. Page wasn't sharing any details. Didn't even come himself, just sent a messenger to say that he couldn't come until his little ones were out of danger." He shook his head again. "Magistrate ain't well pleased, I can tell you that. Plenty o' work won't get done until he gets back."

Underneath her cloak, Lily clenched her hands into fists around the handle of the small valise she was carrying. "Is anyone handling the matter of Mr. Martin Forrest's death while the constable is with his family?"

"I don't . . ." The clerk hesitated. "I don't know. P'raps the magistrate? I'm not supposed to share details of what . . . That is, did you have some information about it?" he asked, sitting up a little straighter. "I can find out who to pass it along to."

Lily shook her head. "No, I thank you," she said, giving him a polite, meaningless smile. Inside, her thoughts were in a turmoil, but she let none of that show. "I was merely curious."

★   ★   ★

"They're sleeping, at the moment," Judith Page said in a low voice at the door. "You are kind to inquire, Mrs. Adler, but I would not wish to risk spreading any infection."

"Is there anything more that needs to be done for them?" Lily asked, not insisting that she be admitted, though part of her wanted to. Poor Miss Page looked exhausted. Lily wanted to tell her to put herself to bed, that she was no good to her niece and nephew if she was run ragged. But she did not say that either. "Have you summoned a doctor?"

Judith gave her a tired smile. "We have. He says he suspects it is the same infection, since they fell ill the same day. But their complaints are so different, he cannot begin to guess what it could be. They seemed the most ill the first day. Now, though, they do not seem precisely ill, just . . ." She shook her head. "Just not well. All we can do is care for them the best we are able and wait to see how they progress. Fanny shows some signs of improving, and George . . . well, he is sleeping more peacefully today. So that is something." She sighed, distracted for the moment, then started, as if she had just remembered that she was holding the door open. "But was there any other reason you called, Mrs. Adler?"

"There was." Seeing Miss Page in person, Lily didn't want to ask, but there was no avoiding it. "Is Mr. Page at liberty to speak for a few minutes? I promise I'll not keep him from the children for long."

Judith Page nodded. "I will send him out. The fresh air will do him good, I've no doubt." Her slight smile caught Lily off guard. "And so will a distraction, which I think you have come prepared to provide."

Simon Page, when he appeared at the door, looked as fatigued as his sister. He sighed when he saw Lily. "How did you know to find me here?"

"I called at your Bow Street office first. The clerk would not have told me where you lived, of course. But luckily I already knew." She studied him. "You will do them no good if you wear yourself out, you know."

He scowled at her. "When you have children to care for, you may tell me how to do so."

Lily's chin snapped up, and she barely restrained herself from giving him a sharp answer. But a look at the shadows under his eyes pulled the fight out of her. She took a deep breath. "No one has taken over the investigation into Mr. Forrest's death in your absence," she said softly.

He rubbed his eyes, lowering himself to sit on the steps before his door. Lily stared; it was the least composed she had ever seen him. "I know. But what would you have me do? Hurst has been sent to deal with a matter in Norfolk. The Bow Street force is small, Mrs. Adler. There are not enough of us to manage it all."

Lily hesitated a moment, worried that it would seem too familiar. Then she shrugged and took a seat beside him, sweeping her skirts forward so they would not snag on the rough stone of the steps. No one there knew her, after all. It hardly mattered if someone saw her. "Fortunately, sir, I am terrible at following your instructions."

Mr. Page had stared at her in astonishment when she sat down; at her words, his eyes narrowed. "What did you do?"

Lily pulled the valise, which she had set down at her feet, closer. "I went to see Dr. Ivey's widow. And while her description of his death was entirely unlike that of Mr. Forrest—and also unlike Colonel Halliday's illness—there is something which gives me pause." She unlatched the top of the bag and withdrew Dr. Ivey's journal, flipping through the pages until she came to the one that mentioned Captain Forrest and Private Carver. "Your neighbor, Mrs. Carver, had a husband died in France. Was his name Louis?"

Mr. Page nodded slowly. "I believe it was."

Lily turned the diary to face him. "Dr. Ivey mentioned him in his battlefield journal. Mr. Carver served as Mr. Forrest's body man in France. They were in the same regiment. Along with Colonel Halliday. And Dr. Ivey."

Mr. Page stared at the diary for a long moment, as though his mind were working more slowly than normal. At last, he looked up at her. "You think someone is targeting the men of that regiment."

Lily nodded. "I do. What I do not yet know is who—or why. But it has become too many coincidences to ignore. And it all seems to center around Martin Forrest, even though he was not the first to be targeted. Dr. Ivey, Colonel Halliday, and Louis Carver were all directly connected to him."

Mr. Page sighed. "Someone needs to look into it. But I cannot be absent from the children," he said quietly. "I would never forgive myself if . . ."

"I know," Lily replied. "I was going to ask for your permission, but not your escort."

"Escort to where?"

"To Newgate," Lily said, hiding her nervousness behind a pretense of confidence. She had only paid one visit to the prison in her life, and it had not ended well. "I wish to speak to Mr. Clive. Now that we know about the military connection, I wonder if we should ask him more questions. He might have seen"—she let out a frustrated breath—"something. Anything."

Mr. Page sighed and stood. Without a word, he disappeared back inside the house. Lily stood herself, waiting, and a few minutes later he emerged once more. The wax seal on the letter he handed her was impressed with the crest of the City of London, used by the Bow Street force on their batons and communications.

"Present this to the warden," he said quietly. "He will, I hope, allow you in without too much trouble or too much of a bribe."

Lily nodded, concealing the paper in her cloak. She was glad it was daylight still. Newgate was a forbidding place at night.

"They will be well," she said, laying her hand on his arm once more. "I am sure of it."

"From your lips," he said, his smile grim. "Please be careful, Mrs. Adler. I do not need anyone else to worry about just now."

"You never need to worry about me, sir," Lily said confidently, hoping that it was true.

CHAPTER 26

M r. Clive looked a good deal the worse for wear.

The State Side of Newgate Prison, where he was detained, was far nicer than the alternative, though only for those who could afford to pay for it. He had a room to himself, a bed whose linens were not entirely filthy, and an empty basin with some soap beside it. There was a blanket on the bed, and a basket of food that looked like it had been purchased from a grocer, likely by one of the wardens after a substantial bribe.

But Henry Clive himself still seemed determined to play his part in spite of his surroundings. He stood quickly when she entered, pulling on the wrinkled, dirty jacket that had been hanging over the back of the chair. And he bowed, saving his surprise until the warden, glaring around the room in a suspicious manner, had closed the door behind him.

Lily heard the bolt thrown, and she could picture the surly man stationing himself just outside the door. She shivered a little—that, too, brought back an unpleasant memory—but pushed the thought from her mind. She had other things to deal with just then, and she could not afford any distractions.

"You look well, all things considered," she said politely, taking a seat at the rough table that occupied slightly more than half of the room's space.

He gave her a sour look. Had she not been there on so serious a purpose, Lily would have been amused to note that prison had done nothing to dampen the sarcastic edge with which he approached the world. "You may skip the pleasantries, madam. We both know you don't mean them, and I've no interest in them."

"As you like," Lily said mildly. "I will come directly to the point, then. Your situation here is not comfortable, however much you pay. I imagine you would like to leave it as soon as possible."

His gaze narrowed. "And how likely is that to happen, if I may ask?"

"That depends on your willingness to answer my questions honestly."

"I've already been more than honest with you."

"Have you?" Lily regarded him thoughtfully. She drummed the fingers on one hand against the table in a slow, steady rhythm. "We shall see. I am here today because I wish to know the exact order of events in which Miss Forrest became convinced that her uncle was stealing from her. Were you there when her suspicions began?"

He shook his head. "Not right at the beginning, no. I think she was suspicious from the moment she found out that her inheritance had disappeared. A worry that Miss Waverly—have you met Miss Waverly yet?" he asked sharply.

"I have."

He snorted. "Well, then I'm sure you can imagine how she encouraged Miss Forrest in her suspicions. That woman would like nothing better than for her life to resemble the plot of a novel as exactly as possible."

Lily kept her amusement at the observation hidden behind a cool expression. "I see. And the night of Mr. Forrest's ball, did you notice anyone—either when you were there with Miss Forest or when you returned on your own—who looked like they might have been an acquaintance from the army?"

Clive frowned in thought, then shook his head. "I don't recall seeing anyone in uniform, if that's what you mean. I wouldn't know anything about his military acquaintances."

Lily's stomach dropped with disappointment. "Did Miss Forrest ever mention her uncle's time in the army to you? Did she know anything about it, or about anyone that he might have kept up with from his regiment?"

"By the time I met Miss Forrest, she was already living in Hans Town and had very little to do with her uncle."

"But she had to have had some communication with him. Do you know if the subject was ever mentioned between them?"

"I don't think—"Clive broke off. "Why are you asking me?"

"Because I wish to know your recollections on the matter," Lily replied, her tone giving nothing away.

"Sarah would be the better person to ask such questions." The sarcasm was gone from his voice; instead, he sounded deadly serious, and his eyes were fixed on her with startling intensity.

Lily sighed. He was not wrong, but Lily suspected that the young Miss Forrest would still refuse to see her if she called. "Because—"

But Clive wasn't listening. He gripped the back of his chair so tightly that the wood—which was not sturdy to begin with—creaked alarmingly. "Why are you asking about Sarah?" he demanded. "You think she did it, don't you?" Lily could see his breathing growing faster, and she tensed, hoping she would not need to summon the warden. But Clive did not move, just stared at her, white-knuckled hands still wrapped around the chair.

"What would you say if I told you I did?" Lily asked, not taking her eyes from him. He might not be able to answer her question about Mr. Forrest's military connections. But she had a feeling he was about to answer at least one lingering question about himself.

She saw his sharp intake of breath, the flinch of his chin pulling back. But his voice, when he spoke, was firm. "I would say you are wrong."

"Her guilt would prove your own innocence," Lily pointed out.

Again, the flinch of his chin; again, the calm firm voice. "But still, I wouldn't believe it." He shook his head. "Even with everything he did to her, I can't believe she would harm him."

Lily had listened silently, her expression giving away none of her thoughts. Now she leaned forward, her arms crossed on the table in front of her. "You do love her."

She could see him swallow nervously. "I told you I did already."

"You did," Lily said. "But I did not believe you then."

If anything, he looked angered by the statement. "But you do now? And here I thought you were supposed to be clever."

Lily took in the play of emotions over his face, the tension in his shoulders, the tone of his voice. She was almost certain he was telling the truth now.

She was equally certain that he had been the morning he told her he'd had nothing to do with Martin Forrest's death. She did not believe he was a murderer.

Clive was still speaking, quick and sarcastic. "My thanks, madam, for your kindness. But I will not accept any proof of my innocence that involves her guilt. She did not do it."

Lily raised her brows pointedly. "I never said she did."

He stared at her for a moment, until understanding dawned. "What a lovely model of generous womanhood you are," he drawled. "Truly, the gentlemen must swoon at your feet."

If he had thought to offend her, he had chosen poorly. Lily had heard far worse insults. And she found that she had some sympathy for his situation as she looked around the room. Prison likely brought out the worst in a man.

She smiled at him as she stood up and walked to the door, glad to be leaving at last. She might not have believed he was a murderer, but that didn't mean she had to like him. And she liked being inside the walls of the prison even less. "Perhaps, sir," she replied. "But I am the model of womanhood who can get you out of here. And then if we are both very lucky, we will never need to see each other again." She paused at the door. "I asked you and not Miss Forrest, by the by, because the last time I called, she did not want to see me. These past days have been trying for her."

"Wait."

When Lily looked back, he was staring at her, his sarcasm and bravado gone. "When you did see her . . . did she speak of me at all?"

"She did," Lily replied a little coldly. He had just insulted her, after all, even if she had decided not to let it ruffle her composure. "I do not think she expects to see you again. Or to be able to trust you, if she does."

His face did not fall. But he seemed to shrink into himself a little, like a hot air balloon slumping to the ground after a disappointing flight. "I suppose she has a right to such feelings," he muttered.

"She does." Lily rapped her knuckles against the door. When the warden opened it, he peered inside suspiciously. "We have finished here," she said to him, then turned to incline her head very briefly to Mr. Clive. "My thanks for your time."

★   ★   ★

Jack wanted to pull out his hair in frustration, but he settled for swinging his cane with unnecessary vigor as he strode down Half Moon Street.

Jem had spent the morning and half the afternoon asking his questions in Hans Town. Jack had given him a full pocket of ready money to spend, on goods and drinks alike, to loosen as many tongues as possible. The young man had passed what was likely a delightful time getting to know both the local shopkeepers and their assorted urchins, coming home half foxed and grinning broadly. But he had kept his head for all of that and asked the questions he needed to.

To no avail. Mr. Blunt's neighbors had nothing but praise for their local apothecary. "Honest and respectable," Jem had reported, swaying only a little. "And according to more'n one report, ever so good with sick children."

Mr. Blunt had no connection to the army either, and nothing odd or untoward in his care of his patients. Jack found himself feeling far more disgusted than he would have expected from the report of a skilled apothecary. But it was yet another useless line of inquiry that he was not eager to share with Lily.

But when the butler showed him into the cozy drawing room at Half Moon Street, it was not Lily who waited for him, but his sister.

"Hello, Raffi," Noor said, glancing up from her book. "Mrs. Adler is out, if that is who you are looking for. I do not know where. She was gone when I came down after breakfast."

Jack felt his heart speed up with worry, though he tried to appear unconcerned. "She did not leave word with the servants? Or a note?"

"I am afraid not," his sister said. There was an odd look on her face, as though she were waiting for something and impatient that it had not yet arrived. "Surely you are not disappointed to see me instead?"

Jack frowned as he took a seat next to her. But he tried to speak kindly, in spite of his worry about Lily. No doubt Noor was nervous and worried as well, and perhaps even feeling neglected, as nearly all his attention had been occupied since he arrived in London. "Of course I am not disappointed to see you. But Mrs. Adler ought not to go about alone, not after what happened at Vauxhall—"

"Yes, indeed." Noor sat up even straighter, casting her book aside, and fixed him with an accusatory look. "Do let us discuss what happened at Vauxhall."

Jack stared at her, bemused and not a little irritated. He did not have time to indulge one of his little sister's rare moods. "I know no more than you do, Noor. So if you are going to be difficult—"

"I am not being difficult. I just hoped that you would trust me more. It seems I was wrong," she said, standing up and looking as though she would walk from the room.

"What?" Jack sprang up after her, grabbing her arm. "Noor, I have hardly kept you in the dark, even when I might have wanted to. You know about Mr. Forrest and the blackmail and—"

"Good God, Raffi, have you always been this obtuse?" she demanded. When he only stared at her, still baffled, she said, her words coming out in a rush, as if she were afraid she might lose her nerve, "I saw you together. You and Mrs. Adler. At Vauxhall."

Jack dropped her arm as though it had burned him. She had turned away from him, and he couldn't see her face clearly, but he could only imagine what she was thinking. "Noor," he said, his voice coming out a little strangled. He cleared his throat. "Whatever you thought you saw—"

That earned him a glare, and he stopped talking instantly. "Do not speak to me as though I am a child," she said fiercely. "I can recognize the evidence of my own eyes, thank you."

For a moment neither of them said anything. At last, Jack sighed. His reputation, while hardly unsavory, was certainly that of a flirt and a charmer. Few people thought him a serious man, even those who knew of his sterling service as a naval officer. And Noor had not only known Freddy Adler her whole life, but she had also come to admire and depend on Mrs. Adler in these last few months.

"Noor," he said quietly, "you must know that my intentions toward her are strictly honorable."

That earned him a blank look. "Strictly honorable?"

He took a step back, offended. "Do you really think I would—"

"Dear God, Raffi," she said, the exclamation seeming to slip out without thought. "I have never heard you sound like such a stuffy bore in my entire life. Your intentions are strictly honorable?" She made a sound of disgust in the back of her throat.

"It may sound stuffy, little sister, but it is true, and—"

"Of course it is true," she said, rolling her eyes. "You are the most honorable man I know, you overbearing idiot. My concern was that someone *else* might have seen you. Or that they might come to certain conclusions, especially when the two of you do things like stand apart whispering together, as you did last night. Idiot man," she added under her breath, rolling her eyes again.

Jack stared at her in confusion. "Then you are not—you were not distressed by what you saw?"

"You and Mrs. Adler embracing?" Noor asked, in the dry, sarcastic voice that only a younger sibling could manage so perfectly. "Truly, my innocent soul has been wounded for life." She was silent a moment. "Though what I cannot figure out is why you must be so secretive about it. If your intentions are honorable, then why not simply—" She broke off, suddenly looking unsure, as though she had just realized that what she had been about to suggest might not be what he or Lily wished.

Jack sighed, sitting back down and running his fingers restlessly through his hair. "It is more complicated than that."

"Does she not wish to marry you?" Noor asked, sitting beside him.

The blunt question made him flinch. "We have not discussed it. The situation is hardly of long standing," he said, shifting uncomfortably in his seat. His little sister was not someone with whom he wanted to have this conversation, but he could not get out of it now. "The complication has more to do with the person who first brought our lives together."

Noor fell silent, and he knew she understood. But a moment later she scooted close enough to poke him in the arm. "That is nonsense," she declared. "I cannot think of anything that Freddy would have approved of more. Can you imagine that he would want anything other than for the two of you to be happy? Or that he would think it anything less than a marvelous joke if you found that happiness together?" She shook her head. "Overbearing idiot," she muttered again, poking him in the arm once more. But she gave him a fond look as she said it.

The words were like a weight lifted from Jack's chest. She was right: it was exactly the sort of thing Freddy would have had a grand sense of humor about. Jack shook his head. "When did you become so wise, little sister?"

"I have always been the most intelligent of my parents' children," she said, looking pleased with herself. "You were simply away from England too long to realize it. Though I must say, Mrs. Adler's wisdom is now in question for me. Truly, I thought she had better taste than—" She broke off, smiling, as she saw his face. But the expression faded as she glanced toward the door. "I wonder where she is now."

Jack was wondering the same thing, and he did not like it.

★　★　★

The warden had summoned a carriage for her—the prison was only three miles from her home, but it was in the middle of the City of London, an unsavory neighborhood where it would have been unwise for her to walk alone.

But she felt restless and stifled in the carriage, and as soon as they were past Covent Garden, she knocked briskly on the roof and asked to be let out. The driver looked askance at the request but did not argue, for which Lily was grateful.

She turned down Piccadilly, walking briskly against the chill spring wind, wanting to move her feet while her mind sifted through everything Mr. Clive had and had not said.

She needed to speak with Miss Forrest, but there was no saying whether the young woman would—

"Mrs. Adler! Dear lady, is that you?"

Lily recalled herself to her surroundings with a start, aware that she knew the voice before she recognized it. A carriage stood just ahead of her, and paused before it, leaning heavily on a cane and with a footman close at hand, stood Colonel Halliday, staring at her with no attempt to conceal his surprise.

Lily stared right back at him. "Colonel, what a surprise to see you here. What can have brought you to London? Is something amiss at Highwood?"

He shook his head. "Not at Highwood, fortunately. Only with me. My son and the doctor in Gravesend finally persuaded me to consult with a physician here in London regarding the lingering effects of my illness. A dashed inconvenience, I must say, but if it puts their minds at ease . . . " He looked about. "You are not alone, I trust, madam?"

"My maid had to return for a package I left behind," Lily said, thinking quickly and giving the lie with a polite smile. She had not brought Anna with her that morning, worried about being recognized as she went to Bow Street. And there had been no opportunity to retrieve her since then—nor, indeed, a true need, as even a maid would not have lent any propriety to her trip to Newgate. "I decided to continue home on foot."

"An intrepid walker, I see," the colonel said, smiling genially. "But these spring winds are growing sharp. May I perhaps offer you a place in my carriage and my escort to your home?"

Lily almost said no on instinct; she was not far from home, and she did not, truthfully, know him well, for all he seemed gentlemanly and pleasant. But she stopped herself before the refusal passed her lips. "I thank you, sir, that is very kind. Especially as there is something particular I would like to ask you, and a short conversation will save me the trouble of writing and you the expense of postage."

"I am at your service, of course," he said, but his genial expression had grown grave. "Is it about Mr. Forrest again?"

"In a manner of speaking, yes." Lily gave her instructions to the driver before she took the colonel's hand and let him help her into the carriage. It was not far to Half Moon Street, so she did not have much time. As soon as they were settled and she felt the carriage sway into motion, she leaned forward. "You mentioned, when we spoke, that two men from your regiment had died."

"Captain Forrest and Dr. Ivey," the colonel said, nodding. "Tragedies, both, though nothing in common between them, as I told you."

"I spoke to Dr. Ivey's widow, and she said as much herself," Lily agreed. "And though she did not know Mr. Forrest's name, she was kind enough to pass along one of the doctor's battlefield journals."

"I cannot imagine it was pleasant reading for you."

"It was not," Lily said quietly, suddenly very much aware of the fact that, for the man across from her, those battlefield notes were but the shallowest edge of a deep well of experience. "But she thought I might be interested in it—that Mr. Forrest's niece might be," she amended quickly, "as the doctor's writing mentioned him at least once."

"Ah, must have been an account of that injury to his hand?" When she nodded, the colonel looked grim. "A bad day, that, though it could have been worse. He could still use it, though he needed assistance from time to time. And luckily it was his left, as he shot and wrote with his right hand."

"Fortunate indeed," Lily said, a little absently as she tried to decide how best to phrase her question. "But Mr. Forrest's was not the only name I recognized in that particular passage. It mentioned his body servant as well, a Private Louis Carver. Do you remember him?"

Colonel Halliday's face had darkened as she spoke. By the time he answered, he was very near to glowering. "I do, yes. I saw him often enough, as he was friendly with my own body man, Private Hansen. Though I would rather now that I had not, the coward."

Lily, about to question him further, paused. It was not the reaction she had been expecting. "Why do you mean by that, sir? And why did you not mention his name with the other men from your regiment who had died?"

"Who told you Carver died?" the colonel demanded.

"His widow, if it is the same man, which I believe it is," Lily said even more warily. "She sells lace from her home in Clerkenwell."

"Ah." Colonel Halliday shook his head as the carriage rolled to a stop in front of her house. His shoulders sagged, with fatigue or distress she could not tell. "I suppose I cannot blame her for saying so. And no doubt it is easier for her to think of it as a death. But so far as I know, Mrs. Adler, Louis Carver is not dead."

Lily stared at him as the carriage swayed with the motion of a groom climbing down. "Not . . . What do you mean? Are you certain?" she asked as the door swung open.

"As certain as I can be," the colonel said, shaking his head. "He is not a dead man, Mrs. Adler. He was charged with escorting Captain Forrest to London, to assist him when his injury made it difficult to manage. But he abandoned his post and never returned to the regiment after Mr. Forrest sold out. Louis Carver is a deserter."

CHAPTER 27

Lily closed the door behind her but did not move, replaying everything Colonel Halliday has said. If Louis Carver was a deserter . . . did his wife know? What about Mr. Forrest?

They had been traveling back to England together; at what point had Louis Carver disappeared? Had Mr. Forrest been part of the deception? Temperate and moral, Colonel Halliday had said about him, almost to a fault. Surely a man like that would not have allowed a desertion to stand?

But he had been happy, the night before he died, to accept Jack's help cheating at faro. Clearly, Mr. Forrest's morals were flexible in the face of enough profit. Had Mr. Carver been able to take advantage of that flaw in his character?

Had that been what led to Mr. Forrest's eventual death? It was impossible to know.

Except . . .

Lily pressed her hands against the wood frame of the doorway, suddenly feeling unsteady. In her mind's eye, she could see the man who had shot at them in Vauxhall, the panicked look on his face before he took off through the trees, Jack tearing after him.

Who better to engage in a crime than someone who was already a criminal? No wonder he had refused to give his name.

"Mrs. Adler?" Amelia poked her head out of the drawing room, looking relieved. "Thank goodness. My brother and I were wondering where—" She broke off, her tone becoming more urgent. "Raffi, come at once. Mrs. Adler is unwell."

"I am perfectly well," Lily said quickly as Jack bolted into the hallway, looking her over in a head-to-toe fashion that was both irritating and endearing. "I am perfectly well," she repeated. "But I think . . ."

"What is it?" Jack demanded while Amelia hovered nervously behind him.

Lily met his eyes. "I think I know who attacked us at Vauxhall."

★　★　★

"Are you sure you wish to come with us?" Lily asked as Amelia tucked a bottle of cordial into the basket. "Fanny and George have been ill, after all. There is no reason for you to risk your health as well."

They were in the hall at Half Moon Street the next morning, and the basket at Amelia's feet already contained an assortment of breads, several jars of broth, spearmint tea, puzzles, and two new picture books.

"I am," Amelia replied, tying on her bonnet. Jack, who had arrived soon after breakfast, stood at her side, taking a second basket from Anna. That one held beef pie, apples, cake, and two bottles of mild wine. "I liked Miss Andrews. I want to make sure she is all right."

One basket for the children, one for the aunt and uncle caring for them. Lily and Jack had agreed that they would not call on Mr. Page the evening before, as it had already grown late by the time Lily arrived home. But they could not wait any longer.

Lily was looking things over to decide whether there was anything else she ought to add, when there was a knock at the door. When Anna went to answer, she held the door so that whoever was on the step could not see who was in the hall. That meant that Lily could not see the visitor either. But she recognized the voice, and she could hardly conceal her surprise when she realized who it was.

"Is Mrs. Adler at home?" Sarah Forrest asked, her nervousness plain.

"I'm afraid—" Anna began, but Lily cleared her throat.

"Come in, Miss Forrest, please." Given her visit to Newgate the day before, she could guess what the girl wanted to talk to her about. And as much as she wanted to hurry to Clerkenwell, she did not want to pass up the chance to glean any bit of information that might be of use. She glanced at Amelia and Jack. "Mr. and Miss Hartley can go on without me, and I will join you as soon as I am able."

Jack didn't look happy with the arrangement, but he couldn't leave his sister to travel to Clerkenwell alone, and they needed to deliver their news to Mr. Page as quickly as possible. He nodded, saying something polite to Miss Forrest before ushering his sister out the door.

When they were alone in the drawing room, Lily could finally take a good look at her visitor. Miss Forrest was still dressed in mourning, of course, but there was more color in her cheeks than the last time Lily had seen her, and a feeling of nervous, anxious energy radiated from her.

She perched on the edge of the settee, her hands clasped in her lap. "You must be wondering why I've come to see you," she said, not quite meeting Lily's eyes.

"I could hazard a guess," Lily said. "But I would prefer that you tell me directly."

"I need someone to talk to about Henry," Miss Forrest said, her mouth trembling. "You are the only other person in London who truly knows him. And I am not sure what to do."

"You seemed quite certain a few days ago," Lily pointed out, wishing she had rung for some kind of refreshment. She wanted something to do with her hands. Instead, she laid them on the arms of her chair, very still as she watched Miss Forrest. "What changed?"

The girl seemed a little cowed as she met Lily's eyes. "He wrote to me. I received the letter this morning. And he . . ." She swallowed. "He was truthful, at last. He told me about his parents, about his life in Hampshire. His determination to become a gentleman, even through less than savory means. That he came to London looking for a wife who would help make that happen, and he met me and decided we would suit well enough." Her voice dropped to a whisper. "And he told me that his plans went astray when he fell in love with me."

"And you want me to tell you whether or not you should believe him?" Lily asked.

Miss Forrest lifted her gaze at last. "He said he decided to write to me after you visited him in prison yesterday. Please—do you think he killed my uncle?"

Lily took a deep breath. "I do not. I am not yet certain who did. But I do not believe it was he."

Miss Forrest swallowed back a sob, pressing her fist against her mouth while she fought to get herself under control. "And do you think he truly loves me, or are his words simply another ploy?"

"I think you know I cannot answer that for you," Lily said, shaking her head.

Miss Forrest made a face, but she nodded. "I wish someone could." A note of bitter humor entered her voice as she added, "My cousin Miss Waverly would like to, but she is no help at all in talking over such questions."

Lily tried not to sound too pointed as she said, "I can imagine her style of insight might be more confusing than helpful at a time like this."

"That's right—you met her, did you not?" Miss Forrest sighed. "She practically raised me, and she did so with a great deal of affection, for which she will always have my love and gratitude. But she is not . . ."

"The people who love us in childhood are not always the best suited to help us as we make our way in the world," Lily suggested delicately.

Miss Forrest let out a short laugh. "Well put, ma'am." Then she sighed again.

Lily was surprised to realize how much sympathy she felt for the girl. Perhaps if she had been better raised and better advised, she would have a stronger character. But she was young yet. There was still time.

"I think," Lily said slowly, "in the end, despite all his deceptions, you know Mr. Clive better than I. What do you believe?" Lily studied the girl. "You must love him a great deal, to be so hurt by him."

"I did," Miss Forrest said. She looked away again, her fingers plucking at one another nervously. "I do. And I want to believe that he loves me back, for myself and not for whatever wealth or position my love could bring him. But . . ."

"But it is hard to trust your own judgment after so many betrayals," Lily said quietly. "Your father. Mr. Clive. Even your uncle."

Sarah Forrest nodded. "Yes. I suppose I ought not to feel betrayed by my uncle at least, as I knew him not at all, and he did not know me. But his actions were a betrayal of my father, at least." She sighed. "It is all a muddle."

"I do not know if it helps, but—" Lily hesitated. "I spoke recently with the widow of a doctor who served in France, and she reminded me that men do sometimes return with nervous complaints or distress of their sensibilities." She did not believe what she was saying—it was not a nervous complaint that had made Mr. Forrest send his body man to shoot at Jack. But Miss Forrest needed something to comfort herself with if she was going to move on with her life. "Your uncle was at war for a long time. And then there was his wound, which I am sure was frustrating and painful, and possibly injurious to his sense of himself as a competent, independent man. Perhaps it would ease your mind to think of him as a man with his own afflictions rather than the betrayer of you and your father."

She realized, as she stopped speaking, that Miss Forrest was regarding her with complete befuddlement. "What on earth can you mean?"

"He took a wound in France that damaged his hand," Lily said, spotting her opening. "I think he was careful about hiding it, perhaps not wanting to appear weak. Did you ever meet any of his acquaintances from the army? They might have—"

"If he was injured, he never told me about it," Miss Forrest interrupted, her voice rising in volume. There was bright, angry color in her cheeks as she stood. "Nor would I have cared if he had. Whatever wound he took in battle, it was no excuse for his keeping my money from me. And for you to defend him thus is *abhorrent* to me."

Lily stared at her, astonished at the sudden snap of anger. But even as she was trying to decide how to respond—how to calm Miss Forrest and find out what she needed to know—the young woman sighed and shook her head.

"I am sorry for speaking to you like that," she said, looking embarrassed as she took her seat once more. "It's been a trying week. But you are someone I have no wish to quarrel with. Indeed, I owe you my thanks." She pulled a small paper package from her reticule as she spoke and held it out.

Lily took it gingerly. "What is this?"

"A small token of gratitude. It is not much, but . . ."

When Lily unwrapped the paper, she found several packets sewn of muslin that crackled beneath her fingers and smelled of tea.

"My cousin and I have got in the habit of making our own blends with what is sold at the end of the day. To save money, I mean." Miss Forrest blushed. "Though I suppose I will not need to worry overmuch about that anymore. It is a relief, but it will be another adjustment. In any case, I thought . . ."

"I thank you for the gesture," Lily said, distracted with trying to decide how to return the conversation to anyone Miss Forrest might recognize from her uncle's military days. "It is very kind."

"I am trying to be kinder," Miss Forrest said, sighing again. "I have not always been. A defect of my upbringing, I suppose." Her smile had a surprising degree of self-awareness in it. "Perhaps that is why Mr. Clive and I always got on so well."

Lily caught a whiff of licorice from one tea packet and tried not to grimace. She had never enjoyed licorice. But perhaps one of her servants would like it. "I do not think his was a defect of upbringing," Lily pointed out as she folded up the paper once more.

"No." Miss Forrest looked away. "Perhaps I cannot blame my upbringing then either."

She stood, clearly preparing to leave, and Lily decided there was no point in trying to be discreet. "Miss Forrest, one more question, if I might. Were any of the guests at your uncle's party acquaintances from his time in the army?"

Miss Forrest looked taken aback by the question, but she laughed shortly. "I cannot say that I would have recognized any of them if they had been," she said tartly. "My uncle made no effort to introduce me to any of his friends, old or new, before he sent me away." Her mouth twisted as though she had tasted something bitter. "Why would he have? He had no intention of letting me remain in his home."

"Of course.' Lily nodded, trying not to let her frustration show. She had expected as much. But she still had hoped for more.

Miss Forrest held out her hand. "That, at least, is in the past. And you can be sure, Mrs. Adler, when I am back in my proper home on Queen Anne Street, you shall be one of the first of my acquaintance to be invited to call."

It was not an entirely pleasant statement for her to make, given the way that home had returned to her possession. And Lily could not help thinking of the last time she had been there, of the gruesome scene in Mr. Forrest's bedroom, Mr. Clive pleading for her help across the rough wood of the housekeeper's table. She wondered how he would feel about the prospect, now, of living in that house.

Still caught up in her thoughts after Sarah Forrest left, Lily absently sorted through the small handful of cards that had been left on the hall table. She had been so busy over the past few days that she had missed several callers. As she did, her eye was caught by the one on top. It belonged to a Mr. Mitford, and it took her a moment to recall the name.

He was the neighbor who had dropped off the package from Lady Adler. Lily sighed, her attention pulled away from the questions that tumbled through her mind without clear answers. If Mr. Mitford had called that morning while she was out, he would no doubt be returning soon, and if he left without a return missive from her, Lady Adler would worry that what she had sent had distressed or offended Lily. With Jack and Amelia having gone ahead to speak to Mr. Page, she could afford to delay by a few minutes. Better to write her response now and have it done with.

And no doubt it would do her good to think about something else. She had learned too much that was new and confusing in the last day, and she knew full well that her mind would work through it all better if she let herself be a little distracted, at least for a short while.

Lily went upstairs to her writing desk. She had put Lady Adler's letter out of sight in the bottom drawer, but she paused in the middle of retrieving it. She had, without thinking, left it next to her pistol. The long-barreled dueling pistol had been one of a pair Freddy had bought at university, wanting to impress his friends. His brother John had kept one and given the other to Lily, though she had never been a good shot.

Now, the sight of it made her shiver a little, remembering the sound of a gunshot echoing through the gardens at Vauxhall. She pushed the thought out of her mind. Louis Carver was in a prison cell, and no doubt once he was confronted with their knowledge of his identity, it would be easier to persuade him to reveal what they needed to know about Mr. Forrest. Besides which, she was supposed to be distracting herself.

Lily pulled out the letter and closed the drawer quickly, not wanting to look at the pistol any longer. Freddy's portrait was still propped up against the mirror of her dressing table; she went to retrieve it as well. But instead of returning to her writing desk, her steps slowed, and she lingered in the middle of the room, staring at his familiar face.

She traced the lines with one finger, her heart catching at the way the painter had captured his too-long hair, the hint of a smile he could never hide, even when he was being serious, the funny way he always stood with his hand at one hip. It was a good likeness.

It was a good likeness . . .

Lily caught her breath. There was a way to prove that the man who had attacked Jack was indeed Louis Carver, proof that she could take to Mr. Page and he in turn could take to his magistrate. Her hand tightened around the miniature before she took a deep breath and set it back against the mirror, Lady Adler's letter abandoned beside it. She had seen something similar recently.

She needed to see it again.

★　★　★

"You are kind to return, Mrs. Adler." Mrs. Carver stepped out of the doorway and gestured for Lily to enter. She rubbed her hands against her skirts nervously, smiling eagerly at the prospect of another sale so soon. "Though I've not finished a new batch in the last few days, I'm sorry to say. I've only got what you saw before."

"That will not be a problem at all," Lily said, snapping her parasol closed and stepping into the front parlor. "My maid has decided the gown will look best with another layer of trim around the sleeves, and I think I remember that there was more of the same pattern I purchased before. May I see it?"

"Of course." Mrs. Carver bobbed her head. "May I offer you some refreshment first? I could step through and brew some tea if you'll have some."

"Thank you, I will," Lily said, inclining her head graciously, playing the part of a dignified lady to her fullest. She had no interest in tea, though Anna had, in fact, mentioned that Lily had not bought enough lace the first time. But she wanted to keep Mrs. Carver out of the parlor for as long as possible. She took a seat on one of the stiff-backed chairs. "I will wait here."

Mrs. Carver, looking anxious to please and a little awed, assured Lily that she was indeed welcome to make herself comfortable, before hurrying from the room. As soon as Lily heard a clattering from the kitchen, she rose from the chair and went to the cabinet in the corner. Mrs. Carver would set the water to boil, and then she would go fetch the baskets of lace. Lily had only a handful of minutes; it would have to be enough.

It was hard to be silent while opening cabinet drawers and rifling through them, and she could only hope that she was looking in the right place. If not, perhaps she could introduce the topic of Mr. Carver somehow, and—

Lily's thoughts pulled to a halt. The drawer she had just opened contained a cluster of letters, a broken pair of scissors, and—nearly buried under the papers—a painted miniature only a few inches tall. She slid it out with careful fingers.

Louis Carver. The artist had inscribed his name carefully on the painted scroll that curled across the bottom of the portrait. It was not so well done as the painting of Freddy. No doubt the Carvers had not been able to afford as skilled an artist. But . . .

Lily stared at it, her heart pounding, feeling as though the floor had dropped out from beneath her feet.

The likeness was good indeed.

"What are you doing?"

Lily fell very still, her mind racing. Her back was to the passage door; in all likelihood, Mrs. Carver could not see what she held. Carefully, Lily slid the portrait back into the cabinet, closing the drawer before she turned around. She fixed a haughty smile on her face, the sort that said she was accustomed to getting her way and unaccustomed to anyone who would gainsay her. "I was looking for a pencil, Mrs. Carver," she said, feigning unconcern, though the anger and nervousness on the other woman's face was plain. "Surely you have such a thing?"

She saw Mrs. Carver's eyes dart to the now-closed drawer, and her lips drew together tightly. Lily wondered if the widow who was not a widow would have the nerve to accuse her of what she had clearly been doing.

"I'm afraid I spoke in error, ma'am," Mrs. Carver said at last. "I haven't got any tea in the house. But I do have four more yards of the same pattern of lace you bought before. Shall I wrap it up for you?"

"If you would be so kind," Lily said, inclining her head. "I have another appointment to keep and must be on my way."

★　★　★

"I'm sorry, Mrs. Adler, but Miss Hartley and her brother have already left us. They returned home at least an hour ago."

"No matter," Lily said, trying to keep her voice calm. Judith Page still looked exhausted and harried; she did not need to be further distressed. "It is Mr. Page I really need to see. Is he at liberty?"

Miss Page shook her head. "No, he was called away."

Lily stared. "But . . . where is he?"

"I haven't the faintest idea," Miss Page said, pushing an errant lock of hair off her forehead and tucking it behind her ear. "One of the mounted watch came to fetch him—some sort of disturbance in the Dials. They needed all the help they could get, I suppose." She glanced over her shoulder, clearly distracted and trying not to show it. "I'm sorry, ma'am, but I oughtn't to stay outside. The children are doing better but are still terribly weak and fretful, and I don't like to leave them alone for too long."

"Of . . . of course." Lily forced a smile, stepping back from the door. "Of course you must go to them. Will you tell Mr. Page I called, when he returns?"

"Certainly." Miss Page's polite smile was already distracted. "And thank you for the deliveries that came with Miss Hartley—it was terribly kind."

Lily stared at the door as it closed in her face. Dusk was already gathering around her, and she knew she shouldn't linger. She was away from home unaccompanied, and no one there knew where she was. She didn't want them to be worrying over her absence yet again. But she still didn't move.

It had not occurred to her that Mr. Page might be gone when she needed to speak to him so urgently. But a disturbance in the Seven Dials might take hours to quell, and he would likely be exhausted when he returned. She could not stay to wait for him, even had she been invited to.

Lily gritted her teeth against the urge to shout in frustration. But what she had learned about Louis Carver could wait for one night more. She sighed, turning her steps toward home.

She would call on Mr. Page first thing in the morning. It would keep until then.

CHAPTER 28

By the time Lily returned to Half Moon Street, the evening had grown dark, and Amelia was clearly beginning to worry. Jack had already left, but when Lily would have disappeared into her room to write to him, Amelia reminded her that there wasn't time.

"We are expected in Portman Square," she pointed out, watching Lily a little nervously. "It would be terribly rude if you were to be absent."

"I think this takes precedence over Mrs. Fox's feelings about her guest list," Lily said with more irritation than she usually let herself show.

"You are the one who always says not to make a statement without thinking through the consequences," Amelia said quietly. "And Mrs. Fox is well enough connected that missing her party would be seen as a statement."

She was right, and Lily knew it. Besides, there was nothing, truly, that could be done that night.

But the evening of dancing and gossiping in Portman Square grated on Lily's already jittery nerves. The Foxes were a political family, and Lily's invitation had come through her connection to Serena and Lord Walter. Few of her other friends were present, and though the atmosphere was elegant, the talk was mostly of Parliament. By the time she returned home, Lily's head ached from smiling and making conversation with strangers and distant acquaintances. But she consoled herself that Amelia, at least, had enjoyed herself; the youngest

Hartley, it seemed, had a head for politics. Amelia even asked to stay longer when Lily finally made her excuses; fortunately, Serena and Lord Walter offered to bring her home in their carriage.

Lily wondered absently, on her own carriage ride home, whether Amelia would ever have the opportunity to put her interest to use.

But as soon as she walked in the door at Half Moon Street, Lily could tell something was wrong. Carstairs was not in the hall when she came through the door, and the noise of the house was all wrong, though she could not have put her finger on exactly why until the sound of feet hurrying down the steps made her turn abruptly toward the staircase.

Mrs. Carstairs was so shocked to see her that she nearly lost her footing and had to grab the banister for balance. "Gracious, ma'am, you gave me a fright," she gasped, clutching one hand against her chest. "I'm sorry—we lost track of the time. Someone should have been here to welcome you home—"

"Mrs. Carstairs, what has happened?" Lily demanded, stepping toward her.

Her housekeeper's face fell even further, and she wrung her hands anxiously. "It's Anna," she whispered. "She's taken ill. Sick in her stomach and shaking . . ." Her voice had fallen to a whisper. "We're keeping her comfortable, ma'am. But we don't know what brought it on."

Lily felt cold all over, and for a moment she was frozen in place. Then she stepped forward. "Take me to her."

Anna was in her bed on the third floor, her eyes pressed tightly shut and sweat standing out on her forehead.

"Mr. Carstairs went for a doctor. She doesn't seem to know we're with her," Mrs. Carstairs whispered.

Lily took her maid's other hand, her mind blank with fear. Too many people had been taken ill. She had known it was no coincidence, even if she hadn't wanted to fully admit that truth. But now . . .

She had known Anna for half her life. If something had happened to her, it was because of what Lily had done, because of who she had scared.

Mr. Forrest was dead. But the person who had killed him was not.

"What happened?" Lily asked in a low voice. "What was she doing?"

"Sewing," Mrs. Carstairs said, her voice hoarse with worry. "She was working on your new dress while she had her tea and we all sat downstairs in the kitchen together."

Lily felt like a hand was squeezing her heart. "What tea was she having?" she demanded.

"What tea?" Mrs. Carstairs frowned. "I don't . . ." She shook her head, clearly at a loss. Just one from the cupboard. It smelled a little of licorice, perhaps. Do you think that was what made her ill?"

"I do not. . . She might have . . ." Lily's heart pounded as she stared at her maid, who was tossing and whimpering, half delirious. "Perhaps it had gone off. I will throw it out, right away, to be safe." There was a cloth in the basin next to the bed; she wrung it out and laid it across Anna's sweating brow. "I shall wait for the doctor downstairs. Will you stay with her?"

"Of course, Mrs. Adler." Mrs. Carstairs pulled herself together and patted Lily's shoulder. "Don't fret, ma'am. It'll do neither us nor her any good to fret. Young as she is, it will pass quickly, I'm certain of it."

"Yes, of course," Lily agreed, purely out of reflex. She barely heard what Mrs. Carstairs was saying as she left the room.

She waited in the hall, pacing restlessly, until the doctor arrived, rumpled and recently roused from sleep, but pressing her hand and giving assurances that he'd see her girl to rights. Lily nodded, wanting to believe him, and she sent Carstairs up to look in on his wife as well. Then she took a deep breath and went downstairs.

In the kitchen, Lily cleared away the empty teacups and pot, setting the teakettle to boil with all the emotion and awareness of a clockwork figure. When it was whistling, she pulled on the spare apron that hung by the hob and began to scald the dishes, wondering the whole time if it would be best to throw everything out.

If she hadn't been so distracted, she would have never accepted the tea from Sarah Forrest. Mr. Clive had said from the beginning that Sarah had been the one convinced that Mr. Forrest had wronged her. She should have listened to him. Lily scrubbed the teapot fiercely, tears on her cheeks and her hands smarting from the heat of the water.

That was where Amelia found her when she returned at last from the rest of her evening. "Mrs. Adler? Whyever are you washing dishes?"

Lily poured another kettle full of boiling water into the basin, rinsing everything one last time, before she turned to Amelia.

"Anna took ill suddenly," she said, pulling off the apron. "In much the same way that Fanny and George Andrews became ill."

Amelia frowned. "But . . . that does not . . ."

"What better way to ensure that a Bow Street constable cannot do his duty?" Lily said, turning for the stairs. "Mr. Page has been unable to attend to the matter of Mr. Forrest's death since his niece and nephew have been unwell. If you are a murderer and want to ensure that the trail you left behind grew cold, that would very much serve your purposes, would it not?"

"But—but then—" Amelia did not know what to say as she followed Lily up.

Lily went straight for her book-room. "I need you to go upstairs, Amelia. Tell Carstairs to go to Piccadilly and summon a carriage. And then you will need to change. Choose sturdier shoes and a less elegant cloak."

"Why?" Amelia whispered.

"I am going to write a letter to Mr. Page. And then you will take Carstairs and deliver it to Mr. Page."

"At this time of night?"

"It cannot wait. You will pound on that door until someone answers, and I do not care how many neighbors you wake with the racket. Mr. Page must read the letter tonight—do you understand?"

"But . . ." Amelia shook her head. "Should you not be the one to go?"

"I cannot go anywhere until I know that Anna is out of danger," Lily said, swallowing. "It is because of me that—" She broke off, taking a deep breath. "I need you to do this."

Amelia's eyes were wide and afraid, but she nodded. "Of course, Mrs. Adler. Of course I will." She hesitated, then laid her hand on Lily's arm. "She will be all right."

Lily didn't waste her breath arguing. "Go. Please."

Amelia went. Lily sank down into a chair at last, staring at the cold fireplace. For a moment, she was too scared to move.

Then she stood. She had a letter to write. And she needed to stay with Anna for as long as she could. And after that . . .

She would bring the woman who had done this to justice.

CHAPTER 29

It was just past dawn when Lily climbed out of the carriage at St. John's Square. Her steps were heavy, and her mind felt fuzzy with fatigue and worry. Amelia had eventually returned and crawled into her bed, worn out with worry and the late hour. But Lily had remained awake with the doctor, watching Anna's breathing and pulse until at last she was resting quietly.

"Is she out of danger?" Lily had demanded in an anxious whisper.

He had shaken his head. "I cannot tell yet. If she wakes, she will be well. But there's nothing more I can do."

Lily had wanted to stay by Anna's side. But she had made herself dress and repin her hair and walk out the door.

The door opened before she even had a chance to knock, and Mr. Page stared down at her. "Miss Hartley was very insistent in her delivery," he said quietly, stepping aside so she could come into the house. "How is your maid?"

"Resting," Lily said. "We do not yet know if she will wake."

"And you think it was deliberate?" he asked as he closed the door.

He spoke in a low voice, and Lily did the same. "I know it was," she said. "And I need you to help me find a way to prove it."

He nodded. "Tell me what you know."

Lily paced around the room as she repeated everything she could remember of her conversations with Mr. Clive and Miss Forrest, her suspicions about Mr. Forrest and Mr. Carver. Miss Forrest's visit.

Lily's discovery of the miniature portrait. Through it all, Mr. Page listened silently, nodding at each point.

"And your maid?" he asked. "You think it was the tea Miss Forrest left that was responsible?"

"I do not know what else it could have been," Lily said, pressing her hands against her eyes. "It is too much like what happened to Colonel Halliday. And her symptoms were just as you described Fanny's. She was drinking tea . . ." Lily trailed off, sudden understanding seizing her like a fist squeezing her chest.

"Drinking tea?" Mr. Page prompted when she did not finish right away.

"She was drinking tea with my other servants," Lily breathed. "There were three cups in the kitchen." She looked up at Mr. Page. "But she was the only one who fell ill."

"Do you mean to say it was not the tea that made her ill?" Mr. Page frowned at her. "Then Sarah Forrest would not be to blame. But if it was not the tea, was it something else?"

"There was nothing else except . . ." The possibility hit her like a slap, so sharp that she could have cursed herself for missing it. "Where does Fanny keep her botany books? I need to see one about English flowers."

"Flowers?" Mr. Page frowned. "I don't know. There is a stack of them in the kitchen, I think. Why?"

Lily was already heading toward the passage. "I need to look up the properties of aconite and how it is administered." There was indeed a stack of books on a chair by the fire. Lily began to look through them until she found two with promising titles.

"Aconite?" Mr. Page frowned from the doorway. "What's that?"

Lily met his eyes. "It is another name for wolfsbane."

"Wolfs . . ." Mr. Page drew in a sharp breath. He looked as though he wanted to demand more information. But instead, he nodded. "Hand me one of the books. I'll help you look."

Lily passed it to him immediately, and for several minutes they were silent except for the crackle of each turning page. Lily's heart was hammering painfully against her ribs by the time she found what she was looking for. "Here," she said. "It's here."

"Let me see it." Mr. Page stared at the book, his expression drawn and tight. "When taken in food or drink . . ." he read slowly. "If there is contact with the skin, it is most likely to be fatal if there is an open wound."

"Anna had no injuries, so far as I know," Lily said, nearly sagging against the wall with relief. "So she might be all right."

"But it was meant for you," Mr. Page said slowly.

Lily could have smiled if her chest hadn't felt so tight with worry. It meant she was correct. "Yes," she said, nodding. "It was."

"And the children? Was that meant for them or . . ." He took a deep breath. "For me, do you think?"

"I had thought it was a distraction, to prevent you from looking into the matter any further," Lily said slowly. *"Likely from eating too many sweets,"* he had said when the children first fell ill. "But I think now it was meant for Fanny all along. Did she bring anything for them? Anything to eat or drink?"

Mr. Page dropped into a chair at the kitchen table, covering his face with his hands. "Yes," he said in a strangled voice. "She said it was to thank Fanny for bringing new business to her door." When he opened his eyes, they were sharp with anger and frustration. "But I do not know how to prove it."

"I can think of a way we might," Lily said slowly, taking took a seat across from him. "But you are not going to like it."

He let out a slow breath. "What do you want us to do?"

★ ★ ★

"The children are in their room."

Lily could hear the footsteps coming up the stairs, the creak of the floorboards as they came down the hall. Judith Page sounded nervous, but that could be accounted for by worry. There was no reason anyone would assume—yet—that she was playing a part.

"The doctor said we could expect them to continue to improve. But they are still fretful, especially Fanny. I thought you might give them something . . ."

"Of course." The sound of Mrs. Carver's voice made the hair on Lily's head stand up, now that she knew what the woman had tried to do. "I brought a tonic for the nerves that should settle her right away and help her rest more easily."

Simon Page, at Lily's side, glanced at her. She nodded back, going to stand beside him so their bodies were in between Mrs. Carver and the two beds. A moment later, the two women appeared in the door, Mrs. Carver still nervously extolling the virtues of her tonic.

"My grandfather used to make the same thing, God rest him, and his patients always said—"

"Mrs. Carver," Lily broke in. "How good of you to come to care for the children."

The woman froze on the threshold, staring at her in uneasy disbelief. "How are you—" She broke off, clutching her bag to her chest with both hands. "What are you doing here?

"What a curious slip of the tongue," Lily said softly. She could see a sheen of perspiration on Mrs. Carver's forehead, and the hands clutching the handle of her bag shook.

"I think perhaps the first question you wanted to ask was the better one," Simon Page said, his voice impersonal and icy. "Like you, Mrs. Adler is here because of the children."

That seemed to give Mrs. Carver some heart. She straightened her spine and nodded, reaching into her bag to pull out a bottle of medicine. "In that case, if you'll all care to step out of the room—"

"Oh, certainly. But first I must ask you to do one thing." Lily's smile held no warmth. "The children have been so unwell, and Mr. and Miss Page have understandably been so worried for them. To set their minds at ease . . ." She nodded to the bottle in Mrs. Carver's hand. "Would you be so good as to sample a taste of the tincture you have prepared?"

The stillness that came over Mrs. Carver at Lily's words was eerie in its suddenness. The two women stared at each other, and Lily knew they both understood what she was saying. She felt no triumph at discovering that she had been right, nor relief at having answers. She did not take her eyes off Miss Carver.

The woman was still dangerous. And while she may not have been a clever person—she was too impulsive, too afraid of her own actions—she was also too desperate to give up just because she knew someone had seen through her.

"I'm afraid I can't do that," Mrs. Carver said, shaking her head and attempting to smile. "A medicine should only be used for the ailment it was intended to treat—"

"Is that something your grandfather taught you?" Lily asked, stepping forward. At the door, Miss Page inched along the wall; they had told her to get away from Mrs. Carver as soon as she was able. Lily had hoped she would leave the room entirely. But she could not blame Miss Page for wanting to see what unfolded. "Your grandfather, the apothecary? You must have learned a great deal from him, Mrs. Carver. What ails, what cures . . ." She did not look away from the woman in front of her. "What kills."

"If you won't permit me to help the children, then I see no reason for me to be here," Mrs. Carver snapped, shoving the bottle back into her bag with shaking hands. She wheeled around, already ready to head for the door.

"Before you go, can I offer you some refreshment?" Mr. Page asked. When Mrs. Carver turned back, confused, he nodded toward the table. "Fanny and George weren't able to finish the sweets you gave Fanny. With gratitude, I think you said, for two new customers. Would you care for one?"

"No, thank you," Mrs. Carver declared, bold and brash and clearly afraid. Lily did not miss the hand that was slowly sliding inside her bag. "I never eat sweets. But if you will—"

The quiet click of a hammer being pulled back filled the room. Mr. Page pulled his hand from under his coat, the pistol in it raised and pointed directly at Mrs. Carver. "Set your bag on the floor, Mrs. Carver. Carefully, if you please. We know exactly what manner of terrible things you have in there," he added, his eyes blazing with fury. "My niece was right about you from the first. I should have listened to her."

Mrs. Carver hesitated, but the barrel of that gun did not waver. Looking scared, she began to slowly lower her bag to the carpet. Then, with a motion that was almost too quick to follow, she threw it toward Miss Page and ran from the room.

CHAPTER 30

Simon cursed, grabbing his sister with one hand and hauling her to him. The bag crashed to the floor only inches from where her feet had been. There was a sound of glass shattering inside it, and liquid began to seep out.

Simon pointed the pistol toward the doorway, but Mrs. Carver was already gone. They could hear her feet pounding down the stairs of the small house.

"Mrs. Adler?" Simon asked, panting a little.

"Do not touch it," Lily said as calmly as she could manage. She was pressed against the opposite wall, swallowing as she stared at the puddle of liquid slowly forming. There was no knowing what had been in there, but she could guess. "You niece's books said that aconite can take effect quickly, and you do not have to ingest it for it to begin working."

"We ought to leave," Judith Page said, her voice shaking. "Quickly. We can deal with the mess later."

Neither Lily nor Simon argued. From below, they could hear the sounds of struggle, and Mrs. Carver's voice raised, shrieking curses and demanding to be unhanded.

Mr. Page glanced at Lily. "That proceeded rather as you expected."

The praise was satisfying, but Lily still shook her head. "I wish I had not been right."

"Do you want to go to the children?" Mr. Page asked his sister.

There was a grimmer look in her eyes than Lily had yet seen, even at the height of her worry about Fanny and George. "I do," Miss

Page said. "But first, I want to know what happened. And I want to hear what she has to say."

They did not linger upstairs. The scene, when they came into the downstairs parlor, was much as Lily had expected. Adelaide Carver was still struggling, but Jack held her arms behind her back. His face was drawn into a tight grimace, and Lily knew his arm must be paining him, but he did not let go. Mrs. Carver looked up as Lily and the Pages came downstairs, but her eyes locked instantly on the pistol Simon Page still carried. She shuddered, and the fight seemed to go out of her. She slumped in Jack's arms, and he hissed with pain as her weight pulled on his bad shoulder. But still he held her tight.

Lily met Jack's eyes. He did not quite smile at her—the situation was too grim for that. But the single nod he gave her made her throat feel tight with relief and gratitude. She had sent him a letter with instructions when she realized who was truly behind Fanny and George's illness, begging him to be at the Pages' house in time to assist them. And she had known without question that he would be there, that he would do as she asked.

She had known he would trust her.

"Let me go," Mrs. Carver pleaded, but her voice was dull and thick, as though she already knew it was useless to ask.

"Not a chance in hell," said a stern voice. Lily looked to the doorway, where Sir Nathaniel Conant, the current chief magistrate at the Bow Street Office, stood with his arms crossed. He was a broad-shouldered, glowering man, and Lily felt more than a little nervous as he looked them all over. She had, in the past, met magistrates who were less than honest in their dealings. But Sir Nathaniel was said to take his duties seriously, and Mr. Page respected him. Lily hoped that respect was not misplaced. "I want to know what has happened here. What evidence do you have against this woman?"

"None," cried Mrs. Carver, growing more animated. "I've done nothing wrong, sir, I'm just a poor widow who—"

"Sir Nathaniel," Lily interrupted, stepping forward. "You are good to come at Mr. Page's summons. The woman being held is Adelaide Carver. She has assisted a murderer in his crimes, turned killer herself, and attempted the destruction of at least three other people who have, fortunately, survived."

"I didn't, on my honor, sir, I never—"

The magistrate held up his hand. "Mr. Page said as much in his message," he said, nodding to the constable, who was standing at very straight attention, though he still gripped his sister's hand comfortingly. With the magistrate present, he had lowered his pistol. "But he offered no proof."

"We hope to present some," Jack said, managing a polite bow of the head without loosening his grip on Mrs. Carver.

The magistrate looked him over. "And you are?"

"Jack Hartley, sir. Until recently a captain of His Majesty's Navy, and honored today to be of assistance to your esteemed constable."

Lily glanced out of the corner of her eye at Mr. Page, who looked surprised by the praise. He and Jack had not always seen eye to eye in the early days of their acquaintance.

"Hartley," the magistrate said slowly, nodding. "You have given evidence to us before."

"I have had that honor, sir," Jack said, giving another bow. Lily held her breath. Jack had indeed spoken before the magistrate's court regarding a case some years before. She hoped that would count in their favor today.

The magistrate looked him up and down, then turned his steely gaze on Lily. "And you, madam?"

It was a fearsome look, but Lily was determined to be equal to it. She lifted her chin. "I am Mrs. Lily Adler."

That made him pause. "I think I have heard your name as well, madam."

That caught her by surprise. Though she had been involved in the work of the Bow Street constables more than once, she had done her best to ensure that her name was not whispered in connection with any of it. And she would not have expected any of them to share credit for their work with—or even admit to making use of assistance from—a lady.

Lily glanced at Mr. Page, whose brows rose as he met her eyes, as though to ask what she expected. Behind the magistrate, she could see Jack smirking, looking pleased at the news. Lily wasn't sure she was equally pleased—she had little desire to become notorious. But she could not say so to the magistrate's face.

"I hope that is to my credit and benefit," she said calmly. "I suppose we shall see. Captain Hartley." She turned to Jack. "Did Jem arrive?"

"Here, mum." The boy popped his head out of the kitchen, looking uneasy as he eyed the grim assembly in the parlor. "Captain told me to stay out of the way until you came down."

"And we are all grateful that you heeded him," Lily said. "Were you able to find the portrait?"

He shook his head. "Me 'n' my boys looked everywhere in her house, soon as she was out the door to come here. Right mess we made of it," he admitted, shrugging. "But you said we needed to work fast."

"That means she likely has it on her person, unless she was wise enough to throw it away. Which I do not think you were," Lily added, turning back to Mrs. Carver. "Or you would have done so the moment your husband returned to London and pulled you into his scheme."

"And what will you do to find out?" Mrs. Carver demanded. "Have these men rummage through a poor widow-woman's clothes? Disgraceful, that would be."

"Of course not," Lily said, refusing to rise to the woman's bait. "But Miss Page and I will not hesitate to search you if we must."

"Never know what might be hidden in my stays and petticoats," Mrs. Carver taunted. "Might be dangerous if it touches you."

Instead of intimidating Lily, however, the threat made her smile. "Do you admit, then, to carrying poisons on your person?"

That made Mrs. Carver snap her mouth closed. She glared at Lily, her jaw working as though there were so many words bottled up there that she could not decide which to utter. At last, she tried to yank one of her arms away from Jack; at a nod from Lily, he let go. Mrs. Carver pulled the miniature portrait from her bodice and threw it to the ground. A sharp crack echoed through the silent room.

Lily picked it up carefully. The wood back had split, though it was still attached. The portrait itself was still whole. She held it out to the magistrate. "You will be able to see, sir, that the name on it is Louis Carver, who was Mrs. Carver's husband." At his nod, she offered the portrait to Miss Page. "You knew him. Would you consider it a good enough likeness?"

Miss Page stared at the painting, then nodded. "Yes, and any neighbor who knew him would tell you the same."

Lily held it out to Mr. Page. "I recognize him as well, Constable, though I never met a Mr. Carver in my life. Do you?"

Simon stared at the miniature. "It *is* Martin Forrest," he said. He had known what to expect, but still, his shock was too obvious to be feigned. He looked at Lily, then to his magistrate, and straightened up once more. "It is Mr. Martin Forrest, the man whose death I have been investigating. I wrote up—"

"Yes, I recall the details," Sir Nathaniel said, brisk but not dismissive. He fixed Lily with a stern eye. "Explain, please, madam." Then he glanced at Jack. "But let that woman sit down. Page is armed, and she is well outnumbered. She will not escape us."

Jack obeyed. While Mrs. Carver slumped into a chair, burying her face in her hands, he went to slap Jem on the shoulder. "Good man," he said approvingly, while the boy seemed to nearly levitate with pride at the praise. "Duck outside now, and make sure the horses are still standing easy." Jack stepped back as Jem obeyed, positioning himself by the mantle but still within arm's reach of Mrs. Carver.

Lily could see that he was holding his arm stiffly at his side, and she wanted to go to him. But the magistrate was still looking at her expectantly. She took a deep breath.

"Mrs. Carver's husband was a private in the army and body servant to Captain Martin Forrest of the Twelfth Light Dragoons. As Mr. Forrest had sold out his commission and was returning to England ahead of the rest of his regiment, his commanding officer, Colonel Halliday, permitted Mr. Carver to travel with him. Mr. Forrest had been injured some months before, you see. Mr. Carver was to assist him with the crossing and establishing himself in

London. But during the crossing, Mr. Carver disappeared, and the army considered him a deserter. Mr. Martin Forrest arrived in London alone, where he became the heir of his recently departed brother and the guardian of his niece, Miss Sarah Forrest." Lily crossed to the mantlepiece as she spoke, where she had left Dr. Ivey's diary that morning. She held it out to the magistrate. "You will find the details of Mr. Forrest's injury, as recorded by Dr. Ivey, in here. And Colonel Halliday, who resides in Gravesend, can confirm the rest."

Sir Nathaniel examined the book for a moment, but his eyes returned to her. "But you said Mr. Forrest was *not* Mr. Forrest," he pointed out, eyes narrowing. "Carver took his place?"

"There was enough resemblance between them to make it plausible," Lily said, nodding. "Especially as Mr. Forrest had not been seen in England in more than two decades."

She heard a loud sigh from Jack. "The colonel said that Mr. Forrest had a loose tongue about his family troubles," he said, slapping his hand down on the mantlepiece as he put the pieces together. "Carver must have heard all about them, along with the rest of the regiment. It probably gave him plenty of information with which to begin his impersonation. And any lapses could be accounted for by years of absence."

"There were such different reports of his character," Simon Page put in. "Unpolished, the servants said."

"And I found him despicable," Jack added with a grimace.

"But the colonel called him a pleasing, well-mannered man," Lily said. "All explained by the simple fact that there were two different men being described."

"I do not suppose your husband told you what happened to the real Mr. Forrest?" Jack said, his voice quiet and fierce as he stared at Mrs. Carver. "Tossed overboard into the Channel, perhaps, or just one of the many bodies found in the alleyways of the City? He was an officer in His Majesty's Army. He deserved better than that."

She shrank back from him. "I don't know," she muttered. "Louis never said, and I didn't ask. There's things it's better not to know."

There was a heavy silence in the room. Jack drew himself up, composed once more, but Lily's heart ached for him.

At last, the magistrate pointed to Mrs. Carver. "How does she come into it, then?"

"At some point, Mr. Carver made her aware of his presence in London, and eventually of his deception. I am afraid I do not know the timeline precisely," Lily said, giving Mrs. Carver a cold smile. "Would you care to share it with us, ma'am?" She was not surprised when Mrs. Carver only glowered at her. "Very well, I shall hazard a guess. Knowing what we do of his character, I think Mr. Carver might not have wanted to let his wife know he had returned to London. But there were people in London, or near to it, from his old regiment who might reasonably cross paths with Mr. Martin Forrest and thus reveal his deception. So he went to his wife."

"She was an apothecary's granddaughter," Judith Page murmured, nodding even as she looked ill at the thought. "Of course. He needed poison."

"It is easy enough to guess at what he promised you, Mrs. Carver," Lily said softly, watching the other woman as she spoke. Mrs. Carver's hands were clasped tightly against her knees, her mouth set in a thin line, her eyes blazing as she stared at Lily. But she said nothing. "A better life for you both—much easier than an existence as a half-pay soldier or as the widow of a deserter. And all you had to do was supply him with poison for two men." She looked at Mr. Page. "Fanny was right about the wolfsbane."

"I should have listened to her sooner," Simon sighed. At his side, Judith reached out to press his hand.

"Two men," Sir Nathaniel rumbled. They all turned toward him, as if they had forgotten for a moment he was there. "Who were they?"

"Dr. Ivey treated Mr. Forrest after his injury," Lily said, nodding to the diary. "Had he seen Mr. Carver in his new role, even from a distance—or had he even spoken to someone else about the real Mr. Forrest—the sham could have been uncovered. And Colonel Halliday was his commanding officer, residing not far from Mr. Forrest's home in London."

"Dr. Ivey took a tincture for his nerves," Jack put in. "Easy enough to replace, for either of them to deliver it and say it was from the apothecary. But his death had little in common with Halliday's illness." He gestured to Mrs. Carver, who turned her glare on him. "Did she use a different mixture?"

"No." Lily shook her head. "We should have asked Fanny earlier. Her love of botany would have come in quite useful." She glanced at Mr. and Miss Page. "She is a frightfully intelligent young lady, you know."

Mr. Page put his arm around his sister's shoulders. "We know."

Lily turned back to the magistrate. It was he, after all, that she needed to persuade. "Apparently people can react differently to aconite poisoning. Some will experience a sensation like a gastric attack; others may seem to suffer from palpitations, or headache and trouble breathing—as George did," she added, glancing at Miss Page. "His and Fanny's illnesses seemed so different as well. That was why."

"And this colonel?" Sir Nathaniel asked. His look had grown even more severe as he listened to Lily speak, his brows drawing together into a glowering frown.

"Mr. Carver paid a visit to his home in Gravesend, knocking on the door mere minutes after the colonel had departed in his carriage." She shook her head. "I am sure it was no difficulty to watch the door and time his call for shortly after he saw the colonel leave. He left a gift of French brandy, knowing from his time with the Dragoons that the colonel loved it. But he had no way of knowing that the colonel was already ill. Had he not been, the poison would no doubt have taken his life as well."

Mr. Page made a sharp, surprised noise, and they all turned to stare at him. "You speculated that it might not have been Mr. Forrest," he said, shaking his head at Lily, "when you first grew suspicious of the brandy. You pointed out that, since the colonel had not seen the man, it might not have been Mr. Forrest who called."

She smiled a little. "If I was correct, it was rather by accident. I did not suspect at the time that Mr. Forrest was not in fact Mr. Forrest. But the brandy was poisoned. If you recall, Colonel Halliday had some, hoping that it would improve his illness. And that was the night that his servants feared he was in danger of dying. No doubt he would have had he not been so ill that he was already . . ." She cleared her throat delicately. "That is, I do not think the aconite was able to remain in his body for long."

The magistrate barked out a laugh. "Too busy casting up his accounts to end up poisoned, you mean. Fortunate man." He shook his head, his expression growing more serious again. "Well, and so, they conspired to poison these men, and once succeeded. How did it come, then, that this Mr. Forrest"—he grimaced—"this Mr. Carver was stabbed?"

"He tried to do me in first," Adelaide Carver snapped, as though unable to restrain herself. "Hired a scoundrel to try to stab me on my way home one night. Lucky I was that one of the mounted patrol happened by just then and chased the blackguard off." She looked between the magistrate and the constable, her expression earnest. "I've always had a great deal of respect and gratitude for the Bow Street force."

"But not for their families?" Mr. Page demanded. "Or for the children of those families, perhaps?" When Mrs. Carver fell silent, looking stricken, he glanced at Sir Nathaniel. "She was attacked in the street, that much is true enough. The night before Mr. Forrest died."

Lily closed her eyes, feeling suddenly exasperated with herself. "She must have been the person the servants were trying to find in the house the night of the ball," she said, shaking her head. "They stumbled on—" She broke off, glancing toward Jack, who was hiding a small grin in spite of the tense situation. She quickly looked away, fixing her eyes on the magistrate so she would not be tempted to look at Jack again. "Mr. Forrest threw a ball the night of his death, with the intent, apparently, of announcing his engagement to a young lady named Miss Crawley. I can only imagine how Mrs. Carver felt, realizing that her husband had attempted to get rid of her so that he could marry a new woman."

"He would have assumed the role of Mr. Forrest completely," Mr. Page said quietly. "Though he might have been in for an unpleasant surprise when he realized his poison had failed to eliminate Colonel Halliday."

"But he did not have the chance," Lily continued. "Mrs. Carver hid in the house, intending to confront him when he came upstairs. One can assume they quarreled. She found a letter opener at hand, and . . ."

The magistrate shook his head. "An unpleasant business, to be sure," he said, his eyes resting on Mrs. Carver. She flinched away, her hands twisting in her skirt, and said nothing.

Sir Nathaniel turned his scrutiny on the rest of them, a frown drawing his brows together. Lily wondered nervously what he was thinking, and she glanced sideways at Jack, who gave her a brief, encouraging flicker of a smile. But he looked nervous as well.

For a moment, no one spoke.

"A question, Mr. Page, before I decide what to do next," said the magistrate. "How the devil—beg your pardon, madam, Miss Page—but how did Mrs. Adler come to be involved in this matter?"

Simon Page cleared his throat a little uncomfortably, clearly not sure of what to say.

Lily had no such hesitation. "Mr. Forrest had a niece, sir, who expected to inherit her father's fortune. When she did not, she became convinced that her uncle had somehow undermined her father's will and stolen the money from her. She wanted help uncovering the truth and sought my aid."

"Had this Mr. Carver done so?"

Lily shook her head. "Her father changed his will shortly before his death, with the expectation that his brother would approve her choice of husband and dower her generously. *That* Mr. Carver did not do. It seems he thought he could provide the smallest possible maintenance to her and her companion and keep the rest in his own pocket."

Sir Nathaniel's lip curled. "A fine man, this Mr. Carver." He shot a glance at Mrs. Carver. "Seems like he was destined for a bad end, at your hand or someone else's."

"It wasn't me," Adelaide Carver muttered, but there was no conviction in the statement. "I didn't mean—I never would have—" She broke off, pressing her lips together, and dropped her gaze to her lap.

"So if this Louis Carver killed the real Mr. Forrest and took his place, then who the devil attacked us in Vauxhall?" Jack demanded. "Who is the man locked up in Newgate?"

"I cannot say for certain, but I believe it may be a man called Hansen, another private who was body servant to Colonel Halliday." Lily glanced at Mrs. Carver as she spoke and was gratified to see confirmation of her guess in the woman's face. "He and Carver served the same sort of role in the regiment and likely became friends. And unlike the rest of the regiment, Hansen would still be in London, waiting for the colonel's health to improve so they might return to the Continent." Seeing Mrs. Carver's furious expression, Lily added, "Though I do not know whether she recognized Hansen during the attack or put the pieces together later when she went to see her husband."

"Stupid man, that Hansen," Mrs. Carver snapped. "Too foolish to realize that if Louis was getting rid of me, it was only a matter of time 'til he stuck a knife in Hansen's back too."

"Likely true," Mr. Page said with a short laugh. "But in the meantime, he kept making use of him. He must have feared, after running into you twice under such odd circumstances, Captain Hartley, that you had somehow uncovered who he really was."

"He was a dreadful, greedy man," Mrs. Carver burst out. "The world is better off with him gone."

"That is not for you to decide," Sir Nathaniel said, his voice a threatening rumble.

Adelaide Carver shrank back into herself. "I was better off when he was nothing but a deserter who would never come home," she bit off, her face twisting with anger. "It was all his doing, you know, I never wanted any of it! I'd never harm a hair on—"

"On anyone's head?" Judith Page burst out. "What about Fanny and George, then?"

"George wasn't even supposed to eat the sweets! And Fanny . . ." Mrs. Carver's voice turned pleading. "She isn't dead, is she? And I could have killed her easily with those poisons Louis made me grow. You know I could have," she added, fixing Mr. Page with a desperate look.

"That is not the persuasive argument you seem to think it is," he said, while Miss Page pressed herself more deeply into the protective curve of his arm.

Mrs. Carver shook her head. "I just needed to buy a little time while I decided what to do. And I didn't want her telling anyone else until I had."

"Telling anyone else what?" Miss Page demanded.

"That she had seen Louis Carver," Lily said quietly. "Is that not right?" Mrs. Carver, glared at her, but she gave a single, jerky nod as Lily continued. "When Fanny first took me to Mrs. Carver's home, she innocently mentioned seeing a man leaving the house one morning. There was a neighbor visiting at the same time, and I thought Mrs. Carver was so upset with Fanny that day because the neighbor speculated that Mrs. Carver was entertaining gentlemen to support herself. But she was really worried that someone would realize that it was her husband and figure out what he was doing."

"I just needed a little time to decide what to do," Mrs. Carver repeated eagerly. "That was all."

"Then what were you planning to do today?" Mr. Page demanded. Mrs. Carver pressed her lips together and said nothing. "And what about the poisoned lace you sent home with Mrs. Adler after she saw the portrait of your husband?"

"What poisoned lace?" Mrs. Carver insisted. "She's standing here, isn't she? She don't look like a poisoned woman to me."

"Because I was not the first one to handle it," Lily said, her voice shaking. She did not bother to hide the full weight of her anger as she stared at Mrs. Carver. "My maid was."

There was a beat of silence in the room. "What happened to her?" the magistrate asked.

Lily glanced at him. "We are waiting to see if she will wake," she said quietly.

His expression grew even more grave. "You had best pray, then, Mrs. Carver, that the maid recovers. Or hers will be another death laid at your feet."

"It was all Louis," Adelaide Carver pleaded. She glanced around the room at each of them in turn. "He was bad, through and through. You saw it yourselves. He stole from that Miss Forrest—and you said he sent Hansen to attack that man!" she added, pointing at Jack. "I never would have hurt anyone without him."

"You attacked children, Mrs. Carver," Sir Nathanial said coldly. "Not only children, but the family of a principal officer of Bow Street. A man charged with keeping the peace and protecting the citizens of this city, who could not fulfill that duty because of your actions. That is besides your role in the poisoning of this Dr. Ivey, the death of your husband, *and* the threat to this lady's life, the life of her servant, and that of the colonel." He strode across the room and hauled Mrs. Carver to her feet. "I have very little sympathy, whatever you may have suffered at the hands of your husband. But it is not up to me to decide what happens to you." He pulled a heavy pair of handcuffs from his coat and snapped them onto her wrists with a decisive click. She let out a sharp sob and hung her head. "Pray you find a jury more sympathetic to your tale than I am at the moment. Constable."

Simon Page stepped forward. "Sir."

"Take this woman to my carriage, which awaits outside. Perhaps this gentleman can assist you," he added, glancing at Jack.

"With pleasure, sir," Jack said, nodding. He paused by Lily as he walked toward the door, as though he would speak. But a moment later he seemed to change his mind, only bowing to her and to Miss Page before he joined Mr. Page in escorting Mrs. Carver out the door.

Sir Nathaniel cleared his throat once it was only the three of them left in the room. He looked suddenly tired. "An unpleasant business, to be sure. But I suppose I am grateful for your assistance in bringing it to light, Mrs. Adler. You have the mind of an investigator." He shook his head. "A shame. Were you a man, I would make good use of you."

"I enjoy being myself well enough, sir," Lily said mildly, knowing that it would be useless to dispute the point. "And I am glad to have been of some assistance."

Sir Nathaniel turned to Miss Page and held out his hand. When she placed hers in it, he bowed over it gallantly. "I am sorry such trouble was brought to your door, Miss Page. I know it is no easy business to live with a man who serves the law."

"It's the work he was meant to do," Miss Page said quietly. "But I'm grateful for your sympathy, sir."

"You and your family both have my gratitude. And I will keep you no longer from the children. No doubt they are distressed with missing your care." Sir Nathaniel bowed to them both and moved to leave. But he turned back at the door, frowning a little. "I have to say, though, it was a risk, summoning her to treat them. It made for a clever trap, but the consequences could have been dreadful had things not gone according to plan."

Judith Page let out a shaky breath that was almost a laugh. "But the children aren't in the house, sir. We wouldn't have let her walk through the front door if they had been." She blinked back tears. "It was hard to leave them, as I'm sure you can imagine. But Mrs. Carver would have been suspicious had I not been here with Mr. Page. She knows too well our concern for them."

"Ah." A ghost of a smile was on the magistrate's lips. "Very wise. But then, Page has always had a good deal of foresight." He glanced at Lily, and she knew he had guessed accurately where the children were. Sir Nathaniel, it seemed, was no fool. "I thank you again, Mrs. Adler. And rest assured, your name shall not be made public, whatever happens with Mrs. Carver's trial."

Lily inclined her head. "You have my gratitude for that, sir."

As soon as the men were gone, Miss Page turned to Lily, no longer bothering to hold back her tears. "Take me to them, please."

Lily nodded. "Jem!" She called out. A moment later, his head popped in the front door. "Find us a carriage, quick as you can. We need to go to Half Moon Street at once."

CHAPTER 31

Lily left Judith Page in the guest room, fussing over both children, who were sitting up in bed and starting to look like themselves at last. The doctor was at hand once more, tending to Anna down in the servants' quarters.

Lily had examined the lace that Anna was sewing onto the gown as soon as she returned home, and the powdered traces of dried wolfsbane had been evident once she knew what to look for. They burned the whole gown and all the poisoned lace out in her patch of garden, where the wind carried the smoke far away.

Amelia had been fussing over the children. Once Lily returned and collapsed into a chair in her sitting room, worn out even though it was barely noon, she was fussed over as well. When she protested that Miss Page was more in need, Amelia informed her that all the Pages had been attended to. Placated, Lily let Amelia help her undress, then crawled into bed.

She woke up disoriented, unaccustomed to sleeping during the day. Someone had drawn the curtains, but enough light peeked through that she could see if was late in the afternoon.

"Feeling better, ma'am?"

Lily jumped, but it was only Amelia, sitting with a book in front of the fireplace. She laid a ribbon between the page to mark her place and let it fall closed. "You slept for hours."

Alarm gripped Lily's chest as she struggled upright against what suddenly felt like too many bedclothes. "Anna—"

"Is resting," Amelia said quickly. "The doctor said she was out of danger. And Miss Page and the children have returned to their home. Lady Carroway came by, and she offered her carriage to convey them when I told her I would not wake you up."

"That was kind of her," Lily said through a yawn. "I ought to have seen them off, though."

"They understood," Amelia said quietly, setting her book aside. "Miss Page told us what happened. I think you must be terribly proud of yourself, Mrs. Adler."

Lily closed her eyes, pressing her hands against her forehead. "She told Lady Carroway as well?"

"Yes." When Lily opened her eyes, there was a smile on Amelia's face. "Her ladyship said that she would understand if you needed to miss her grand ball tonight, but I do not think she meant it."

Lily groaned. "I had forgotten that was tonight. No, we cannot miss it. I will simply have to rally myself for it. Did anything else happen when I was asleep?"

"My brother called to see you. But when I said you were sleeping, he took himself off."

Lily sat up. "Did he say what news there was? Anything from Bow Street? You ought to have woken me."

"I would have. He would not permit me. But he said to tell you that Mrs. Carver has been taken to Newgate to await her trial. And that Mr. Clive has been released." Amelia picked up her book once more. "He also asked me to assure you that he would see you tonight."

Lily fell back against the pillows, relieved. "Good."

"There seemed to be something else he wished to say, though perhaps not with his little sister as a messenger." Amelia flipped the pages of her book with a great deal of studied unconcern. "Is there anything particular you wish to tell me, Mrs. Adler?"

Lily felt her cheeks heat, resenting the embarrassed smile that wanted to spread across her face. Instead, she gave Amelia a stern look. "Why should I, when you clearly already know?"

Amelia's smile grew as she set her book aside and rose. "I shall ring for the tea tray. You ought to have something to eat before we dress for the evening."

But before she could reach the bellpull, there was a gentle tap at the door. When Amelia called out permission to enter, Mrs. Carstairs peeked in.

"Ah, Mrs. Adler, I'm that glad to see you awake again, ma'am. Miss Hartley told you the news about Anna?"

"She did," Lily said, sitting up quickly. "Is she resting as well? How does she seem?"

"She is resting, yes," Mrs. Carstairs said, coming to the bed and patting Lily's hand in a reassuring fashion. "The doctor said it will be a few days until she is feeling herself again. I told him I was sure our Mrs. Adler would not insist she return to her duties before she was ready."

"No indeed," Lily said firmly. "If I did not think a long journey by carriage would make things worse, I would even say she should return to her parents while she recovers." Seeing the hesitant look on her housekeeper's face, Lily felt a prickle of unease. "What is it, Mrs. Carstairs? Did the doctor say something else?"

"No, not at all. But I actually didn't come up here because of Anna. You've visitors downstairs, a man and a woman, and even when I said you weren't receiving anyone, they were insistent that they needed to see you."

"Did they give their names?"

"A Miss Forrest and Mr. Clive." Mrs. Carstairs shook her head. "It might be difficult to get rid of them, ma'am, though of course we will if you don't wish to see them."

"No." Lily shook her head, tossing back the bedclothes. "I shall be forced to see them at some point, so it might as well be now. Will you help me to dress?"

★ ★ ★

"You know, you have a very pretty house," Miss Forrest said as soon as Lily walked into the drawing room. She was at the mantelpiece, examining a pair of candlesticks that rested there. "I had not really looked around when I was here before."

"Thank you," Lily said mildly, taking a seat by the window. She had not ordered refreshments, not wanting to give her guests an excuse to linger. She glanced at Henry Clive, who was seated opposite while Miss Forrest prowled around. "You look well, sir."

"For a man recently released from prison, you mean?" he said, his ironic smile back and displayed in full force. "Never have I appreciated the luxury of a hot bath more than I did today."

"And you two have reconciled, I see?"

"We have." Sarah Forrest sank down next to her sweetheart, beaming at him as he took her hand and pressed it tightly. "He came to my doorstep as soon as he was released from Newgate—well, almost as soon; he went home to bathe first—and threw himself at my feet in the parlor. It was terribly romantic."

"Miss Waverly must have been very impressed," Lily said dryly.

Miss Forrest laughed. "She was near to swooning with admiration. And I decided it does not matter to me what his origins are. He is a gentleman now, surely, and we care for each other so very much. What more could a young lady hope for in a husband?" She took a deep breath. "But that was not what we came to talk to you about. The man from Bow Street came to see me this morning, Mrs. Adler. And the tale he told was"—her eyes were wide—"extraordinary. Is it true that Mr. Forrest—the man I knew as Mr. Forrest, I mean—was not, in fact, my uncle?"

Lily didn't want to relive the whole business again so soon, but the girl deserved to hear it from her in all its confusing, messy detail. She told them quietly how it had come about, from the death of the real Mr. Forrest to the death of the false one. She did not venture much beyond that—they did not need to know the details of the Page family's involvement, and she had no wish to mention Ofelia or bring her fears for Jack's safety into it. Miss Forrest drank in the whole tale, exclaiming at each extraordinary revelation.

"I wish I'd had the chance to know my real uncle," she said sadly. "Do you think he would have been good to me, Mrs. Adler? Or would he have borne a grudge for my father's treatment of him all those years?" Her voice trembled as she spoke.

"I think, from what we learned of the true Martin Forrest's character, that he would have done his best to treat you well," Lily said gently. She thought it was true, but even if it was not, she had the feeling that Miss Forrest needed to hear it. "He came at his brother's summons, after all. Even if he did still bear some resentment, I think he would have wanted to be a good guardian to you."

Mr. Clive had been watching her the whole time with a thoughtful look on his face. "I think there are parts of your story that may be missing," he said, smiling a little when she finished. "Do you not trust me with them, then?"

"They are not relevant," Lily said firmly.

"Hmm." He shook his head. "Well, I suppose I can't blame you for that, given all that has passed."

"He would never truly have blackmailed you," Miss Forrest said earnestly, leaning forward. "You must believe that, Mrs. Adler."

"If you say so," Lily replied. "I will admit to having a higher opinion of his character now than I did when he was first taken to prison."

"Praise indeed," Mr. Clive said. "How much higher?"

Lily smiled coolly at him. "A very little."

"I shall take what I can get," he said, rising. "Come, Sarah. Mrs. Adler no doubt needs peace and quiet after these last eventful days. And we have an engagement to announce."

"Oh yes, indeed, my love. You will have to visit us in Queen Anne Street, Mrs. Adler. You didn't get to see it to its best advantage, you know. It is even prettier than your home and ever so much grander. I think I shall throw a splendid ball once we are married, to chase away all the unpleasant memories of the past months."

"You plan to settle in London, then?" Lily could not help asking as she followed them to the door.

"Oh yes," Miss Forrest said eagerly, not noticing the wry note to Lily's voice.

But Mr. Clive did, and the look he sent her way was amused. "Never fear, Mrs. Adler. I am sure you will be able to escape my company most of the time."

"But not all the time?" she could not help asking.

"Adversity builds character," he said with an ironic bow. But his expression, when he straightened, was more serious than she expected. "Perhaps even for someone like myself."

CHAPTER 32

The ballroom glittered with candlelight, and the couples circling around it were like bright bits of silk floating on a breeze. Everywhere Lily looked, there were people, a crush of bodies that shifted and flowed through the beautifully decorated rooms. And everywhere she turned, she could hear whispers and rumors.

It made her smile a little, even as she shook her head. Serena had once joked that if London lost its gossip, half the walls in the city would topple to the ground without the normal amount of hot air to hold them up. Lily had laughed at the time. But she had come to realize there was a great deal of truth in the sentiment.

"What are you smiling at?"

Lily turned to find Ofelia at her elbow, looking splendid in emerald-green silk, piles of curls framing her face and diamonds winking at her ears. Beside her, Ned beamed proudly, offering Lily one of the glasses of wine that he held.

"All this," Lily said, taking the glass and raising it in a toast. "A grand success, I would say. You must be pleased."

Ofelia looked around the ballroom and nodded decisively. "I am pleased. Absolutely *everyone* came tonight. I do not think there were more guests even at Mrs. Drummond-Burrell's soiree last week."

"Still carriages lined up in the street, trying to get to the house, you know," Ned added, looking at his wife with a great deal of pride. "London loves Lady Carroway."

"London loves someone to talk about," Ofelia said with a roll of her eyes. "And I provide that, it seems, whether I do anything to merit it or not." When Ned's face fell, she patted his arm, smiling. "Tonight I do not mind. Though," she added with a laugh, "I think just one of these a year will be enough for me. I am perhaps not meant to be a true society hostess, as I find I much prefer *other* people's parties to the headaches of my own."

"You could always simply change the size of the guest list," Lily suggested, nudging her friend's shoulder with her own. "Twenty couples, perhaps, rather than two hundred."

Ofelia's eyes glittered with pleasure as she surveyed the crowd. "Indeed not, Mrs. Adler. You know me too well for that. I shall do everything at the grandest scale possible or not at all." Ofelia cut a sideways glance at her husband, then looked back at Lily. "And are you all right, Mrs. Adler? It has been . . ." She hesitated, searching for the right words to use in so public a setting. "A trying week."

"It has," Lily agreed quietly. "But it is done, and I am grateful for that."

Ofelia seemed to sense that Lily did not want to continue down that road. After a moment, she smiled and said, as if the matter were of no consequence, "It is a helpful thing, of course, that we planned our ball for so early in the season. We will be able to spend our time at home now, should we need to. Or leave London altogether if it becomes necessary."

"No plans to leave London," Ned said, looking confused. "Not this time of year, certainly."

Lily took a sip of her wine. "Fortunate timing, indeed," she said in response to Ofelia, her voice as diffident as the young Lady Carroway's had been. "Should your plans need to change."

Ofelia let out a small giggle. "What gave it away, ma'am?"

"You cannot abide the smell of tea right now," Lily pointed out.

That made Ofelia laugh outright. On the dance floor, the spinning circles of couples were smiling as the musicians drew their playful reel to a flourishing end. A cello drew out the first gentle notes of the next song, and there was a dignified shuffle of bodies as everyone checked their dance cards and saw that a waltz was next.

"That was what made me suspect as well," Ofelia admitted. "That and eggs."

"Breakfast must be torture," Lily speculated dryly, which made Ofelia giggle again.

"The eggs have been mysteriously absent for the last two weeks," she said. "I think the servants have also guessed."

"But otherwise you are well?" Lily asked, trying not to look her friend over too obviously.

Ofelia's smile seemed to make her whole person glow. "I am very well," she said. "And very happy. Just a bit hungry."

"Here now," Ned grumbled as both women laughed. "Not amusing, being the only one left out of the joke."

"Not to worry, my love," Ofelia said, patting his arm. "I am sure you shall figure it out in the next, oh, perhaps six months? Especially as it will soon become too obvious to miss."

Ned stared at her, confusion slowly growing into absolute delight. "Really?" he whispered. "Are you certain?"

Ofelia smiled. "As certain as one can be about such things. But keep your voice down, if you please. There is no need to go shouting *that* all around London."

Ned lifted her hand to press a kiss against her gloved knuckles. "Dance with me."

Ofelia's brows lifted. "Your mother will have some pointed words for you if we do."

He slid his other palm down to her waist. "Dance with me," he said again. "Or I'll be forced to make even more of a scene than dancing with my own wife."

Ofelia's smile deepened. "A persuasive argument, sir." She waved over a nearby servant to take her glass and placed her hand in Ned's. Just before he led her away, she glanced past Lily. "And I feel no hesitation in abandoning you, ma'am, as I suspect you will not be without company for long."

Lily watched Ofelia and her husband take their place among the dancers, smiling when she heard footsteps behind her. "How is your arm, Captain?" she asked without turning around.

She felt him at her shoulder, standing as close as propriety would allow. "It hurts," he admitted. "But it has been worse."

Lily turned to look at him at last. They had not seen each other since he'd left the Pages' house; now, they stared at each other, Lily wanting reassurance that he was well and safe after everything that had happened.

He seemed to want the same. His gaze drank her in from head to toe, until she began to worry that people would notice.

"You are staring, sir," she said quietly.

"You are worth staring at," he replied, giving her a playful grin.

She gave his uninjured arm a light smack with her fan. "Stop that," she ordered sternly. "You know how I feel about flirting."

"Is it flirting if it is the truth?" he inquired too innocently, but he looked away as he said it, following her gaze to where the Carroways were sweeping their way around the floor. "You know," he said, his voice growing thoughtful, "Carroway said something earlier that surprised me." He gave Lily a sideways glance. "He believes that after the business with Mr. Clive and being faced with the risk of exposure, you will have been persuaded to give up such inquiries."

"By which he means that his wife will give them up as well?"

"Doubtless, yes." Jack's expression as he watched her was serious.

She could feel the question, even though he had not asked it aloud. Lily watched the dance floor without really seeing it. It was not something that she and Ned had discussed. But it had certainly been on her mind. "Lady Carroway was in more danger than I was. And you, as it turns out, were in more than either she or I." She glanced at him, her eyes lingering pointedly on his arm. "Yet again. What do you think?"

Jack rotated his shoulder slowly. Then he surprised her with another grin. "It was not the first time someone has shot at me," he pointed out.

"Yes, but . . ." Lily took a deep breath. "It is hard to know that I have, once more, put the people I care about in danger."

"Do you care about me then, Lily?" he asked, his smile growing even wider.

Lily scowled at him so that she would not smile back. "You know I do."

"Just as you know that we made our own choices," Jack said. "You did what you felt was right, and so did I. So did Lady Carroway. Besides which," he added, turning his gaze back to the dance floor, "I think there are some among your acquaintance who have a good deal of cause to be grateful for what you have done."

She could guess that he was thinking of the Pages. But there were others he could have meant as well. The thought was like a warm flame under her breastbone, burning away some of the doubt that had been gripping her. "You do not think, then, that I should give it up."

"I think you will do as you feel is right," Jack said quietly. "As you always do. As any of us must. And until then . . ." He held out his hand. "Will you dance with me?"

Lily gave him a narrow-eyed look. "You said not five minutes ago that your arm hurts."

He laughed. "I did. But a waltz will not trouble it. And even if it did, I will brave the discomfort if you will waltz with me." His voice grew softer. "I would brave a great deal more, Lily, to hold you in my arms."

Lily could feel the warmth of his gaze all through her body. She thought of the portrait of Freddy that Lady Adler had sent, carefully wrapped once more and placed in the drawer of her dressing table. It would have made him smile to see them together, she was certain.

And more importantly, it made her smile too.

She placed her hand in Jack's and let him lead her to the floor just as an argument broke out in one corner. Lily spotted Ofelia hurrying over to speak with Mrs. Carter and Mrs. Peters, whose children had so recently not become engaged, and who were both very red-faced as they sniped at each other.

"What has you suddenly so entertained?" Jack asked. When she looked up at him, he grinned at her, sliding his arm around her waist. "Not me, I hope."

"No, you are not nearly as entertaining as you think," Lily said tartly, which only made him laugh. Her expression softened. "But you do make me smile, Jack."

"A rare privilege," he said, more serious as he watched her closely. "We had said that when all that business with Mr. Forrest was resolved, we had a great deal to discuss. Including . . ." He took a deep breath. "I can imagine that you have been thinking of Freddy—"

"No," Lily said, shaking her head. "I do not think he needs to enter into this, except as someone we have both cared for, who cared for both of us, and who would want us to be happy."

Jack did not hide his relief. "Then what . . . what do you think happens next, Lily? For us?"

"I confess, I am not quite certain. There is a good deal . . . that is, there are many changes to consider. In both our lives. And I am not quite certain how we will wish to resolve them."

"There is that," he said softly. "But I hope that whatever comes next, we can meet it together."

Lily let herself sink more deeply into his arms, not caring, for once, who might see or disapprove. "I would like that, Jack," she said softly. "I would like that very much."

"Mrs. Adler!"

The quiet, urgent whisper at her elbow made them both fall still, turning to find Ofelia waiting there. There was a polite smile fixed on her face, but Lily could see the nervous edge to it. "Would you be so good as to lend your assistance, ma'am?" she said, barely loud enough to be heard. "It seems no one can find Mrs. Carter's youngest daughter, and her parents are dreadfully worried that she may have . . ." Ofelia lowered her voice even further. "Her cloak is missing from the hall."

Lily glanced back at Jack, who let his arms fall. "Go on," he said, smiling. "I will be waiting when you return."

Lily felt a little knot of pleasure squeeze inside her chest. She turned and, her steps unhurried but her mind already working, followed Ofelia from the ballroom.

AUTHOR'S NOTE

Aconite is a plant that has had many names throughout the years, including wolfsbane, monkshood, and leopard's bane. It grows in the wild in Northern Europe and was eventually brought to the United States. Every part of it is toxic.

If ingested, aconite can cause vomiting, palpitations, and paralysis. It can stop the heart and cause death by asphyxiation. Even touching it can lead to tingling or numbness of the nerves, as well as palpitations, headaches, and cardiac symptoms. Ancient Greek hunters are said to have used aconite on the tips of poisoned arrows, and it had a reputation in the Middle Ages as a choice ingredient in witches' potions.

And yet, aconite has also been found in gardens for centuries due to its lovely blue and purple flowers.

To learn more about the deadly plants that are all around us, there are few more enjoyable and informative books than Amy Stewart's *Wicked Plants: The Weed That Killed Lincoln's Mother and Other Botanical Atrocities.*

ACKNOWLEDGMENTS

There is a point in writing every book when finishing it feels impossible, when I become convinced that *this* is the one that will defeat me. And yet, even knowing that, this one very nearly did. I am more grateful than I can say to Faith Black Ross for helping me pinpoint everything that was and wasn't working so I could find my way to the end. I am beyond lucky to have an editor who knows this series and these characters so well, and who loves them as much as I do.

The team at Crooked Lane put in tireless hours to get this book from idea to shelf. My thanks especially to Melissa Rechter, Madeline Rathle, Dulce Botello, Mikaela Bender, Thaisheemarie Perez, and Rebecca Nelson. And to Nicole Lecht, who designs the most beautiful covers.

Whitney Ross has an answer for every question, a pep talk for every moment of panic, and clear vision for guiding both books and writers. (She also puts a lot of excited, all-caps notes in the margins during *certain* scenes.) I truly couldn't ask for a better agent.

The year in which I wrote this book was a difficult one, especially the last few months of it, and I am so thankful for the loving support of so many people in my life: Jim and Andrea Schellman, who first taught me to love books and now have a shelf for all of mine; Laura and Ryan, who always come through with a meal on a hard day or a soft space for my kids to land; Jason and Hayley, who show up to so many events and put my books in their Christmas letters; Meg, who fangirls at me even though our kids have sleepovers together; all the

Paljugs, especially Joe, who I love more than I can say; Brian, who had some stern words for me when he finished the last book, and who knows where everything is in the grocery store so I don't have to.

I am grateful for Mary Ann, who always welcomed me as a daughter and friend, and who told me four years ago that she couldn't wait to see what was in store for Lily and Jack. You were supposed to be here to see that this book is dedicated to you. I wish so much that you were.

And finally, to you, dear reader. I am so very, very grateful to you.